P9-COP-609

Paula Egolf

Tristan Egolf (1971–2005) was born in Spain and resided in Philadelphia; Paris; rural Indiana; Vienna; Oxford, Mississippi; Amsterdam; New York City; London; and New Orleans. He published two novels during his life, *Lord of the Barnyard* and *Skirt and the Fiddle*. At the time of his death in May 2005 he was living in Lancaster, Pennsylvania, a city with a sizeable Amish population. In addition to *Kornwolf* he had written a rock opera and recorded a CD with Doomed to Obscurity, his Philadelphia-based band.

Kornwolf

Also by Tristan Egolf:

Lord of the Barnyard

Skirt and the Fiddle

TRISTAN EGOLF

Grove Press
New York

We gratefully acknowledge permission to reprint lyrics from the following songs:

Library of Congress Cataloging-in-Publication Data

Egolf, Tristan, 1971–2005
Kornwolf / Tristan Egolf.
p. cm.
ISBN 0-8021-1816-X (hc)
1. Amish—Fiction. 2. Werewolves—Fiction.
3. Pennsylvania—Fiction. I. Title.
PS3555.G37K67 2006
813'.54—dc22 2005052574

Grove Press
an imprint of Grove/Atlantic, Inc.
841 Broadway
New York, NY 10003

06 07 08 09 10 10 9 8 7 6 5 4 3 2 1

For Emmanuel Augustus—Long live the underdog.

Kornwolf

. . . tearing through bull-thistle, jimsonweed, supplejack—brittle with mid-autumn coming of frost—and of pulsating crimson, appendages thwarted and stumbling, slam into fallen timber, as worm-ridden slick with organic decay—to meandering blindly through goldenrod, inkberry, sheep laurel, bladdernut, Solomon's seal—a prickling rash of woodland nettles—cries emanating from lurch of within, as of burning in flame now, at once underfoot—down embankment and plunging headlong into watercress, chilly with runoff from fertilized fields, and of crippling thirst satiated in excess—then up again, scrambling, mud on the incline, a jagged escarpment, then over to stillness . . .

Gulping of air / equilibrium reeling as pounding inside, as of inner combustion . . .

. . . a sharp edge of sassafras borne on the wind—and of chimney smoke, rising from miles in the distance—and rosemary, slash pine, chicory, hemlock—replete with a tang of synthetic emissions . . . And traces of crimson in putrefaction . . . Of hunger awakened to ravenous burning . . . Responding—by light of the moon, with intent now—through corn-cockle, snakeroot and billowing milkweed to wax-myrtle, buckthorn and snapping of aster—then out to a rolling expanse of stubble . . . with shackles unbridled—elation of freedom, release and ahead, moving / charging—amok . . .

Into blackness.

. . . then routing through pestilent cubicle—vinegar, trappings and fat of the lamb—in a large metal box full of scum-lining, refuse and sourly rancid, fermented barley—a groaning of door hinges, outside . . . Footsteps . . . Crossing of pavement . . . The roar of ignition . . . A panning of lantern light, sweeping the property . . . Leaving . . . Then back to the gristle of crimson . . .

More blackness.

To voices now: haltingly. Startled . . .

. . . the sweet smell of fear and confusion . . .

Retreat . . .

. . . cries of alarm from behind, fading quickly . . . return to the stubble, and darkness enveloping / stars overhead in a shower of pinpoints—onward proceeding, alive in the night . . .

PART ONE
Introductions

Owen

For years, had it been suggested that Owen might ever again reside in Stepford, he would have endeavored to let it slide, but not without having been vaguely insulted. In over a decade away from the town of his birth, he had always defined it outright as the "source of his lasting discontent," the one place on earth he could never *live*. . . Weekends "home" were bad enough: fraught, as they were, with urges to seize on the nearest suburban dolt in passing and pummel him into renunciation. In time, the farther he strayed abroad, the brighter such impulses flared on return. By early adulthood, more than an evening in town was a field-tested nonpossibility. He wouldn't have lasted a week as an actual resident. Stepford County. *Jesus* . . . Better off dead than a prodigal son. The mere idea would have left him reeling.

In youth, on many an afternoon, he had climbed the neighborhood water tower, and, from thirty rungs over the treetops, regarded the rolling, unbroken expanse of forest (three thousand years of native prosperity, two extended colonial wars, an influx of German and Swiss migration and a meltdown at Three Mile Island, upriver, gone by and *still,* by appearances, Penn's Woods, in the actual lay of the treaty) set to emerge from a decade of semi-privileged suburban honky conquest with all but scattered clumps of fauna lost in a maze of development housing—the *"gingerbread eyesore modules,"* he called them—and overlapped highways and treeless lawns, to the mall, and beyond: to the outskirts of town, hazily gray with industrial smoke, and nary a cropping of overgrowth fit to sustain the groundhogs in between: where once this valley had thrived with game, now it was crawling with Astro Vans. Regarding it thus, Owen felt odd, if ill-suited, in knowing that he, at the age of thirty, remembered *the good old days.*

As good old days they had rarely been.

On most of those afternoons, staring across the as-yet undefiled valley, with nowhere to go, in particular, no one who knew what to make of *Blonde on Blonde*, no parlors or pool halls, and unbelievably, *not one God damned sidewalk, for miles*—just a Quik Mart whose owner prohibited loitering, a half-buried junkyard off in the woods, a couple of churches per every mile, and a ten-acre asphalt and Plexiglas hamburger factory known as Hempland High, from out of the stifling vortex of which only fleeting points of light would escape, through the plasticine tarpaulin thrown over everything, pinpoints suggesting a *world* out there, a place where pedestrians wandered the streets, where music drifted from open windows, where blankets of smoke and aromas of coffee and laughter filled dimly lit taverns at night—around fountains, through courtyards, cathedrals, down riverbanks, into the shallows by light of the moon—where young people met under streetlamps in cobblestone plazas to shuffle and mumble and dance—(instead of resorting in boredom and sheer desperation to feats of vandalism: from hurling garbage toward oncoming traffic on back roads at seventy miles an hour, to golf balls driven through schoolroom windows, dung from the overpass, spray painting, brush fires: anything able to quell the furnace, to strike some *terror* into these people)—where public schooling wasn't a daily incentive to go on a shooting spree, where the architecture reflected the most remedial grasp of human aesthetics, where open discourse was considered a virtue, and everyone read on buses and benches, and people like Owen would not go forever unnoticed by members of the opposite sex—a place suggested in celluloid images, songs from the dustbowl, Keaton and Garbo, late night shortwave radio broadcasts, veiled accounts from the roaring twenties—instead of the universe Owen had inhabited (captive stooge in the honky tundra) where nothing quite passed for sublime or dismal, discreet or brash, even fair to midland—just solid, implacable, unbroken gray, with the least of all plausible worldly variance.

Owen had grown up dreaming of nuking it. Stepford could render such impulses rational.

So then, the question begged of its own: how did he find himself driving up Old Route 30, heading east in "Chiffon" (his locally insured Subaru Legacy), Owen Brynmor, East Zone Cops Reporter for the *Stepford Daily Plea*: a gainfully employed, taxpaying registered Independent and downtown resident?

Right now, swamped in rush hour traffic, it made no sense. He couldn't get his mind around it. Everything was vaguely incomprehensible—adding to which, his nicotine fits hadn't let up for twenty-four hours and counting . . .

(His "patch" had been tossed in the can that morning, prompted by nausea, fever and madness. From there on out, he had gone cold turkey—*so* much worse than he could have expected: black as the cosmos, noxious bobbing, as bad as withdrawing from any drug.)

He gripped the wheel.

The road before him was jammed on an angle. The sky was red. And the drivers around him, clearly intending to thwart him at every turn, were to blame. Traffic was tied up for miles. He hadn't been caught on this stretch of highway in years. The landscape had been overhauled completely: more motor resorts, more developments, dining and shopping outlets to every side: another campaign of de-sanctification gone by, and no one the wiser, apparently.

Sickened, impatient and reeling with visions of bombing it all, he could take no more.

He shifted his Legacy into gear and gunned it across the highway divider. Veering in front of oncoming traffic, he vaulted into a parking lot. From there, he blew by a taffy emporium, rounded a corner and shot up a one-lane strip running under the elevated monorail system of the Dutch Land amusement park. To either side, enormous metal support columns flashed in rapid succession. Off to the left, a moat full of porcelain Dutchies appeared in a fountain basin. The park had been closed for the season, apparently. None of the rides were moving. Horror.

Continuing: under an overpass, back onto Old Route 30 a mile up flow, then three more lights until finally, a left onto 891—a two-lane road winding north through a stretch of forested gray. Owen, relieved to have shaken the clot of humanity, maintained excessive speed. Traffic like that, back there, enraged him beyond all limits of human endurance. Traffic like that was apocalyptic. And like it or not, it was back in his life.

He suddenly found it incredible, shocking, an earth-rendering bolt of primordial awe—to think that he'd actually *chosen* to reimmerse himself in this world of shit. What on earth had gotten into him? Had he come here expecting a rebirth of wonder? If so, he was in for a rude awakening. That's what this was. The traffic proved it . . .

Five turns later, a road sign appeared for the Lamepeter Township game reserve. Owen followed it down a gravel path cutting into the woods for a mile. Beyond a rickety wooden bridge, he came to a field of matted grass, on one end of which sat a tiny cottage with stacks of timber out front.

This was it.

He parked. Releasing his white-knuckled grip on the wheel, he got out of the car and stretched. He drew in the air, then looked around. Alone, it appeared. In an open clearing. With one other vehicle—a pickup truck.

Above him, a network of juniper limbs extended across the afternoon sky: for miles on end, gnarled and twisted and stark, with occasional hatchings of pine.

He made for the cottage—across the clearing and up a wood-chipped path to the entrance. A plaque read: "NO DRUNK SHOOTING"—facing outward. Then: "VIOLATORS WILL BE SHOT." Signed: "KRATZ."

Kratz, Owen had to assume, being Joel, his contact, the Lamepeter Township game warden—Kratz, who had claimed to have "something bizarre" which the paper would "definitely" want to see (though he hadn't known how to explain it by phone, and "no one would ever believe it anyway"), Kratz, the smallish, rigidly coiled, if typical make of a warden inside, beckoning hither, all scruff and grizzle: pure Kascynski behind his desk . . .

Owen swallowed and stepped inside. The room was hot and stunk of mold. A pair of antlers hung on the wall—and beside it, a VFW flag.

The warden spoke first: "You the reporter?"

Owen nodded, displaying his press badge.

Kratz looked him over, appearing uncertain. A wrinkle creased his brow. He was tentative.

Then he broke off and, shrugging, produced a manila folder. "Here's your story."

As Owen himself would reiterate back at the office, the explanation followed.

The morning before, October 6th, one Dwayne Gibbons, a native of Blue Ball and longtime hunter on Kratz's reserve, had come by the office with a puzzling set of negatives from his photographic "motion detector." Motion detectors, the warden explained, were battery-operated mechanisms used in the tracking of game—in this case deer. Entirely legal, these common devices consisted of two very basic components, two small plastic boxes to be mounted on separate trees in close proximity. Between these units, a laser transmission was maintained. In the event of the beam's disruption, a built-in camera was triggered, recording the scene—with a flash, if needed—and the time. The purpose and function being: to determine the herding patterns of local deer. By such means, both effective stalking and the placement of tree stands might be determined.

The use of motion detectors was not at all unusual, Kratz explained.

"But this," he continued, shaking his head while presenting the folder, "*this* is a first."

Not knowing what to expect, Owen took it and, flipping the cover, looked inside. There were photographs in there—a stack of enlargements. Grainy, underexposed and off angle, the first one appeared to be shot in the dark: a falling leaf in the flashbulb's range. The second exposure wasn't much clearer, just brighter, having been taken at dawn. The third and fourth prints showed a tangle of hooves and hindquarters, shot by the light of day. The fifth was a buck in profile, marked 9/28, 17:49. The next four shots featured groundhogs digging. Certainly nothing to fire up the presses . . .

Then he flipped to number ten.

Years down the road, he would hearken back to the very first image that came to mind: a fuming heap of scrapple some Philth Town waitress had served him, back in the drink—a brazenly heedless order placed, the arrival of something unfit for display, scarcely to be recalled, until now: something which shouldn't, and *won't* occur naturally. Something right out of a waste dump in Jersey. Or up from the depths of a portable toilet.

In days to come, opinions would vary with wild extravagance, far and wide: some people claiming this blotted image resembled a dog—only backwards and rearing with some kind of horrible skin disease. Others would argue those "weeping lesions" were actually calluses. Or parasites, maybe. One man would claim that it looked like Richard Nixon plastered in mud or feces. Others would lean toward a five-legged brown bear entangled in hawk wire, down from the Poconos.

No one would know what to make of the face. The jury would go out on every feature. A knotted mound of what might be considered a cheekbone was really a snout, some would say. Others would doubt it, seeing the bulge instead as a cyst on a back-turned head—or maybe an angry boil, hives, a case of the shingles, cauliflower ear . . .

In truth, there would be many takes on which end of the photo was even supposed to be *up*—and which direction the "figure" within it (if even conceded) was actually facing. Skeptics would howl, of course—but to little effect, overall, and with dismal wit. Regardless of what else was said of the photo, it naggingly begged some basic questions. Such as: who would have gone to such crafty, elaborate lengths in staging this image but not followed through with a sharper photo? Why leave out a discernible profile? Why the contusions and the hairless patches? Why would anyone go so far without adding the final, convincing touches? After all, as long as Gibbons didn't check out as an anarchist yahoo, his alibi couldn't have been any tighter. It was brilliant—too brilliant *not* to be true. Why allow room for controversy?

Of course, maybe that was a part of the plan: befuddle the public with imprecision. Which *would* have accounted, in part, for Gibbons, whose record would complicate matters further. Domestic charges. Bankruptcy. Drunk driving. Outstanding warrants for unpaid fines—all of which would be held up to rigorous public review in days to come, yet none of which fingered Gibbons for a practical joker.

In a word, he was simply a wretch.

For Joel Kratz, the answer lay elsewhere—as yet to be fathomed, though pressing, surely: either somebody was running amok in a steel wool jumpsuit, at risk of drawing fire, or something ungodly was loose in his woods.

Either way, it gave him the creeps.

For Owen, the case was less in doubt. Moreover, it called for a tip of the hat. Somebody—*other* than Kratz or Gibbons, most likely—had whipped up a fabulous hoax. Its presentation, down to the last detail, made Owen flush with envy. It also managed to take his mind off of smoking (or not), if just for a moment. For that much, he would remain indebted, and moreso, amazed: he had actually *laughed* . . . It was truly a first-rate piece of work. The least he could do was publicize it.

Back at the office, his (questionably mad) city editor, Terrance Jarvik, agreed. On viewing the photo, the old man broke down in laughter. Emerging from which, he was game.

His rival pulpit, the *Horaceburg Screed,* would be livid, he claimed. They had no sense of humor.

Thereby, Owen was handed not only the story, but his very own "Halloween" series (he couldn't dispute the title just yet), beginning with five hundred words by midnight—an order which, after speaking with Kratz, then delving into the public files, would yield his unearthing a long-forgotten chapter of Stepford County's past: something familiar to none but an aging resident few. The caption would follow: a lead that, upon publication, would cast a tenuous line into area memory, something to prompt many locals to ridicule, others to barring their doors at night, and the rest to a vague, bewildered disquiet.

Indeed:

The Blue Ball Devil was back.

JACK

By noon, the West Side Gym had begun to warm up from the early autumn chill. Sunlight spilled through the windows to the rear of the ground floor, bathing a rack of free weights. Swirls of dust kicked up from the ring mat, over which Calvin and Marty Boy shuffled in time with the music of Gil Scott-Heron—"The Bottle," from 1976. Two other junior competitors, Franklin and Holy War, stood by the glove rack, tying up. Everyone present had arrived on time, yet still, there was no sign of Roddy Lowe.

For Coach Jack Stumpf, this didn't bode well. It was certainly no way to kick off training . . .

Once upon a time ago, Roddy had been the most promising amateur The Coach had ever worked with. In truth, he was probably one of the very best fighters the West Side had ever turned out— and that would date back to the turn of the century—whole generations of durable prospects. Here, in a state renowned for its barrios, Roddy, a humble suburban white boy, had torn through the ranks with a transcendental vengeance. The kid had been tough as a Jersey fireplug. Discipline, focus, listening and (hard to imagine) *punctuality* had never been issues. He'd always been cool under fire. His performance had always been purely driven and spirited. What's more, his conduct outside of the ring had been flawless, thanks, in part, to his father. Aldo Lowe, one of Jack's best friends, a fellow trainer and the gym's former bookkeeper, had always been a rigid stickler for discipline (at times to a fault) with his only son. Outside of the ring, Roddy had been known, in the early years as "Gentleman Lowe"—a moniker that stuck until he grew a bit older, giving way, in due course, to "The Unbelievable." Such, as it happened, appropriately so: by fifteen, he had scored several *unbelievable* upsets—a trend that would only continue that season at the Golden Gloves finals, upstate—where Roddy, with his usual corner—Aldo, Jack and Syd—would go up against Choppo Suarez, the state champ at 132, in his backyard—and drop him with a hook in the first.

He hadn't made too many friends in the crowd, but Roddy had caught the public's attention—and, in stripping Suarez of his title, the nation's.

He had held that title for the next three seasons.

By the time he'd turned pro, at nineteen—too early, in Jack's mind, regardless of Aldo's insistence—the local promoters had been lined up. In a world where black and white made green, Roddy, as fresh meat, had been in demand. His excellent amateur record and his limited professional experience had marked him for booking. On appearance alone—ruggedly handsome & cool—he was sure to be sought out by every regional promoter, from D.C. to Boston, intent on grooming a star for the networks. His name would have looked good on any contender's record: solid, career-building stuff.

Yet again, when the time came—right from the opening bell—Roddy would fail to "cooperate." Three more upsets, and heads would start turning. His public appeal would go up with each outing. Before long, big-time promoters had been calling. Which had led to a short-lived but glorious series of matches that steadily jockeyed him up the ladder to primary undercard pickings for Thursday Night Fights, national broadcasting. There, at last, he'd been robbed of a decision that most (if not all) broadcast and ringside observers scored a shutout the other way. Even now, it ranked among the top five worst decisions Jack had ever seen. He still found it hard to believe the judges had made it out of the club alive.

That was the first night Jack had seen Roddy dive straight to the bottom of a fifth of bourbon. It was also the evening when Aldo and Roddy at last reached an overdue fork in their road—the specifics of which, in all likelihood, no one would ever know. The Coach still didn't. He only remembered waking to crashes and screaming from down the hall at the hotel—after the show, it was five a.m.—in responding to which, he'd found Aldo raving and clutching his jaw by a soda machine (*"The little son of a bitch hit me!"*)—while random explosions of porcelain and glass and furniture, mingled with bursts of profanity: (*"*&$% this $#!+—if I @#$% come back here, I'll &*$%—"*), boomed out from behind Roddy's door.

He was tearing the room to pieces. He sounded like some kind of animal.

Jack could relate.

Almost a third of their evening's pay—the biggest of Roddy's career, to be sure—went to covering damages rendered that night. A mortified Aldo had withheld the rest, claiming Roddy could have his share if and when he atoned for disgracing his team and the gym. Despite all attempts to mediate between them—as well as to straighten out finances fairly—Jack had not been able to salvage the wreck of Team Lowe. The damage had been done. Father and son had gone separate ways—Aldo to cool his jets for a while, and Roddy, disgusted, following one more bout on his own (which he'd lost), to Horaceburg. There, as persisting rumor would maintain, he worked as a plumber for the next five years—never, in all that time, once getting in contact with Jack, much less his father. Talk of debaucherous evenings and mishaps with women would filter back to The Coach. But nary a phone call or visit. Disgusted, Roddy had turned his back on boxing.

For his part, Aldo would continue to handle the gym's finances—monthly utilities, rent, taxes—the fund-raising end. But he wouldn't be working as Jack's assistant, or in any training capacity, again. The quasi-fraternal bond that existed between them had lost its mortar in Roddy.

Five years later, just three months back, coming home on the turnpike late one evening, Aldo, while riding his Harley, had merged from a service station ramp in the pouring rain to collide with an eighteen-wheeler. Instant.

Jack and Roddy had been reunited at the funeral, if only momentarily. On first appearance, it was obvious that Roddy had never gotten over falling out with his father. In fact, it was clear that he'd harbored hopes of reconciliation, one day, if possible.

Those hopes were dashed for eternity now. And the grieving of lost opportunities begun.

At some point during the ceremony, somebody, one of the elder Lowes, perhaps, reminded him—whether in consolation or out of some pending legal concern—that, according to documents, Jack was his godfather.

Which was about to take on a new meaning.

Within a week, Roddy had gathered his things from the floor of a squat in Horaceburg, rolled back over the Susquehanna, mournfully entered a houseful of Aldo's belongings—as designated by his will—found his box of gear in the attic, unpacked it and slunk back into the West Side . . .

Of course, Jack was happy to have him back. He too lived with grief over lost opportunities. But as to whether Roddy belonged in the ring, just yet—The Coach had his doubts. It wasn't that Roddy had lost his edge, physically, as anyone at 140 dumb enough to stand right in front of him would have discovered quickly. And his trademark lead right hook was still lethal . . . The problem, if problem there be, was psychological. Which is to say, by appearances: his head was on crooked and his heart wasn't in it.

In youth, his instincts had been superb. He had known when to jump on a staggered opponent. He had never taken shots without angling, at least, toward far more damaging counterpunches.

Jack could only assume then that, based on what he was seeing (dissociation), Roddy was dealing, in some way, with Aldo. But one could never be certain with Roddy. In fifteen years, The Coach still hadn't been able to figure out what propelled—or derailed or arrested—his inner workings. Roddy's mind was truly confounding . . .

In the meantime, back on earth, he was taking entirely too many shots to the head. And that was no way to walk into a match. That was no mind frame to place in harm's way.

Such, above all, was The Coach's concern. As the young man's trainer and manager, he hadn't—and wouldn't have—taken a bout with a sleek young contender like Fido Jones. Not yet. Roddy, the bonehead, had blundered into it—enticed by Ronald "The Shark" Travers, a ruthless Atlantic City promoter and Jack Stumpf's absolute nemesis.

Travers's latest (and hottest) commodity, Fido "The Cobra" Jones, a current alphabet contender professionally, was facing a late hour cancellation. His scheduled opponent, a Baltimore journeyman, had sustained a fractured hand in training. During their scramble for a seminotable, however dependably safe replacement, Travers's people, having caught wind of Roddy's "return" from Jerry Blye (a longtime rival trainer of Jack's), had telephoned Roddy at home, on the sly—bypassing Jack, his official manager. Roddy, with only a four-round bout in the can since emerging from a sixty-month layoff, had taken the fight without so much as notifying Jack, to say nothing of seeking his approval. By the time this deal had been brought to The Coach's attention, it was already too late. He could've *killed* Roddy. Everyone, including and *especially* Roddy, knew Jack would never let him step into the ring without a West Side crew behind him. Through circumstances beyond his control, Jack now faced going back on a vow he had long ago sworn to uphold without variance: not to engage in dealings with The Shark—even if at the expense of his livelihood. Jack had witnessed, and suffered firsthand, what Travers could do to a fighter's career. Numerous photographs lining the walls of the West Side Gym were a constant reminder: by the double-end bag, Larry McKreetz, broke after seven title defenses—behind the ring, Demitrius Yarrow, jailed for direct assault of his trainer—then Eustace Kermon, officially a "suicide," even though a letter had not been produced—all of them former

West Side fighters gone over to Travers on turning pro—and all overshadowed by the finest boxer Jack had produced in his years at the gym: as still on display in a gilded frame at the building's entrance, off to the right, and across the walls of the training room floor—photographs, signatures, newspaper articles—many beginning to yellow with age: Hernando Valdez, the "Stepford Cyclone," the one-time lightweight champion of the world, last reported miserably friendless, broke, on parole & divorced in Maryland . . .

Even now, after seven long years, the taste of it hung in Jack's mouth like poison. Scarcely an hour went by when he didn't, in some way or other, mourn Hernando. "The Cyclone" was still the best fighter he had ever turned out. And, on mornings like these, it was evident. Hernando had always been right on time. Hernando had always weighed out on schedule. Hernando had systematically disassembled opponents without hesitation . . . In matters of punctuality, discipline, focus, drive and finishing instincts, the early Hernando—the one who was pictured all over the gym—was sorely missed. Yet, his image was also a constant reminder that, in this profession, certain defeats—or "plummets from grace" —were guaranteed. If Hernando could go down, anyone could. The fighters on hand were at similar risk . . .

Like him, the juniors assembled for sparring today had come from "broken" homes. Calvin's father was serving forty to life in prison for murder one. Holy War Jackson's mother dealt crack; five of his seven brothers were in prison. Franklin Pendle had been on the streets or in juvenile halls since the age of five. All of these young men had been in trouble, at one point or other, throughout their lives. The only thing Jack could do for them, one and all, was nurture their self-esteem. Which, in turn—providing initiative—might grow into respect for others.

And that brought matters right back to Roddy.

Sighing, Jack looked at his watch. It was 12:35.

The kid was unbelievable.

"Hey, Coach!" called Holy War, breaking the silence. He nodded through his head-guard. "You mind if we warm up?"

Shaking his head with exasperation, Jack waved: "Go on!"

He turned and plodded across the floor to his unlit office.

Once inside, he placed a call to Roddy, just for the hell of it. Ringing . . .

(—Fido Jones was a powerful puncher. Regardless of all else that might've been said of him—yes, he'd been brought along nicely, protected and sheltered, somewhat—he still packed a wallop. And his footwork was good. He was highly elusive. Without a doubt, he knew how to move . . . Roddy, years back, might have taken him into the later rounds by making a brawl of it—cutting off the ring, then pinning him into the corner with alternating hooks and uppercuts. However, right now, from what Jack had witnessed in training, such needed aggression was lacking. If Roddy didn't hop on the ball, as in yesterday, the fight would be over inside of four rounds.)

He dropped the receiver back in its cradle. One more ring and that message would've picked up—Roddy's laconic, gurgling drawl: *"I'm not home now. Leave a message, y'all."* Click.

Beside him, the answering machine was blinking. Jack hadn't bothered to check it before. There were three new messages. Hitting the button, he played the first. It was Stepford Electric, announcing a forthcoming shut-off date. The second was Thurston Bach, a lawyer, in reference to overdue property taxes. The third, it got better, was someone—a stranger—demanding his "boy's" ten-dollar deposit . . . No word from Roddy among them. And every one pending.

Jack felt sorry for wondering.

He leaned slowly back, his chair creaking under him, and buried his face in his hands with a sigh.

This wasn't the first time that, suddenly, from out of the grind, he'd missed Aldo for practical reasons. Aldo had always kept track of this mess, leaving Jack to coach. That had been their dynamic.

Which isn't to say that Jack couldn't have made the transition for lack of common sense. The problem was: Aldo had kept all his figures in longhand—his phone numbers, addresses, contacts. And Jack, for the life of him, couldn't make sense of them. He couldn't decipher the penmanship.

His own proactive intuition, i.e., personally calling around, had amounted to less than he liked to admit. He had never been good with soliciting funds. Coaching itself wasn't paying the bills—especially not with absent fighters. And he couldn't rely on most of his juniors for monthly dues. They couldn't afford them. That was the reason this place was needed: without it, these kids would have been on the streets. The only thing standing between, say, Franklin and a juvenile home was the West Side Gym—the only community youth center left in the downtown area that was open year-round. And, for all of the millions in public taxes funding the local prison system, The Coach couldn't raise enough money to pay his electric bill.

The cycle continued.

A figure loomed into the doorway, disrupting the sunlight that spilled across the floor. Jack, from his desk in the dark, looked up. It was Jarret Yoder.

Of course it was.

Even in adolescence, Yoder's knack for timing had been uncanny. Then, as now—only twenty years later, as a juvenile attorney—he appeared on cue. Jack could assume that his oldest friend had come by to make a donation—his routine check at the first of the month. He'd been pledging the same amount for years.

"What's new, Yul?" Straightening up in his seat, Jack was able to muster a grin. "You know the best thing about short people?"—(someone had told him this joke the week before)—"They're the last to get wet when it rains."

Quietly, Yoder stepped into the room, unsmiling.

The Coach looked him over. *"Ba-dump?"*

No laughter.

Shit, thought Jack. He slumped in his chair. Yoder's expression was tentative, humorless. Something was wrong. Which was also a knack of his: bearing bad tidings. The "Harbinger," Jack called him—either responding in deed for the better, with financial contributions, as such, or appearing with some kind of bombshell announcement to complicate further existing disorder. This was apparently one such occasion. One of their juniors was probably in trouble . . .

"All right, then . . ." Jack finally broke down: "What happened?"—braced for the drop hatch to yawn beneath him.

Jarret stared at him, seeming to gauge his response with a shade of uneasy reluctance.

Jack didn't like it one bit. "What's wrong?"

After another uncomfortable silence, Yoder broke out of it, shaking his head. "Man," he groaned in resignation. "I was afraid you were going to say that." He exhaled forcefully. "I don't believe this."

He dropped a newspaper onto the desktop.

Slowly, Jack turned it over, expecting the worst, as the possibilities flared (limited only by Jarret's ambiguous cool and The Coach's imagination). He spread the copy out in front of him. Stepford's *Plea*.

He regarded the lead.

At once, even fording the jolt of adrenaline, he thought about Scarlet and Broken Rubber. The two of them, yukking it up out there. Only *they* could have done this, the snickering bastards. Probably testing a new computer.

But *why*?

And *no:* they wouldn't have dared.

It was too much to process.

This couldn't be happening.

What did this paper say? What was this newspaper? Oh, yes—*The Plea*, that's right. The daily . . . Or maybe a mockup, a counterfeit copy, as part of a grander practical joke . . .

Any moment now, Scarlet would show in a Little Red Riding Hood suit, with tassels.

According to the text, no hoaxes or frat pranks had ever come out of the game reserve.

According to the article, lab results cleared the photo of having been treated or modified.

According to the story, the photograph's exposure date coincided with recent reports of a wild dog, a "rabid stray from the hills," on the loose in Lamepeter Township.

According to the paper, other complaints had been lodged regarding a "nocturnal prowler" whose commonest going description varied from "gross" to "one of them toxic avengers."

And *man,* the writer was something else . . .

According to an *Owen Brynmor,* listed as a freelance investigative reporter: *"Sightings concur with an area legend which holds, in spite of Warden Kratz, that a nuclear defect stalks the hills of Blue Ball, Intercourse, Laycock and Bird-in-Hand."*

Jack got up and wiped his brow. He felt nauseous. His heart was pounding violently.

"Feeling all right?" asked Yoder.

The Coach appeared more incensed than offended. "Come on now."

Jarret shrugged. "Then how's the family?"

Dismissing the question, Jack lifted the paper. "First things first—who the hell *wrote* this?"

Just then, a figure appeared at the door. It was Roddy. Along with a pasty-faced white boy.

"Hey." Roddy spoke with evident caution. "I wanted to get my friend here a membership. This is—"

Jack waved him off with a snarl. "You're late, Mr. Lowe. This is no way to start . . ."

What might have amounted to dragging his fighter over the coals only moments before had fizzled for Jack into muted bewilderment. Then: "Get changed!" he blurted. "Move it!"

"Yes," droned Roddy. "I just want my friend here to—"

"Fill out a form!" yelled Jack, thrusting a clipboard into the white boy's hands. Then, back to Roddy: "I want you back up here in five minutes."

He slammed the door.

Totally thrown off his game as a trainer, Jack went back to reading the paper.

"The 'Blue Ball Devil' Returns," read the headline. So inappropriate, nothing could figure it.

After a lengthy, weighted silence, Yoder's question was sensibly posed. "So what do we do?" His tone was sincere.

Jack stepped away from the paper, exhaling.

At length, he mumbled: "I'll have to call Scarlet."

"Scarlet?"

He offered no explanation. Reading the paper again, he was. Sweating.

He straightened up. More than surprised, he felt worried. And angrier still with the paper's reporter.

"Who *is* this guy?" he asked, dissolving the silence. He thumped *The Plea*. "Who is he?"

Yoder shrugged. "I've never heard of him."

Somebody knocked at the door—that white boy again. Jack opened up in silence.

"Excuse me," the kid said with measured reserve. He held out the clipboard that Jack had given him. Both of the forms were completed. On top of them, under the clip, there was twenty-five dollars.

Absently, Jack accepted it. "Right," he said, dismissing him. "Go warm up."

As Jack resumed pondering, Yoder walked over to close the door and turn on a light. Having done so, he cast a random glance toward a pile of papers, letters and bills heaped up on a table by the doorway—on top of which Jack had just tossed the clipboard. He bent over, looking at something, apparently. Then he let out an exhausted laugh.

Torn from his reverie, Jack looked up. "What's so funny?" he asked in annoyance.

Yoder, shaking his head as though punch-drunk, mumbled in reply. "You *know* it's October."

Grabbing the clipboard, Jack, who was already lagging behind the press, regarded in print, as signed (the ink was still wet on the paper), the name of *Owen Brynmor*.

Ephraim

The carload of Redcoats had just appeared when the one-man plow beneath him jammed, and Ephraim, thrown from its plank in a splay of appendages, pitched facedown in the dirt. A flock of gulls burst up all around him; scattered from picking alfalfa seeds out of the crooked and twisting wake of the plow. They hovered above him, cawing defiantly. Already caked in manure, he lashed at them—only to meet with a splatter of gall. Streaks of it blotted his face and chest, his trousers. Squinting, he rubbed his eyes.

The carload of English erupted with laughter—all hooting and *"man, did you see that?"*s and ridicule. Their vehicle rocked to a halt at the edge of the yard. It shrouded the road with exhaust. A clamor of music blared out of it—sounding of rape in a trough, or a freighter derailing.

One of them shouted, "Nice bowl cut, Zeke!"

A bottle flew out of the driver's seat window. It clouted the mailbox.

Ephraim got up.

Behind him, the hinny kicked and brayed. It was caught in the crupper, jammed on an angle. The blade wouldn't give. The animal panicked. Ephraim attempted to calm it with gestures: *easy, now . . .* He reached for the bridle. The hinny reared. He fell back in the dirt.

A screech of rubber vaulted the cackling Redcoats south on

Weavertown Pike—in between fields of corn and alfalfa, rolling around the bend, then west on Welshtown Road, still blasting that music.

Ephraim lay on his back, listening.

Above him, parallel bands of altocumulus clouds drifted over the sky. A cold front was coming. The wind had picked up. There was rain on the way. Before nightfall, probably.

Allowing his gaze to wander across the overhanging shelf of gray, Ephraim drifted slowly back to earth, dipping below the tree line. Behind him, a waterwheel gently turned, its long arm rising and falling in time, directing a steady trickle of creek water over an aqueduct, into the stables. Beyond, across the gravel drive, a chimney stack rose from a weed-choked garden, dividing the house's white facade and three separate levels of pine-green shutters. Farther back, in the distance, the oval-shaped side of a barn, with its crumbling trim, sat flush with a wall of tall, old evergreens—after which the wreck of a windmill stood, the fence surrounding it, lined with gulls.

Ephraim sat up to wipe their gall from his brow. It was starting to burn his skin. He trudged to the creek to dunk his head.

Inside of the swirl, he listened—as one might press an ear to the railroad track—for *some* intimation of death to the English, whether by famine or flame, to come . . .

He emerged with little assurance of hope.

No, these people would only multiply. Their housing would only continue to spread. The coming years would bring legions of rental cars, neighborhood catfish carts and tour buses—and even more Amish imposter craftsmen, bakers, clerks and buggy ride drivers—stalking the roads for a glimpse of the Plain Folk in whatever context—preferably working; or riding a scooter, even better: for Ephraim, many a slow pursuit down back roads had already left him no option but barreling into the corn for cover. Those occasions would grow more frequent. So would the drive-by camera corps. And the "scenic" motels that had sprung up all over The Basin in recent, the past five, years—as the one that now bordered the Bontrager property: a ninety-yard wall of linoleum siding, with ten upper-level "observation" platforms that were built and designed for the purpose of "viewing" the local Order at work in the fields—in this case Ephraim alone, as the building had driven off most of their closest neighbors, leaving tourists to settle for the image of a solitary plow boy working his yard. Twenty-five windows per level—and often, at harvest, on weekends, filled, every one of them. Children observed him in vague confusion—as now, with the red-haired kid on the ground floor, pressing his tongue to the window, gurgling—his mother and father standing over him, training their camera's eye on Ephraim. And worse, in an upstairs window, with little attempt at concealment and zero remorse (not to mention regard or consideration for the Ordnung's stance on graven images): a video camera perched on a tripod, left unattended to film his whole day . . .

Every crop he had ever attempted to grow had been surveyed by English cameras. They felt to be bleeding him thinner each year, as they called him to account for the state of his harvest: a crop being only as good as its master, the master, only as good as his seed, and Ephraim's tobacco, Lord have mercy, the whole rotting lot of it, sealing that verdict.

After a season of improper fertilization, drought and multiple parasites, all thirty plants had been cut in the wake of a storm, leading to massive spoilage (soon to be worsened by subsequent overexposure to sunlight to curb the wilting, then speared, too close to the butt on the lathe, then hung to smother and shed-burn high in the rafter beams of a stuffy shack) so that now, including the plow being jammed and the hinny enraged, chewing its bit, the Bontrager home could boast of a haul that would probably roll down to fifty cigars.

Disgusted, Ephraim charged the gulls. They burst and fluttered, then settled nearby. He slumped back into the dirt on his haunches. He glared at the plow, still lodged on an angle. One of its blades had been caught on a root . . . The rows of his plot were unworkably crooked. The soil was dry and craggy in spite of his every attempt to enrich it with dung. Even Bishop Schnaeder wouldn't have known what to do with such mistreated land. In horror, the Bishop had already turned to the Minister, Ephraim's father, to that end: tobacco was the absolute worst crop someone like Ephraim, alone, could hope to produce—as, for one factor: it was hardly profitable; two: it was brutally labor-intensive; and three: no one had taught the boy how to work his land. He did *everything* wrong. Watching the neighbors tend their fields from a distance had only crossed his signals. With the Minister off at the mill by day, and Ephraim an only, motherless child, no one was there to catch his mistakes when he made them. And so, they would only continue.

Time and again, the Bishop, and others, had appealed to Benedictus on the matter: it was wasteful, they'd argued, for his son to be working at home. He belonged in the fields at harvest.

But Minister Bontrager hadn't conceded: the boy would remain on the property, alone. It didn't appear to matter, at least insofar as the crops were concerned, what he *did* with it—just as long as he watched the house, from dawn to dusk, every day of his life.

A vehicle topped the hill, approaching. Its engine dropped. Ephraim looked up. It was one of those "pickup" trucks, that's what they called them—an older model. Obnoxiously large. And faded red . . . It was slowing down. It had come to a halt. At the edge of the field, it was sitting there now. Slowly, its driver leaned forward and looked at him. Ephraim stared for a moment, annoyed. Then he waved, as though to say *move on—the parking lot's over there, you moron!*

It worked. The driver, spotting the entrance ahead, moved on. And no sooner gone than a clopping of hooves from the north to replace his engine sounded, at once familiar . . .

Jonathan Becker rounded the wall in his topless, two-seated courting buggy. High on the box he roosted, leisurely guiding his groomed and ever-immaculate saddle-bred pacer across and over the small, meandering creek's stone bridge—one hand on the whip-socket, empty, beside him, the other with reins in a steadied clench, and the running gear quietly gliding below, oiled from axle to perch, down the shafts—from crupper to bridle, bridle to bellyband, breeching to bit—the entire wagon.

Jonathan's penchant for organization infuriated his supper gang members. The Crossbills, all thirteen of them, had never understood it—with Ephraim included among them. *Rumspringa* came only once in life. And, at twenty, Jonathan's clock was ticking. At the most, he had three more years left to run. Now was no time, in their frame of thought, for tuning equipment or steaming trousers. Or *working,* for that matter, not the way *he* worked—or *had* worked, of late—as an auctioneer. Now was the time to imbibe and partake. And to chase after women. Beautiful women . . .

He should've been savoring every moment.

His buggy swung into the Bontrager lane. Clearing the stables, it slowed to a halt. He dismounted. He adjusted the blinds of his pacer, then, turning to Ephraim, flashed a grin.

"Ach!" he exclaimed in English. "Look at the state of you, Bontrager. Wonderful soiled."

Ephraim glared in silence, streaked with gall and manure.

Jonathan caught himself. "Sorry." He switched to Pennsyltucky Dutch: *"All right, then. It's payday at market. You coming?"*

Leaving the hinny on the plow in the yard, they got into the buggy and started south. Ephraim would have to return in an hour, ahead of The Minister. Plenty of time.

Pulling away from the house, they ascended the gradual slope of Eshelman's Hill. Charlock and pennycress spilled from the ditches on either side like wild ivy. Leveling out, a gentle plateau stretched on toward a rising bluff to the west—crowned with a plot of forgotten tombs, their headstones dating to 1750—while off to the east, maybe two hundred yards through a stretch of evenly cropped stubble: a wall of oak and hickory forest, its ecotone jumbled with barren thickets—what used to be Isaac Tanner's woods, before the family had moved to Ohio. The English couple who'd bought their house had let the property run to seed. The fence surrounding their barn had crumbled. Tent worms had eaten their giant oak. And, after the turn onto Welshtown Road, piles of garbage marred their lawn.

Continuing on, there unfolded a more pristine expanse of unsullied farmland. Holstein cattle on the hillsides, grazing in black and white. A wind of manure. Fields of alfalfa in yellow and green. A patchwork of District Seven at harvest: devoid of the Redcoats, if only in stretches. Layers of orange and magenta, stratums of brown and puce and viridian green washed over in cooling, violet hues with the rolling approach of an evening shower. Storage silos appeared on the tree line. A Lutheran steeple was nestled among them—stable yards, orchards and farms below, all of them teeming with harvest activity. Every hand in the valley was out. Those who had already brought in their corn were now sowing the last of the year's alfalfa. Horse-drawn wagons appeared on all sides. Crews of men and women and children labored in packs, with the gulls at their heels.

With no sign of traffic, Jonathan drifted slowly into the middle of the road. He straddled the center line, easing up on the reins. On their nearing the Ziegler farm, a white picket fence loomed up to their left. It ran toward a water tank and onward to a barn, where three or four members of the family were manning a cutter that chopped and blew corn to storage. Above, from a second-level window of the barn, across the yard to the porch of the house, ran a clothesline, hung with the customary black and white and blue of the Orderly vestiture. Below, young Katie Ziegler was driving a push-mower over the lawn in starts. Jonathan smiled as they drifted by. He winked at her, then pulled back to his lane.

"So," he finally broke the silence in Py. Dutch, leaning forward. *"I don't know if anyone told you what happened . . ."*

He launched right into recounting the previous weekend's stomp at the Metzler barn—how somebody, one of their English neighbors, presumably, had called the police to complain, how Officer Beaumont and three other deputies had driven their cruisers right up on the lawn—how everyone had scattered and broken for cover—some for the corn in a wild dash, others back into the barn for a hiding place, down in the stables or up on the roof—how four of the Crossbills—Gideon, Isaac, Samuel and Colin—had been arrested and held at the precinct until the next morning, and how they would now be obliged to attend an alcohol counseling session downtown—and all of the rest of it, everything Ephraim had already known at the outset, as, unlike Jon, who'd been working the auction that evening and hadn't even gone to or stopped by the party, Ephraim had been on the roof of the barn, looking down, observing the course of events. He might have explained this, had it been feasible. He might have elaborated in detail.

But clarifying all such matters had always been next to impossible.

Ephraim was mute.

Bearing north onto Laycock Drive, they came into view of a one-room schoolhouse. Shading its tiled belfry, a pair of chestnut oaks stood over the building. A blanket of acorns covered the yard. An outhouse stood by a fence, and beyond it: a porch, with a row of scooters lined up to it.

Jonathan slowed his buggy in passing. He and Ephraim gazed toward the window. They spotted an outline of figures inside, seated at desks in the first two rows. Some of them turned at the sound of the buggy. Then Fannie appeared, if just for a moment—out from behind the instructor's desk.

Fannie had turned eighteen that summer. This was to be her last season teaching. In less than a month (on Sunday, November 14th) she would take her vows of baptism. Shortly thereafter, as a member of the church, she would pass on her duties to Mary Brechbuhl.

She waved. Grinning, Ephraim and Jonathan waved in return.

They continued east.

A ways up the road, on Harvest Lane, Jonathan sat upright on his box. He wavered intently, sniffing the air. *"Hey,"* he eventually spoke up. *"Do you smell something . . ."* He paused to consider his choice of words, settling, at length, on *"strange?"*

Ephraim looked toward the Byars farm, at the edge of which Samson and Jeremiah were busily manning a "honey wagon," churning a ton and a half of manure. He pointed.

Jonathan shook his head. *"No, it's more like . . ."* He paused. *"Can't you smell that?"*

Ephraim gazed ahead, unblinking. He didn't respond. There were geese in the road.

Jonathan slowed up. *"Strange,"* he repeated himself, this time in English, with doubt.

Ephraim sat watching the waterfowl waddle across the pavement and down an embankment. They seemed to be spooked by the weather. They moved in a huddled rush. They were plump and healthy.

He turned around just in time to catch Jonathan casting a furtive, sidelong glance at him—one that was quickly diverted, but which still left a boldly indelible imprint of worry. Ephraim had seen that expression before. It didn't much bother him now, or ever. Leaning back, he steadied his gaze on the road, as Intercourse loomed in the distance.

Once onto 341, it was less than a quarter of a mile to the auction lot. They pulled in, crossing a set of railroad tracks, then parked among several buggies. Jonathan tethered his steed to a post. They walked down an aisle of open-air stands—most of them piled with fabric and tools. The aromas of fodder and hay and roasting chestnuts permeated the lot. There were chickens and rabbits and goats in cages, stacked to the rear of the auction barn. A peddler trumpeted *"Groundhog filets!"* in Py. Dutch from behind a grill. Somebody else with a bullhorn announced a sale on lighters and nine-volt batteries—everyone haggling, everyone twisted on coffee and grease, by appearances.

Ephraim and Jonathan entered the main building, walked by the produce and butcher displays, then turned through a door to the livestock area. There, Ephraim waited impatiently, surrounded by crates of ducklings, rabbits and leghorns, as Jonathan stepped into one of the offices.

Moments later, he was back with a paycheck. "All right, then," he announced. "I'm finished."

Ephraim took off in a flash, winding back through the cages and out to the flea market area. Jonathan scuttled to keep up, darting through wandering packs of tourists and visitors. After a row of antique displays, they came to the record collector's stand—and, as fortune would have it, the longhair was working. He spotted them coming and cracked a grin. "Well." His gaze came to rest on Jonathan. "What's up, Abe?"

"Jonathan."

"Sorry. Whoa, you're dressed to the nines, my man."

Jonathan looked down—"What?"—in confusion.

The longhair laughed. "I'm kidding, I'm kidding."

Jonathan still didn't understand.

The longhair shifted his gaze to Ephraim, who stood in flannel and mud-stained pants, with no hat on his head and three days' worth of stubble. Excepting his haircut, he bore little outward resemblance to an Orderly, even one in *Rumspringa*. The longhair looked back to Jonathan, frowning. "Well, this won't do," he said, shaking his head. "I can't sell you anything dressed like *that.* Your people might see." He got up and, turning, opened a door to the parking lot. "Here."

Ephraim picked up the case marked "2 for $5" and walked out. Jonathan followed him.

Once on the dock, Ephraim got down on his knees and started to sift through the tapes. From the doorway above, the longhair remarked: "A couple of recent additions in there."

Ephraim looked up with a glimmer of hope. He motioned one hand in a half-circle, questioning.

Puzzled, the longhair watched him, trying to make sense of it.

Jonathan ventured a guess. "He's talking about last week, I think."

The longhair's expression brightened suddenly. "Ah! You dug that Possum. Is that it?"

Ephraim appeared confused, if hopeful.

Grinning, the longhair went on to explain: "That's what they call George Jones, his moniker."

Ephraim nodded emphatically *yes*.

"No," said the longhair. "Sorry 'bout that. But I'll keep my eyes open. Try me next week."

Satisfied, at least insofar as the longhair *identified,* Ephraim nodded his head. Between them, a torch had been passed, an exclusive understanding sallied forth.

He returned to the bargain box, much relieved. He sifted and picked with a gratified air. One of the tape covers featured a group of (women?) in war paint stalking a scrap yard. Another showed figures with plastic geranium pots on their heads, entitled: *Devo.* Continuing, someone who looked like the Minister Bontrager lost on a drunk: *Aqualung.* Finally, a creature named Ponharev leaned on a wall with his barn door flap hanging open.

"Forget that, kid," said the longhair. "You want something wicked? Try this." He brandished a tape.

Turning it over, Ephraim regarded the cover design. Very little was clear: a wash of darkness streaked with burgundy red and what looked to be creases of light. On closer examination, a host of misshapen figures began to emerge. In the center, strapped to a chair: the head of a goat on the shoulders and chest of a man. Beside it, a body, inverted, possibly hung by a hook from the roof of a cave. To its left, a five-pointed figure entangled in hieroglyphics. And down below, a lake of crimson bobbing with limbs and appendages, reading: "REIGN IN BLOOD."

Ephraim looked up to the longhair, as though to ask, *This is good?*

"That," said the longhair, grinning with relish "is *wicked* shit."

Outside, the crowd was steadily thinning. The clouds hung heavy now. Rain was imminent. Jonathan's pacer, tied to the hitching post, shifted restlessly, stamping the gravel.

Time was short. They would need to return via 341 at a steady clip.

Ephraim climbed into the buggy ahead of Jonathan, fixed on manning the pacer. Always the more assertive driver, he gripped the reins and parried about. Within moments, the railroad tracks had passed under them. Turning west, they rolled through a stoplight, moving by quilt and basketry outlets—then under a bridge and onto an overpass, into the thick of a traffic jam . . .

At once, it was clear they had made a mistake. And terribly, *irreversibly* so—there was no way to angle the buggy around with a full lane of steadily oncoming traffic. Their own lane, devoid of an adequate shoulder, was backed up for three hundred yards from the Sprawl Mart—a ten-acre superstore complex—ahead: one week away from its grand opening, and still, after fourteen months in construction, mobbed with resident protesters, area farmers and small local business owners.

Ephraim and Jonathan hadn't foreseen this delay. For them, as with most of the Plain Folk who normally veered from this road on principle, the Sprawl Mart was just another English atrocity. In appearance, it wasn't much worse than the rest. They certainly hadn't expected the roads to be tied up this badly in both directions.

An oncoming tour bus gradually slowed to a crawl on approaching Jonathan's buggy. Ephraim looked up to see wall-eyed Redcoats staring down on them, angling cameras. One of them slammed his head to the tinted window in mute incapacitation. The others didn't really appear to know what they needed or wanted to say, they just stared. The driver's voice came over the intercom: "Don't worry, folks, these people are guaranteed *non-violent*. Just try to remember: the camera steals their souls." (Laughter.) "So, if you *must*, try and shoot on the sly . . ."

Flashbulbs exploded. Ephraim winced.

Behind the bus, a line of drivers began to honk and rev their engines. The bus driver paid them no mind. Ephraim looked up, blinking away the static. He singled out one of the cameras and pointed. The Redcoat blinked, apparently startled. Ephraim threw him a middle finger. Jonathan gasped. The bus driver took off.

Slowly, their lane began to move. But it didn't proceed more than twenty yards—they had just drifted into view of the road crew—when everything slowed to a halt once more. A traffic director had flipped his sign from SLOW to STOP. The delay would continue. Three more lanes of traffic would now be allowed to pass, one at a time, before the next chance to get through came around, and even then, there was no guarantee . . .

Ephraim, losing patience quickly, hopped out of the buggy and scouted ahead. He passed a line of motionless vehicles. Most of their drivers regarded him warily. Scowling, he batted the hood of a station wagon at random, then turned around.

He climbed back into the buggy. His body felt overheated. He clawed at his forearms . . . Something was wrong: out of nowhere, it seemed, he was terribly thirsty. His throat was burning.

Ahead, in the distance, a tractor-trailer was angling out of the superstore lot. It swung around to the west at a drag. Ephraim spotted it slowly approaching.

He whirled on Jonathan, agitated, motioning: *Where's the stereo?* Jonathan glanced over one of his shoulders, into the trunk. Ephraim followed his gesture and, presently, pulled up the battery-powered player. Then he inserted the *Wicked Shet* tape.

At first, once the leader had rolled and the opening notes had begun, booming out of the speakers, Ephraim was forced to assume there was something wrong with the tape. This equipment had never emitted such grating, cacophonic belches. It sounded like a chain saw, whining and rising in sharp, sporadic bursts, then leveling . . . Adding to matters, the longhair had sold them faulty goods. Or so it seemed—till the bashing commenced: like a trash can lid being whacked with a crowbar—*ONE,* overtop of the chain saw, then—*ONE, TWO*—more menacing now, more deliberate—*ONE*—as a serpent coiled to strike—*ONE, TWO*—the strike giving way to a gallop: the pound of a broken fan belt slapping the underside of an engine hood: approaching, over the fields, preparing to sack and pillage and raze and defile—*ONE, TWO*—with the chain saws winding, the crowbar, the fan belt, pushing to a head, then: *"AAAAAARRRRRRGGGGHHHHHHH"*—a scream, like ten thousand demons plummeting hell-bound, end over end . . .

Ephraim's equilibrium reeled. He fell forward, bracing his weight on the dash.

A series of turbulent images flared in relief on the screen of his inner eye. He watched them tumble and weave and recede into blackening madness.

Then came the vocals:

Slow Death
Immense Decay
Showers that cleanse you of your life
Forced in
Like cattle you run
Stripped of your life's worth
Human mice for the Angel of Death

Back to the galloping, chain saws, crowbars, visions of torture beyond comprehension:

Angel of Death
Monarch to the kingdom of the dead . . .

Beside him, Jonathan reached for the stereo, desperately trying to silence the roar.

But Ephraim, in white-knuckled rapture, blocked his attempt with a sweep of one leg and then went on, much to the shock of surrounding motorists (if equally geared to the protesters' cheering) to tighten the reins, angle the buggy out into the oncoming lane and charge.

Jonathan nearly flew off his box.

A bystander shouted. *"Get out of the way!"*

Gripping the reins even tighter, Ephraim lashed the pacer's haunches, lunging. Above the wind and the pounding of hooves and the carriage wheels grating on asphalt beneath him, the *Wicked Shet* blasted.

Surgery with no anesthesia
Feel the knife pierce you intensely

Inferior, no use to mankind
Strapped down screaming out to die . . .
Angel of Death
Monarch to the kingdom of the dead
Infamous butcher
Angel of Death . . .

Jonathan cried out. The protesters screamed as the oncoming trailer blared its horn. The rest of the traffic joined in with it, over which Ephraim, holding steady, howled.

Benedictus

What felt to be three or four centuries back—in a time so gone it was hard to imagine it having existed in this day and age—the essence of compound filth had preceded The Crow's arrival well in advance: ahead of the corn liquor rasping his palate, ahead of the musk of his perspiration, before his appearance—dragging one leg that had never recovered from gout in childhood—scowling sternly, his brow in a furrow of ruts, underscored by his graveyard eyes.

And so, now, after all this time . . .

Some things never changed.

They just ripened.

From two hundred yards in the distance, his arrival by carriage was heralded in on a plague wind. Twenty years later and no less rancid. In fact, the stench had only intensified.

He pulled to a stop alongside of the waterwheel. Slowly, the carriage door opened outward. A dung-crusted boot touched down on the platform and pivoted. Another boot dropped to the gravel. Rocking forward, the old man stood to position, slightly cocked to the left—in profile now, and, as might have been expected, of wider girth, having bloated with age. His beard was almost entirely white. His pitted nose had swollen and flattened. The passage of years had exacted a toll, to be sure. But his aura was undiminished. The rancor was deeply imbedded and festering—instantly, jarringly identifiable . . .

And still, he was dragging that gimpy leg.

The only significant, nonbiological change in his appearance was the hat on his head—a creaseless, wide-brimmed, black felt hat—which, at last, confirmed the nigh to implausible: he, Benedictus, was now a minister.

Certainly, stranger things had happened. But few, if any, less appropriate.

The idea of Old Man Bontrager reading the Book of Isaiah—or delivering the *Es Schwer Deel*—in the presence of an organized body of worship was so preposterous, so perverse, so obscene, it begged the question: what could have happened to District Seven? What in the world had become of the church?

Clearly disgusted, though, given his sour expression, equally unsurprised, the old man stared at the upended plow in the yard, and the hinny, gnawing its bit. Removing his hat, he spat in the dirt, then wiped his mouth with one dirty sleeve. Frowning, he pondered the image intently. Then he made for the summer kitchen.

He got to the door, unlocked it, went in. A pile of crockery fell from the windowsill—rattling, crashing. A moment of silence. He reappeared with a bottle of corn whiskey.

Nothing had changed.

Minister Bontrager. Lord deliver.

What came next?

Officer Rudolf Beaumont, of course . . .

Ludicrous though it may have sounded: Rudy "The Great White Chickenshit" Beaumont—fishtailing into the drive in what would've appeared to be his very own township cruiser—his yapping in bursts from the driver's seat window discernible even at seventy yards. His nasal bleating, as unmistakable—down the lane it proceeded, approaching . . .

He slammed to a halt. He got out of the cruiser and yelled toward the house: "Get out here, Bennet! This motherfucking kid!"

He was heavier. Balding.

He looked like a swine in tights.

That much, too, hadn't changed.

In early adulthood, Rudolf had been pronounced unfit for military service (the navy) due to acute asthma. In order to spare him disgrace in the family (three generations of low-ranking sailors) he'd been assigned to "domestic" service, stateside, overseeing "highway patrols." The closest he'd come to "the shit" was an unpaved stretch of road outside of Philth Town. There, he had "monitored" thirty-man labor teams made up of conscientious objectors—most of them Orderly draftees working the pavement in lieu of active duty. In other words, he had stood guard over pacifists—mostly young Amish and Mennonite men—some of whom recognized him from Blue Ball, and none of whom knew how to take him seriously.

Back home, his father had been renowned as the laughingstock of the Amish Basin: by day, a scarcely respected mining executive and would-be community man, by night, a chauvinistic bigot who, after steadily hosing his mind with drink for the better part of a lifetime, had gone off the deep end, much to the shame and lasting disrepute of his family, by first becoming an honorary member of the Pennsyltucky Nazi party—Rudolf was named after Hitler's deputy—second, shooting all five of his dogs for "chronic insubordination," and third, coming out of the closet on a gin-blown, ass-naked yodeling public rampage—one that had led to a padded cell, leaving Rudolf behind as an angry young short man.

And Rudolf was most undoubtedly short. That much was clear in his one-to-one dealings, as had been the case with the Orderly COs—most of whom, once again, had known him for years, and who certainly bore him no personal favor. At first, his insistence on being addressed as "sir" had been greeted as vaguely hilarious. However, soon—after three or four tantrums—the whole thing had started to lose its charm. Soon, as the only non-Orderly present, he'd been shut out: the use of English had been dropped. He had wound up in conversational exile. His every command had gone unacknowledged. The only time anyone had paid him the first bit of mind was to crack a short-man joke. That much, he'd gotten without a translation. And it had driven him green with anger. When he'd threatened to call in the National Guard and have them all cited for insurrection, the Orderly COs had heard enough. All twenty-five of them had dropped their shovels and walked to the nearest service station. After lodging a formal complaint with the army by phone, they had gone on an all-night drunk.

The next they had heard, he'd been back in The Basin, working as a meter maid.

Eighteen years ago.

Now he defended the public trust.

"Get out here, Bennet!" he yelled at the house.

Benedictus stepped from the kitchen.

At the sight of him, Rudolf jerked a thumb toward his cruiser: "Stunk up my whole backseat!"

A motionless figure was sitting in the vehicle.

Beaumont opened the door and grabbed him. Headlong into the dirt he was tossed.

Stepping forward, The Crow looked down on him.

Already marked with cuts and bruises, the boy looked up in evident terror. The boy: the poor, unsightly wretch—as blighted to God-awkward, all out of sorts.

It hurt just to look at him.

He looked like his mother.

This was entirely too much to process . . .

Rudolf continued to blather hysterically: "—going upstate next time, so help me—"

In all likelihood, the boy had already outwitted The Chickenshit once, if not many times. No doubt, there would have been multiple incidents—and more than spontaneous cow-tipping sprees. The kid would have proven a considerable nuisance. And gotten away with it, largely.

Till now.

Benedictus loomed over him, seething. The boy cowered. A moment went by. Then, as if signaled, he got up and slunk through the yard toward the house with his head hung low. Rudolf clouted his face in passing.

Class act(s). Benedictus and Beaumont. The Church and The State. The Crow and The Chickenshit.

Fighting again, they were—back and forth:

"This one'll cost you!" Rudolf yelled.

Bontrager yelled back. "What do you *want*?"

Rudolf went into the summer kitchen. Gone for a moment, he reappeared with a jug of corn whiskey.

"And double the weekly," he said on his way to the cruiser. "Move it."

Benedictus climbed the stairs to the porch, went in, was gone, came back. Then—by stroke of outrageous fortune—he handed Beaumont an offerings box. Beaumont opened it, pulled out a wad of bills, and—incredibly—even counted them.

Score.

Long Live The Celluloid.

Perfect.

And just ahead of the rain, no less. From over the hill in a wall of gray—sweeping the fields with a pattering rumble.

Rudolf's cruiser moved off down the lane. Benedictus was left on the porch, enraged, confused and in evident thirst.

Scowling, he turned and went into the house.

Fannie

While most of The Order explained away Ephraim's behavior by branding him not only damaged, but insolent, reckless, antisocial and, somehow, inherently cursed by nature, Fannie knew more than to blame superstitions and old Amish lore for her cousin's condition. No, he hadn't been doomed to clumsiness owing to the fact that he was born on a Wednesday. He wasn't a mess on account of the household chores not having been completed that morning. The storm outside at the time of his birth had *not* foretold of an early passing. The fact that his gums had broken early, and all such nonsense, wasn't to blame. Fannie knew better, as Fannie remembered in vivid detail too much of their childhood, too many early impressions of Ephraim—before he'd been taken away by her uncle, the Minister—back when her mother, Grizelda, as Ephraim's surrogate, had tended them both—back when, side by side, they had crawled through the autumn wheat on their hands and knees.

As common seed brought to term under vastly disparate conditions, the two now existed: from kindred ilk in flesh and bearing to polar extremes, by appearances.

To begin with, most of the district mothers had been at a loss to distinguish between them. Having been born less than eight weeks apart, they'd been taken for twins on several occasions—both being fair-complected, blue-eyed, healthy and plump, with similar temperaments. Whether at rest in the crib or, together, on hands and knees, exploring the kitchen—the misunderstanding was natural enough. Fannie's mother, Grizelda Hostler, the Minister's long-estranged sister, maintained that both children had always been characteristically well-mannered, calm and untroublesome. And once upon a time they had *spoken,* as well. Both of them. He no less than she. Even now, Fannie could still hear him striving to eke out his first attempts at expression. *Fang,* he had called her in one bursting syllable, then broken into a satisfied grin. Most of the Plain Folk had missed that part—as Ephraim, in early boyhood, had been reserved, and had rarely spoken in church. Very few members knew just how *well* he'd been learning to speak at the time of the accident.

Up to a point, he and Fannie had grown and developed in nearly identical stages. Only when Minister Bontrager intervened had their paths begun to diverge.

First, by a stroke of misfortune, Ephraim had lost his voice—with no hope of recovery. Fannie, conversely, had gone on to speak three languages, then undertaken to teach them.

Ephraim had blundered through numerous farming endeavors alone, and to ruinous ends, while Fannie had worked in the fields alongside of her family, embraced by a whole community.

Presently, she was on a first-name basis with at least thirty members of the district every day (in addition to teaching, she worked the fields and played in a Mennonite volleyball league), whereas Ephraim, since finishing school at thirteen, had been spotted in public during daylight hours, usually racing like mad on his scooter, once or twice a month, at the most—and always unbeknownst to his father.

Only at night, when the Minister faded with drink, had the boy been free to wander. For years, he'd been roaming the fields by moonlight while, usually, Fannie had lain asleep.

In effect, then: she was the oldest of three healthy siblings, functional, well-adjusted—adept in the arts of agriculture no less than teaching, with shining prospects—he was a single child, unapprenticed and a one-man agricultural bust in a world that revolved around time-honored notions of family, skill and communal prosperity . . .

Given this, the contrast would only grow more pronounced in the seasons to come:

After twenty-five months in *Rumspringa,* Fannie would soon face taking her vows of baptism—thus becoming an active, devoted member of the church, however early—Ephraim, who'd always remained at a wall-eyed distance from most of the area's youth, had become a Crossbill in recent months and, at this rate, wasn't likely to be accepted as a member of the church at all. His future within The Order at large was in doubt. And his gang wasn't helping matters.

Isaac and Colin had been the first to take him on one of their nightly rounds—the "rounds" which consisted of tooling the roads in a beat-up car they had bought from a scrap yard. Over the course of the past few months, they had goaded him into all manner of mischief—from plastering traffic on 30 with dirt bombs to swabbing construction equipment with honey.

Yet, what had begun with bread and butter had led to more serious episodes recently—the latest of which was now being relayed by Jonathan, perched on a stool near the window.

"Ach!" He faltered, still at a loss over how to explain what had happened that day. "I've just never—*ever* seen anything like it."

Fannie gazed out the window in silence.

The walls around her felt vaguely confining.

She and her two younger siblings had used this loft for as far back as they could remember. The room was furnished with chairs and a table. There were cushions and blankets and bales of hay. On evenings like these, with the rain coming down and the drunken English weaving around in it, Abe and Grizelda Hostler took comfort in knowing their children were home, in the barn. This evening, Hanz and Barbara, Fannie's brother and sister, were already sleeping. Along with their father, most likely. The crops were still out. Gravitation began at dawn.

Fannie, not due at school until six, could afford to burn the midnight oil. (Not that she would have been *able* to sleep.) As burn it did: from a lamp on the table between them, Jonathan's countenance flickering.

Shaking his head in bewildered frustration, he mumbled: "It weren't the Ephraim I know."

Images jumbled chaotically, pleading to Fannie for placement in some kind of order: the marketplace, late, her cousin impatiently roaming through motionless traffic on foot—a busload of English, passing, an altercation with someone in one of its windows, then blasphemous, truly malevolent music, *"enough to make Lucifer's blood run cold,"* an English trailer, a jolt of momentum, the sudden appearance of movement oncoming, a chorus of horns—more onlookers screaming, Ephraim undaunted, even encouraged—refusing to veer, the trailer deferring and *SLAM*ming into a telephone pole—power lines tearing in showers of sparks, ensuing confusion, panic and rage until Officer Rudolf Beaumont appeared to dispense with a loudly demanded beating—which Jonathan somehow eluded in passing (Rudolf had targeted Ephraim alone) and Ephraim's hideous, puckering grin through blow after blow of the officer's nightstick—till someone or other, one of the demonstrators, maybe, stepped forward to intervene—and a small riot later, the whole thing stopped making sense . . .

Fannie knew not what to make of it.

For Jonathan, only one thing was clear: the Ephraim he'd known all his life and the fiend he had been with that day were opposed diametrically—this one, a relative boon to creation, that one, the literal bane of a species. The idea that anyone might have played host to them both was decidedly hard to imagine.

He shook his head, looking down at the floor. "I don't understand," he groaned in English.

Rainfall pattered against the roof. Outside, the evening was black and turbulent.

"—don't know what happened." He switched to Py. Dutch: *"It's like something took over. I don't—"* He tapered off, pressing one palm to his forehead. Then, in conclusion: *"I just don't know why."*

Something occurred to Fannie abruptly. A look of mortal dread came over her. *"You didn't tell him?"* She held her breath.

Jonathan shook his head. *"Of course not. And now I* really *don't know what to say."*

The oil lamp flickered as, off in the distance, a rifle shot cracked through the pouring rain.

Fannie, more bothered than prompted to curiosity, tried to change the subject: *"You think they're shooting at The Devil?"*

Jonathan sat up. The question had caught him off guard. He looked over, trying to gauge her bearing. *"Don't joke of such matters."*

"I'm not," she said.

Jonathan held his peace for a moment. Then he ventured a word in reply: *"They were talking about it at market today."*

Fannie cocked her head, unimpressed. *"They've been talking about it at market for weeks."*

"Yes, but—" Leaning forward, he elaborated: *"The Graberses spotted it Saturday night."*

"I heard that too," she continued, unfazed: *"And the Hershbergers lost three cocks on Monday."*

"And now the English are writing about it."

She nodded.

"They think it's a ruse," he said.

Fannie looked over. *"What do* you *think it is?"*

He stared at the ceiling in hesitation. Finally, he shrugged. *"I don't know."* He bit one thumbnail, gazing into the lantern's flame. *"It might be a coy dog."*

Fannie seemed doubtful. *"I don't think so."*

He followed up quickly: *"Then* you *think it's real?"*

She didn't know how else to phrase her reply: *"I think it's something we don't understand."*

Jonathan got up and arched his back. He walked a circle around the table. A halfhearted grin appeared on his face. He muttered: *"My grandfather says it's your uncle."*

"Your grandfather's crazy."

"True," he conceded. *"But so was your uncle. Or so I'm told."*

She looked up. *"'Was'?"*

He clarified: *"Not the Minister. I mean—"*

She waved him off. *"People say all kinds of things."*

To which he was forced to acquiesce. *"OK. I'm just thinking out loud here."*

"Of course." She frowned, wringing her hands in frustration. *"You think it's your gang, then?"*

He looked at her doubtfully. Logic precluded the need to respond: yes, perhaps the Crossbills *were* involved in this mess, to some extent—at least insofar as the pranks were concerned. As little as Jon had seen of them lately, he probably wouldn't have known the specifics.

However, could they, or *would* they have been killing chickens and goats?

Probably not.

Fannie shifted, no longer able to feign distraction. *"I just wish he'd get here."*

And no sooner spoken than the sound of a door swinging open went up from the dark on the ground floor. Jonathan shot from his stool and leaned over the ladder. *"Ephraim!"* he called.

"Is that you?" added Fannie. Her body was tense in the stillness.

Grizelda's voice came back in reply: "I'm sorry."

She stepped into view from the shadows, raising her lantern. Her bonnet was soaked—her upturned face, a mask of worry. She stared. *"Are you OK?"* she asked.

Fannie relaxed with a heavy sigh. *"We're fine."*

Grizelda glanced between them. *"He hasn't arrived,"* she stated flatly.

They shook their heads.

She lowered her gaze.

"Rest assured, missus—he'll be all right," said Jonathan, doing his best to sound comforting. *"He was released from the station earlier—hours ago. I've already checked. He's probably just been detained by the Minister."*

Which was exactly what she feared—and certainly not what she wanted to hear. Now, at this hour, her brother was normally blacked out with drink, and her nephew, roaming.

Tonight, however, would probably be different. Surely, the old man would still be awake—and in God only knew what frame of temper.

Nights like these had always been hard on her.

"Damn," she whispered. Then, peering up: *"You haven't told him yet, have you?"* she asked.

Fannie responded: *"No. We haven't."*

Grizelda peered away from them, frowning.

She lowered her lantern and whispered, again, to herself in a forceful hiss: *"Damn it."*

Slowly, she made for the door. Before leaving, she paused to look up for a final remark. She gestured toward Fannie while speaking to Jon: *"I trust you'll have her inside by midnight."*

Jonathan bowed deferentially. *"Yes, ma'am. Of course I will. Have a good evening."* He smiled.

Grizelda stared at him, seemingly unimpressed by his awkward show of servility. Jonathan lowered his gaze uneasily.

After a moment, she left in silence.

Once the weight of her presence had lifted, Jonathan heaved a sigh of relief. *"I don't think your mother likes me,"* he said, understating the matter, to his way of thinking.

Fannie returned to the corner and sat. She drew in her legs and embraced them, muttering distantly: *"Mother just worries for Ephraim."*

Unconvinced, by the look of it, Jonathan got up and wandered around the room. His shadow, crossing the walls erratically, back and forth, made Fannie dizzy. Sheets of rainwater crawled down the window behind him, steadily blurring the lights of a distant, flashing radio tower.

Another gunshot boomed in the distance.

Suddenly, Fannie got up. She walked to the ladder and looked down. "He's coming," she said.

Jonathan, gently: *"Of course he is, Fannie . . ."*

She shook her head. *"No, I mean now. He's here."*

A thud went up from the ground floor.

Jonathan leapt with a start.

Fannie hushed him.

Hinges groaned. A draft blew over the floor. Footsteps.

Fannie called to him: *"Ephraim!"*—her voice like a trapped canary inside the barn.

Below, a mop of tangled hair and dripping fabric stepped into view. Glancing up, he was lost in shadow.

Fannie beckoned tenderly: *"Come,"* she said, with her arms outstretched.

Slowly, Ephraim climbed the ladder. Into the light he rose, his countenance gradually brought into stark relief.

Jonathan took a step back at the sight of him. Fannie choked in a horrified gasp.

Ephraim stood in the half-light. His right eye was blackened and swollen. The bridge of his nose had been cut. His garments were badly ripped. A pool of water was spreading around him . . .

He squinted toward them.

Fannie broke down. She seized his collar and jerked him about. She was sobbing convulsively—torn between hitting, embracing and throwing him out of the loft—until Jonathan got to and managed to steady her.

Slowly, he led them both to the corner. Ephraim slumped in a pile of straw. Fannie remained on her feet, standing over him, tears cascading down her cheeks. Jonathan signaled her, motioning: *Keep it together*—and pointing to Ephraim.

She sat.

Even though Jonathan did his part by ejecting the *Weckit Shet* tape (he had characterized this music as "evil incarnate") from out of the deck of the unit he'd brought along for precisely this occasion, and, setting it off to one side for disposal / incineration by flame later on, then inserting George Jones, track one, side one, "A Good Year for the Roses," Ephraim's favorite—even though the opening notes thereof settled over the room as a sedative haze, lulling the almost unbearable pain to recession, if anesthetically so—there was only one thing that would ever bring Ephraim comfort, one person to quell the furnace—not Jonathan, for all of his noble intentions—not Auntie, who seldom, if ever, laid eyes on him—not the Crossbills, whatever their purposes, past and present, and not even Possum. Only Fannie, for all of their differences growing up, could bring him relief.

That was one matter which Jonathan already understood, maybe better than they. Having grown up with them, he had been forced to accept that the bond which existed between them ran deeper than even blood being thicker than water. It transcended family, love and death. In a sense, it was larger than they, and, as such: nothing would ever come between them.

For Jon, this kinship had to be frustrating.

Here, indeed, was relief for Ephraim: nestled into his cousin's embrace, with rainwater tapping the roof overhead, an oil lamp glowing softly beside them and Possum's velvet delivery crooning of imminent safety, salvation, deliverance . . .

Meanwhile, Ephraim had nearly gotten him, Jonathan, killed that afternoon—not to mention placing his wagon and pacer in danger, and his person at risk of a beating—for all of which, he didn't even look apologetic.

No doubt: Jonathan should have been furious.

Instead, he looked more disturbed by something—a creeping stench that had entered the room. It seemed to be coming from Ephraim. It was . . . Even while soaked to the bone, he exuded it.

Fannie had trouble accepting her senses. Ephraim had never been overly pungent. Somewhat *stale* perhaps, but in keeping with life as an only son, and not much of a wash keep, understandably so. Quite often, his clothing was mussed and bespattered with scratch, but his person was normally clean. At worst, he gave off the scent of manure.

This was *not* the scent of manure.

Ephraim himself seemed oblivious to it. He offered no gesture of explanation.

But Jonathan smelled it. He blinked in poorly concealed astonishment.

Fannie blushed. A feeling of helplessness overcame her—heartache and helplessness. Leading to pity. Then desperation. Then panic. Then anger: *rage,* above all, with her uncle, the Minister.

No matter what the community maintained, or how many questions she harbored herself, Fannie knew, she felt certain, that Benedictus was wholly to blame for her cousin's condition.

She would never understand how the old man could treat his only son so deplorably. Even by Orderly standards, it was criminal—far beyond biblical precepts of discipline, far beyond sparing the rod, as it were.

Yet Fannie, like Jon, could do little about it.

For now, "A Good Year for the Roses" would have to suffice for their part in restoring the peace. Despite the Ordnung's stance on it, music was good sometimes. It served a purpose. Soon enough, Fannie would have to forsake that knowledge. But not yet. Tonight it was good . . . For the roses, of course. And the rain. And the silence: the three of them settling down in the straw to drift in a speechless, recuperative reverie—this during what had been slated for possible anguish earlier. And just as well: moments like these were as precious as rapidly vanishing land, and weren't to be rushed.

By the end of the tape, they were sleeping soundly.

Fannie dreamed of a quartered mule.

She awoke to the crack of a rifle, later.

Still raining outside. Jon lay wrapped in a shawl, on the couch, breathing peacefully.

Thunder rumbled across The Basin.

Ephraim was gone.

And the *Weckit Shet* with him.

PART TWO

Let It Roll

Whatever the reason for Owen's return to Stepford, finances weren't the problem. Although he had less than a grand to his name (which wouldn't have gotten him off to so much as a working start in New York City), the fact was: the cost of living in Stepford was really no lower than in Philth Town or Baltimore.

Neither were matters of employment the cause of it, as—even though, yes, he had just been fired, with disdain, as a crime beat reporter in Gorbach (pop 10k), Louisiana, and couldn't rely on references there—he had nothing, no business connections in Stepford, to fall back on in the event of disaster.

And as much as he might have preferred to blame his parents, they weren't responsible either. In point of fact, they had left the area, bound for Connecticut, seven years earlier: his father in seeking out long-distance bicycle routes, on which he was given to foray, his mother in search of that New England light—her "acrylicist's dream"—by which to paint.

In retrospect, they would claim to have stayed in the area for so many years for the *land*. Once it was gone, they had left, went the story.

But not before Owen had shouldered the brunt of it.

Whatever, family matters had nothing to do with the situation at hand.

And he couldn't consider himself to have *gotten over it* (that is: *The Angst*) either. Worldly experience hadn't succeeded in galvanizing his tender hide. He certainly hadn't returned with outstanding hopes of recapturing lost youth.

No, he wasn't in town on account of a personal crisis or taxes or bankruptcy. No, he hadn't burned all of his bridges—or exhausted the last of his options . . .

He had returned for one reason alone. And a long time due, it had been:

The fight game.

Owen had seen his first boxing match (Clay v. Liston II) at the age of five. Since then, nothing of any significance to happen in the ring had escaped his attention. Much of his "traveling road show" (the heap of things he now carted from town to town) consisted of a sizeable video library—roughly three thousand bouts on tape—five or six boxes of memorabilia: gloves, pictures, trophies, wraps—dozens of books and hundreds of magazines, all of which Owen had read through repeatedly, tracing the history of the sport from gladiatorial Rome to the present day . . .

Over the years, he had dreamed of one day committing related knowledge to print. Yet, to date, he had published a mere two articles touching on the subject. The reason being, as he was aware: he couldn't evaluate any contender's performance—that is: critique it in print—without ever having stepped into a ring, without ever having taken a punch in his life.

While his love for the sport had never faltered, it had remained, thus far, vicarious. In youth, the allure of music, books and film (along with a field of grass) had piqued his interest as much as the fight game. He hadn't played organized sports in school. Most of his adolescence had gone into priming the noggin for freelance reporting. His twenties had passed in a flurry of same, with all the attendant indulgence in vice. His body had held up remarkably well, considering. So had his mind, for the most part. Until now, plenty of time had remained for "salvaging mortal wreckage," as he termed it—or, less dramatically, getting in shape.

Decidedly, that was no longer the case.

At present, his physical constitution, though not yet waning, had certainly peaked. His tide was now all the way in, so to speak. (And he hadn't even *tried* to quit smoking in a decade.) The number of seasons remaining to pick up the sport, from the inside, proper, was limited. Learning the ropes could go on for years. Owen had five of them left, at best.

If ever he planned on entitling himself to write on the subject, or even to watch it, then now was the time to find a gym, quit smoking and work like never before. He couldn't expect to have anything up on the matadors, cops and bear hunters out there—the algebra teachers and ATF agents and all the wrong cowards at large on the rock—who wouldn't have lasted a round in the ring, who would've been spat on and booed and insulted and driven right out of the house as disgraceful (not to mention the legion of half-witted journalists already plaguing the sport) without having warded off incoming blows on his own, and throwing a few in return.

His conscience simply wouldn't allow for it.

He had come "home" to get punched in the face.

With that in mind, he had settled on Stepford for two basic reasons, both of them practical: first, between Philth Town, Pittburgh, Rudding, Horaceburg, Alleytown, Stepford and Yorc, Pennsyltucky probably harbored the richest boxing tradition on earth. Residing in any one of these towns would have tapped him into the source directly. And, like it or not, despite his absence, he already knew his way around Stepford—adding to which, as importantly, *second:* he also had ties to Roddy Lowe.

Three time Golden Gloves state champ and, presently, accomplished professional junior welterweight, Roddy was truly a hometown legend. He and Owen had met through a mutual friend. (Which is to say: their medicine dealer.) Courteous, humble, attentive, impeccably groomed and tailored—and charming to boot—he often prompted the same remark from strangers: *"I've never met anyone like him."* Dependably brimming with euphemistic vernacular, Roddy had always presented a figure more suited to 1940: one part dying breed / old-school gentleman—a deferential ham with the ladies—one part dutiful Christian soldier / chevalier of the righteous light, and one part anachronistic cross of beatnik, homeboy and wharf rat brawler: a throwback in every regard, if incongruous, more: a decidedly singular character. *And* he was loyal. Roddy would've bent over backwards to help out a friend in need. Owen had known he could count on as much. It was taken for granted ahead of the move.

While puttering north in his overstuffed Legacy, Owen had accepted, then embraced, his decision. Fifteen hours behind the wheel, nonstop, and he'd surfaced from Dixie intact: as usual, Stepford appeared and seemed to straddle the Mason / Dixon equally: not quite the South, yet a hundred miles shy of New England, and vaguely Midwestern all over, Pennsyltucky consisted of Philth Town and Pittburgh. The rest was West Virginia.

The apartment, it seemed, had been waiting for him: twenty-five classified listings and, clearly, the choice of the lot: a one-hundred-year-old colonial flat near the Beaver Street projects. Instead of immersing himself in the well-to-do cracker suburban ring around town, he would settle with the resident poor therein, who hadn't the means or desire to ruin it. This would resolve his sidewalk issues. Along with the gingerbread eyesore modules. As a new Caucasian, he preferred the old ghetto.

His lease was secured in an afternoon.

Landing a job had been easier still.

Even though he'd come back willing not only to put his profession on hold, for the moment, but to tackle the grind, if necessary—be it temp work, dishes or pick-hoeing mule apples out of the cracks on Route 21—he was still able, somehow, by stroke of unlikely fortune, to land a job reporting. In truth, he'd submitted his file to *The Plea* on a whim while heading to an interview with a dog-walking agency over on Lime Street. Passing the five-storied glass-front building, he'd decided, for the hell of it, to go on in.

The lobby's receptionist, a scowler with her hair pulled back so tightly it was thinning down the middle, had examined his resume. Her tag read "Josie." Frowning, she had mumbled, "I've got to use the phone."

Her pronunciation of "phone" had been laden with the Dutch Anal Pucker—the Stepford drawl. Owen hadn't heard that lilt in years—the nasally rolling *"oe"* (with an umlaut) of "Br*oe*g's" a regional microbrewery. Of "p*oe*nies" galloping over a field. Of "p*oe*ms" by moonlight. Of "t*oe*tem" poles. And of secretaries named "J*oe*sie" on "ph*oe*ns" . . . By slowing down the enunciation and rolling over, forward and back, the *"oe"* while simultaneously curling the top lip sharply toward the nostrils—thereby exposing the two front teeth (hence the "anal" pucker) and pressing one's tongue almost flush with the roof of the mouth, then forcing a tonsillar bleat through that opening—one may hope to re-create this phenomenon within a controlled environment. Anyone who's ever left the county would have to recognize it as local stuff. Only the people of Stepford Town could demand of their faces the work of an anus.

Owen had turned to walk out the door when she snapped her fingers, still holding the ph*oe*n. He had turned back. Annoyed, she had motioned to *hold on*—flexing a finger. Again, she had looked away. Someone had picked up the line on the other end. Soon, the receptionist had glanced up to ask, "How soon are you available?"

Incredulous, Owen had shrugged. "What time is it?"

The voice on the other end must have overheard him. There was laughter, cawing. The receptionist hung up. "Mr. Jarvik will see you now"—handing him back his resume.

"Mr. Jarvik?"

She nodded. "Terrance Jarvik." Her voice had gone flat. "The city editor."

Upstairs.

He sat on a chair in the waiting room, convinced that his time was being wasted. He figured his background check was running, and shortly, somebody would give him the boot.

(As soon as he landed a job, he would have to quit smoking. That was the goal he had set. Which left him in no kind of hurry, for the moment. The four-alarm hell ride was fast approaching.)

Laughter drifted out of an office. Followed by: "Where is he?"—coughed with delighted approval, by the sound of it. "Send him in here!"

A woman in blue secretarial gear appeared in the doorway. She beckoned to Owen.

For the next better part of the afternoon, he had sat in a comfortable leather recliner being lauded with undeserved praise by a stranger—a gaunt, wiry old ferret of a man, overdressed, in a gabardine number—who couldn't stop laughing and shifting in starts at his desk, and who hadn't introduced himself yet, although Owen was naturally left to assume he was dealing with Editor Terrance Jarvik. That much was likely. The rest was unclear.

It seemed that the old man had gotten a hoot out of Owen's "reason" for leaving Gorbach—which, admittedly, sounded preposterous, but which had been at least *half* true: his boss in Louisiana, a mouthpiece for corporate land deal interests (the true half), had made inappropriate "advances" toward him—an allegation intended to ward off inquiry more than to entertain. The fact is: the charge wasn't meant to be funny. Yet Jarvik, strangely, was all busted up by it. Stranger still, he hadn't appeared to believe the story, and yet, for that reason, was all the more thrilled and, evidently, impressed. By admitting, thus, to horrible references, Owen had bought his way out of them—out of the need to address them.

Or so it appeared.

He hadn't the first idea of what to make of it.

On walking in, he had taken Jarvik for simply eccentric, a cracked old goat of a very-big-fish-in-an-empty-pond type, a lettered Yankee from old southern money, perhaps—with no one around him at present to pose any challenge or threat to his eminence—which, in itself, had grown flaccid, as such—full of bluster and affectation, he was.

However, as the meeting had proceeded, the old man's fervor began to appear less than voluntary. He must've been pushing seventy plus, so maybe his mind was just falling apart. But his gaze had appeared alert and attentive. And his energy level was through the roof. He may have been nearing retirement, yes, but he hadn't seemed ready to go out quietly.

Apparently (being the operative term), the gist of his current dilemma was this: in the previous month, an unexplained rise in disturbances—or, as the old man had coined them patronizingly, "rural mishaps," had swept the eastern—almost a third of—Stepford County. Notably similar incidents of breaking and entering, arson, criminal trespass, robbery and senseless destruction of property had been reported across the area known, unofficially, as the Amish Basin. Accounts of livestock assault, theft and harassment were unexplainably numerous (twelve by the last count) from Laycock to Bird-in-Hand, Intercourse to Paradise and all through Blue Ball. The highest frequency of incidents appeared to be occurring in the less residential expanses of corn and tobacco fields south of New Holland, off of Route 21, along the township borders. Statistically, the area couldn't have boasted a recent history of much less crime. Low-key barroom brawls had let out in the local taverns from time to time, and there *was* a significant biker culture, with multiple road gangs headquartered locally. But most of the resident "underworld," so to speak, usually kept pretty much to itself. Cases of actual breaking and entering had never been filed on the present level. The willful destruction of property was almost unheard of, even toward Halloween.

October had always been strange in The Basin. But rarely, if ever, to such extremes. The public records, according to Jarvik, reflected as much in no uncertain terms. "Trouble in Paradise isn't the norm," he claimed, unable to skirt the term. The Basin was characteristically dull and uneventful in most regards, to the point where even *The Plea* didn't opt to retain a full-time farm beat reporter. Any news worth printing was normally gathered once a week by a "hack" for inclusion in Sunday's "Lifestyles" section.

That particular "hack," it seemed, had quit the paper two weeks earlier. Meaning: *The Plea* was critically understaffed one dependable field reporter. Attempts to fill the position had, for whatever reason, come to naught. For the moment, two city reporters were splitting the sudden barrage of complaints down the middle. This, in effect, had demanded their overtime, travel through unfamiliar terrain and, as Jarvik pronounced, "more common sense than either fool can manage to summon."

"Besides which," he kept on, "they don't know a thing about farm equipment. *And* they can't write."

These were the circumstances into which Owen had blundered haphazardly, however strange. Even though he probably knew less about farms, and farming equipment, than anyone in town, he had managed without even trying, somehow, to land a position writing about them. Which, in general, seemed to be one of his stronger and more consistent talents. "The luck of the Celts," his grandfather called it. Despite the fact that he hadn't exactly been offered a shot at deposing the mayor, he *had* secured a job he could not only live with, but work without blowing his focus.

Or so he had thought on accepting the offer.

Then he had gone to the game reserve.

From there on, nothing had happened as planned. And nothing had been short of frantically paced.

His second day on the job, Friday, October 8th, as the perfect example:

He was called to the office at two p.m., an hour early, on Jarvik's orders. Two other daily reporters were present, neither of whom extended him a greeting, or even a handshake, upon introduction. They both seemed annoyed with him right off the bat. And so did Jarvik's assistant editor, a pasty-faced honky named Timothy Kegel. They all struck Owen as miserable assholes.

Then he found out why they'd been called in.

The *Blue Ball Devil Returns* edition had already gone into four printings. By evening, a fifth was expected to go to press, with further demand projected. Regional TV was phoning nonstop, along with a paper from nearby Rudding—and numerous local residents calling to verify similar "sightings" of their own.

So much for the cozy reception, thought Owen: his basket looked like a public spitoon. It would overflow the next morning, when the *Philth Town Inquiry* ran his story, front page . . . No doubt, the regular staff was irate. And not without reason. After all, who was he?—this Owen Brynmor, this slovenly kid drifting into their midst on an unscreened, trial-run basis, apparently, to fall under some kind of cracked and delirious favor of their aging city editor—who, incidentally, introduced him as "someone who might help you idiots think"—then go on to triple circulation by landing an AP smash on his *first* report—and with tales of Bigfoot, no less . . .

They all looked insulted beyond their capacities.

Owen himself found it hard to believe.

Beforehand, of course, he'd expected a smash. There was no way this story could *not* have sold. But to watch something actually rip as intended was a rare and genuine marvel to behold. Twice in the past, he had lost what should have been national copy to turn of luck—the first to a presidential scandal, the second to the fall of the Berlin Wall. He knew not to blink till the check had cleared—and even then, with residual caution.

Jarvik, on the other hand, was openly thrilled. (Tripling circulation tends to have that effect on city editors.) Having called everyone into his office, he assigned his regulars each to a task—two of them to telephone duty, and the third, a furious Kegel, to screening messages, while Owen, overtly exempt from the old man's disdain, was encouraged to follow up his story. He could start by reporting to the Intercourse Market to verify rumors of livestock attacks.

Already, Owen could feel the resentment building around him. He left quietly.

Outside, in the car, his window jammed. While rolling the handle, his fingers locked up. Nicotine: worse than he'd ever imagined possible, hurting like none of these people could . . . Day number two. It would never get worse. This nightmare would never seem more insurmountable. He would feel crazed, overdriven and sick for the next thirty hours, with little improvement. His hand would continue to wander involuntarily, à la Dr. Strangelove. The sweat would continue to roll in flashes. His heart would continue to palpitate violently. He would be tempted to give up, but wouldn't be able to. He would feel optionless, ruined: either back to the toxins, or life as an unending heart attack.

This would take years to get used to.

The coming week had been put on reserve for expected trauma to mind and body—compounded by which, the effects of his workout with Roddy that morning—his first afternoon at the West Side Gym—were beginning to register. He hadn't been out of the club for an hour. Yet already, both of his lats felt torn. Hard as The Coach had pushed them—and, Jesus, he certainly hadn't shown any mercy—Owen was having a great deal of trouble just lifting his keys to start the ignition. His arms and legs were a throbbing mass of quivering, mashed and achy muscles. Earlier, coming down the stairs, his knees had threatened to buckle beneath him. Now, he felt nauseous—so out of shape, it was something of a miracle the session hadn't killed him. There was no oxygen high on this trip. He wasn't enjoying the pump, so to speak. The only reward was a fleeting reprieve from the nicotine cravings. Which wouldn't last.

One hour later, twenty miles west, in the steadily darkening afternoon, he had managed to alienate most of the Intercourse Market's outdoor livestock vendors. Having started out casually, broaching the subject with palpably brazen nonchalance, he'd been quick to pick up on the sweeping derision his inquiries seemed to be eliciting. Before long, he'd felt less at home in the stands than he had at the paper that afternoon. Being spurned by the Plain Folk was highly unsettling. It made Owen feel like a cancer cell. He was suddenly given to wonder if Jarvik's reason was altogether intact. In avoiding his questions, these people were not only unresponsive—there was hostility. Which couldn't have come as any surprise. The Plain Folk had always been ill-disposed toward the press. Jarvik must have known that.

Yet, checking back into the office was unreassuring. The old man had stepped out for dinner.

Thus, Owen took the initiative to follow up several reports from the previous week.

The first was a breaking and entering call from the "venison farm," a fenced-in, four-acre pasture stocked with exotic deer. The farm was privately owned by an elderly couple, Robert and Nancy McConnel—according to whom, their herd of seventy rare and, primarily, imported animals had been terrorized by a loping, bipedal "freak of creation" for the past two weeks. When asked to elaborate, the couple fell silent, as neither, it turned out, had sighted the creature. Nevertheless, Mrs. McConnel was willing to go on record as stating that, based on events of the week before, the sounds she had heard from the yard after midnight (howling above the stampeding herd) undoubtedly / certainly / had to have been that "thing" in the paper: *"Jesus help us."*

It wasn't much better a mile down the road, where a local tavern—the Dogboy—owner, an aging coot with a widow's peak, reported a "one-man pack of dogs" having scattered garbage all over the parking lot. Several regulars claimed to have spotted a "creature" on leaving the bar that week—and while no one could say what it looked like for certain, or even agree on the species, for that matter, going consensus held that the newspaper's Blue Ball Devil was close enough. As far as Owen could tell, the Dogboy's owner was speaking in dead earnest.

Owen left him a contact number, one he was free to give out to the locals.

Finally, he drove to the Holtwood Development, a ten-acre neighborhood under construction a mile down the road, between Smoketown and Bird-in-Hand. There, amid eyesore module foundations in varying stages of half-assembly, a contractor hoarsely explained how the houses had fallen prey to nightly sabotage. And no, Bigfoot wasn't suspected—or any fraternity prank, for that matter. One needed only consider the "evidence" left behind to confirm as much: a purplish goo, some kind of spray paint, marking the sides of several plows. In other words: *people* (gasp) and the contractor reckoned he knew just whom: *"Them hippies."*

As though on cue, Owen's clunky cell phone rang in his jacket pocket. It was Jarvik's assistant reporting a "riot" on 341, back east, toward Intercourse. Leaving the contractor, Owen climbed into his Subaru and took off, bewildered by now. Since when had The Basin gone apeshit, he wondered. This place was amazing. He couldn't believe it.

He arrived on the scene of the "riot" to find that the road had been sealed off and traffic rerouted toward Bareville and Ronks, to the north and south. He parked his car and walked toward the scene of what looked to be a fairly serious accident. A telephone pole lay across the road. A clean-up crew was attempting to move it. Aside from a couple of Lamepeter troopers, a tow truck driver and some volunteer firemen, only a handful of elderly locals with cardboard signs remained on the scene. These were the hippies, no doubt: as defined by exercising their right to assemble—though most of them, based on appearance, had probably been too old to draft even back in the sixties. Owen had trouble coaxing a clear account of proceedings from anyone present. The most he could ascertain was that a "crazy-ass Dutch boy" had challenged an eighteen-wheeler to a game of chicken in an open buggy—and, afterward, paid a terrible price in a brutal beating by one of the cops.

The farm boy's name, as determined through a call to the Lamepeter precinct, was Ephraim Bontrager. No further details regarding his case were available. The suspect was being "interrogated."

Owen returned to the office at dusk. But the office would bring him little relief.

To start, the Associated Press had been calling all day for verification of text. Demands had been made to speak with "the lucky reporter." Congratulations were offered: *"most convincing hoax in years,"* and *"should go down in the books with Nessie."* One caller had asked what the suit was made of, applauding the editor's sense of humor. Another deplored his sheer audacity and willingness to stop at nothing for sales. For most of the afternoon, Jarvik's assistant had kept her cool while fielding questions. Along about five, however, someone had called her a hayseed. From there, she had lost it.

As Owen entered the copy room, most of the rest of the staff appeared equally frazzled. He walked down an aisle of partitioned cubicles, feeling the glares from every side.

Telephones all through the building were ringing. Even the weatherman's line was tied up. And not just with press calls, either. As many complaints had been pouring in from locals—some in urgent need of assurance, some in jabbering, high-flown panics, the rest either tickled pink or disgusted, with glimpses of vague uncertainty between. Several subscribers had threatened already to cancel their daily delivery service in opposition to what they considered the creature's "pornographic" namesake. Others were simply embarrassed—one lady claiming a brother in Yorc had been teasing her. As well, the game warden, Kratz, had phoned to complain that he, too, had been swamped with calls. Everyone seemed intent on discrediting him as the "hoax's" perpetrator. But, as that went, Kratz hadn't taken the photograph. He was demanding a public disclaimer.

And then there was the mail—by fax, by telegraph and, later, by post it would flood the office.

Throughout the week, Owen would come in to parcels from every enthusiast geek of the paranormal this side of Billings: allegations of similar "sightings," and going speculation per this one.

Someone in Blue Ball was willing to wager the Jersey Devil had come to town. But the problem with that was: the Jersey Devil, by legend, had the head of a horse, the wings of an eagle and the body of a giant serpent. The Blue Ball Devil looked more like a mud-thrown kangaroo with a scorched pompadour. So then, perhaps the fabled Goat Man: one caller certainly seemed to think so. Years earlier, according to a Michael Hoober of Windmill City, Virginia, a neighbor had clipped the beast while driving home on a back road, late one night—and even had a wiry clump of hair that was pulled from the radiator grill to show for it. The catch was: the Goat Man, a laboratorial fugitive gone amok in the hills, was described as having the upper body of a man, and the legs and hooves of a goat. Here, too, the descriptions clashed. A closer match, one anonymous source contended, was Mo Mo, the half-man / half-ape creature from Louisiana, Missouri. While closer to the Blue Ball Devil in appearance, there was little to account for the distance between them, or the fact that Mo Mo hadn't been spotted in over twenty years. And so with the Beast of Truro, a savage, catlike creature from Massachusetts. And Saskatchewan's mythical Red Coyote. And El Dientudo of Buenos Aires . . . The list continued: a regional entity / legend from most existing cultures, and hundreds of former marching band geeks here at home to keep them all on file.

Owen wound up at a loss for anything even remotely similar in profile. The Blue Ball Devil, as urban myth and enigma, appeared to be one of a kind. The only related reference on file—three one-paragraph blurbs on the subject, all of them upward of twenty years old—had been pulled from the *Stepford Daily Plea*'s archives. The microfiche files had been milked for their worth, and from them was woven to print the tale of a creature—what one local farmer was quoted as calling a "wingless goblin with quills" —purported to have wandered the eastern half of the county in 1974. The creature was said to have rendered extensive, community-impacting levels of crop damage. None of *The Plea*'s current staff members, not even Jarvik, as the longtime city editor, could tell him much more than that. And being that Lindsey Cale, the reporter who'd covered the story originally, was dead (her car gone into a roadside ditch in the early eighties, cause unknown), Owen would have to rely on the here and now in following up his story. Which should have been simple enough: the calls that were pouring in to the paper at present were *not* in reference to previous sightings so much as they were in regard to a creature trashing their compost heaps that week.

For his follow-up article, therefore, he gathered the choicest reports from the previous days, and, with minimal formatting, gave them to Jarvik.

The old man couldn't have been more pleased.

He burst into laughter on reading the text. He dabbed his face with a handkerchief, giggled, then nodded approvingly. "This will do."

Owen went home feeling relatively satisfied, if intent on a few basic changes.

For one thing, he wanted his story, for as long as it ran, to be more than a public ledger. One time around, that format worked. But the impact would lessen with repetition. He would have to find a new angle, somehow. He would have to explore The Basin . . .

More confusingly, he didn't know what he was after, exactly. What was he getting at? Mass hysteria? As in: the provocation thereof?

—Most likely, yes.

But, theatrics aside, was that justifiable?

—Sometimes it's right to do the wrong thing . . .

Beyond all of which, there was also the matter of what exactly did *he* "believe"? Now, there was a question worth considering.

When his mother had called him to talk that morning, things had been plenty confusing already. Explaining to her the situation had proven no easy matter for Owen. Mostly, she hadn't been able to figure out where he was coming from, why he was doing this. By her estimation, he was one of what he called those "paranormal geeks" himself. Yet his tone was imbued with the glee of a prankster.

Moreover, she couldn't have known the extent to which he and his coverage were having an impact.

On Thursday morning, however, that changed—as the story began to appear in newspapers all across the nation, including her chosen daily in rural Connecticut. *"Beelzebub in Pennsyltucky"*—disgusted, she quoted the lead by phone. And a caption beneath the photo: *"It Came From Blue Ball."*

"I suppose you think that's funny."

Even though neither term was Owen's, his mother was sure to blame him for both.

What she didn't, and couldn't, have known was that Owen, despite his giggle on breaking it down, had questions himself—and couldn't entirely write this matter off as a hoax.

On first appearance, he'd taken the motion detector photo for having been staged—and brilliantly so: far and away the best thing ever to come out of Stepford. But after a day in The Basin, he'd been given to wonder—*not* so much by the tavern and deer ranch debacles, which barely held water, but owing more to the hostile reception afforded him that afternoon at the market. Those vendors had been more than simply unfriendly. They had been spooked. There was no doubt about it.

Whatever the case, he was certain of one thing: the Blue Ball Devil was a bonafide smash—a syndicated humdinger, national copy. And as a result, in spite of his initial resolve on returning to Stepford to begin with, Owen found himself back in reporting as never before.

He felt like a rock star.

An estimated three hundred papers across the country had printed the story and photo. There was talk of coverage in Europe too. And on TV: at one point, a network executive called to speak with "the werewolf reporter." A late night radio DJ from Texas had gotten himself in trouble for claiming the creature was Uncle Shrub in drag.

A brick had been thrown through the station window.

Just down the street from *The Plea*, the Press Room Deli was humming with talk of the matter. On stopping in before work that day, Owen had silenced the room completely. While standing in line, he could feel their contempt in a noxious, stifling cloud all around him. Slowly, their conversation resumed, but in hushed mutters, with awkward pauses.

Bess, a sickly attractive, chain-smoking thirty-something from Format approached him.

"Man," she squinted unsmilingly, leaning forward to whisper. "These people hate you."

For what it was worth, he hated them back—especially Kegel, the junior editor: chronically dour, with a bulging vein that divided his forehead in times of duress: Kegel, the Stepford Anus incarnate . . .

That afternoon, he pounced on Owen straight out of the elevator: "Mister Brynmor." He sidled up, waving some papers. "I don't know how it's done elsewhere, but here we *staple* submissions. It's clear that you haven't consulted your style book."

Blam.

He probably went golfing every Thursday.

He would make working the bag less torturous.

For Sunday's edition, Jarvik ordered a "week in review" piece—intended not only to recap the story's development to date, but to focus as much on worldwide coverage the photograph, and thereby Stepford, was receiving: interviews with recognized "experts" in Tucson who claimed that the beast was an astral traveler, to locals from Washington Avenue, Brooklyn, who yodeled of Pumpkinhead's return.

Somewhere in the article, mention was made of a bid for the photo's original negative (quoted at $2,000) being surpassed by a TV executive's offer. In truth, the original bid had been placed by a comic book collector from Delaware, who, like his corporate competitor, had been referred directly to Dwayne Gibbons. Apparently, Gibbons, who owned the original negative, had not received their calls—or at least had yet to benefit by them—as, Sunday morning, he phoned *The Plea* to complain. "It says here two thousand dollars." His tone was belligerent. "What's this about?"

He wanted to speak with the "author" in person—and, yes, he had news—an update, of sorts. He was down at the Dogboy, east on 21.

Owen hung up.

He knew the address.

The tavern was nearly empty at that hour. Most of the regular crowd was sleeping. A couple of stoolhuggers sat at the end of the bar. The air smelled of lovely tobacco.

The barkeep, a ruggedly fierce-looking woman, came over. She looked at him blankly.

"I'm here to see someone named Dwayne Gibbons," he told her.

She nodded, turning.

Behind her, down at the end of the bar, a figure sat up. He was wearing a hood.

"The reporter's here to see you," the bartender called to him, jerking a thumb toward Owen.

The figure let out a belch. Then, getting up: "So he is." He started to weave down the aisle. "You think he'll buy me a drink?"

Owen nodded to the bartender.

"One for yourself?" she asked.

He nodded again.

As Gibbons approached down the length of the bar, Owen turned for an introduction.

"I'm Brynmor," he said. He held out his hand.

Sliding onto a stool before him, Gibbons looked back in silence, frowning. "I know who you are." He wiped his chin.

Gradually, Owen dropped his hand.

Right off, he didn't like what he saw. There was something overtly obscene about Gibbons. More than shady, he was all-out beady-eyed.

"Look," he commenced, producing a paper. "It says here an offer for two thousand dollars."

"That offer was forwarded straight to you," said Owen. "I gave him your number myself."

Gibbons blinked. "It says here offers."

"—were forwarded straight to you, as I said."

Surely, this weasel had more to say.

The bartender brought over two pints of beer.

Owen placed a five on the counter.

Shaking his head, Gibbons continued with a forced, unnaturally casual leer. "The way I see it, you owe me some money."

Owen stared at him, trying to pinpoint the physical features that most repulsed him—maybe the way his eyebrows intersected just over the bridge of his nose—or his scrawny neck, marked with cuts and a horribly razor-burned Adam's apple—the way his back was bowed to a permanent C—his darkly tobacco-stained lips.

Yet even in combination, none of those features surpassed his venomous gaze.

It was disappointing to think that the Blue Ball Devil, and thereby the current renown of Stepford (let alone Owen's career), had been triggered by one with the eyes of a viper.

"You won't get a dime out of me," said Owen.

He stood up. Twenty-five minutes he'd wasted driving here. "Check your answering machine." He chased his beer in clear disgust.

Gibbons cracked a hideous grin: you could follow it back to his fortieth aunt. "I didn't expect a dime out of you," he said. "I was talking about your boss. But now that you mention it—" Sliding his empty glass across the counter, he nodded. "Buy me another drink, and I just might tell you something."

The bartender cut in. "Don't buy him anything, mister."

Furious, Gibbons glared at her.

Ignoring him, she added, "He's just trying to tell you what everyone in here already knows. And that is—"

"Shut your mouth!" snarled Gibbons.

She followed up: "The Devil was here last night."

Until then, Owen had been intent on walking out with no further remark.

He lifted a finger. "Give him a drink."

A heap at the end of the counter sat up.

"And that one too," Owen added. "And one for yourself."

He pulled up a stool and sat.

They were silent at first, the four of them hitting their beers, until finally, the bartender spoke: "It came in at midnight."

The Heap interjected. "It was closer to one."

"It was midnight exactly. Bob had just left. I remember."

"Bob worked late last night."

They argued the point. Owen allowed it to roll for a moment. Then he cut in: "So what did it look like?" he asked, not knowing where to begin.

They shifted uncertainly.

The Heap was the first to venture an effort: "He looked like Nixon."

"Right," said Gibbons. "Maybe after a beating."

The bartender shook her head. "It weren't Nixon. More like an ape in overalls."

"Dirty ones."

"Smelled like it . . ."

"Ugly."

"—as Nixon."

"And talks like him."

Owen's head was spinning. "Hold on now." He stepped in, reeling. "Do you mean to tell me this thing wears *clothing*?"

He could hear how ridiculous the question sounded.

They stared at him.

"*And* that it talks" he continued, trying to justify having spoken.

(The Blue Ball Devil as Richard Nixon?)

"That's right," said Gibbons. "He's a regular guy. Though to my ear, it don't speak English too good."

"He's *not* a regular guy," said the barkeep.

"He ain't a guy at all," said The Heap. "He's a devil. Just like you called him, mister."

Owen gestured to Gibbons's newspaper. Sitting faceup on the counter, the motion detector photo begged his retort. "That doesn't look like a person to me."

"Of course not." Gibbons said, shaking his head. "That picture was taken on October first."

Owen stared for a moment. "And what does that mean?" he asked.

Gibbons stared back. "All I can say is: check your calendar."

Suddenly, Owen felt disadvantaged, as though the ground were sliding beneath him. What did these people know that he didn't? What did that sneer of Gibbons's mean?

Just then, a beverage delivery man stepped in. He was older, grizzled, stocky. The door swung shut behind him. The barkeep directed him back toward the take-out coolers. She picked up a clipboard and moved to join him.

The Heap kept talking: "I heard The Devil's a chimp they shaved and taught to speak."

Gibbons dismissed him. "The Devil's no chimp."

"How would you know?"

"Cuz." He glowered. "I seen it."

Another argument started up. Owen listened in disbelief as they went back and forth on the creature's appearance, then onto theories of nuclear accidents just down the river and Nature's revenge . . .

In spite of his prior insistence, The Heap was now sure that the Blue Ball Devil, the original, was dead: some local farmers had shot it. The freak that had come in the night before was a fake, he claimed: an imposter, a charlatan.

Down the bar, at the end of the counter, the beverage delivery man overheard them. He looked up from tallying invoice figures to chime in, calmly: "It's definitely dead."

Everyone looked at him.

"What would you know?" Gibbons demanded. "You don't even live in this area."

"True," said the man, unfazed. "But I used to."

"So, then?" asked The Heap. "Have you seen it?"

"No," the man admitted. "But it ripped the handle off of my grandfather's whiskey still, if that counts." He laughed out loud.

"I thought you said it was dead," Owen followed up.

"I said, the Blue Ball *Devil*'s dead. You folks are talking about something else."

"Like what?" asked Gibbons.

The man shook his head with a grin: "The Mennonites call it the Corn Wolf."

"The what?" said Owen.

The Heap added: "What is it?"

Grinning still, the man came back. "Hey, you tell me. I don't live here, remember?"

At last, The Heap and Gibbons fell silent.

But Owen continued to press the issue: "How do you know for certain it's dead?"

The man replied with a casual shrug. "Because," he said, reaching into his pocket to pull out a Swisher Sweet cigarillo. He lit it, puffed and concluded: "His name was Jacob Speicher. He died in The Nam."

Jack was on the telephone with Jarret Yoder the moment Scarlet walked into the gym. Her appearance found him, The Coach, in ill humor. It had been a hell of a morning already.

To start off, somebody—probably one of the heroin dealers from down the street—had blown two holes in a neighbor's car hood, and planted a third in the gym's back wall.

Then the plumbing had gone out downstairs: a septic pump flooding a third of the level. It smelled like a field of outhouses, wafting up, halfway over the training floor . . .

To add to which, a collection bureau had called on behalf of an ambulance depot, seeking in excess of two thousand dollars in tournament dues—a debt which Aldo Lowe had incurred, unbeknownst to Jack.

And crowning the heap, his watch was missing—a silver Timex awarded him early that year by the Stepford Commissioner's Office for "outstanding work with city youth." Ironic, of course, that it wind up stolen. Which certainly seemed to be the case. Twice now, Jack had combed the building. And he wasn't given to losing things . . . Nor was he overly prone to theft. Sure, missing wraps and gloves were common. Headgear came and went with the weather—and some of it borne away on the sly, perhaps. But nothing right out of his office. That was another game entirely—one that The Coach was relaying to Yoder, suspecting, between them, Franklin Pendle.

Of course, there was no way of knowing for certain. Franklin had already left the building and probably, if, indeed, he had taken it, wouldn't hold on to the watch for long. Besides which, it could have been somebody else. Scores of locals belonged to this gym. In theory, somebody could have slipped into and out of the office unnoticed that morning. Jack hated jumping to any conclusions . . . However, his own recollections were clear: other than Franklin, just Roddy, Holy War, Calvin, Rhya Deeds and her class—which consisted of two girls from Weight Watchers, one Cuban schoolboy, their junior starlet, Denise, the Brynmor kid and a Horaceburg drunk in recovery—had been in the building all morning. And Jack was pretty much certain on them. Whereas Franklin, while he hadn't been *caught* in a while, had a mile-long record for petty theft. Moreover, he'd been in the office that morning, using the phone with The Coach's permission—and would have stood right there, above the desk, looking down on the Timex where Jack had left it.

Beyond that, he just had a feeling, did Jack—something he couldn't deny much longer. He had known Franklin for half the boy's lifetime. Twice, he had taken him into his home. Twice, they had gone to the semifinals. Twice, he had kicked him out of the gym for indiscipline. And twice, he had taken him back. He knew all the writing on Franklin's wall. And right now, it didn't look good. Not at all.

Only a few months earlier, the young man's uncle and guardian, a small-time pusher, had been shot holding up a convenience store. Franklin had been on the slide ever since. Former habits had quickly resurfaced: running with trouble, shirking on training and smoking—and now it seemed *selling*—grass.

Just that week, he'd been picked up for dealing—along with a carload of homies, joyriding, windows down, smoking a blunt with the stereo blasting, straight through a four-way stop sign. (Reasonable *what*?) And the fools had been carrying *seven* ounces—which, worse, had been split into multiple bags. They were all being charged with intent to sell. It was everything Jack had been able to do to keep Franklin out of the juvenile hall. And this, it appeared, was how Franklin repaid him. The little bastard.

Another one down.

As much as it saddened him, Jack was compelled to relay his suspicions to Yoder by phone. Maybe they'd made a mistake, he submitted. Maybe the kid belonged in jail.

"Don't take it to heart," he was told in a well-meant, if futile attempt at consolation. "There's only so much a person can do."

But that brought little solace to Jack. He'd never been able to throw in the towel without beating himself up.

"We'll handle it," Yoder assured him. "Anything else I can do for you?"

Yes, as a matter of fact, there was . . .

He began to explain.

Then Scarlet walked in.

In a sense, it was better this way: forgoing the pleasantries, skipping the awkwardly overjoyed greeting, a whiff of the giant past, and proceeding, instead, directly to business.

Of course, she looked great. She was still Talutah. A few years older perhaps—some touches of gray where the hair had once flowed down her back and shoulders in pure, obsidian black—some lines of age underscoring her eyes, though in fact, they were probably creases from grinning. That much hadn't changed a bit: beaming down on him now from the doorway.

She overheard most of his conversation. Which spared him having to paraphrase later. Once he had hung up the phone, she slumped in a chair to the right of the door and looked at him. "Well," she sighed, as though most of her worst suspicions had been confirmed already (yet bidding, still, on a doomed appeal): "There's still time to call this a false alarm."

He raised his hands in helpless apology.

"I *will* forgive you." Upping her bid, she ignored the gesture. "I'll tell you what: cover my expenses and we'll call it even?"

Torn between less than witty comebacks, Jack was left shaking his head in silence.

She frowned. "Well, how about we just call it even, then? I'll even act like I wasn't enjoying my first vacation in twenty-two months."

Finally, The Coach had heard enough. "How in the hell do you think *I* feel?"

And at last, with an instantaneous dissipation of mirth, she accepted it. "Damn." She leaned forward, holding her head in her hands. She looked up and sighed again, puffing her cheeks. She was no longer smiling.

"Word is: you've got exactly a month."

He leaned back, expressionless. "That's what I figured."

The rhythm of bag work lingered between them.

Then she sat up. "Well, let's have it, then." Gone was the sarcasm. "What have you got?"

Jack pulled a folder from a drawer in his desk. He handed it to her.

She looked inside. An angled rut furrowed into her brow. "And you think this will work?"

"It better." He nodded.

"And where does one . . . *buy* . . ." She trailed off.

Jack took the folder and closed it, tucking it back in his drawer. "From a farrier," he answered.

She blinked. "A what?"

He waved her off. "Don't worry about it."

A pained expression came over her face. She closed her eyes and rubbed her temples. Then she sat up, remembering something. "And who's the reporter?" she asked, as though broaching a whole different subject: the insult to injury.

Heaving a short, delirious sigh of his own, he peered through the glass behind her.

She sat up and followed his gaze out the window to center floor. There were six of them, jumping rope.

"Which one?" she asked.

"Which one do you *think*?"

She looked closer. Two Caucasians. And one of them sweating profusely, suffering, starched . . .

"Whoa." She drew back. "He looks like he's dying."

"Don't worry," said Jack, with the only grin that would crease his expression all day. "He'll make it."

But that much remained on the table. The Coach had seen too many white boys who looked just like him: the washed-out, flabby, repentant lush on an early to midlife panic attack. Most of them lasted no more than a week.

"So what do you know about him?" Scarlet asked.

Shrugging, Jack relayed his findings:

. . . Owen Kelly Brynmor. Age: thirty. Born and raised in Stepford, Py. Received his bachelor's in journalism from PSU in 19–. Graduated sixth in a class of four hundred. Subsequently stationed in New York City, freelance reporting for seven years. Thereafter, headed south for a string of primarily rural and small-town assignments. Recent positions included police reporting for a daily in Roswell, New Mexico. Followed by film reviewing in Little Rock. Then on to crime reporting for the *Gorbach Daily* in western Louisiana.

His record was clean, for all practical purposes. One count of discharging illegal fireworks. A couple of unpaid traffic fines. A suspended driver's license in West Virginia. Possession of cannabis, two grams.

"He's harmless enough," Jack declared. "He just can't hold a job for long."

They watched him heave and wheeze through the glass.

"And he just walked in here?" she asked, very matter-of-factly, almost asserting the question.

Jack nodded yes: "Strange as it sounds."

Scarlet shook her head, incredulous.

Out on the floor, Owen could feel them watching. It caught him completely off guard. Until then, aside from their first encounter,

The Coach had ignored his side of the planet. Not once had he met Owen's gaze directly. Not once had he deigned to return his greetings. In fact, his only acknowledgment of Owen's existence had come indirectly, and that—*"Go easy, we've all got to start somewhere"*—in hushing his juniors from poking fun. Owen's footwork had made them laugh. The Coach had forced them to quiet down. Which hadn't exactly amounted to contact, but Owen *had,* at least, felt visible.

He still didn't know what to make of Jack's attitude . . .

Roddy had warned him about it beforehand, down in the locker room, just before noon.

"Coach gets lost in his world sometimes. You know what I'm sayin'?"—in trying to explain: "He gets distracted. It's nothing personal. Just don't bum-rush him."

No worries there.

Whatever the state of his graces—financial, domestic, the plumbing situation downstairs—The Coach was someone you wouldn't cross paths with. On size alone he commanded respect: at 6'5", 240-plus and maintained, he was bearlike in stature—with steely arms, enormous legs and a powerful frame. And his tempered, even disposition imbued him with rare, uncommon authority. The fact that his juniors refrained from the use of profanity here in the gym spoke volumes. Eliciting such obedience testified to The Coach's strength of character.

So did his taste in women. *Yowza*—assuming the matron saint was his. She was striking. She looked like a Native American Goddess.

What were they doing here, both of them? And why were they staring at him? Lordy. What? . . .

Locking his gaze to a photo of Lupe Pintor hanging above the mirror, Owen grew painfully conscious of the jump rope's every pass, just over his head. The floor beneath him was streaked with sweat. It was dripping, rolling, pouring out of him—steadily, two and three drops at a time.

Surrounding him, two fantastically obese women, a quiet Hispanic kid, one tough-looking dark-haired girl whose confidence, movement and strength betrayed her experience and one old man in a *Kansas* shirt paid vigilant heed to Rhya Deeds—Rhya, best known for shattering one-time media darling Katherine Collier's well-protected title reign in a thrilling, nationally televised upset. Owen remembered that fight as a smoker. Of course, the idea that he might ever *train* under Rhya would never have occurred to him then. Yet, here and now, as the gym's assistant instructor, she faced him, barking orders.

Behind her, Roddy was working the bags, to Owen's marvel and incomprehension. When Roddy tore into that hundred-pound trainer, the building roared like a firing range. You could hear his punches from down the block. It was hard to imagine anyone *taking* them. For Owen, less than a round of the same activity left his body spent. Just landing on target at full extension felt like driving his arms through quicksand; on impact, he carried no wallop at all. His right cross wouldn't have staggered a girl scout. His cardiovascular state was worse. And his bowels were churning. He couldn't keep up . . .

But he had to—even when every muscle was still on the cross from the session before. Even when most of the damage had only begun to register early that morning, even while every inch of his body was pushing spontaneous disassembly . . . Realistically, all of that was to be expected, and no doubt more: a hell ride—what salvaging bodily wreckage *should* have entailed, at least to begin with—as meanwhile, back in the grueling now, Rhya shouted for double time (*"Thirty more seconds!"*) and Roddy laid into the bag with his hooks, resounding like cannon fire—and, even more humbling, numerous greats of the game looked down on him, gazing from hundreds of photos and posters and foldouts and programs all over the room, every inch of the walls—(*concentrate on them*): Sugar Ray Robinson. (*Keep it together.*) Benny Leonard. Sweet Pea. Little Red. (*Lopez.*) Alexis Arguello. Duran in a panama hat . . .

In addition to premium standards in women, The Coach had impeccable taste in fighters: many of Owen's brightest beacons were on display throughout the room. Their appearance alone made him place a good deal of faith in Jack as a competent trainer, even if, thus far, his social skills had fallen short of ingratiating. Anyone who mounted a portrait of Mathew Franklin over his door could be trusted. And right on across, as methodically showcased: Salvador Sanchez, minus the halo. Carmen Basilio digging an uppercut. Archie Moore playing stand-up bass. Battling Siki in gangster apparel . . . And, front and center, the one that had caught Owen's eye in a flash upon entering the gym: the "Human Windmill," Harry Greb, in the prime of his short, magnificent life—Greb the enigma, the legend, the myth, whose record, conversely, was rooted in fact: in 299 fights, he'd won 264, lost 23 and drawn 12. And his quality of opposition, on the whole, was nearly unrivaled in boxing history.

Two hundred ninety-nine fights. Against some of the brightest and best of a glorious era. The figure was crushing. Owen was hoping to spar three rounds before it was over.

Or, right now, to make it through jumping this rope.

At last, it snared on his dragging feet. He sprawled.

The class erupted with laughter.

Rhya stood over him, choking it back. "Are you OK?" She offered a hand. He got up without it, disgraced. "I'm sorry."

Apologizing just made it worse.

She turned away, yelling: "Thirty more seconds!"—then back to him: "Whenever you're ready."

They booed—all of them, still jumping rope.

The Coach and his lady had drawn the blinds.

Owen got back on it, heaving to lift his feet from the floor without twisting an ankle. He tripped again with ten seconds remaining.

"Thirty more seconds!" Rhya repeated.

Somebody yelled at him: "Come on, man!"

It was all he could muster to finish the round without spraying his innards across the mirror. At "TIME!" he tripped to the water fountain, but found himself panting too heavily to drink. His legs were trembling. The face sweating back in the mirror was starched. He looked like a crowd control hose had been turned on him. Nobody else in the group looked as bad.

Managing somehow to slip to the toilet unchallenged, he locked himself in the stall. For a moment, the nausea almost receded. But no. It was coming . . .

He vomited beans.

Fitting enough, he thought to himself: after years of indulgence, it served him right. He should have been thankful, really—to still have a chance, that it wasn't too late already. *Assuming* it wasn't too late already . . . The agony of training confirmed its need. He was lucky to suffer in relative youth.

The bell rang. Out there. Miles away . . .

With his vision fogged over in static pinpricks, he leaned on the wall. His lungs were burning. His chest was tight, full of garbage and phlegm. He couldn't imagine smoking a cigarette . . . Something was wrong with his hearing, too—a blockage. He couldn't yawn it away. Through a high-pitched ring, Rhya was shouting: "Seven more minutes!"

Jesus Christ.

Leaning forward, he flushed his breakfast. He opened the stall door and limped to the sink. He turned on a faucet and cupped his hands and splashed his face and neck with water.

Afterward, staring despondently into the mirror—into one of his dilated pupils—he drifted in silent, void suspension . . .

That's when the roar of intrusion sounded.

To start, there was garbled hollering, what might have been Calvin and Holy War having an argument.

Then came a booming *"Yo!"* and what sounded like somebody kicking the gym's back door.

Right away, Owen thought of the heroin dealers Roddy had told him about: the ones who had shot up the alley that morning.

His scalp went hot with a burst of sweat.

But then, rising over a chorus of shouts, he heard taunting. The unequivocal ring of a challenge.

He opened the door for a look.

The first thing he saw were the card girls, two of them—long-legged, busty and far too scantily clad for the weather—framed in the doorway. They sauntered in like advertisements.

Behind them, a couple of muscle-bound goons in trench coats followed along from the alley.

Then, a cameraman stepped in. He leveled his lens and moved away from the door . . .

A honky in skin-tight jeans, with a handlebar mustache, appeared, crowding the shot. He looked like a queer iguana. His eyes were narrow, hateful, venomous slits. His expression was so far beyond malicious, it could have been taken, at first, for play-acting. However, once he spotted Roddy, he let out a yell of real hostility. "There he is!" Pointing, the man looked possessed. Owen had never seen anything like it. It gave him the creeps. Who was he?

All of them took a step back from the door and, with swagger and gall, The Cobra stepped in.

Now it made sense. A publicity stunt.

To date, Owen had never seen Fido Jones in the ring, on or off of television. The "Philth Town Destroyer" was still on his way up and hadn't, as yet, received national air time. He *had* been featured in *Boxing Digest,* and mentioned on *Thursday Night Fights* on occasion. But, so far, his bouts had been broadcast regionally, mostly here on the eastern seaboard. Owen had been in the South for years. He'd never witnessed The Cobra in action. But, based on all that he'd learned that week, he felt like he pretty much knew the deal. Jones was one of a recurring breed—a showboating fool who, by grace of his natural talent, could fight—but whose greatest a$$et lay with his knack for riling the crowd. In fourteen undefeated bouts, he had probably made a small fortune already. Whether by verbal assault of opponents at weigh-ins, or calling out critics in public, he knew how to rope them in, get their temperatures boiling and, as a result, sell tickets. His manager, Ronald

Travers, encouraged such antics—going so far as to stage them. Which seemed to be what was happening here. The Shark had ordered a raid on the West Side, with regional media droogs in tow. The camera was marked with a Channel Ten logo—the Philth Town nightly news at six.

The Cobra was dressed in a pin-striped suit. He was twirling a cane. He looked like a pimp.

Smirking, he stepped in and walked toward Roddy, waving a glistening T-bone steak.

"You're just another piece of hamburger, son," he announced.

He threw the steak on the floor.

A moment of indecision commenced—everyone gawking dumbly, wide-eyed—even The Cobra's goons and the card girls—nobody knowing quite what to make of this—and less so, how to react, exactly. The only one able to stay on his game without freezing up was the cameraman—who steadied his lens on the pitiful glob of meat lying still on the sweat-soaked floor.

Then, in a flash, there was pandemonium.

Calvin and Holy War flew off the canvas, yelling and lunging against the ropes. Travers's goons hollered back at them, jeering. Rhya let out at the top of her lungs. The class joined in. The iguana gyrated, as Jack, at last, appeared from his office.

Desperately, Owen ran for his bag. He got to it, reached in and pulled out the camera . . . unloaded. (My God, would he *ever* keep up?) New rolls of film in the side pocket. *Move it . . .*

Off in the cluster, he spotted Roddy, alone at center floor in confusion. Just *hold on,* Owen thought—five more seconds, I'm on it, just—*one*—to feed the leader, as everyone hollered and stomped in pitch—*two*—activating the power, switching the focus to auto and lifting the cap for—*three*—maneuvering into the fracas without calling undue attention to self—*four*—to set up the shot, a beautiful angle of Roddy and Jones on the face-off, though Roddy was obviously having a good deal of trouble keeping a straight expression, Jones with a hiss, craning his neck in spirals, leering into the camera, then—*five*—losing his footing either in Owen's sweat or the juice from the steak and, all too suddenly—legs out from under him, upended—falling down flat on his ass . . .

Owen could never have seen it coming. His shutter had snapped in mid-collapse. No one could see what had happened until it was over, by stroke of a minor miracle.

The silence to follow was broken, at length, by howls of laughter from Calvin and Holy War. Everyone else, excepting the goons and the queer iguana, followed suit. Rhya doubled over in stitches. The tough-looking girl shouted: "Smooth, you *idiot*!" The cameraman struggled to keep it together. Even the card girls were hooting out loud.

The Cobra got up, wincing in pain. Owen snapped a recovery shot, this one of wobbling, pigeon-toed Jones with a hammy lip and his eyes half-shut. It was perfect. The consummate—no, the *ultimate* jackass. And, standing over him: Roddy, grinning. Unbothered. *Amused,* by the look of it.

One of the goons went after the camera. Owen shielded it, stepping away—into the reach of the second goon, who got ahold of his collar and pulled. While falling back, Owen spotted a face in the fleeting downward blur, beside him: The Coach's girlfriend, reaching out. He fumbled the camera into her hands.

Then his head hit the floor with a smack.

Everyone—Jack, Roddy, Holy War, Calvin and Rhya—charged the group. Caught unawares, the goons retreated, stumbling back, if not leaping in terror—with one of them falling into the alley. The cameraman followed. Then, by moderate force (a medicine ball to the torso, hurled by Rhya), The Cobra himself. And finally, hoisted aloft by the seat of his pants, squawking and kicking, the queer iguana (who must've been out of his mind to come here), tossed to the pavement by Jack.

Rhya slammed the door in their faces. She locked it.

The queer iguana got up. Behind him, regrouping, the others looked stunned.

The Coach's girlfriend blew them a kiss. They fired back with a slew of curses. She laughed at them. Stomping back and forth, they glared at her—twitching with murderous rage. Their game had been totally blown off the planet. And their hometown cameras had caught every moment. The Philth Town Destroyer had just made a blithering, almost *unparalleled* ass of himself. Channel Ten had caught the whole thing going off in his face, and despite Ronald Travers's objections, the footage was sure to be broadcast all over Pennsyltucky by fight night. As long as the tape wasn't bought off or stolen, the footage was simply too good not to air. The news at six would replay it for days. The cameraman, likely, would be a celebrity.

This was the greatest thing Owen had seen since Reagan was shot. He couldn't believe it.

Shaking his head, Jack peered through the window. The Cobra was throwing a fit out there.

"Try wearing tights next time!" Rhya shouted. She lowered the blinds and turned away.

Holy War, Roddy and Calvin escorted the trembling card girls, the only intruders remaining inside the gym, out the front door. Nobody else in the room had stopped laughing—except for Jack, who looked calmly disgusted.

He walked up to Owen. "Are you all right?"

Owen gawked in amazement. The Coach was *addressing* him.

"Yeah." He nodded self-consciously, rubbing the back of his head. "I'll be fine."

Jack picked up the steak and walked off.

His girlfriend replaced him, grinning at Owen. "You might want to sell these." She handed him back his camera. "But don't get carried away."

Still grinning, she turned and, shaking her head, went back to the office.

Confused, Owen watched her.

She still looked like a Native American Goddess.

From his desk at the window, Ephraim sat watching a one-man crop duster circle the neighborhood. Only a moment before, he had spotted it topping a line of trees in the distance. Now, he was riding the pilot's eye: though washed out, overexposed and bowed at the edges for a spherically oblong effect, the earth beneath him passed in vivid detail, igniting a sensory overload. Hovering south, over courtyards and oak-lined streets on the eastern half of the city—with layers of orange and autumnal gold and wild ivy passing beneath him—emptying out to a public park, at the end of which stood the county prison, its wing walls jumbled with razor wire, enclosing a massive, hexagonal yard and connecting a prominent central tower with smaller towers at both extremes—appearing as one part carnival fortress / one part medieval torture dungeon . . . Continuing, over a stickball diamond and sweeping the rim of a water tower, above a congested intersection—bumper to bumper, a blast of exhaust and emissions, the humming of motors below—down the slope of a weedy embankment, an upcoming rush of organic decay—to the edge of a shabby housing development (Isaac Hoeker had called it "The Ward") where hundreds of home units dotted the hillside in varying states of dilapidation, with auto parts, garbage and slabs of concrete strewn down the incline, leveling out to a fenced-in military compound full of rusty cannons and draped machinery . . . Veering east, with a change in the wind, a lessening glare and the rising coolness of moss and trickling water below, the freshening sweetness of fertile earth—skirting a bridge, over white-water shallows and rivulets, quivering pools of foam—hugging the edge of the county park, a rolling expanse of overgrowth marked with occasional open fields and pavilions—and on, toward a wind of manure from The Basin—around, heading north toward the juvenile hall, another fenced-in, razor-lined compound, ending right back at the rehab center: an overhauled sanitarium commonly known as the "The Tank" or "The Barley Stockade," its parking lot dotted with shoddy bicycles, up-to-date sports cars and Old Order buggies.

From start to finish: affluence, poverty, crime and captivity—cluttered extremes: a castle, the slums, artillery, the stockade—all in the course of a two-mile run.

The center itself was no more consistent. Paisley walls with barred windows. Plastic seats with old wooden desktops. Polished floors and windows, yet stains on the ceiling. And low-powered halogen lighting . . . The odor of solvents and buried asbestos offsetting, by contrast, the smell of manure and sweat and cologne emanating from the crowd of juvenile offenders seated around him: four other Crossbills—Gideon, Samuel, Isaac and Colin—two Beachies from Smoketown, a Mennonite girl from District Eight and upward of ten inner-city kids dressed in jackets that read: "The Beaver Street League"—all of whom looked more fit and limber than, last, the fifteen English on hand, each of them splotchy, obese and coiffed in appearance—some in stickball caps, with goatees, halitosis and hair-gel . . .

Only a juvenile alcohol counseling session in Stepford could host such a gathering.

So far, the class had been uneventful. Ephraim hadn't been paying attention. He was too busy riding the crop duster's eye. There was also a groundhog out by the creek. And, more distractingly, he was thirsty. His tongue was like leather. His throat was burning.

Somebody knocked on the door. As the session instructor stepped out, a small piece of metal, a coin, hit the back of Ephraim's head. Ripples of laughter spread around him. Ephraim turned. A fleshy, uni-browed Redcoat was sitting behind him, leering. He was bigger than the others—considerably bigger. His hair was cropped in a dirty-blond flattop. Something was clogging his left nostril. His skin was pink. He smelled like a diaper.

"Hey, Zeke." He pinched his nose, wincing. "Man, you stink like wild ass."

The Redcoats laughed in quiet agreement. Expressionless, Ephraim peered around at them.

A voice cut in: "Don't worry 'bout them"—from a Beaver Street kid who was seated beside him. Ephraim looked over. The kid shook his head. He shifted, assuming a guarded air. "Check this out." He looked both ways, turning his shoulder away from the Redcoats. He leaned forward, sliding his hand in one pocket. "Here." He flashed a silver watch.

At first, it seemed like an English trinket, one of no particular worth . . .

Ephraim stared for a moment, unblinking.

Then something started to hold his attention—the radiant luster and glare of the band. His vision narrowed.

A wall of blackness flashed before him.

Behind him, the Redcoats were snickering still. But he couldn't make out what the fuss was about.

Then, as quickly, his focus returned. He nodded to the Beaver Street kid: *"How much?"*

"Fifty bucks," he was told in a whisper.

Without hesitation, he dug into one of his pockets and pulled out a wad of bills. A collective gasp went up behind him. The sight of his money had filled them with awe.

Somebody whistled. Ephraim ignored it, quickly peeling three bills from the roll. He handed them off in open view. Out of nowhere, the Beaver Street kid looked nervous. He shoved the watch into Ephraim's hands. And no sooner done than Riggs, the session instructor, poked his head back into the room. He pointed to the Beaver Street kid. "Pendle."

The kid raised his hands, looking guilty as sin and ready to lie through his teeth, if needed. Everyone yukked and whinnied around him.

Riggs yelled: "Quiet!" Then to "Pendle": "Come here."

Smirking, the kid got up from his chair and swaggered slowly out of the room.

Unconcerned with him, Ephraim pulled on the watch and adjusted its silver band. Again, he was soon transfixed by the shimmering gleam of the metal, the points of reflected light dancing over his scope in patterns. Again, he couldn't make sense of the conversation going on around him. And again, a flashing wall of blackness engulfed his vision momentarily. Jumbled images coalesced in semidiscernible, grotesque profusion—visions of moving in darkness, pain, the tearing of mulberry thorns on flesh . . .

Returning, he sensed a level of muted alarm now filling the room around him. What had just happened? Where had he gone? How long had he been there? . . . He had no idea. He couldn't account for these fleeting lapses any more than the cuts on his arms, or the odor he seemed to be exuding, or all of this money filling his pockets . . .

The voices outside in the hall remained flat-toned. Riggs didn't glance back in for a follow-up. Ephraim sat quietly still in his seat while his Redcoat antagonist held back in silence. Only when the voices grew louder, more heated, did Ephraim begin to squirm uncomfortably. The hairs on the back of his neck stood up. His shoulders twitched. His breathing quickened.

This only added to the sense of alarm. He could feel it around him, from everyone present. He knew he was making them terribly nervous—panting, fidgeting, flaunting money and buying a watch from the Beaver Street kid. Certainly, charging a trailer in Jonathan Becker's buggy was stranger still—an act for which, incidentally, he had been slapped with a routine drinking charge.

That part, too, would have left them guessing. Ephraim had gotten off easy, somehow . . .

But nothing would ever begin to contend with the spectacle set to unfold momentarily.

Fed up, annoyed or somewhat nervous (probably all three in combination), the Redcoat seated behind him tossed another coin at Ephraim's head. In a flash, before it hit the floor, Ephraim whirled, gripping the back of his seat and, to everyone's utter shock—even the Redcoats', who couldn't have known he was mute, and the Crossbills', who couldn't know otherwise—snarled, with his cuspids bared and his narrowed eyes in a flash, with conviction: *"Genug!"*

For the Redcoat, this would've been strange, to be sure—and obviously not what he'd been expecting.

Likewise, the Beaver Street League sat speechless, as though a phantom had just blown in.

Yet nobody could've looked more astounded than Gideon, Samuel, Isaac and Colin. For them, this would have brought into question the testimony of their own senses.

As though in corroboration thereof, Ephraim turned to address them directly. *"Sieht er nicht wie ein rosafarbener Gorilla aus?"*—he motioned to the Redcoat.

The Crossbills gawked in stupefied silence. For a moment, they couldn't breathe. There was stillness.

Then, blown away as they were, Colin and Isaac could no longer hold back from laughing. After all, it was true: that Redcoat *did* look like a pink gorilla. His skull was enormous, his skin was flushed and his nostrils were gaping, outturned chasms.

Ephraim peered into them, squinting one eye. *"Sie konnen fast Halfte die seines Gehirns von hier aus sehen."*

Snapping out of their daze at last, the rest of the Crossbills exploded with laughter—soon to be joined by the Beaver Street League.

The Pink Gorilla sat gawking dumbly. He couldn't have known what was being said, but clearly, it ran to his expense . . .

Actually, the Crossbills seemed to be having their own deal of trouble following Ephraim. And *not* because of his use of language. After all, he was speaking a legible, however garbled High German. They had been raised on sermons in the mother tongue. The language would not have been lost on them. Beyond the fact that he was speaking at all, which would have been their biggest shock, the actual content of what he was *saying,* the tenuous links in the chain of images (threading wire into one of the Redcoats' nostrils and back out the other, like a *"Fisch au der Leine,"* then tying both ends to a bumper and dragging him down to a chunk of meat), had them gawking in proper disbelief.

The Pink Gorilla, on the other hand, was furious—and making no attempt to conceal it. By now, it was clear that what had begun as a one-sided leaning on a beat-up Dutchie who stunk like a roadkill and wouldn't speak English was taking a backfire turn for the weird, full of snickering gibes at *his* expense. He couldn't seem to figure out when, or why, the Plain Folk had started talking back . . .

At last, he stood.

As quickly, Ephraim rose to his feet, sneering greedily.

All around them, hooting went up.

Startled, Riggs looked into the room. "Quiet!" he yelled with a show of force. He looked at the Pink Gorilla. "Sit down. And *you!"* He pointed to Ephraim. "Come here." Again, he turned his back on the class.

Ephraim blew the Gorilla a kiss and quietly whispered *"next time"* in English.

While turning away, he carefully pulled off the watch and slipped it into his pocket. Then, amid murmurs of wild excitement, he walked down the aisle and out the door.

Hanging his head, he presented himself to Riggs. The Beaver Street kid was gone. Riggs deferred to a short man in spectacles, forty and balding, dressed in a suit. He smelled like a courthouse. His bearing was firm.

"Ephraim Bontrager?" He spoke with civility.

Ephraim stared at the floor in silence.

(Termites were eating the wall behind him.)

Offering no introduction, the short man ordered him quietly: "Roll up your sleeves."

Ephraim complied, presenting his arms on command. They were lacerated.

Looking them over, then turning each wrist, the man demanded: "How did this happen?"

Ephraim's gaze remained on the floor.

Finally, the man took a half-step back. He removed his glasses and leaned on the wall. Briefly, he closed his eyes and rubbed them, sighing in torn deliberation.

At last, he announced: "I'm taking him with me."

Riggs shifted back on a heel. "For trial?"

"No." The man shook his head with an air of beleaguered dismay. "He's going to the hospital."

By Sunday morning, the property of Jonas and Marcelyn Kachel was all but immaculate. Hosting their district's worship service had called for extensive preparations. Abraham and Grizelda Hostler, along with their children, Hanz and Barbara, regarded the fruits of the Kachels' labor while rolling up their gravel drive. On one side, freshly churned soil ran clear to an empty stable yard; on the other, the last of the year's alfalfa stretched to the edge of a hickory forest. Ahead, a small wooden bridge passed over a creek, its bank cleared of stones and kindling. Beyond, two rows of empty horseless carriages stretched down a small dirt path.

Their buggy rounded a bend in the drive at the urging of two young men who stood waving. Abraham guided his steed past another row of horseless carriages, seven deep. He stopped before a sloped embankment that rose toward a Swiss barn's second-level entrance. He got out to help young Shamus Kachel unhitch the steed.

"Where's Fannie this morning?" the young man asked.

Grizelda heard Abraham answer. "Fannie's at home today, Shamus. She won't be attending."

Together, they disappeared into the stables.

Grizelda, Hanz and Barbara waited. The yard around them was freshly raked.

Abraham reappeared from the barn. He walked down the bank to rejoin his family.

Across the drive stood a pair of corn bins. Their concrete flats had been swept of kernels. Behind them, an oak tree shadowed a pantry house. The Hostlers walked around it.

The Kachel home came into view—a three-storied farmhouse with pine-green trim and a tall brick chimney, overlooking a yard. Dozens of men in split-tailed *mutzes* and flat-crowned hats milled about on the grass—offset by the bright white caps of the married women, and the organdy capes of the girls—while the young people, clean as the morning air and on best behavior, crowded the drive.

With thirty-one families in District Seven, and worship being held in the homes of members on a fortnightly basis in constant rotation, each household might expect, realistically, to host one service every year. For the hosting family, this amounted to an annual inspection by the whole community. Preparations began several weeks in advance with weeding and hedging the property, barn repairs and home front maintenance—all, in the Kachels' case, on top of the already grueling demands of harvest—then winding down to interior work in the days and hours preceding the service—clearing out every article of furniture, save for a cupboard or two, on the ground floor, removing partitions between the rooms to accommodate over two hundred persons, then cooking, baking, cleaning, scrubbing, canning, washing, kneading, pleating: a lengthy and manifold undertaking, and one not to be carried out secondarily. Any failure to meet with accepted standards could be seen as a lack of devotion. The family was expected to shoulder the labors of preparation among its own. Aside from limited help in the kitchen, outside assistance was clearly discouraged.

So then, the question naturally followed: how was it, just as Grizelda had feared, that behind the assembly, on the farthest end of the yard, between a flatbed wagon and the side porch, bent beneath the weight of a prayer bench, Ephraim, in view of the whole district body, was hauling furniture into the house?

Not only would such preparations normally have been dispatched by one of the Kachels—as opposed to a young man in *Rumspringa,* who hadn't been baptized and, like his cohorts, normally wouldn't have attended this service at all—they would have been completed hours, days, even weeks before the assembly's arrival. The fact that Ephraim was even present could mean only one thing, as would have been clear: Benedictus had ordered his son to task as a public disclaimer, of sorts. Even though Ephraim's recent behavior had yet to be brought to the council's focus, his father had reached a verdict already and wanted to make his position known. In two weeks' time, this case would be ruled on. Until then, the boy was to be avoided.

Grizelda wasn't able to reach him in time. She got to the porch as the door swung shut. She wouldn't be able to go inside until Bishop Schnaeder gave the signal.

She walked back down the stairs and proceeded to circle the house in agitation. An image of panic, impatience and rage, she parted the crowd, neighbors and friends, without greeting in search of an open window. She added to an already tangible air of unease that hung over the scene like a pall. While everyone else seemed inclined to maintain a veneer of normality, or subtle disquiet, Grizelda alone made no attempt to curb her outward display of worry. Embarrassed, Abraham, and even to some extent Barbara, attempted to cover for her, to pose a distraction, with awkwardly forced outpourings of joy at the sight of neighbors. These attempts were unsuccessful. Grizelda's presence was undeniable. And no one dared step forward to calm her—Abraham, her husband, least of all. While essentially respected, Grizelda was known as a problematically willful woman. Which is to say, she ruled her household. Abraham Hostler couldn't control her.

And neither could Benedictus, for that matter. Though he and Grizelda, as brother and sister, maintained an unwarlike repose in proximity, the two hadn't spoken a word in years. Long ago, they had come to an impasse.

Following the death of Ephraim's mother, Benedictus had gone on a three-week drunk. Beyond any doubt, by his own admission, he hadn't been fit for the task of parenting. Thereby, Grizelda, herself a new mother at the time, had been given charge of the boy. Which, on the whole, had been accepted by most of the community as being for the better. For three years, she had raised him as one of her own. In that time, Benedictus had shown no interest in having anything to do with him. Even after becoming a minister, he'd never stopped by to see his son. It was only when community demand had come to bear that he started to press for custody. An ordained minister should have been able to raise his only child, it was felt.

Staunchly opposed, Grizelda had taken the matter straight to the district council and, to it, before him as one of its members, pronounced him completely unfit for the task.

Even though Benedictus had been granted custody with little deliberation, the Minister had never gotten over the fact that his sister would dare to defy him in public. From that day forward, he had distanced himself from not just the Hostlers, but most of their relatives. He had forbidden Ephraim from more than required contact with any of them.

It seemed that an eon had passed when Bishop Schnaeder called the assembly to file. Responding, the women and girls dropped their bonnets and shawls in a basket brought out from the pantry. Members of the Kachel family gathered overcoats from the boys and men.

First to enter the house were the ordained men. They were followed by the district elders. Then came the middle-aged men. Then the adolescent boys—in single file, down to the youngest—then switching over to the opposite sex, beginning with the unmarried girls and working back up to the crones at the end of the line. At forty-three, Grizelda wound up toward the rear. It took her a while to reach the door, and longer to greet the ordained men inside—as usual, passing her brother in silence—and continuing into the kitchen to drop her bonnet on top of a wooden table, around which several mothers sat cradling newborn infants and younger children. The walls were painted a cool shade of turquoise and mounted with brass-handled oil lamps. A woodstove crackled and spat in the corner, emitting a field of gentle warmth. A bookshelf lined with scripture stood next to a doorway that led to the sitting room.

She went in.

Most of the assembly was present already.

Copies of *The Ausbund,* the Old Order hymn book, were sitting, face-up, on every bench. A row of chairs toward the front of the room had been reserved for the ordained men. The oldest men in attendance sat with their backs to the wall or in rocking chairs. Behind them: a body of younger men. To Grizelda's right: the unmarried women. And square in the eye of the district body, at peak visibility, front and center, just as she had been dreading all week, seated on the "Sinner's Bench," as it were (the plank on which those who faced social avoidance were (un)customarily placed during worship), with Gideon Brechbuhl and Colin Graybill on either side of him, likewise staked—his shoulders locked in a clench, his head tilted forward, his posture twisted crookedly: Ephraim, guilty until proven innocent.

Fannie would have broken down crying at the sight of him.

Grizelda could hardly bear to look. As though he weren't in for enough already—this morning, this service, this day, the whole season—Ephraim was set for a public shaming.

Benedictus held nothing sacred.

Finally, Bishop Schnaeder called the assembly to order. Grizelda assumed her place toward the rear of the congregation.

Soon, a *Vorsinger,* Jan Pratt, an auctioneer colleague of Jon's by day, addressed the assembly by raising *The Ausbund* and calling for hymn number ninety-eight.

In a doleful, trembling falsetto, Pratt began to sing. Once his pitch was set, the assembly joined in, a cappella. It was painfully slow. The hymn extended for several minutes. Upon its conclusion, the ordained men withdrew to a room upstairs, as scheduled, for *Arbot,* or counsel. Its being two weeks into the final harvest, custom demanded that autumn affairs and related concerns be brought to the council's attention this morning, before the service. Even though Ephraim's predicament wouldn't have qualified as an autumn affair, the visible rash of welts on his neck was all the excuse Grizelda needed.

As several young men left their benches and filed to the right toward a doorway that led to a staircase, Grizelda rose to her feet and followed them—edging ahead of the wary crowd, forcing everyone back an obliging step—and then up the stairs to the council room door.

She knocked on it, waited for only a moment, then slapped it flush with an open palm.

A startled murmur went up all around her.

Minister Zook opened up, looking visibly shaken. Behind him, around a table sat Bishop Schnaeder, Deacon Byars, Minister Grabers and Benedictus. Before them stood Jonathan Becker, struck with alarm at the sudden appearance of Grizelda. But Grizelda hadn't come for him. He just happened to be there, that was all. Her purpose lay in demanding her nephew's removal at once from the Sinner's Bench: placing him out on display, as such, would accomplish nothing at all, she told them. It was ridiculous, inhumane and thoroughly idiotic treatment—and the boy faced plenty of *that* already . . .

At the table, Benedictus threw up his hands, as though to say *"Here we go again."*

He turned away, refusing to look at her.

In spite of him, Grizelda, gently barred from entering the room by Minister Zook, continued to rave, insisting her brother had never been fit to raise beans in a jar, to say nothing of children. One needed only consider the state of his business to know that. Johann Schnaeder got up from the table. He raised his hands while approaching her. *"Please,"* he spoke in German, cutting her off. His tone was firm.

The Schnaeders had always been thought of as sturdy, dependable, scrupulous, God-fearing people. Johann, in keeping with all of those traits, was known as a man of equal compassion. In the ten years he had served as a bishop (the briefest tenure among the ordained men), he had opposed in theory and (unsuccessfully) in practice the Sinner's Bench. For him, social avoidance without a ruling was unjust, pure and simple. He stood alone on that principle—not even Minister Zook would defy tradition. Nevertheless, alone he *stood*. And not without drawing considerable attention.

Some district members considered the Bishop too soft, too lenient, far too permissive—unlike his predecessor, Bishop Holtz. Schnaeder had succeeded a disciplinarian. Time was, Ephraim—with Colin and Gideon, would have been shunned from The Order already. But Schnaeder was made of different stuff. So was Minister Josef Zook. Of the five ordained men present, the church stood virtually split down the middle on discipline: Grabers and Bontrager favoring more traditional, stricter, hands-on enforcement, Schnaeder and Zook being less inflexible—and Deacon Byars, at eighty-seven, in latter-day geriatric oblivion, vacillating between them, and somehow preserving the church, if only symbolically. Byars, the last of the district's founding clergy, had long been considered the mortar by which the assembly held together. Upon his much-anticipated passing, the church would dissolve into three separate bodies. The Bontrager crowd would remain in place, consigning the district, at last, to ruin; Zook, with a party of fifty less rigid, though fervent souls, would join District Ten; and Schnaeder's group, nearly half of the current church, would found a whole new assembly.

Grizelda felt certain that Schnaeder, of all the ordained men, would be the most sympathetic. Not only was he more progressive-minded, he had issues with Benedictus. Having grown up down the road from her brother, Schnaeder knew Bontrager all too well. He had never considered him fit for the cloth. Ideally, a minister's role in the church involved upholding standards of basic decency—including in business and family matters. Yet Johann Schnaeder had always considered the Minister's line of work obscene.

And as for parenting, one needed only consider the state of Ephraim's tobacco . . .

Seizing the Bishop's arm and twisting, Grizelda pitted her weight against him and desperately, mournfully begged him to do something, anything please—this couldn't continue.

Again, the Bishop attempted to calm her, gently dislodging himself from her grasp, then imposing his own with a firm command: "Be quiet, Grizelda," he whispered in English. He fixed her gaze, overriding it. *"Please."*

Abruptly, the young men crowding the stairwell behind her, watching, caught Schnaeder's attention.

He backed her into the hallway, shut the door behind them, turned and, gently leading her by one arm, proceeded down the hall to a second door. He opened it, pushed her inside and stepped in. She flinched at the sound of the door slamming shut. Turning to face her, he spoke in hushed frustration. "Now *listen* . . ."

She took a step back.

Holding his voice at a low, intent whisper, the Bishop explained how first, aside from their placement on the Sinner's Bench—an informal, draconian custom observed (almost) exclusively in District Seven—the boys were not to be singled out in speech or deed throughout the service. Their case was to be discussed in two weeks' time at the regional autumn council. Judgment would be reserved until then, Sunday, October 31st. The council, arranged to convene in New Holland, would be comprised of selected ordained men from thirty-one districts throughout the state. When the moment arrived, Schnaeder explained—leaning forward and dropping his volume further—this matter would be addressed to the whole of the regional panel for a detailed review. Bishop Schnaeder himself would see to it. Ephraim's recent encounter with Officer Beaumont had struck a community nerve. Demand had arisen not only to chastise the boy—by excommunication, if needed—but to figure out what in the world was wrong with him, and to make sure it never happened again. Being more than a nuisance, he had become a cultural hazard /

liability. Simply removing him wouldn't suffice. His condition would have to be sorted out. Meaning: a long-awaited assessment of Minister Bontrager's role as a guardian—and thereby, his place in the whole community—would be up, at last, for a proper review.

The Bishop had waited a long time for this. He couldn't let anyone jeopardize it. Creating a scene here would only hinder his coming appeal. This was a critically delicate juncture. A service devoid of strife was imperative. Grizelda, for all of her good intentions, was placing the chance of a lifetime at risk.

Aside from that, he understood her concern—and promised her this, on his word of honor: he would do everything possible to have the young man removed from the Minister's home. The coming storm would be long overdue, and would justly purge a good deal of The Basin. Once it was over, with God's blessing, Ephraim, absolved of all culpability, would remain in the fold—under her care, presumably.

But until then, Grizelda was interfering. As much as it pained her to stand back and watch, she would now have to do exactly that. If left unprovoked, her brother would surely hold his peace—for the moment, at least.

Acquiescing to Schnaeder's command, Grizelda stood nonetheless unconvinced. Johann Schnaeder was not to blame for his ignorance. And clearly, his intentions were noble.

He just didn't understand what he was dealing with.

Two weeks from now, it would be too late.

She turned away without further comment. In silence, the Bishop watched her slowly walk to the door with her head hung low.

Before leaving, she turned to look back at him—standing there, bathed in the glow of an oil lamp. He nodded solemnly.

Staring back, Grizelda lost all hope in the church.

The *Lobleib,* traditionally the second hymn of every service, was underway as she slowly reentered the sitting room. Drawing stern, wholly unamused looks all around, she resumed her place at the bench and ignored them. She made no attempt to join in the singing. She didn't pick up her copy of *The Ausbund*. She didn't even look at her husband or children. All she could do was fixate on Ephraim, staring intently at the back of his head. Flanked by Colin and Samuel, deliberately centered, though lesser in stature and width, he was sweating already: a flow from his scalp, down his neck. The Sunday shirt clung to his back.

Jonathan, appearing from the kitchen, reentered the sitting room, an image of sainthood in contrast: walking tall, bespectacled, oiled and powdered and clean as an April shower—with every snag in his trousers hemmed, every hook and eye on his vest well-polished. Down the aisle, he attracted the gaze of the whole assembly. He sang as he walked. He returned to his seat, to the right of and four rows behind the Sinner's Bench.

The *Vorsinger*'s lead had been shifted from Pratt to Josef Hertzler, who was droning his way through *"S Lobg"sang,* The Hymn of Praise. Hertzler signaled to Jonathan now. In a clear, ringing falsetto, Jonathan took the lead. He guided the assembly through the *Loblieb*'s final verse.

Like many an auctioneer, he'd been attending church for years without having been baptized. This was common practice in honing the voice, the tool of his trade, to perfection. There was no greater training than worship, and no greater challenge than leading this hymn, in particular.

After a while, the ordained men filed back into the room from the stairs, to the right. They walked to their chairs, to the left of center, as the *Loblieb* wound to its burdensome conclusion.

From the moment she spotted him, Grizelda felt certain her brother would never hold his peace. The feeling took root and wouldn't abate throughout the hours of worship to follow. Only the closing hymn would settle it. And that was a long way off at the moment.

Presently, Minister Zook got up, came forward and turned to the congregation. Upon his signal, everyone sat. Folding his hands beneath his beard, he commenced with the *Anfang,* the opening sermon. Beginning in a low, subdued mumble, his voice attained to coherence gradually, rhythmically dipping from English to Pennsyltucky Dutch to High German.

He bade the assembly good morning and wished it the power of God and the Holy Ghost. In times of abundance, as these, he claimed, man needed to offer special thanks unto Him, our creator and life eternal—as man's harvest was God's blessing. The coming days would attest to as much. As written in the Book of Ezekiel (34:25): *"And the tree of the field shall yield her fruit, and the earth shall yield her increase, and they shall be safe in their land, and shall know that I am the Lord."*

He went on to praise God's mercy by quoting the Book of Isaiah, from 44:6: *"Thus saith the Lord, the king of Israel, and his redeemer, the Lord of hosts; I am the first, and I am the last, and beside me, there is no God."*

The room was unusually warm, for some reason. Already, foreheads were starting to glisten. The house felt stuffy, stale and unventilated. Marcelyn Kachel sealed the stove in the kitchen and quietly opened a window.

Never appearing to notice, Zook continued by stressing the importance of family, tradition, community, respect of one's elders, humility and hard, honest work. His sermon ran for twenty-five minutes, toward the end of which he offered an apology for weakness.

He hadn't intended to infringe on the morning's *Es Schwer Deel,* the main sermon. He would ask everyone present to pray for Bishop Schnaeder in his coming delivery.

He closed by admonishing the congregation to *"Work out your own salvation with fear and trembling"* Philippians 2:12.

"If you're all agreed, let us pray."

Everyone knelt. Muffled coughing disrupted the moment of silence to follow. By the time Minister Zook signaled to rise from prayer, his collar was damp with sweat.

Calmly, he turned and walked to his seat.

The assembly remained on its feet as, sluggishly, Deacon Byars hobbled forth to deliver a selected reading from the Bible. The passage had been determined already. The register of scriptures began every Christmas with the birth of Jesus and ran through the year, service by service, to the Book of Revelations. The date being October 17th meant the Epistle of James was slated for delivery. Byars, a portrait of mental deterioration, assumed position before the assembly and, after a silence, commenced in a high-pitched, quasi-melodic chant: *"Ye adulterers and adulteresses, know ye not that friendship of the world in enmity with God? Whosoever therefore will be a friend of the world is an enemy of God . . . Submit yourselves, therefore, to God . . . Resist the devil and he will flee from you . . . Cleanse your hands, ye sinners, and purify your hearts, ye double-minded . . . Be afflicted and mourn and weep. Let your laughter be turned to mourning, and your joy to heaviness . . . Humble yourselves in the might of the Lord, and . . ."*

At which point the Deacon, having already skipped four chapters (twenty minutes' worth of reading), looked up from his text in sudden distraction. His nostrils flared. He seemed confused.

Losing his spot in the scripture, he grimaced, then stumbled back to his seat in a daze.

Were it not for the fact that the congregation had long been accustomed to similar lapses, the sudden wash of an odor, like solvents and dung, to which Byars had been responding, might have caused an embarrassing stir.

But for now, the assembly sat calmly perturbed. Somebody opened a second window. A gentle draft rolled over the floor. The heat and the odor began to subside.

Sighing, Bishop Schnaeder stood and signaled the congregation to sit. He walked to position as everyone sat, then turned to face them, nodding humbly.

"Grace be with you, and peace from God, our father," he said.

The sermon had begun.

In opening, he posed a reminder as to the importance of obedience to the Bible and our elders, as designated by the vows of baptism. He praised *Das alt Gebrauch,* the old way of life, the *Regel and Ordnung,* the rules of the church, and the idea of pilgrims in a hostile world.

The preface extended for several minutes.

In delivering the sermon, the Bishop's voice would also attain to a chantlike rhythm. Reflecting first on the Old Testament, his pitch would rise in a plaintive sustain, then abruptly drop at the end of each phrase. After several phrases, a silence would settle. Then, trembling, the Bishop would continue.

So proceeded the *Es Schwer Deel.*

For the next two hours, the assembly sat motionless. Save for an occasional disturbance from the kitchen, where mothers were quietly suckling infants, no sound went up from the congregation. And gone was the unexplainable smell. Discomfort was now the biggest concern. The backless benches would only grow harder and more unforgiving throughout the morning. Parents and children alike would shift on their seats, flexing their aching shoulders.

As Schnaeder proceeded from the Old to the New Testament, beginning with the story of John the Baptist and moving toward Paul's Missionary Journeys, the room began to feel stuffy and heated again. The children were growing restless. Marcelyn Kachel passed a tray of cookies and crackers down the aisle. This was followed by several glasses of water, including a glass for the Bishop.

Pausing to lean on a chair, Schnaeder drank. He dabbed his gleaming brow with a handkerchief, then continued with Paul's journeys.

At last, the sermon came to an end, at which point the Bishop redirected the assembly's attention back to the Epistle of James, as Deacon Byars had scarcely touched on the text. From the beginning, he read through the exhortations of chapter one, through disseminating faith without works in two, then halting at three to remark at length against strife and envy (3:13), followed by four, an exhortation to patience, and five, on the power of prayer, by the end of which Schnaeder's overall intensity was starting to lag and wane in the heat. With a sigh, he ended by calling for *Zeugnis,* the testimonies of the ordained men: general corrections or comments regarding the Bishop's delivery of the *Es Schwer Deel.*

This was the point at which Grizelda sat up in her seat, squirming, tensely expectant. She drifted through Minister Zook's innocuous commentary on Paul's journeys. She ignored the corrections by Minister Grabers, then endured Deacon Byars's mumbling.

Finally, after a minor eternity, the moment she had been dreading arrived: Benedictus favored one leg to the front of the room, then slowly turned around. Unsmiling, he faced the congregation in silence, scanning every row. His expression was stern and what was beginning to feel inappropriately overextended.

Before even speaking a word, he had exceeded his given role in *Zeugnis*. The assembly had never been *stared* down. Even Grizelda was taken aback.

He began in a level, somber tone by commending Bishop Schnaeder's delivery. Little fault could be found in his lengthy accounts of the Old and New Testaments. Likewise, his reading of James had been flawless. Along with the subsequent commentary. He, the Minister, took no exception to any point that the Bishop had stressed. In particular, given the season, thoughts on wisdom and righteousness were appropriate. No one could fault his presentation for what it succeeded in bringing to light. Contrarily, he could think of just one other passage that hadn't been emphasized fully.

Stopping to clear his throat, he scanned the assembly again. The room was still.

He resumed: the passage of which he spoke concerned faith without works. The Epistle of James, chapter 2, verse 20: (He raised his hand in exhortation):

"But wilt thou know, O vain man, that faith without works is dead? 21. Was not Abraham our father justified by works, when he had offered Isaac his son upon the altar? 22. Seest thou how faith wrought with his works, and by works was faith made perfect? 23. And the scripture was fulfilled which saith, Abraham believed God, and it was imputed unto

him for righteousness: and he was called the friend of God. 24. Ye see then how that by works a man is justified, and not by faith only. 26. For as the body without spirit is dead, so faith without works is dead also . . ."

He folded his hands behind his back, turned to the right and, in weighted silence, walked a slow, deliberate circle around the single chair beside him.

So what does that mean? He posed the question. How did works of faith relay to everyday life in District Seven? And what could each of its members do to carry out the will of God?

Bontrager sighed, folding his hands, as though to say: *Allow me to be more specific . . .*

If, he said, in these times of harvest, it came to pass one unfortunate day that a nuisance were plaguing the family orchard (he leveled his gaze on Jonas Tulk, whose tobacco field had been ravaged that week) or a virus had broken out in the flock (he turned to Aaron Ziegler, who'd lost a goat and two chickens the night before) or that a scavenger had raided the grain store (to Ethan Becker, whose silo had just been sabotaged under cover of the night)—then how, as a Christian, would God have expected his children to handle the situation?

Several district elders squirmed.

The Minister was broaching a previously unacknowledged subject in public worship.

Indeed, he continued, as any harvester worth his weight in salt understood: parasites, when left unchecked, only multiplied. Without proper diligence, labor and care, the orchard would be overrun very quickly—and a poorer man he who had stood idly by. As the Bible read: *There was a Time to Act.* And, just as the Bishop had quoted from the Epistle of James, "Faith without works is dead," so it was equally true to say that "The Lord helps those who help themselves." After all, there was also *a Time to Kill . . .*

The assembly rippled with consternation.

Bontrager circled the chair once more, his narrowed gaze running over the crowd, his hands locked tightly behind his back.

Had he really just called the assembly to arms?

Reactions varied across the room.

The Zieglers and Tulks, both having suffered no minor setback in recent losses, approved of the present address: if talking about it, no matter how poorly timed, meant saving the harvest, so be it: proceed.

Others appeared more apprehensive—those for whom the events of this season, as any that might have gone before it, were manifestations of God's displeasure with his people—a curse, of sorts, that could only be lifted through prayer and meditation.

Everyone else appeared overwhelmed with discomfort by Minister Bontrager's words, yet no more partial to standing by while the fruits of their labor were stripped to nothing.

"Amen!" cried Jonas Tulk. His voice carried over the room like a gunshot. Several cries of approval went up. But just as many of opposition.

In the midst of the uproar, the odor returned—and more pungent now, curdling into a haze of limburger, garbage and rotting entrails. Everyone choked in mid-sustain. Teary-eyed faces were buried in handkerchiefs.

Four aisles back, Jonas Tulk only added to matters with another announcement, this one submitted at top volume with no hypothetical pretense implied: volunteers for road patrols would assemble that evening on Kreiner Road. Traps would be set in surrounding fields. A nightly circuit would be determined.

A dozen assembly members stood and shouted.

Bishop Schnaeder got up, imploring the congregation to come to order—this matter could be discussed . . .

Benedictus, appearing grimly content with his work, returned to his chair.

Schnaeder was left at front and center, beseeching families not to walk out—and bearing the brunt of conflicting hostilities. He looked distraught to the point of mania.

After much resistance and shouting, the standing members reluctantly sat. Another minute went into restoring a semblance of order, along with attempting to filter in a breathable draft.

At length, the Bishop's imploring tone gave way to righteous indignation.

First, he admonished the assembly—and specifically the Minister—to bear in careful mind the *Regel and Ordnung*'s stance on violence. Christ had taught nonresistance to worldly enemies.

Someone shouted. "*Worldly* enemies?"

More yelling ensued.

The Bishop continued, overriding it: the road to salvation lay not in wrath, but in prayer and atonement and fear of God. Perhaps the Minister *did* have a point—insofar as the harvest itself was concerned. But metaphors hardly sustained his message. His message itself was utterly blasphemous. To stand before his own assembly in recruiting—and here, the Bishop chose his words carefully—a "pitchfork brigade" was to break with the faith irreconcilably. Moreover, quoting James to that end wasn't just misleading, it was false interpretation. The passage which Minister Bontrager held to justify the use of force preceded chapter three's conclusion: *"Righteousness comes by peace alone."*

Sadly, in this situation, he said, perhaps 3:6 was more appropriate: *"And the tongue is a fire, and a world of iniquity: so is the tongue among our members, that it defileth the whole body, and setteth on fire the course of nature; and it is set on a fire of hell . . ."*

Again, an uproar swept the room.

In twenty-five years of church attendance, Grizelda had never seen anyone *leave*. Entire families were flooding the exit. And those left behind were left arguing bitterly: the Tulks and Zieglers and Stoltzfi on one end, calling for action in spite of the Schnaeders and Beckers, who clung to salvation through prayer and atonement, whatever the cost, on the other.

While Bishop Schnaeder stared defiantly into the fragmenting congregation and Minister Bontrager, slumped in his seat like a bandit king, watched with cold acceptance, everyone else, save for Ephraim, Colin and Gideon, hovered in between, till the caustic odor intensified, reaching a pungency hitherto unimagined—wafting of vomit and toxic bile, so thick and restrictive, so utterly rank as to choke many cries in mid-sustain. The uproar cut to an agonized choir of sneezing, coughing, retching and heaving. A wave of shame overcame the assembly. How it could generate such an execrably hellish odor was beyond comprehension. Only one thing was clear: this service was over. Already gone to the chao, as it were: with the horseman of pestilence galloping through, the rest of the morning would have to be cut.

Deacon Byars, whose neck was breaking out in hives, at last stepped forward. As the fading lock on a past that had little future, his present might still serve a purpose: to end this madness. Or so it was hoped . . .

Instead, he removed a sheet of paper from his pocket, unfolded it and, coughing into his sleeve, then peering through fogged bifocals, began to deliver baptismal announcements.

The congregation could have killed him.

Grizelda herself could have murdered the fool.

Clamping her mouth with the cuff of one sleeve, she strained for a fleeting glimpse of her nephew. Along with Colin and Gideon, hunched in a quiet trance, the boy sat motionless. All of them looked to have gone into shutdown.

Behind them, in contrast, Jonathan followed the Deacon's announcement in rapt attention.

Here it came . . .

As the congregation hacked its way into a chorus of gurgles, he read the list. For what it was worth (all ceremonies were sure to be put on delay, for the moment) there were seven names. As had been expected for several months, Fannie Hostler was one of the first. But less foreseeably, the seventh, most recent addition was announced as: "Jonathan Becker."

All at once, Ephraim snapped to attention. Colin and Gideon stirred from their daze. Confused, all three of them looked to Jon for an explanation—a motion of denial, an assurance that someone had misunderstood. Granted, Jon had been out of the running for weeks, which hadn't gone unnoticed. However, his regular church attendance, as they had always understood it, had served as ongoing vocal training—a means of getting ahead in the game—not as an actual rite of conviction. The Crossbills had never suspected as much. He'd given no indication of joining The Order / leaving his gang, or whatnot. Surely, he wouldn't have quit without telling them. Surely, there had to be some mistake . . .

But apparently not. Coughing, he nodded in confirmation of Byars's announcement. Colin, Ephraim and Gideon watched in disbelief from the Sinner's Bench. In a roomful of suffocating Plain Folk, they seemed uniquely unaffected by the stench. Jonathan, suddenly aware of their attention, didn't look back. His gaze remained locked on the Deacon. Grizelda watched as, slowly, Ephraim turned away in apparent bewilderment. He might have remained in that state all day had the Deacon not kept on with autumn announcements, during which Jonathan's name was mentioned again—this time to surprise all around.

With the hives on his neck in angry splotches, tears streaming into his beard and the room in a state of fuming pandemonium, Deacon Byars lifted his head to announce the betrothal of Jonathan Rubin Becker to Fannie Gwendolyn Hostler, scheduled to marry November 20th.

Ephraim fell to the floor, unconscious.

Forty-three-year-old Hector Shlem had just clocked in for his midnight shift with three other Sprawl Mart security guards—had taken a seat in a cubicle overlooking the superstore's parking lot, and scarcely broken the seal on a can of sardines—when "the whirlwind" appeared from the south. At first, as it came over the hill in a flurry of movement, Shlem had mistaken the flash for a motorbike—somebody tooling the fields. But then he'd picked up on the silence, the notably total lack of an engine's roar. Shlem put down his can of sardines and stood, prompted to curiosity. He watched as the movement blazed down the weedy slope from the edge of 342, rounded a light pole and leveled out to the parking lot, heading directly for him. It seemed to be gaining momentum steadily. Its features were blurred in the swarm of activity. Nothing was clearly visible, save for the fact that it wasn't slowing down. On the contrary, it was accelerating. Without any question, approaching fast . . . No sooner had Shlem begun to wonder than impact became undeniably imminent. He dodged to one side with scarcely a moment to spare before it crashed through the cubicle. Thirty-five square feet of reinforced glass exploded inward, raining oblivion. Shlem ended up in a crouch on the floor, uninjured. The spray of glass had blown over him. The whole thing was finished before he could stand.

His sardines would later turn up in cosmetics.

A swath of destruction was torn down an aisle, back to the exit and, no less explosively, straight through another wall of glass.

"It was kind of like having a freight train plow through your greenhouse," Shlem would be quoted as stating.

It nearly measured up in damages, as Rudolf Beaumont would have to concur. As the first responding officer present, he would call in a six-figure estimate. Strange as it may have appeared first-hand, the sheriff's dispatcher was oddly unfazed by his spluttered attempts to describe the scene. This was due to the fact that the precinct was now being swamped with disturbance reports—the latest of which was about to go out as an APB from Sheriff Highman: priority one on a "high-speed maniac" said to be wrecking the Holtwood Development.

Hector Shlem was left in the rubble with several meandering Sprawl Mart officials while Rudolf Beaumont throttled his cruiser directly to Holtwood, a mile up the road.

He arrived to find four other officers, three private watchmen and one angry contractor present—patrolling the craggy terrain on foot between visibly damaged house foundations, cutting their flash beams over the wreckage.

Officer Beaumont got out of his cruiser to join them. He overheard one of the watchmen complain of not having heard or seen *"them"* coming and, once under siege, having been outrun. "They were too fast," he kept saying. "Too fast."

Rudolf approached them. "How many were there?"

Visibly shaken, the watchman snapped in reply: "How should I know?" He pointed across a series of paths to the opposite bluff. "It started up there, then headed this way. I don't know. They were just kind of everywhere at once." He shook his head. "It happened too fast."

Irritated, Beaumont turned from the group and, unlatching his flashlight, started up the hill. He unholstered his .45 and clicked off the safety.

An oddly unseasonal chorus of locusts split the midnight calm from the ecotone.

Almost immediately, Rudolf felt certain the prowler(s) were gone. For the seventh time in a month, and by far the most damaging yet, they had gotten away. Between Holtwood and Sprawl Mart, lo$$e$ were sure to exceed all accumulated wreckage to date.

Down the hill, Sheriff Buster Highman's cruiser drifted into view. He slowed to a stop and got out. He leveled his speaker horn. "Bring it in, ladies!"

Beaumont retraced his steps down the path, joining Officer Kutay along the way. Kutay, a bungling doughboy known as the "precinct pussy," looked good and spooked. Their radios squawked of intrusion at both the Mayweather stables and a liquor store in Paradise—the first having something to do with a burning scarecrow posted along the drive, and the second a forced intrusion report. As they wound down the slope, talk came through of a wolf chasing traffic on Dillerville Pike.

The sheriff hollered: "Turn off that radio, Beaumont!"

Rudolf cut the volume.

Two more cruisers appeared from the highway, bringing the number of officers present to seven. Highman, pivoting tensely on one heel, got to the point, addressing them.

"I don't know what we're dealing with here," he said, for lack of a better approach. "But whatever it is—kill it."

Simple.

Order confirmed with no objections.

For over a week, while everyone else had been yukking it up at The Basin's expense, law enforcement officials therein had been running in circles, to worsening ends. Hoax or not—whether juvenile vandalism or, as had been suggested already, a moonsick wild man roaming the fields, the Blue Ball Devil had to be stopped. This situation was out of control.

Just that evening, Philth Town 10 had aired a five-minute broadcast dubbed "A Week in the Lamepeter Public Ledger," which featured sarcastic, embittered and frightened remarks by longtime area residents—something he found less irritating than the newscaster's subsequent laughing fit. ("Sounds like a serious case of the blue balls—I mean, excuse me: a *bad case in Blue Ball.*")

Millions of people had heard the report. And others like it were sure to follow. And with them would come a new wave of visitors—thrill seekers, Wiccans and gothic trash—flooding the local hotels for a week in hopes of catching a glimpse of the creature and adding to the already harrowing plight of nightly patrol in the townships of late. Every cop in the county, by now, was chomping at the bit for a shot at the culprit(s).

Officers Kreider and Hertz were dispatched to a three-mile stretch of Dillerville Pike. Officers Keiffer, Billings and Koch were assigned to the burning scarecrow reports, while Beaumont and Kutay wound up stuck with investigating the liquor store. Rudolf quietly damned the sheriff. Now was no time to be weighted down. Whatever was running amok out there, it was fast—or, in any case, highly elusive. Officer Nelson "Fatty" Kutay was probably the slowest man on the force. In every respect, he would only serve as a ball and chain around Beaumont's neck.

Furious, Rudolf got into his cruiser. He followed the typically idling Kutay back up the drive to 342 and swung onto it, instantly punching the gas. With his siren and lights in a wailing blur, he shot past Kutay's black and white, then widened the gap between them, leaving Fatty stuck at an intersection. Once in the clear, he left the highway, moving east on Harvest Lane. He was reaching to cut the lights when, ahead in the oncoming lane, a buggy appeared. There were three of them, gliding along in the dark.

What were the Orderlies doing out at this hour?

Beaumont slowed his cruiser to see, as Fatty came over the radio: "-**Rudolf*-?"

Ahead, more buggies topped the hill. The first two drivers were unfamiliar. But Jonas Tulk was manning the third. No doubt about it: Jonas Tulk—and a posse of Amish patrolling the road. Something was happening.

"-**Officer Beaumont?**-" Again, the radio.

Rudolf considered not responding. Then came thoughts of the sheriff's orders.

"Officer Beaumont, where are you?"

He grabbed the receiver. "En route. Where the hell do you think?"

Kutay sounded ready to cry. *"But I lost you,"* he burbled.

"Try the accelerator."

One of these seasons, the sheriff would drop dead of colon cancer or high cholesterol. When that happened, Fatty—along with Officer Koch, the sap, would be out of a job: two walking-the-dog-to-the-breadline, no-house, barbecued-pork-eating welfare cheats . . .

A sizeable crowd of angry locals had gathered in front of the liquor store. The building's center bay had been shattered. Sirens were blaring from wall-mounted horns. Every soul in The Basin was sure to be walking the floors. It sounded like war.

On arrival, Beaumont spotted a figure attempting to climb through the ruined display case. He didn't appear to be looting the store. He seemed to be trying to find the alarm.

As Fatty Kutay pulled in to join them, the crowd turned its anger on both officers.

"Can't you make it *stop?*" one man in camo-fatigue pajamas demanded.

Beaumont walked to the front of the store. What he could see inside was a mess. He climbed through the scattered remains of the main display and hopped in. After a bungled attempt to locate and deactivate the security board, and with no sign of personnel forthcoming, he climbed up onto a crate and proceeded to bash the interior horn with his club. On try number three, he succeeded in tearing it out of the wall, but not killing the siren. The siren jammed on an even higher, more shrill and grating pitch than before. Outside, the locals hollered angrily. They hoisted a cinder block into the display case—"Here, try this, God damn it—hurry!"—while others ran to their pickups for crowbars.

All together, they beat the alarms into silence. The last one sounding was blown from the eastern wall by a shotgun blast. The boom echoed back from a nearby rail yard, reverberating west through the settling calm.

For everyone present, it seemed as though all of creation let out a sight of relief.

Except Fatty: "Who fired that shot?" he demanded.

The crowd ignored him. Instead, someone shouted: "Can't you people control those hippies?"

Cries of disgusted agreement went up.

Beaumont came forward, throwing his shoulders back, warning the group not to test his patience.

"Screw you, Rudolf," someone replied. "We pay our taxes. You work for *us.*"

Both officers blinked, abruptly aware of the silhouettes tensed in the darkness around them. Officer Kutay's breathing deepened, breaking the otherwise total silence.

Then came a distant barrage of gunfire off to the north. Everyone jumped. Torn from its daze, the crowd had already begun to disperse before Fatty stepped forward. "You people go home. This situation is . . ."

"Eat shit!" came a call in response. On pulling away, someone yelled from a window: "If you won't do something about it, *we* will."

Several pickups took off in succession, barreling north toward a stretch of forest from which more gunfire was sounding steadily.

Rudolf and Kutay were left behind in the parking lot, weighing their yearly salaries.

At last, Beaumont spoke. "Go get 'em."

Kutay blanched. "*You* go get 'em."

"I will," said Beaumont. "I'll block the road at Bareville Pike. You drive 'em in."

Fatty didn't like the sound of that. "No way," he refused. "You're just gonna leave me with the dirty work again."

Beaumont shook his head. "You want to block the road yourself?"

"Yes!"

Sucker.

Rudolf conceded. "Fine with me. Just stay off your radio."

Kutay got in his cruiser and drove off, easily rid of.

Now for the compound.

Ivan Grabers and Eli Stoltzfus, one with a spade and the other his rifle, stood in the drive of the Tulk estate, looking none too pleased by Beaumont's appearance. Behind them, torches were posted along the outer fence, surrounding the building.

He rolled to a stop and got out of his cruiser, expecting a howling din from the building. Instead, it was quiet. Nary so much as a peep from within. Just the humming of locusts.

Cleon Stoltzfus, with two of his sons, James and Ezekiel, appeared from the shadows. All three of them were carrying rifles. They stopped.

Rudolf approached them, demanding, "What's happening?"

"Nothing," said Cleon, turning away.

He unlocked the gate to the yard and, speaking no more, walked off.

James and Ezekiel hung back quietly.

Beaumont wrangled a statement from Grabers, who claimed that nothing had happened, as yet. "The hounds went crazy an hour ago."

"And now they're quiet," Rudolf observed. He scratched his head, regarding the building. "Where's Bontrager?"

Ezekiel pointed toward the back gate.

"And Tulk's on the road?"

All three of them nodded.

Officer Kutay's voice squawked over the radio, booming from Rudolf's cruiser. "They're shooting again! They're shooting!"—just as a flurry of bursts went up to the west.

Everyone listened intently.

Then more from the radio: talk of "an animal under attack" near Cry in the Dark . . .

Cry in the Dark was a seasonal (Halloween) theme park open for most of October. Featuring hayrides, a haunted barn and the not-so-impressive hall of mirrors, the park had most recently added a new attraction: the Blue Ball Devil Maze—a complex labyrinth chopped out of two square acres of withering Indian corn.

Beaumont grabbed his receiver. "I'm on it."

Behind him, Ezekiel Stoltzfus snapped to attention. "What?"

"An attack?" said Grabers.

"In Ronks," added James, turning away.

As quickly, Beaumont got into his cruiser.

In the headlights, Grabers and both of the boys were already moving to bridle their pacers.

Ronks was fifteen minutes away by buggy.

Beaumont was there in three.

On the way, he attempted to gather more details, but only wound up in the gray as the dispatcher, given no further information, repeated: "-**an animal under attack**-"

Before he could make any sense of it, Cry in the Dark loomed up to the side of the road, and, before it, a crowd pointing urgently west. Beaumont took his cue. He pulled onto Dillerville Pike and gunned his engine. He rolled up a hill between plots of forest. On rounding a bend, he nearly flattened them: five or six figures with painted faces, blocking the road in a pitted huddle. They seemed to be kicking the shit out of something. Rudolf screeched to a fish tailed halt. The figures scattered into the woods.

A deposit was left behind on the road. It looked like a heap of quivering rugs. Beaumont got out of his cruiser, holding his pistol in one hand and casting the beam of his flashlight across the road with the other. The beam moved over a mound of fur on the pavement. It seemed to be whimpering lightly.

Rudolf looked closer, not understanding. He poked the deposit of fur with his flashlight.

"Ow!" came a voice in response. "Take it easy!" A bloodied face turned into the beam.

He was seventeen, maybe. His nose had been bloodied. He was wearing a suit.

"What *are* you, a cop?" he said.

Beaumont took hold of the young man's collar and hoisted him, groaning in pain, upright. Something fell to the pavement between them. Not letting go, Rudolf looked down.

A rubber mask lay torn on the road.

"What?" Beaumont looked closer, squinting.

"I work for the park," the kid announced. His tone was notably apprehensive.

Beaumont nudged the mask with his foot. It turned over. The face of a wolf looked up at him.

"Listen," the kid pleaded desperately now. "Just call my boss. He'll tell you about it."

Beaumont unhooked his nightstick.

"My father's a doctor. He won't . . ."

A blow to the side of his skull put him back on the pavement, unconscious.

As he stood over the motionless body, everything came to Rudolf at once. After three weeks of fruitless, confused pursuit, the "Blue Ball Devil" lay captured before him. The whole thing would now be revealed as a hoax—its perpetrator locked up, caught red-handed. And Beaumont due for some recognition . . .

As long as Fatty stayed out of the way.

Again, the radio: "*-*Officer Beaumont?*-*"

Headlights approaching from over the hill . . .

Snapping out of it, Rudolf dragged the kid to his cruiser and threw him in the backseat. A pickup appeared. He waved it onward, then climbed back into his driver's seat.

The western stretch of Dillerville Pike went by like trees on the side of a runway.

"*-*Officer Beaumont*-*"

It was the sheriff.

Rudolf picked up. “Yes, sir?”

“Where the hell are you?” Highman screamed. *“Officer Kutay needs your backup.”*

“I’ve taken a suspect into custody.”

The line went dead. Then: *“What did you say?”*

Beaumont answered: “Sir, it’s a kid in a wolfman costume. I’m bringing him in.”

“In a wolfman costume?” Highman echoed.

“Affirmative, sir. I’m bringing him in.”

The sheriff’s voice trailed off in the background, yelling at a dispatcher: *“Get a load of this!”*

Officer Kutay continued to squawk, as Keiffer chimed in: *“Did you save us some, Rudy?”*

Beaumont turned his radio down.

The media wouldn’t bother with Highman. *Rudolf*’s name would be the one in the paper. The *“Cop Who Uncovered the Blue Ball Devil.”* With photographs: *“Captor and Prize on Display,”* like a fisherman flaunting his catch on the dock.

In the midst of his reverie, a tree limb dropped to the road in his headlights, directly ahead. Shrieking, Beaumont swerved to avoid it. The cruiser jolted. One of its wheels drifted off the pavement, tearing and grinding.

A voice went up from the backseat: “What are you *doing*?”

The kid was awake.

“You *asshole*!”

Again, the cruiser lurched with a bang.

Rudolf managed to straighten his wheel. He angled his front left tire from the rim of the ditch, then leveled out on the pavement. And no sooner done than the sheriff was back on the radio, yelling—though no more than patches of clarity broke through a wash of static. Beaumont reached for his volume dial, but it didn’t help. He pounded the box. Only part of a statement trickled through. “*-*kid* woRks foR -&%$#@—yOu’ve G*t thE *wrong—* *#$”

Beaumont turned his radio off.

"Jesus." He looked in the rearview mirror, still not clear as to what had just happened.

With Kutay and Highman dropped from the mix, he felt like he'd just boomed out of a dust storm. Dillerville Pike was as calm as before. The sound of his breathing filled the car. He dabbed the clammy sweat from his brow.

The backseat was quiet. He looked around. The kid was unconscious again. What had happened? Another blow to the skull? Or just terror . . .

Turning to face the road once more, Rudolf's heart continued to race. He shook his head in bewilderment. *Jesus* . . .

Later that morning, a couple of rum and sodas would go down nicely. Stiff.

The sloping, weed-choked banks to either side of the roadway glowed in the headlights, plunging into the ditches below while rising up to a series of pastures. Gripping the wheel, Beaumont angled his cruiser between them, straight down the middle.

He was plotting his course of return to the precinct, torn between Groffdale and Eby Hess Roads, when everything seemed to go strangely quiet.

It wasn't a drop in sound, or any reduction in visible movement, so much as the sudden, eerie sensation of being watched, and *closely,* that caught his attention. The hairs on the back of his neck had already begun to bristle when something flickered—a flash of movement, off to the left. Just out the window. Directly beside him . . . Stiff with hesitation, he looked over—slowly turning his head to see. At first, nothing appeared to him clearly. What looked like the lights of a distant radio tower flashed across a lake . . . (?) . . . Or *was* that a lake? And, actually, wouldn't those flashing lights have been blocked by the road bank? For that matter, how were they holding steady beside his cruiser for hundreds of yards?

The sudden loss of perspective confounded him.

Then, to skew his bearings further, the "lake" disappeared—as though a haze had drifted across the moon's reflection. That's when

Rudolf nervously started to reconfigure his visual take. What he came up with coursed a chill to the farthest extreme of every appendage. No, that wasn't a radio tower. Those weren't signals off in the distance . . . No, that was a pair of eyes—red and beaming, directly beside him. And no, that wasn't a lake. That was a tongue, a mouth, glistening, panting—fogging the window, just inches away. A hideous face was staring at *him*. And not just staring, but laughing, cackling . . .

Paralyzed, Beaumont's stomach dropped. Suspended in breathless, flatline shock, he could only await the return of his senses.

It looked like an overgrown jackrabbit, bounding . . .

- at sixty miles per hour, at least

- glaring in mockery, jeering

- it smiled . . .

Rudolf lost control of his cruiser.

PART THREE

Ride It Out

Unsurprisingly, Dr. Elias Kepple, MD, the Stepford General's resident authority on genetic disorders, was either unable or unwilling, based on the findings of a single examination, to link under oath the Bontrager boy's condition with chronic physical abuse. Seeing how the area's 20,000 Anabaptists had descended, by and large, from twelve families (roughly 200 people) of Swiss and German extraction who'd settled The Basin in the early eighteenth century—that is to say: being that most of the community had been a closed genetic population for twelve generations—a host of related disorders had come into being, the symptoms of which were all too commonly taken for signs of abuse. In Ephraim's case, one of two metabolic disorders would have come into question: the first, and more common, being MSUD, or Maple Syrup Urine Disease. This condition was highly prevalent among the Amish of Stepford County. Defined as a disorder in the body's ability to metabolize three amino acids in protein—leucine, isoleucine and valine—collectively labeled the "branched chain amino acids"—MSUD resulted from the inability of mutated genes to convert these amino acids into energy. Because this conversion could not proceed, metabolites built to toxic levels, precipitating illness, coma and, sometimes, death. Often, attacks occurred early in infancy—as early as the first few days after birth—causing grievous neurological damage. If treated in time, victims survived. However, subsequent sicknesses, whether the flu or chicken pox, might induce relapses, even the mildest of which could still render permanent mental retardation.

This would've come into question with Ephraim, given his seemingly muted status. And even though x-ray photos revealed that, at some point, probably in early childhood, the boy had sustained a fractured skull, an MRI under Dr. Kepple revealed no significant traces of brain damage. Officially, Dr. Kepple would've diagnosed Ephraim as having suffered a milder bout of MSUD early in life, and as presently being in the midst of a relapse. Corroborating symptoms coincided: bruising about the arms and neck (which could have been caused by regular seizures), dehydration, hypertonia (excessive muscle tension), spasticity, acidosis (his blood test levels were abnormally high) and, obviously, lesions and rashes, which marked his body in splotches from head to toe.

One of the only problems was: his urine didn't smell of maple syrup. His urine, instead, smelled of cleaning solvents, and was inexplicably bluish in color. What's more, because the MRI had revealed no striking irregularities—aside from an overabundance of testosterone—and no trace of cerebral edema or other accumulations of fluid, the judge or jury might also have been informed of a second possibility: Glutaric Aciduria One. Another metabolic disorder, GA1 occurred most frequently in Sweden, among the Native Americans of Manitoba, Canada and in Pennsyltucky's Amish community: among whom one in three hundred was afflicted. Symptoms were similar, if not identical to MSUD, in several regards. The bruising, the rashes, the dehydration—the hypertonia—all matched up. But again, a discrepancy lay with the fact that, given Ephraim's neglected condition, i.e., the fact that he hadn't been treated—both disorders might easily have put him into a coma, if not killed him.

At the very least, Dr. Kepple maintained, he should've looked "like he had cerebral palsy."

Still, on the record, the doctor would have diagnosed one of these two diseases.

In his private opinion, however, the boy, in all likelihood, *was* a victim of abuse. His speech block appeared to be psychological. And his injuries corresponded with most of the telltale signs of inflicted trauma.

But that didn't mean the doctor was willing to testify to as much in court. On one too many occasions already, Kepple had taken the stand to be cross-examined by infamous Amish and Mennonite public defender Davin Stutz. In twenty-five years of local practice, Stutz had cleared an overwhelming majority (as many as nine out of every ten) clients faced with equivalent charges. His office, which had begun in a roadside apartment on 342 in the sixties, had since been expanded and relocated to a three-story building in Central Intercourse. There, it served as a hub of the whole Anabaptist community's legal front—although a significant many Amish and Mennonites stood opposed to his practice. Stutz, who wasn't a member of The Order—who, in fact, had been Lutheran for most of his life—was considered by some an opportunist, a scavenger feeding off cultural schisms—loyal to none, including legitimate victims of crime, but the almighty dollar: a man with one foot in The Basin and one in The System, with little allegiance to either—someone who knew every clause in the book, and was versed in persuading any jury that, short of felony violations, the Plain Folk were better left to themselves. Seeing as how they paid no social security taxes and, what's more, considered themselves exempt from all laws but the word of God (Obey thy parents, among them), then, Stutz argued, these people's affairs, so long as they posed no threat to the masses, were none of our business. If independent, autonomous coexistence was what they wanted, so be it. Their churches would monitor matters of discipline. And no one disputed their churches' integrity . . .

As members almost never bore witness against one another in English courts, and as, again, MSUD and GA1 (loosely known as "Shaken Baby Syndrome") had numerous precedents of misdiagnosis, the jury was often set to dismiss Dr. Kepple before he took the stand. As such, the doctor refrained from committing to testify in all but the most severe cases—among whom, Ephraim Bontrager, even with a glaring black eye, didn't manage to qualify—for, even in bearing the markings of physical cruelty, he was also, in Kepple's words, "covered in pine sap, stunk like a leper and looked to have gone for a roll in the briars." It might have been argued with little rebuff that the boy simply couldn't take care of himself, and was prone, by mental defect, to injury. Meaning: there was no way in hell he would get around Stutz. The case wouldn't make it to trial.

Jack, in having appealed to Yoder to make the exam, had expected as much. Physical checkups were standard procedure. They rarely, if ever, sufficed in securing a warrant for legal intervention. Yet, one didn't go to court without them. Formally, they were indispensable.

Both men had come to their meeting in Yoder's Prince Street office well-prepared. Jack pulled an envelope out of his leather satchel and dropped it on the table between them. "We don't have much more time," he said.

Yoder picked up the envelope, nodding. "I know." He broke the seal and removed a manila folder. He turned it over.

"There's more where that came from," Jack assured him.

Jarret's expression was unperturbed. He flipped through the documents, print by print—until, halting, he tilted the page on an angle. "What *is* that?"—recoiling—"Jesus, man. What *are* they?"—disgusted, he turned another page. "Who handled this case?"

"Davin Stutz," said Jack.

Yoder rolled his eyes. "That figures." Again, he stopped. "My *God* . . ." He was horrified. "What do you call this, Jack?"

"Inadmissible. That's where *you* come in."

Yoder blinked. He stuck one end of a pen in his mouth and gnawed it, gurgling.

"Nobody's had a crack at these people in years," said Jack. "They're due for a hit. There's a detailed list of contacts in there—customers, clients, neighbors and whatnot. The SPCA's expecting your call."

"I'm on it."

Producing a videotape, Jack nodded gravely. "And wait till you see this."

Ten minutes later, he left the building and wandered up Prince Street, bound for his truck. A couple of kids were gathered around the base of a colonial stoop playing handball. One of them spotted Jack and called out: "Coach!"

With a grin, Jack nodded toward them.

The pang of accord seemed out of place.

While working with Yoder on one thing, he'd been contending with Roddy and Jones on another—with turbulent subchapters back at the gym, the latest of which involved more missing items: someone had stolen his cell phone. Along with some headgear and gloves from the rack.

And nothing had turned up on Franklin's person.

The daily madness of life as The Coach may have taken a backseat, but it was still pressing. Jack was looking forward to getting away from it all for a couple of months. He hadn't been able to breathe in weeks.

He hadn't been able to breathe for years.

A line was queued at the rescue mission. There, too, someone called his name. "Hey, Coach! Y'all better whoop that Cobra!"

Jack raised his right hand, forming a fist.

He cut through an empty lot full of garbage to Water Street, spotted with wreckage and trash. Sunlight bathed the pavement around him, glaring brightly for mid-October.

Less than a block from his truck, he passed a newspaper box and, with a double take, stopped.

The headline, slightly bowed by the plastic viewing glass of the copy dispenser, struck him, at first, as a practical joke or a tabloid gag, if not a mirage. *"The Blue Ball Devil Captured,"* it read. With a subhead: *"Chappaquiddick Revisited."* By: Celebrated Columnist Owen Brynmor. And beneath it, centered, some white kid's high school photo, with a caption reading: *"Menace to Society?"*

Jack stood scratching his head for a moment. When, at last,

he'd managed to dig some change from his pocket and purchase a copy, he still hadn't fully accepted the print's authenticity. Something was wrong.

Indeed.

In the opening paragraph, Officer Rudolf Beaumont was credited with "cracking the case," though only by flipping his squad car into a ditch, then leaving the wounded "suspect," a seventeen-year-old Hempland student, trapped inside, cuffed to the door, while "searching for help" at a local tavern. Jeremy Ruoss, who harbored "acting ambitions" and worked at a theme park four nights a week in the role of the "Stepford Basin's Wolfman," was listed in "stable" condition at sunrise. Police spokesmen, when asked to verify that a perpetrator had been apprehended, confirmed the report. Officer Beaumont himself was being treated for "injuries."

At first, it was everything Jack could do not to laugh. Had he been more surprised, or less calloused by ongoing updates, he might not have held back.

As it occurred, the article only served to confuse him all the more . . .

For one thing, Brynmor's wording—his clearly theatrical, partly sarcastic and wholly disdainful-of-county-authorities bias—wasn't in keeping with the otherwise customarily sterile paper's spirit. Right from the start, that had baffled The Coach. For many years, he'd been reading *The Plea*. He knew more than one of its staff reporters, to whom he had granted numerous interviews. He knew Dale Goodall, in charge of sports, and Terrance Jarvik, the city editor—both on a first-name basis, and both well enough to know that, after hours, they may have been decent-humored enough—but, once at their desks, neither man had distinguished himself as a taker of risks . . . Above all, he knew what the demographic would tolerate in public print. And in that regard, and those preceding it, Owen didn't fit the bill. The fact that his stories were being printed suggested a senior-level malfunction. Something was happening over at the paper, as something was happening off in The Basin, as something was happening back with Yoder . . .

This was a hell of a cycle, thought Jack.

Whatever the case, it was making him paranoid. With Brynmor unknowingly under his nose, recounting the "wildest night in The Basin"—and, as listed upon conclusion: "For more by the author, see Section C (Sports)," having been ordered to couple the photo he'd taken of Jones and Roddy with text—Jack was now beginning to feel at continual risk of investigation. Even during Golden Gloves, he'd never gotten so much publicity—and just when he needed it the least. Again, he might have laughed it off, had the odds against everything not overwhelmed him.

Owen, as unsuspectingly, couldn't have blown more shit at The Coach with a twister. The kid was a serious pain in the ass. And he didn't even know it.

He would have been embarrassed.

Whatever, the photo he'd taken was perfect: Roddy, clearly unconscious of the camera, with a hazily affable grin on his face, unfocused (the moment had passed in a flash), standing over The Cobra, who was halfway pitched over backwards, his torso horizontal, with one leg folding underneath him, the other shooting off at an angle and a grimace of pain and disgrace, going down . . .

And "Ole Broken Dick" standing behind him, horrified.

That part, Jack didn't mind so much. Once he'd come to grips with the fact that Jerry Blye had actually *dared*—it was almost impressive—to enter the West Side (which, never having put the old bastard past it, was still incredibly hard to believe) he couldn't help quietly reveling in it. Ole Broken Dick looked like a horse's ass . . . Jack could hear them in Philth Town already: "You hear about *Blye?*"—with merciless laughter. And televised, leading up to the fight: *"The Cobra takes a flying spill!"*

Although it had already aired from the city, Jack still hadn't seen the footage. He prayed that the camera hadn't caught him tossing Blye out the door *too* explicitly—as Blye was certain to sue already, and, with footage, would probably shoot for broke. If worse came to worse, The Coach would just have to be man enough to accept the damage. In which case, at least Brynmor's article captured the moment, for history's sake.

Without having posed a single question to Jack, Owen had pieced together not only a chronological recap of Jones's public self-abnegation, but detailed rundowns on every party concerned—Roddy, Blye, Travers, Coach Stumpf and the West Side itself—and all with accuracy, relatively speaking—bridging the gap between general reference and the die-hard fight fan's understanding—beginning with an introduction to Roddy—in overly flattering terms, perhaps, but with only the best of intentions—and, soon to proceed, with highly needed results.

The article opened with one of his quotes: "I guess the fella just lost his balance"—delivered with an absence of malice so real, he was sure to capture the public's endearment.

He would be cheered around town all week. Come Thursday night, half of the county would be tuned in to watch the fight. This would only work to Team Lowe's advantage—as Roddy, unlike The Cobra, had always been buoyed by roaring support.

With that much, at least, Jack was pleased.

Moreover, the writing itself was solid.

Brynmor had turned to the public files in compiling a no-less-flattering portrait of Jack's career than Roddy's skill. The Coach hadn't paid the kid his due. Along with a penchant for visual detail: with broader, more detailed strokes than might have been gracing the pages of Stepford's *Plea*, the gym was brought to life on a multisensual level, from cellar to roof-hatch—with posters of Hagler and Chavez and Langford, and even "The Great" Harry Greb, on the wall—from the glove racks, "heaped like treated hides in the half-light," backed by the speed bags' humming, from the medicine balls on a tier by the door to the "sweet smell of wood polish, sweat and the ring mat"—a paragraph devoted to the building, which was founded in August of 1874, including a third-floor showroom, the two-lane bowling alley downstairs—and talk of the "phantom" that haunted it (where in the world had he heard about *that* one?)—to profiles of area trainers and boxers and referees dating back to the forties, all of which Owen could only have gathered by questioning Roddy, and possibly Marty, and carefully reading the hundreds of newspaper articles lining the walls of the gym.

What's more, the prose itself was strong, inspired, informed and factually accurate. On the big board, of course, there was room for improvement. Some of the jargon was a bit academic. He needed some corner time, maybe. But all the essentials, the smarts, the cojones were there . . .

Jack was beginning to see an angle.

Meanwhile, life in reporting continued . . .

So pleased had been Jarvik with the "Week in Review"' piece, submitted to him by midnight Saturday, that, right away, Owen was offered the text on his photo of Roddy and Jones for Monday.

Initially, Owen hesitated—checked by his homecoming resolution. He wasn't about to renege on his vow to step into the ring before writing about it. He wouldn't be able to *cover* the fight . . .

But this had nothing to do with the fight. This was about someone taking a spill. And in that regard, Owen had definite obligations to Mother Discordia.

What's more, his photo had been solicited by *Ring Magazine,* along with the *Horaceburg Screed* and three different private collectors, before even generating AP demand. It was crucial that one of the staff's more competent writers finish the article quickly. And Owen, after all, had *been* there. He'd taken the picture.

He took the assignment.

Dale Goodall, the editor in sports, didn't seem to mind. Unlike most of the paper's staff, Goodall, a bony, dry-humored man, seemed unperturbed by the Blue Ball Devil, and so, bore Owen no evident grudge. Besides which, he knew good work when he saw it.

And that was exactly what Owen delivered.

It had been one of his smoother, less inhibited turns at the keyboard in years. He'd drawn on the pressurized visceral octane and sensory freight of a week in training—clear as the freshly driven snow, like rockets flaring across the harbor. These moments came rarely. They made it all worthwhile.

By seven o'clock, he was high as a kite.

He emerged from the microfiche room at ten, bleary-eyed—toting a sack full of empty Styrofoam coffee dispenser cups. He waded through the hum on an angle to Goodall's basket, submitted the piece with a tug of reluctance, then wandered in search of distraction.

As always, the newsroom was stuffy and tense. Out of the fox-hole & into the frost: these people were nearing the end of another wild shift, and none in good humor.

On Owen's desk sat a plastic Hefty bag full of what Kegel referred to as *Hate Mail*—letters addressed to the paper, the editor and/or assistant editors directly. Kegel had sifted through it already. Its worth had been stripped to slender pickings—mostly complaints re: the boogeyman coverage from semi-illiterate Christian trash.

Two new reports had been dropped in his basket: one, from a lady in Bareville who'd called in twenty-five "encounters" if she'd called in one—the latest involving a chimpanzee gone yodeling mad in a nearby cornfield. The second was placed by a country club owner, who claimed to have spotted a naked "maniac" loping across his seventh fairway—then actually leaping (yes, in a single bound, with a howl) over the pond. It was *"faster than One-Time Charlie,"* he said.

Both reports had been filed by 8:00.

There were also two envelopes. Neither was marked with a return address. Enclosed in the first was a copy of what appeared to be an agricultural newsletter—one without photographs. *The Budget*, it read. Owen began to flip through it. Entries were grouped into columns by order of town: Hutchinson, Kansas. Brown City, Michigan. Danville, Ohio. Boyd, Wisconsin.

It was an Amish and Mennonite newsletter: entries from families around the world—mostly relaying harvest, weather, domestic and church-related concerns. Letters from Stepford, as maybe no longer the biggest, but the oldest, most influential Anabaptist community in existence (the "Hub of the Plain Folk," the "Old Order Mecca"), extended in print for over three pages, more than any other town—on the second, inside column of which an entry was circled in bright red ink: a letter from an Eli Hershberger, dated October 3rd, which read, from start to finish: *"The Time of the Killing Is Back."*

The second piece opened up to a threat: "*We know where you live*"—which Owen stuffed into a pocket to file away at home.

And finally, a memo from "Charlene" in copy: "Your wording is cumbersome. Try to economize."

He dropped her remark in the trash, then picked up his cell phone and went in search of a place to talk without being leered at.

He found a spot by the coffee machine in the break room, and dialed the country club's number. Moments later, the owner was swearing to Jesus by it: *"the damnedest thing I've ever seen: right over the lake!"*

"What time did this happen?" Owen asked him and, in doing so, looked down to realize that Bess, that frumpy vampire girl in Layout, was sitting at the table, directly in front of him. He had been standing there gripping his testicles. She looked disgusted, if vaguely amused.

"An hour ago," the club owner answered.

Owen hung up. "What are *you* looking at?"

She shook her head. "You tell me."

He pivoted, turning away, horrified. "I'm just trying to word myself here . . . "

She said nothing.

Jarvik walked by the window, dressed in a tux. They watched him pass.

Owen, too happy to change the subject, asked: "Has he always been like this?"

Leaning back on her chair, she replied with a shrug: "Only since you got here."

He waited for something, a word of explanation, a guess, anything.

Silence.

Finally, he followed up: "What do you make of it?"

Smirking, she looked him up and down. She was shaking her head. Her grin was ambiguous. "He must like the way you carry yourself."

That busted her up.

She coughed. "Or not."

She got up and made for the door, looking satisfied. "You're the reporter. You find out."

Fine, then: he would find out for himself . . .

But first: a wild night in The Basin.

From the moment the Lamepeter scanners began to crackle and hiss with disturbance reports—just before quitting time (midnight) at the paper—activity would scarcely let up for a moment, carrying through to the early morning. Along with the chimp in the stubble report, and the lake-leaping maniac, already registered, a handful of goblin, werewolf and "negro-streaker" sightings would also come in. Twenty-four emergency calls would be logged in the course of the following seven hours. Among them: one case of "firebombing" an elderly widow's (reportedly one of the resident superstore protesters) mailbox, a "team of derelicts" spray-painting three of the "Welcome to Stepford" billboards on Old Route 30 with "Beware of The Dutchies" in black, and the trashing of an estimated one-acre plot of corn (by uprooting) just south of Paradise. Other damages throughout The Basin would include a six-figure toll at the Sprawl Mart, yet-to-be-tallied losses at Holtwood, four dozen bottles of missing whiskey, three hundred dollars in register cash, and Officer Beaumont's overturned cruiser—along with the injured youth inside of it . . .

In formatting text, Owen would focus on the latter situation specifically.

Having arrived at the accident site less than ten minutes after the call had come in, he had watched as, in view of dozens of witnesses, Russel Commons, the owner of Cry in the Dark, the seasonal horror park had verbally blasted responding officers Corbett, Kutay and Edwards on behalf of the Lamepeter Police Department at large (and, above all, Officer Rudolf Beaumont) for beating, endangering and deserting his seventeen-year-old employee, Jeremy Ruoss.

Ruoss, a slight, gangly type with alleged theatrical aspirations, had been cast by Commons as the lead in the park's latest feature: the Blue Ball Devil Maze.

Through the first seven days of the season, he'd been assaulted on four separate occasions—first by "East Petersburg Hessians" who, according to Ruoss, were "nasty, but couldn't throw a punch," then moving on to "stinking wasted" football players from Muncie Township, most of whom outweighed him by over a hundred pounds, and who charged him in squads.

By midweek, they had been showing up early, jamming the parking lot just after practice to power-slam quarts of Miller Lite through plastic funnel bongs, belching it up. At opening time, the crowd had been charged. A few of them actually paid for tickets. The rest just hopped right over the gate, letting out for the nearest geek in a suit—and the Blue Ball Devil Maze, in particular, where Ruoss and others in masquerade were to spring out of bushes, startling maze-goers.

Commons had been phoning the police all week, to no effect whatsoever, thus far. On two occasions, an officer had come by to take a report subsequently—but only after the squads had gone home, the damage was done and the park had been closed. To date, not a soul had been questioned about it. Police protection had not been provided. The park was on a first-name basis with the 911 operator—yet, so far, no circuit patrols—not even an hourly drive-by had been dispatched. Commons himself had appeared at the sheriff's office, demanding to speak with Highman, only to be turned away without explanation.

The cops had been *zero* help.

That evening (the 17th) Ruoss had been attacked and beaten by one of the squads, after which he'd been chased, driven into the fields, recaptured and beaten again before Officer Beaumont could intervene—and he himself had delivered another beating, followed by a General Lee off the road—and topping it all, a prompt abandonment.

Beaumont seemed to have disappeared.

Commons now regretted having called the police for help at all.

As Jeremy Ruoss would manage to splutter upon being dragged from the overturned wreck, he had come to his senses with power lines floating by the window outside—holding steady, drifting, falling and—SLAM—into darkness. Then waiting, pinned upside down in the wreck. The cop had given him up for dead.

"Who *hired* that asshole?" was Ruoss's final remark upon being escorted away.

That was all Owen had needed to know. A goatboy, maybe—confused, pissed and alone, but *not* the Blue Ball Devil. No further testimony needed on Ruoss.

For now, Russel Commons would deal out the whoop ass—cursing the township police as incompetent morons—and *doomed* in court . . .

The young man's father was a prominent surgeon.

The sheriff responded, as relayed through Officer Corbett, with the incomprehensible charge that Ruoss was also, despite his claims, the primary suspect in "this Devil business"—the lone agent believed to have been behind dozens of sightings in recent weeks.

More than absurd, the contention was self-negating—especially in light of the fact that, even before the cruiser was dragged from the mud by a locally hired wrecker, two more "ape dog" sightings came over the radio. Clearly, nothing was over.

For whatever reason, the Lamepeter P.D. was standing behind—to a certain extent even shielding—Officer Beaumont's conduct, probably in hopes of eluding a brutality suit.

But they couldn't protect him from Owen.

Hence: *"The Blue Ball Devil Captured!"* as next morning's lead. The "Wildest Night in The Basin" opened up with a rundown on not just events at the Sprawl Mart, the state store and the Holtwood grounds, but thirteen robberies, just as many prowler calls and even more motorists claiming to have been chased by a fearsome, repulsive creature—none of which triggered half of the reaction elicited by Beaumont's treatment of Ruoss: the reference to Chappaquiddick had been deserved. The officer had, after all, left the young man to die. And to worsen his image, he would turn up drunk at the Dogboy later that evening. The tavern's owner would place a call to the precinct at 1:38 a.m., complaining of an officer in full uniform guzzling whiskey right out in the open—sweating profusely, mumbling gibberish and "scaring" the regular, paying customers—on top of which, he had "lost" his wallet and hadn't paid for a drink all night.

All of which Owen relayed verbatim.

Jarvik would hold the presses until almost five a.m., a record hour. Owen finished the piece at a booth in an all-night diner at 4:35—before the sightings had even trailed off—and drove it back to submit at the office. He didn't go home until after dawn. And, wired on caffeine, adrenaline, fatigue and momentum, he wouldn't be able to sleep before noon, when Roddy's training began.

As always, he got to the gym on time.

By four o'clock that afternoon, he hadn't slept in thirty-two hours.

The rest of his evening was now accounted for. That is to say: he needed sleep. His mind was beginning to fall apart. He couldn't go on at this rate effectively . . .

Thereby, it wasn't till Tuesday morning that he finally got a chance to look into some matters—a few things he hadn't been able to shake since Thursday. He walked to the library early.

In following up the bizarre claims of the Dogboy's beverage delivery man (the members of whose extended family, it turned out, were practicing Old Order Mennonites) Owen had searched the paper's cross-directory in search of a Jacob Speicher—one presumably born between 1935 and '57. There were ten of them, only three of whom had social security numbers listed. Only two had phones—both of which had been disconnected years earlier. And seeing how the paper's death records hadn't been updated since the early sixties, there was no telling who was even alive . . .

It certainly wasn't much of a start.

(And whoever heard of a Mennonite wolfman?)

Try soliciting door to door:

(The *Troweling.*)

"Hello, does The Devil live here?"

He needed more information than that.

So then he'd gone back to the articles written by Lindsey Cale in '74—the original Blue Ball Devil coverage, which seemed to have been less dramatic in scope than the present campaign, at least on record. Most of The Basin's trouble appeared to have centered on agricultural matters: record-low yields of corn at harvest, along with a handful of livestock "attacks." There were very few entries for breaking and entering. No lynchings. And no one named Jacob Speicher . . .

Owen proceeded by contacting two known sources from the articles by Lindsey Cale.

The first name was "Sergeant Buster Highman," which, one could hope, was unique in also belonging to the present-day sheriff of Lamepeter Township. Highman, presumably young at the time, had been quoted as having "serious doubts" when asked to remark on whether or not the Blue Ball Devil might be a cougar.

Unfortunately, he proved even less forthcoming when questioned as The Sheriff. He hung up on Owen.

The second name to catch his attention was Marcus Diller, veterinarian MD, whose comments had been solicited more in a humorous vein, one was tempted to guess, than his answer might have accommodated. "Yes," he was quoted in whatever context: "There's more to this story than meets the eye."

Dr. Diller, it turned out, was still in the business. Owen had managed to reach him, in person, by phone, at nine that morning. When asked to remark on the situation, the doctor had responded flatly, all posturing aside, strictly between the two of them: "*Do* mind your questions, Mr. Brynmor. You never know what you might turn up."

Which could have been clarified, instead of compounded by: "They'll call you a madman. Don't be a fool."

The warning had gotten to Owen, who suddenly felt overcome with a sense of embarrassment. In effect, however indirectly, the doctor had just assured him of one thing: there were *people* out there—maybe five or ten, maybe half of the Amish Basin—who must have been getting a kick (or not) out of watching him flounder about in this story. Even acknowledging artistic license—meaning: his less than objective intent—there were bound to be parties in awe over just how grievously wide of the mark he was shooting.

That was a bit more than Owen could bear. He needed to figure out what he was dealing with. *Now* . . . He couldn't rely on these contacts. He couldn't rely on the paper's archives. Most of this reference was obsolete. The microfiche slides were out of order—by years, sometimes. And the lighting was terrible.

Nothing would be resolved from this office.

Jarvik, by now in a lavender peacoat, granted him all the time he needed. A follow-up piece to the weekend's "trilogy" wasn't expected for two or three days. If necessary, Kegel would update the Sprawl Mart and Holtwood affairs, not to worry. Providing the scanners didn't go ape again, Owen was encouraged to put all he had into making his next installment a "scorcher."

Which gave him a chance, at last, to find out what a corn wolf was—although only at random, *after* he'd tried and given up. It was really a fluke that he found it at all. Having settled on browsing *Bad Moon: An Unabridged History of Urban Legends,* by Ronald Stoner, he stumbled onto it: *Kornwolf*—spelled with a K. It was German.

Centuries back, at the time of the Thirty Years' War (1618–1648), an age when wolves had still roamed the forests of Germany, farmers had grown to refer to the outlaws, deserters and fugitives hiding in fields all over Europe as kornwolves. Often, these "heretics" were able to live off the land until harvest without being spotted.

Currently, the term had survived in some older, primarily German-American communities. In parts of the rural Midwest, the Kornwolf was still reviled as a spirit of vengeance, a curse of the fields, a "blight," a "pariah."

The term was included in Stoner's history owing to "The Kornwolf of Dole, Indiana"—also known by the people of Blessinger County as "The Werewolf of Possum Turn." This creature had first been spotted roaming the Hoosier Forest in 1970. One person claimed to have witnessed it mauling a goat on the side of the road at dusk. Another reported horrible screams from the forest. Three dozen chickens were murdered . . . For over a month, it had wandered the region—then, just as unexpectedly, vanished. In appearance, it was said to have bridged the gap between Lon Chaney Jr. as the Wolf Man, and Nixon . . .

Owen looked up from the book with a start.

It had taken him almost seven hours, but, finally, he'd stumbled onto something.

Dr. Diller had been on the money.

Now, for gazing into the abyss . . .

By the next afternoon, he had narrowed his definition of "werewolf" down accordingly. Every mythology, every belief, every culture, tradition and creed in history recognized some basic manifestation of the shape-shifter. It was a universal.

Typically, a person assumed the form of the most deadly beast in that part of the world—the wolf or bear in Europe and northern Asia, the leopard or hyena in Africa, the lion or tiger in China and India—each to its own inherent embodiment. The Romans had the *Versipellis*. Italy had the *Lupo Manero.* Portugal had the *Lobo homem.* Mexico, the *Nahual.* France, the *Loup Garou.* And *Werewolf* came from the German.

The modern (Christian) image of the werewolf, culled from the fire and brimstone of medieval Europe, had gelled to its current form in the sixteenth century's Reformation.

Between the years of 1520 and 1630, over thirty thousand individuals were condemned as werewolves—not witches, but werewolves—most of whom were burned, beheaded, dismembered or otherwise put to death.

In 1540, Rainer Yokelman, a friar from Cologne, had devised a key to identifying werewolves in human form.

Indications included:

Pale skin.
Sensitivity to light.
An absence of tears or saliva.
Bad breath.
Excessive thirst.
Cuts and abrasions on arms and legs that do not heal.
An extended ring finger.
Glands that emit foul odors.
Hypersexuality—including a drive toward incest, bestiality and rape.
Speaking in tongues.
Purple or bluish urine.
Intense cravings for meat.
The ability to sense—or "see"—events happening miles away, or even beforehand.
Massive intake of wine or spirits, used to catalyze demonic possession.
Irritability.
Drastic mood swings—spells of lethargy erupting in outbreaks of wild violence.
A bent for long, nocturnal meanderings.
Extreme sensitivity to lunar conditions.
Steadily darkening skin throughout the day preceding a transformation.

According to Yokelman, the "blighted" or cursed individual could also exercise powers of mind control over those around them—particularly those affected by intoxicants.

Continuing, Yokelman ardently maintained that, while most werewolves, or *lycanthropes* (from the Greek: *lykoi,* wolf, and *anthropos,* man), were commonly given to work their mischief by light of the full moon, lunar conditions, in fact, continued to influence not just their behavior, but their overall psychological and physical dispositions, throughout the cycle. The dual natures of human and beast were not at all mutually exclusive. They waxed and waned in flux with one another as much as they did with the moon. The "blighted" was subject to transformation at any time, with varying severity.

Other means of inducing the blight included wearing a "wolf pelt" or "girdle"—one granted by the devil in exchange for the individual's soul—wearing an article of clothing obtained from a werewolf, eating the heart of a wolf, chanting a series of incantations while dancing around a ritual fire, "carnal indulgence" and last, sustaining excessive mental and physical trauma.

During interrogations, suspected werewolves were beaten, often to death, instead of being questioned properly. The verdict was simply a flogging away, went the logic—as long as the suspect was chained to the floor, that is. The old: *"If-she-floats-she's-a-witch, if-she-doesn't-she's-dead"* routine.

Today, a handful of explanations had begun to account for this age of hysteria. Foremost among them, and not to be underestimated, being the fact that Europe had been enmeshed, at the time, in a comprehensive religious cataclysm: many accepted, seemingly harmless sects like the Anabaptists—and even the Quakers—had been lumped in with all manner of heretics, killers and social outlaws, each to be hounded with equal tenacity. Modern physicians would now place anyone afflicted with schizophrenia, rabies, porphyria (the "hairy gene"), psychomotor epilepsy, manic depressive psychosis and hysterical neurosis of the dissociative type—to say nothing of everyday quirks and foibles, *or* an alternative sexual lifestyle—at risk of being accused and condemned as a werewolf by sixteenth-century standards. Most of the people Owen considered worth a damn would not have survived it. In likelihood, he himself would have burned at the stake on a dozen occasions already—and he wasn't even a creep, ho ho.

He *never* would have made it through adolescence.

He checked out *Bad Moon* at 8:45, just before the library closed, and adjourned to *The Plea* to catch up on his basket, the scanner and Jarvik's latest wardrobe.

Through his window, the old man appeared to be lost in thought.

He was seated with his feet on the desktop, staring absently into space. A rose had been tucked into one of his pockets.

Owen decided to leave him alone.

Nothing new had come over the scanner. A couple of vaguely similar calls had filtered in on Monday evening—one from an angry Soddersburg resident claiming to have been pulled over, searched and questioned by "heavily armed Dutchies," the other from Bird-in-Hand, someone complaining of having been tailgated clear from Ronks to New Holland by a Sprawl Mart wagon with high beams.

Little had happened as yet this evening. A call had come in from the Intercourse Getaway's desk clerk, reporting a "posse of vampire types" who were scaring his regular customers.

Otherwise, nothing was cooking out there. No livestock attacks. No kornwolf sightings.

Feeling no less unwelcome in the newsroom than ever, he stopped by the kitchen, filled up on coffee and made for the microfiche vault.

For the next few hours, he read through Stoner's *Bad Moon*. It was organized alphabetically. Owen would make it to H by midnight. Along the way he would read about the Adlet; the bloodthirsty Inuit weredogs that still hunt the icelands in search of human flesh; the Navajo Coyote People, who were able to travel for miles in the blink of an eye; Gilles Garnier, the Hermit of Dole, burned as a werewolf in the 1570s; and more from Germany, the Greifswald werewolves, who plundered that city in 1640.

The last entry he was able to read that evening concerned the "Harvest Sabbath." Dating back, again, to the sixteenth century, this ritual event was defined as the culmination of a seasonal curse. When a group or community lost its faith, or was errant in performing the will of the Lord, *"a blight would overcome their fields, as a madness would overtake their young, as a devil would grow to appear among them, enticing their gentlest hearts to murder."* This devil, this spirit of vengeance, would "bury its seed among them by light of the moon," from which would grow their undoing, in time. The Sabbath itself was a rite of destruction.

Reeling, bewildered, exhausted and drifting in oversuspended disbelief, Owen emerged from the microfiche vault a few hours later to check the scanner.

Someone from Paradise had phoned in complaining of too many locals seated with guns on their porches all over The Basin of late, and how it was ruining the tourist season.

Otherwise, nothing. Still no sightings.

The lull was increasingly disconcerting.

Owen left the building and walked up the street to the empty central plaza. The fountains were still. He leaned on the edge of one basin, sitting beneath a walk light. His temples were throbbing. He rubbed them. The evening was quiet. The air was crisp and clear.

He looked up, into the sky, as framed by an outline of darkened department buildings—and spotted the moon in a solid crescent, as centerpiece, hanging directly above him. A *waxing* crescent, if memory served—working its way to the first quarter. Or was that a gibbous, he wondered. He couldn't remember the order. How did it go?

Whatever the case, it was hanging over him. Which only confused him all the more—as it wasn't full . . .

Lord almighty.

Again, he cradled his head, exhaling.

For all of that afternoon's research, the one thing he couldn't shake—the one thing that hadn't stopped eating a hole in his rambling thought dreams—was Rainer Yokelman's listing of purple or bluish urine as a symptom of lycanthropy, and with it, the one image hanging persistently, now, in his mind, from the past two weeks—more than all of the "sightings" combined, more than the motion detector photo—the observation he couldn't in some way or other attribute to human delusion (which wasn't to be underestimated) and/or deception (by outside parties) was the purplish "spray paint" marking the walls of the Holtwood structures the week before—the bluish goo that, upon inspection, appeared to have rusted around the edges, eaten away by a potent corrosive.

He hadn't been able to figure it then, and he couldn't pretend to shake it now. He was all out of sorts. He didn't know what to believe anymore. He never had.

In the morning, he woke up with less than an hour remaining before he was due at the gym. He dressed, made coffee and checked his original list of goals for the early hours. He hadn't left time to sift through the hate mail. That would just have to wait until later. He wouldn't be able to swing by the bookstore either, not before three o'clock.

One way or another, he definitely needed to turn something in by the end of the day.

He thought about it all the way to the gym . . .

Whatever the case, Roddy looked good in training.

As that went, watching The Unbelievable spar with Calvin that afternoon would not only interrupt Owen's regularly scheduled torture session with Rhya, Coach Stumpf would actually give him cause, by surprise, for pleasant distraction. Owen could never have seen it coming, as, all morning, Jack had seemed even more dour than usual.

He still hadn't mentioned the article.

Earlier, Roddy had outlined a bad situation pending with one of the juniors, Franklin, the one with the lip on him. Jack was in serious straits with Franklin, apparently.

It seemed to be all he could do to focus on Roddy and Calvin's work in the ring. Which Owen took for a good sign, at least insofar as it indicated that Roddy, by sparring like an able-bodied veteran, was rendering the luxury of distraction affordable. There wasn't much Jack really needed to tell him. Roddy had been fighting for twenty years. He knew every gun on his deck, by now. And their plan was solid: attack the body.

A week before, Owen had sensed a current of tension between them, coach and fighter. Jack had seemed skeptical, nervous, reserved as to Roddy's performance & mind-set in training—and

Roddy, in turn, had been tuning Jack out, getting caught with his back to the ropes too often—at times, it seemed, to *spite* his coach. That tension appeared to have settled by now. Beyond his impressive work in sparring, Roddy was regulating his weight—inching down from 148. He was pulling his roadwork every morning. He was sleeping at least eight hours a night. He was drinking his water. And his diet was on track—carbs in the morning, roughage and lean white meat at night.

And no booze, no grass.

Bobbing and weaving, he walked Calvin down with his hands up, chin tucked, unblinking. He looked like a real contender.

Jack appeared more or less satisfied with him. The only time he really spoke up was to jump on Calvin, not Roddy, to keep his hands up—and cut with the shucking and jiving already. Calvin tended to showboat a bit. But only, in this case, by running from Roddy. They wound up hashing it out in the corner. Roddy proceeded to land his hooks, and, although he might have been holding back, they still looked plenty painful to Owen.

Jack hit his stop watch. "TIME!"

The voice of Aretha Franklin welled up in the cease-fire, warbling out of the speakers. Roddy and Calvin tapped gloves and walked back to their corners. Jack was mumbling—hardly a bitter expression about him—but notably humorless, distant, dazed—in spite of his own better efforts, preoccupied.

Thereby, it came in a flash when, on turning to Owen, he mumbled: "You're in on this, right?"

Owen stepped back, looking over his shoulder to make way for whomever Jack was addressing. But no one was there. He swallowed. He looked back, wide-eyed. "Me?"

Jack waited for an answer.

Roddy leaned over the ropes, peering out through his headgear, jawing his mouthpiece to clarify. "You want to work the corner, buddy?"

Owen swallowed again. "Doing what?"

Jack produced a yellow bucket.

Hallelujah.

Spit bucket boy.

At last, O Lord, he was coming home. And for those who had doubted him: *eat your hearts out . . .*

Owen could not have been more elated. The whole thing was nearly too good to be true. Finally: some time on the inside, working the corner, wading through all of the sleaze and the grit and the nervous anticipation—all of the dead time and agony backstage. And he would be there as a part of Team Lowe: spit bucket boy for The Unbelievable . . .

Once again, Jack had acknowledged his presence, albeit with less than an excess of jubilance.

Man, The Coach was a weird dude.

Whatever the case, Owen accepted.

It was almost enough to throw him off his game for the rest of the afternoon. But no matter how thrilled he may've been, he still had a deadline back at *The Plea* and, as yet, very little to go on but incomplete research and dwindling scanner reports.

He arrived at the office to find that a total of one complaint had come out of The Basin the night before—and not even a cooker: that lady from Bareville again, with a random gunfire report . . .

This didn't look good.

A sinking feeling returned to Owen. For three nights now, the disorder in Lamepeter Township had shown a marked decline. What had begun as a drifting lull in the action was starting to make him nervous. The Blue Ball Devil needed a catalyst, something to bring it all together. Synchronization of disparate elements. Mobilization. Order to chaos.

He ended up back at the library, this time in search of astronomical data. Something about the previous evening down in the plaza wouldn't sit with him. The fact that he couldn't remember the lunar phases may have been part of the problem. But maybe the moon's having come up in reference on more than a dozen occasions that afternoon—each in the line of his unbiased fire—bothered him more. He had questions, as always.

According to an article published in *Mythos Quarterly,* the moon's effect on human behavior was demonstrated clearly through statistical analysis. During the first and last quarters of each lunar cycle, the time on either side of the full moon, the level of registered crime in society rose—unequivocally, month after month. From schools, jails and emergency rooms to public zoos across the planet, everything living was somehow or other affected by the moon's gravitational pull—and the fact was, again statistically, behavior was far less rational while it was full. The reasons were purely scientific: over 70 percent of the earth was covered with water. The human body was made up of roughly that same percentage of water. The moon was known to affect the tides most strongly during the time when its gravitational pull on the earth was greatest, i.e., during the phase when the sun, the earth and the moon were assembled in a line, in that order. It followed, then, that the human body was equally affected during that phase.

However, as Owen continued reading, other sources would maintain ardently, in spite of conventional wisdom, astrology, folklore and chronically "skewed" statistics, that levels of registered mayhem increased during *new* moons as clearly as during full ones. Which did make sense, astronomically at least, as new moons occurred when the same celestial bodies in question were lined up directly (only with the moon in the middle this time) and exerting the same gravitational pull. The new moon was known as the "full moon's ghost." Related arguments cited statistical peaks in assault and battery at the new moon. Also, emergency admissions to psychiatric facilities reached a pinnacle. A national poll of radio DJs revealed a surge in "loony" calls, as, by report, did the FBI—from people of all walks of life, irrespective of economic and social distinctions, people complaining of being watched by communists, neighbors and little green men—in the days directly surrounding a new moon.

By these studies, public unrest would appear to have risen *twice* a month (at the full and new moons) and fallen in the days directly preceding and following the first and third quarters.

Other sources conflicted wildly, as Owen was quick to discover through research. For every classroom teacher who swore by student behavior taking a turn for the insubordinate during a full moon, for every claim that delinquent behavior increased, and birth rates soared, and sexual activity reached a peak—along with levels of menstruating females—that bartenders oversaw turbulent evenings from Bangkok to Billings, and murders abounded, there was someone to balk at the claim and, as often as not, dismiss it as superstition. One had to watch out for closed-minded naysayers no less than uninformed crackpot enthusiasts. For most of recorded history, even considering the idea that lunar phases might have a bearing on human behavior—i.e., not rejecting it outright as totally baseless paranoia—had placed many doctors at risk of mockery and even persecution within their fields. Only in recent years had thorough statistical and clinical research, performed and reported in books and recognized medical journals, begun to gain acceptance—or at least appear to warrant review. The field had a long way to go to establish a basic, generally accepted groundwork. Owen couldn't have known what to make of it—not in a single afternoon. He was blown away by the lack of conclusive material. He didn't trust anything, yet. For as far back as humankind had been charting the moon—up to 40,000 years, by evidence—for all of the advances in medicine, science, statistics and human understanding, it still seemed that one of the basic phenomenological entities known to the species remained, at least as reflected in semi-reliable terms, a virtual mystery.

From here on, Owen would have to rely on his intuition. Which led him, as such, to a lunar almanac: four thousand years of monthly calendars.

He found the date.

Thursday, October 21st: Waxing Crescent, approaching first quarter.

He'd gotten it right. Which meant, it occurred to him first by deduction, then by consulting the almanac chart, that the new moon had fallen on Saturday—square in the rising tide of unrest leading up to "The Wildest Night in The Basin."

Owen got up from where he was sitting, and walked a circle around the table. Up at the periodical desk, a slight, mousy librarian looked at him.

He plodded back into an aisle of shelves to process his thoughts without posing a spectacle. There, in the inchoate swirl of computations coming to bear in his head, one voice in particular stood out clearly: Dwayne Gibbons, that rat from the Dogboy—shaking his head almost condescendingly: *"That picture was taken October first"* and *"All I can say is: check your calendar."*

Owen returned to the table and redirected his attention to the lunar calendar. What he discovered, in doing so, beat the odds to a nearly uncanny degree. The moon had already been full that month—on the *first,* at 1:07 p.m. But, as broken down in the almanac's text, the lunar cycle's duration from start to finish was 29.5 days. Meaning, with thirty-one days in October, two full moons would occur that month—one on the 1st, the other at 12:51 a.m. on the 31st.

Halloween.

Owen regarded the date to confirm. *Blue Moon,* it read in italics.

Man . . .

He got up and walked around again.

. . . *where* had he heard that term?

Stoner.

He returned to the table, pulled *Bad Moon* from his rucksack, sat down and opened it up. He'd read about blue moons the evening before. They were characterized in their own entry. Two separate definitions were offered. The first, a "traditional" blue moon, was listed as the third full moon in a season containing four full moons—which occurred, on average, every five or six years. The second had already been defined by the almanac—a single calendar month containing two full moons—something that occurred, on average, every thirty months.

Many folk traditions held these cycles to host all manner of *lunacy*. In parts of Siberia, the blue moon was said to push reindeer into aimless stampedes. In Chile, the whole month preceding it witnessed outrageous behavior by housewives and dogs. In Oklahoma, flocks of sparrows would fall from the sky like "raining death." In Old Germany, werewolves were said to convene in "sabbaths" during the blue moon. These "orgies of madness" revolved around music, dance, fornication and human sacrifice.

Owen returned to the almanac, riding a hunch. October of '74 . . .

This time he walked right out of the building—with Dr. Diller hissing along: *"They'll call you a madman / don't be a fool . . ."*

At last, he would heed the doctor's orders.

By now, Owen was starting to feel less in charge of this story than guided along by it. Something was reeling him in to this mess. He'd been caught in the tractor beam once before . . .

But he had never left the mainland.

Lord, it was hard being Celtic sometimes.

There *was* one advantage to it, though—being Celtic: the Celts had a knack for employing theatrics exactly when they were least appropriate. Charging the Roman garrisons naked. Walking the plank in a fit of laughter . . .

Once he had gotten a chance to steady his nerves, outside, on a public bench, Owen settled down to configuring.

A few minutes later, it started to come to him—etched in relief by his lack of alternatives. Soon, he was laughing out loud on the bench. A lady walked by, looking nervously back at him. He felt like chasing her down the block.

Jesus, Kegel was going to freak out. The vein in his forehead would probably explode. Owen could already picture it now, before the letter was even drafted. There was no possible way the poor bastard would *ever* believe Owen hadn't written it. The same would apply to Jarvik, but Jarvik wouldn't care. Jarvik would eat it up. Kegel would have to deal with the public.

Already, complaints from local business executives had been pouring in for a week. That morning, someone had telephoned threatening to "string up" the paper's entire staff. (The call had been traced to the home of an algebra teacher employed by Hempland High.) And the morning before, a panel of Catholic priests had denounced the coverage as "profane"—for all of which, most of the serious gripes had been handled by Kegel, and Kegel alone.

Jarvik had been holed up in his office—one moment walking the floor in silence, testing his blinds, raising and dropping them, the next with his feet up, reclining, glassy-eyed, mumbling emptily into space. He hadn't read anyone's work, aside from Owen's, over and over, in days. His only real concern appeared to be what came next for the Blue Ball Devil.

Which would've had Kegel honked off already.

But this would seal it.

Owen proceeded.

He got to the office by eight o'clock.

Making his way toward the newsroom, he spotted Bess and managed to bite his lip. Then Jarvik's assistant, across the path. It was all he could do to keep from laughing.

He paused at the fountain to gather his wits.

Then he heard Jarvik around the corner, his voice in a broken, piercing shriek. "Have you heard about *The Screed*?"—being Horaceburg's daily. "They called it a *Nuclear Kangaroo*!"

Owen stepped into view as the old man reentered his office from out on the floor. His blinds had been raised. Through the glass, he was talking to Kegel, dressed in a ruffled tuxedo shirt . . .

His voice boomed out of the office: "Idiot! Can't you see I'm busy. You—"

Flinching, he stopped. He looked over. His face lit up. *"Brynmor!"*

He pushed by Kegel. The shirttails hung from his beltless trousers. His grin was ravenous.

"Greetings!" He tripped up and thrust out his hand.

Owen shook it.

"Please." The old man looked toward his office. "More worthy environs. Coffee or tea?"

Owen could feel the animosity surging around him. "Coffee. Please."

Jarvik nodded politely, then, turning to Kegel, snapped, "What are you, *deaf*?"

Here came the vein in Kegel's forehead . . .

"And bring us some scones," the old man added.

Kegel shifted to Owen, glaring.

Jarvik stepped between them, motioning Owen into the office. Then he whirled on Kegel and shouted, "*Move* it, cretin!"

Kegel stepped back.

The old man slammed the door in his face. He scratched like a chimp through the window. "Yes, I'm talking to *you*!" He laughed out loud.

He lowered the blinds and turned with a grin.

He clapped his palms and rubbed them together. "All right, then—" He smiled, his gaze bleeding through from a parallel vortex. "What have we got?" He glanced to the paper Owen was holding. "What is it?" Cringing in dread-filled glee, he could barely restrain his excitement. He reached for it. "May I?"

Owen began to explain how this letter had come in the morning before.

"Of course!" Jarvik assured him, as though to say *"Not to worry, alibis covered."*

Unfolding the paper, he started to read.

Again, Kegel—like most of the staff—would know at a glance who had written the text. Maybe in parts of the county where nobody knew what to make—or expect—of *The Plea,* or, more likely, off in France, in particular—*Le Monde* had just printed a piece on the latest rural American "horror show"—practical jokers, extremists and paranoid cabin dwellers would get the credit. But not in the office. The staff wouldn't buy it. Neither would Jarvik. Or the Lamepeter cops. Or Owen's mother. (*"You always push it!"*) Or nine other callers who, subsequently, would try to take credit for writing the text . . .

As for the paper, daily subscribers would rue its fall to sub-tabloid standards—one reader branding this letter "the largest call to a public orgy in history."

All of which was sure to place Owen's condition on critical red at the paper.

First, however, Jarvik would have to approve of the text. Which ran as such:

> *Know ye—*
>
> *Sinners and braggarts and harlots and wicked folke of the toen of Steppfort:*
>
> *I am The Kornwolf. And woe unto him what denies mine eminence.*
>
> *Lo, but for korn meal:*
>
> *An hour of reckoning fast approecheth.*
>
> *Come Halloween, of bluest moon, shall vengeance exact of its own unto thee. By midnight's toll shall The Sabbath begin—and none be spared but for him what partakes of fermented barley for bounding through flame to the beating of drums and the union of flesh. In home and market, only the keepers of song and dance may elude retribution.*
>
> *The rest, ye of barren, unscrupulous worth, shall fall as tender wheat to mine sickle.*
>
> *Sinners and cave fish, ye have been warned.*
>
> *Lo, but for Harvest Sabbath—The Kornwolf.*

What started with hollow, muffled grunts from the old man's diaphragm rose to his throat in a steadily building upward gurgle, catching in starts. He was choking in silence. One of his eyeballs rolled to the side.

He dropped to his knees. Losing his balance, he nearly went over—but caught himself—braced on a wastebasket, gripping it—gulping air, gasping "My *God*!" with a cough.

He exploded with laughter.

It was madness: one part rebuff of the naysayers' skeptical take on the blue moon's effect, the other, the living personification of Owen's withdrawal from bastard nicotine.

Jarvik was grimacing, heaving in pain. He gripped his chest.

Owen stood there.

Finally, the old man crawled to his feet. He wiped a tear from his cheek and coughed, then tripped to his door and opened up.

"Boy!" he shouted across the room, still grinning. His face was scarlet red.

The assistant editor looked up—from poisoning Owen's coffee, no doubt, in the break room. Jarvik waved him over, flashing the letter. "Seven days. Half-page. Local."

On reading the text, Kegel's vein began to throb. It darkened to purple. The rest of his face was white as a sheet.

With incredible effort, he looked up and swallowed. "Sir—" He spoke with solemnity, terror. "Sir, I beg you."

Jarvik waved him off with no further consideration. Turning to Owen, he beamed, all rain in the dust bowl. "Now. What can we do for you?"

Kegel stepped forward, not conceding. "Sir!" he squawked on buckling knees. "Please, *please* reconsider . . ."

Whirling, Jarvik bore down on him. "All right, *full* page then!" he screamed. "Section A!"

Silence.

Jarvik slammed the door.

He turned to Owen, held out his hand and, smiling, shook it. "All Hail Discordia!"

Twice in the course of guiding his buggy up Welshtown Road, between Bird-in-Hand and Gordonville, Jonathan had been pulled over and questioned—first by a housing development wagoneer, then by a township officer, Kreider—regarding his destination, cargo and purpose for driving around after dark. An unofficial curfew (sundown) was being enforced across The Basin, apparently, one which effectively granted more nonresidential parties, i.e., the superstore's growing cadre of private guards, even more unofficial (illegal) approval to halt, detain and search vehicles. This state of happenings coincided with heightened black bumper squadron activity. And, beginning that week, residential, non-business-related groups had joined in as well . . . The night before, a posse of English bikers had stopped and sacked Jon's wagon. Later, a couple of young men, drunk, in hunting jackets had tried the same . . . Even though Devil reports had been scarce, and no livestock had been attacked for a week now, the roads were alive with more nightly activity than ever. These were uncertain hours.

Rumors of English media bilge had been floating around the market for days—outrageously hellish tidings by press that were difficult, even now, to fathom. Jon had taken the whole thing for somebody's poor attempt at humor, a joke. The English had always been depraved. But they still had a sensible fear of hellfire.

Tonight, however, while driving to Fannie's house—crossing 342 into Bird-in-Hand, posted in front of Woolly Mack's Tavern—he spotted a billboard with flashing lights, facing traffic, which read:

KORNWOLF HOOTENANNY
OCTOBER 30th
Featuring the Music of
BLUE MOON IN BLUE BALL
(n.k.a. the Dave Stauffer Trio)
Five Dollar Korn Puppies.
Ladies night. Jell-O shots

It had taken Jonathan a moment to process. Seeing the word on a Redcoat billboard had challenged his powers of observation: from *what in the world?*—to—*surely not*—to—*they wouldn't dare*—to—*the filthy bastards* . . .

While driving away, the harder he tried to accommodate for it, the more it incensed him. Leave it to the Redcoats to turn even *this* (what's a korn puppy?) into a money-making enterprise. Nothing was sacred, not even the profane.

And, meanwhile, the roads were increasingly dangerous.

Monday night, on his way home from work, a carload of English had pulled up beside him and pelted his wagon and mount with potatoes. A few minutes later, just down the road, he'd spotted their overturned car in a ditch with a couple of people crawling out of it. Not hesitating, he'd slowed his buggy, preparing to stop and help, if he could. Instead, he'd been driven away with curses, jeering and one more round of potatoes.

The fact that he wouldn't have lasted a day among them—and wouldn't have wanted to either—only compounded his growing sense of isolation in the overall picture. A Redcoat he wasn't, and couldn't have been. But he wasn't an Orderly either. Not yet. And with District Seven in shambles, his prospects didn't look good for the rest of the season. His baptismal ceremony, originally scheduled for November, had been postponed indefinitely. And, as marriage couldn't proceed before baptism, he and Fannie were stuck, as well. Which would please her mother, no doubt. Grizelda had too many family ties to conflicting parties within the district even to *think* about hosting a wedding right now.

Besides which, she didn't like Jonathan.

Adding to all of that, his less than graceful break with the Crossbills the week before (he still hadn't spoken with any of them) and he was now drifting, suspended—a colt with no stable, no gang, no church, no community—only his fellow auctioneers at the market and Fannie, his betrothed, his *verschproche*—between the two of whom, driving the roads unmolested was proving almost impossible.

The whole situation tore at his nerves.

And getting pulled over did nothing to help.

As Officer Kreider probed the trunk with a flashlight beam in search of accelerants, Jonathan couldn't help but reflect on how these were supposed to be memorable days, some of the best he would ever know.

"They ought to change that sign up the road," he remarked.

Kreider looked up. "What?"

Jonathan shook his head, deadpan. "At Woolly Mack's."

Kreider ignored the statement. He clicked off his flashlight, stepping back. "You get to wherever you're going fast."

Moments later, Jonathan angled his buggy back onto Welshtown Road. Kreider's taillights dimmed to a flickering set of pinpoints, ahead in the distance. They veered to the left before vanishing into a jagged line of trees on the skyline. Aside from a couple of glowing porch lanterns, no sign of civilization was visible. The rising stretch of empty pavement before him was bathed in a haze of starlight.

At times, he had to remind himself that, whatever else, he still had Fannie. In spite of the madness, their bond was intact. They would get through this, and more, if demanded. And that was all Jonathan needed to know. The rest would play out as intended by God. Their wedding would come to pass in the springtime. From then on, their marriage would prosper deservingly. Jonathan's standing at market was already well-secured, and would only solidify. God willing, he would always be able to provide for his wife and, in time, their family. Eventually, they would take over his uncle Wilhelm Becker's farm in New Holland, as already worked out with all of the principles. There, they would harvest tobacco and corn, and raise their children to follow suit . . . In time, the events of this season would dim to a rarely discussed, if acknowledged, topic. Relations with Grizelda would stabilize somehow. The media engine would run out of steam. Life on the roads would return to normal. The Devil would go on its way, God willing. And one by one, (most of) the Crossbills would follow Jonathan's present lead—taking baptism, joining the church, getting married, settling down and starting families. Most of them wouldn't hold a grudge against Jon for dodging them unannounced—as they would have found out, by then, for themselves how difficult leaving the gang can be.

He told himself—over and over and over . . .

Something stirred in the ditch up ahead, interrupting his reverie. Scanning the road, he saw no sign of movement. A raccoon, probably.

He went back to guiding the mare through the dark. The moon wasn't up yet. The fields were quiet.

Then more rustling caught his attention—followed by a slap on the asphalt behind him—a muffled patter trailing his wagon, yet no sign of spotlights, no rhythm of wheels . . .

Before he could turn to look, before he could register any cause for alarm, a figure emerged from the blackness behind him. It vaulted up onto his buggy and dropped into place in the passenger seat by his side. Jonathan nearly leapt out of his skin. The mare reared up, came down and, kicking, thrashed in the riding gear. The buggy rocked back on two wheels, then dropped to the road with a crash.

A peal of laughter went up beside Jonathan.

He nearly flew off his perch in terror . . .

While heaving to steady the mare, he *tasted* the smell of decay. He knew that stench.

But the voice to follow was something new:

"Sapperlot!" Ephraim howled maniacally.

Jonathan's blood ran cold in his veins.

He ventured a sidelong glance to confirm.

It was Bontrager, all right—only, he looked even worse, more *diseased,* than he had a week earlier. Jonathan hadn't laid eyes on him since—though he *had* been expecting a midnight visit. Ephraim's appearance was hard to believe. The side of his face was covered with scabs. His hair was shiny with grease in the starlight. His shoulders were hunched. His clothing was torn. His eyes were a sickly, yellowish hue. (In English, the word "abject" came to mind.) And that grin, that predatory, downturned leer was enough to wring blood from a whipping post. There was something so foul and repugnant about it that, even while bearing Ephraim's likeness, it couldn't have resembled him less.

Twitching, he snickered: *"To smell of the fear coming out of you, Becker. For cod-oil rancor."* He hawked a clot of phlegm and gulped it, peering around. *"You'll shet in your hosen."*

Gripped with terror as Jonathan may have been, he was equally flabbergasted. He didn't know whether to ask after cod-oil rancor, or how it was Ephraim had spoken . . .

Almost as though in reply, Ephraim went on. *"Kumfermierung,"* in Py. Dutch, then in English: "talk of a mute hitherto"—and in German: *"Nicht mehr."*

Leaning forward, he started to root through the trunk.

"Where's the stucco, Becker?"

"The what?" asked Jonathan, dabbing the sweat from his forehead.

"The stucco!" Ephraim snapped: *"You know: the spirits—the swallop, damn it!"*

Jonathan cringed. *"I haven't been drinking."*

Ephraim pounded the dash. *"Bah!"* His expression twisted. He snarled in disgust. *"And nary a gleam o' the crimson either."*

Never had Jonathan stopped to wonder how Ephraim's voice, in another lifetime, removed from this setting, might have sounded. Upon reflection, he would have imagined a gruff falsetto—or maybe a low-ended monotone, even a raspy mutter. But never this gurgling, phlegm-clotted basso profundo. It wouldn't have entered his mind.

Again, he was left with the feeling that, somehow, Ephraim was gone, playing host to another. The entity turning his trunk upside down for tobacco and liquor and meat had emerged from a bottomless pit to make off with his friend. And no one would tell him, Jonathan, otherwise.

Fannie, sadly, would have concurred.

"Speaking of whom—" The figure sat up.

Jonathan's body went stiff with terror.

Ephraim cackled. *"Mind your oats!"* He resumed with a hiss. *"In relinquishing grievances: come to announce ceremonial rites!"*

Jonathan tried not to look too confused.

"Gemutlichtzeit!" Ephraim continued, sharply pounding the top of his legs. He leapt from the buggy. *"Excuse us."* He shot off the pavement, dodging back into the ditch.

And no sooner gone than a line of Orderly buggies topped the hill in the distance. Torches were mounted to each of their frames. There were four of them, blazing along at a clip.

They slowed on approaching. Jonathan recognized Jonas Tulk at the head of the pack.

They surrounded his buggy, halting him. Slowly, Tulk leaned out of the driver's seat.

"Riding alone?" he spoke in Plain Folk. *"Yes? What's the matter, cat got your tongue?"*

"No sir," Jonathan said with impatience. *"I'm on my way to visit the Hostlers."*

Tulk's expression, a wall-eyed, cadaverous leer, was discernible now in the shadows. *"Ach!"* He spoke with imperious rancor. *"Your* verschproche."

"And *her family,"* Jonathan emphasized.

Tulk leaned forward and spat on the pavement.

Jon waited.

Tulk shook his head. *"And what about your supper gang?"*

"Sir?" said Jonathan.

A voice from the back of the line called out. *"Where's Colin Graybill?"*—and someone else, seemingly Amos Ziegler: *"And Samuel Hoff?"*

They were lined up in silhouette, crows on a fence post, around him. Their features were lost in the darkness.

Tulk demanded. *"Have you seen them?"*

Jonathan answered, *"No, sir."*

They stared.

He waited.

"Ach! You wouldn't lie to us, Becker?"

"No, sir," he repeated.

From Tulk, more directly: *"And how about Bontrager?"*

Already braced for the question, Jonathan answered it calmly, unflinchingly. *"No, sir. Not for a week now."*

Ziegler's voice (or was that a Stoltzfus?)—cried out: *"He hasn't been home for a week."*

"You know that, Becker," said Tulk with annoyance.

Jonathan swallowed, replying in earnest. *"No. I didn't. He hasn't . . . (?) . . ."*

Tulk completed his sentence, repeating: *". . . been home."*

Starlight shone on the pavement between them.

Jon, having heard enough, gripped his reins. *"If you'll excuse me."*

He angled his wagon around their group and continued east.

He couldn't abide by the Tulks any more than the Zieglers—and, least of them all, the Stoltzfi. It was a good thing the church was dissolving. Maybe these vultures would fly to Ohio.

From up the hill, he turned to spot their line of torches moving west. He continued on Welshtown Road, regaining his breath and, eventually, leveling out. The fields and ditches around him were quiet. He started to wonder if Ephraim had fled . . .

Then a shadow whirled out of the darkness and *slammed* back into the seat beside him.

There was that smell again . . .

"No!" shouted Ephraim, resuming his frantic search of the trunk. *"No tobacco. No transistor. No fermentation."*

He dove to the pavement and circled the wagon, howling. *"No fermentation! No swallop!"*

The pacer reared up again. Ephraim slapped its flank while hurtling back to his seat.

Jonathan's heart was thumping painfully. Sweat ran into his eyes and burned.

"More cod-oil rancor!" his passenger growled. *"Cowardice! Listen to why for have come now to—"*

Suddenly, something caught in his throat. He vomited over the side of the buggy. It splashed on the pavement.

More laughter: *"Excuse us, it*"*—wiping his chin with a sleeve. *"—to deliver an invitation."* He turned, at last, toward stating his purpose: *"Disappointment in Becker's failure to notify cohorts: a farewell in order."* His yellowish eyes went wide in the darkness. He drew a hissing intake of breath.

In the awkward silence to follow, Jonathan ventured a word in reply: *"A farewell?"*

Ephraim snapped out of it. *"Yes!"* He twitched. *"A farewell to Bontrager, not all of wrath unto Becker forgiven, and sister blessed."*

Jonathan reeled. The language was growing more incomprehensible every moment. *"Farewell to Bontrager?"*

Ephraim tossed his head. *"*No reprieve for the wicked* . . . "* He cleared his throat with a gurgle. At once he looked painfully vulnerable. *"*Look at us, Becker. Shall never endureth. Thy neighbor's wife."* He shook his head. *" Shall never endureth."* His vulnerability gave way to spite. *"A parting of ways, then—a celebration!"* Nudging Jonathan's ribs, he bellowed, *"Saturday night"*—his breath a wind of rancid putrefaction. *"The farm."*

Jonathan, staring ahead in terrified indecision, mumbled, *"The farm?"*

Ephraim twisted his neck and spat. *"The Schlabach Farm. What's the matter with Becker?"*

Saturday night was October 30th.

"I have to work until ten o'clock," muttered Jonathan, searching for any excuse.

For the first time, Ephraim turned his bloodshot, burning gaze directly on Jonathan: *"The market closes at eight on Saturday,"* he said with rage underscoring his tone. *"Don't lie to us, Becker. Deception becometh the Reaper. Midnight. Alone. No excuses."*

Jonathan, chilled to the marrow, watched as, without any further remark, Ephraim leapt from his buggy, hopped over the ditch and, fleet-footed, made off into a field of stubble. A few hundred yards to the west, he dropped out of sight—and, along with him, Jonathan's blessings.

After a lifetime of weighing the balances, God had turned His back on the Bontragers.

Jonathan, however anguished, could no longer hope to deny that his friend was The Devil.

Roddy had always been cool as rain in the hours directly preceding a fight. Tonight was no different: delayed in the entry hall, robed and wrapped, with a cap on his head, he looked steady, calm. He was up on his toes. He had worked up a proper sweat. He was ready.

Likewise, Syd Gajecki, a registered nurse from Yorc, stood waiting patiently. Tonight would be Syd's three hundredth bout as a cut man (the source of an earlier toast), and his seventh time in as many years to serve in Roddy's corner professionally.

It would be Brynmor's first, on the other hand. But, to his credit, he looked prepared—standing with a towel draped over one shoulder, his black satin ring jacket catching the glare, "The Unbelievable" woven into his front left pocket, green on black, with rubber gloves on his flexing hands, holding an empty plastic bucket. He stood there eagerly. Game as the wild.

Jack hoped the kid didn't fall on his head.

Flushing, The Coach dug into a pocket and twisted the lid on his medicine vial. He washed two tablets down with water, tossing his head back. Just for good measure.

A door swung open.

The roar of the crowd flooded in. Some guards were beckoning urgently.

Twenty-four hours of maddening downtime had led to this moment.

They started forward.

Even though, circumstantially, Roddy had received more media attention that week than he had in the course of his whole career, there was still no broadcasting crew in place to escort him from the entry hall into the ring. Which was probably just as well, as, for one thing, the network cameramen were famously obnoxious and never failed to test Jack's patience, and two: the sound men ended up blundering Roddy's chosen walk-in music (Funkadelic's "Back in Our Minds"), airing instead some Jimmy Buffett wannabe's ditty on gin-soaked barmaids.

At least they were out of the dressing room, Jack thought—albeit trailing the odor of mold. And, at least, as had already been suggested, Roddy had plenty of friends in the house: down from the balcony, up from the pit and across the floor in a surging roar (the Blue Palomino, Philth Town's most prestigious fight hall, was packed to the rafters)—cries of *"We love you, Roddy!"* and *"Kill this motherfucker!"* went out all around them. In spite of the absence of network coverage, his entry was greeted with loud hosannas—some of it coming from long-term acquaintances, friends of both Roddy and Jack, and the West Side—sparring partners from Yorc and Horaceburg, coaches and colleagues from amateur days—but even more strangers intent on seeing The Cobra go down by *any* means. Whatever the odds, however shadowed by Fido Jones's wider renown, Philth Town belonged, at least in predominant fashion this evening, to Roddy Lowe.

In the ring, the cameras finally got to him, circling, swarming like ravenous sharks. Roddy moved past them with confidence, walked to the farthest corner and raised one glove to a group of supporters above in the balcony. A roaring wave of cheers rained down on him. Grinning, he thumped his chest and waved back.

Down in front, Jack overheard one of the network commentator's referencing Roddy's fight with Rosario five years back. Behind him, Ronald Travers was seated with two of his heavies, yukking it up.

Syd was shaking hands with the referee, Dale Smoger, an upstanding cat. Smoger looked over to Jack and waved. Jack returned the gesture warmly. It was good to have one honest man in the house. The Blue Palomino's management often insisted on appointing its own referees. All three judges at ringside belonged to Travers, but at least the ref was dependable.

After a one-minute cut to commercials, during which Jack stood quietly off in the corner, preparing himself for the schmaltz, the house lights suddenly dropped. Here it came.

All week long, The Cobra's people would have been at work on the consummate walk-in to counter the fact that their fighter had made such an ass of himself at the West Side Gym. Network television normally didn't provide for walk-in coverage at all. But Jones, based on his uncanny knack for whipping up bloodlust with cheap theatrics, was different, apparently. That, or Travers had arranged for a lone exception, $omehow.

Either way, it was hard to imagine that, of all the cards this club had hosted, The Cobra, unlike thousands of journeymen, veterans and contenders from days gone by, would now be showcased sauntering into the ring like a common professional wrestler. He really did know how to make people hate him. Even Jack, who normally wasn't as easily riled by a fighter as by a crooked promoter, couldn't help wanting, on principle, to see this kid get his ass handed to him.

The gradually sloped, carpeted walkway lined with flashing, pinpoint lights extending from the upstairs dressing room area, straight through the crowd and down to the ring must've taken four days of labor to erect. And The Cobra would milk it for all it was worth. But first, he would let the music play . . .

Jack, through the years, had grown accustomed to hip-hop, dance and gangsta rap—and other music he couldn't label. But the blaring, discordant, cacophonous roar from the speakers at present was something new. More like a wood saw tearing through a carload of trapped gorillas, it was downright painful: for the life of him, Jack couldn't figure out what kind of gadgetry might produce such noise.

The crowd, on the other hand, seemed more incensed by The Cobra's arrival, at last, than the soundtrack. The moment his figure appeared at the top of the ramp, a murderous boo went up. His silhouette, bathed in a cloud of dry ice and flashing strobe lights, began to gyrate—flexing his arms and legs, first, then bobbing his head, then bucking his pelvis. The club guards started to line up, forming a human shield on both sides of the walkway.

The spectacle might have been funny—might even have *worked*—had it not dragged on for so long. Jones didn't even emerge from his cloud at the top of the ramp for over a minute. And once he had done so, at last, appearing in tiger-skin trunks and tasseled footwear, he walked down the ramp at a torturous crawl, often backtracking, stalling just for effect. With an almost comically smug leer, he taunted the crowd to no suffering end.

In the ring, the delay was beginning to wear on Roddy, who was pacing spirited circles. At first, he hadn't minded so much. In a way, he had been enjoying the show. However, by now, these antics had exceeded good form and were leaning toward calculated insult. Jack stepped forward to calm his fighter. He gripped Roddy's shoulders. "Don't let it get to you."

Which was sound advice in itself. But not so easily put into practice.

As Jones drew ever nearer to the ring, his rate of advance was stalled even further. The network technicians began to signal their desperate need to cut to commercials. The Cobra paid them little mind. On reaching the ring, he paused at the top of the stairs to blow the crowd a kiss. After playing it up for another delay without taking a flying bottle to the head, he turned and, first getting a hold on the top rope and flexing once, twice, three times, followed through on the forward momentum, with both legs swung to the side, then over the top. He came down, pedaling forward, and reared up in Roddy's face with a cackling sneer.

This time Roddy kept his cool. He was game. They were inches apart, squaring off . . .

The rest of The Cobra's posse, led by "Green Dog" Williams, flooded the ring.

Green Dog, one of the older trainers in Philth Town, had probably burned more bridges than any figure in regional boxing, other than Blye, for the past twenty years. His famously hot-headed temperament had led to more bad relations than should have been possible. Even though Jack hadn't seen him in a while, he had dealt with Green Dog on countless occasions. Ronald Travers was likely the only promoter left who would cut him a break.

Quickly enough, the cameras had gotten between and divided Roddy and Jones. At last, the network cut to commercials. Devoid of a spotlight, Jones backed off. For the next two minutes, the chairmen, judges, physicians and referee were announced. Then the commercials were over. The cameras and, therefore, The Cobra were back for more. An exasperated Smoger ordered everyone out of the ring but the fighters—Roddy and Jones—and their trainers, Jack and Green Dog, at once.

During the face-off, the roar of the spectators swelled to such a deafening pitch that almost no one heard the instructions issued by Smoger, even when amplified. All attention was locked on the heated nonverbal exchange between the fighters—Roddy, expressionless, facing The Cobra, who, grinning back, was playing the crowd.

For his part, Green Dog didn't appear to be sweating Roddy. He did, however, avoid Jack's gaze. Green Dog wanted no part of The Coach.

Smoger motioned for the fighters to touch their gloves in acknowledgment of his instructions. Jones complied with undue force. Roddy, caught off guard for the last time, trundled back to his corner intently. From behind the ropes, Syd and Owen gestured to *lay this bastard out*. Jack kissed Roddy's cheek before leaving the ring. "Strength and skills, young man." He parted the ropes and stepped from the ring.

Roddy knelt and crossed himself.

The pace was furious right from the bell.

Jones opened up with a wild, lunging right down the middle, overcommitting so grievously, his back leg kicked out behind him.

Once he'd regained his balance, he was able to plant his base. His legs were thick. He spread them, maintaining an anchored stance. This reduced his already limited height, and made him a difficult target. From there, his movement would complicate matters—over the canvas in awkward starts, upredictably shifting his weight, he lurched in and out of an orthodox stance.

Roddy, a versatile southpaw himself, would commence at a loss for an opening shot, eating a series of jabs on the way. From the corner, Jack would holler to *"Get on the inside!"*—over and over and over . . .

At 1:50, Roddy would finally do so, landing a solid hook to the ribs. Unperturbed, The Cobra would drop his hands, wiggle and grin defiantly, then come back with a left of his own. Roddy would counter it, landing flush. At which point The Cobra would back off briefly. He circled to the right, regrouping, on alert. Roddy, heeding The Coach, went after him. Jones assumed a conventional stance, shuffled, took three steps back in eluding a left hand lead and dropped his guard. He circled to the right with his back to the ropes. Roddy blocked a looping hook, then missed a counter-shot of his own. Jones drove him into the corner with an uppercut, followed by a hard right hand to the temple. No sooner had Jack and Syd started screaming in desperation to "Get your hands up!" than Jones committed a cardinal sin by rocking back and lifting his chin.

Roddy would capitalize on the opening so unexpectedly, it seemed to come from nowhere.

Later, Jack would rank it among the top five moments of his coaching career—one of those instants that justified all of the heartache and loss that went into the game. He would hearken back to it, time and again, as a source of tremendous inspiration:

that image of Roddy's beautiful counter-right sending Jones to the canvas, sprawling . . .

The crowd, of course, went off its rocker.

Jack, Owen and Syd, in the corner, stamped and bayed like Sheffield hooligans.

As Roddy made for the neutral corner, Smoger watched him, then started the count. It was everything Jack could do to hold back from bounding into the ring with joy. Even though Jones got up right away, albeit in clear and evident bewilderment, the crowd might as well have borne witness to a full-fledged knock-out for all the excitement it generated.

The roar persisted as Smoger finished the count and looked into Jones's eyes. The Cobra nodded, unsmiling now. His bell had been rung, and he couldn't mask it.

Smoger signaled the return to action. Jack yelled, "Get on him!" just as a hollering chorus went up: *"You're Unbelievable!"*

Wobbling, Jones immediately launched a flurry of missed or blocked jabs. Then he caught one of Roddy's left hooks to the liver before being saved by the bell.

At the break, The Cobra's glare of defiant mockery wasn't at all convincing. He seemed to be forcing his grin through a haze of unforeseen humiliation. A confident Roddy wasn't impressed. Neither was Smoger, who voided their face-off. Of course, the audience ate it up. And so did the network commentators.

Jack sat Roddy on his stool in the corner. "That was beautiful, kid! Are you OK?"

Roddy nodded, hardly winded.

"Give him some water."

Owen held up a bottle. Jack took it. Roddy, unmarked, drew a mouthful and swished. He spat in the bucket as Syd pressed an ice pack onto the back of his shoulders.

"Good work."

Roddy looked over to Owen, who nodded. "That was amazing."

The Coach squared off. "OK, now listen: Everything looks pretty good from here, but we need to start backing him into the corners.

He'll just keep running if you give him the chance. So cut off the ring and use your jab to get on the inside, *then* work the body. He won't last more than a couple of rounds if you *work the body*. You understand? And, once you've got him, watch his right. He's not even trying to cover his ribs. You'll see what I mean. Just watch that hand . . . You can set up the hook with a quick short right of your own. You'll catch him every time . . . But don't back away. He's looking for one big shot from the outside. Don't give it to him."

Syd threw the ice pack into the bucket and pulled out a tub of Vaseline. He smeared a glob onto Roddy's brow.

"Are we clear?" asked Jack.

Roddy sat up. "Yes, sir!"

From the center of the ring, Smoger yelled, "Seconds out!"

Roddy stood. Owen removed the stool and wiped the canvas with a towel.

On his way out, Jack looked into Roddy's eyes. "This is your night, son," he said.

The bell rang.

Round two opened as though in deliberate disregard of Jack's instructions. Immediately, Roddy and Jones came together and started right into a jabbing contest. The action was initiated by Jones, the puncher, but was matched, shot for shot, then surpassed by Roddy—who probably hadn't seen it coming. His initial response had seemed involuntary. But once they were going, even with an evident power disadvantage, he refused to back off. On paper it was suicide: toe to toe with an almost freakishly heavy hitter. In practice, however, it worked effectively. Back and forth at center ring, each of them getting as good as he gave until finally, frustrated, Jones attempted to narrow the distance between them, thereby effectively yielding to Roddy's pace—and eating a hard left cross in the bargain. The Cobra barely had time to glare before catching another jab on the chin. Then another. And another. And a hook. And a cross. And an uppercut that sent him reeling back into the ring ropes.

Already standing, the crowd pushed into a frenzy as Roddy got on the inside and managed to land a tremendous right. Jones spun around and was left with one glove on the canvas and the other hanging over the top rope. Before the ref could start his count, however, The Cobra came forward, off balance . . . This time, Roddy caught him on the temple with a beautiful left hand lead down the middle. Jones fell into the turnbuckle. Smoger sent Roddy to the corner. The crowd never stopped.

Again, Team Lowe, with the rest of the house, was ecstatic, whooping and crowing and stomping.

Now The Cobra was angry. You could see it in his face as Smoger issued the count. He hadn't expected this—not from Roddy. Not now. Not tonight, in his own backyard. He was already three points down on the cards, at the very least. And this round wasn't over. What's more, he had taken a couple of good hard shots that had caught his attention directly. He seemed to be stunned. He was doing his best to summon a grin, but it wasn't working. And the crowd wasn't cutting him any breaks. Someone in the balcony shouted: *"You loser!"*

From off in the blue corner, Green Dog's raspy bellow to "Stay on your guard!" went up—to which The Coach and Syd and Owen responded by yelling for Roddy to *"Finish him!"*

Roddy came forward, stepping into and landing a solid right cross. The impact snapped through Jones's body. Wavering, he managed to throw off a hook in return, but it strayed from the mark completely. Roddy blocked two more follow-up shots, then answered on target with a flurry of jabs. The Cobra was driven back into the ropes, desperately trying to land a counter.

He snuck in a rabbit punch, slicker than grease.

It was gone before anyone knew what had happened: a looping hook around Roddy's head to the back of his brain stem, right on the dial. Roddy went back, falling into the turnbuckle. Grabbing the ropes, he regained his balance. But The Cobra, one step ahead of the referee, followed through with a crushing right.

Roddy spun and fell to the canvas.

Boos went up from the rear of the ground floor clear to the balcony's highest row. For a moment, it almost seemed that a mob would rush the canvas to pummel Jones.

An angry Smoger grabbed and shoved him back toward Green Dog. Roddy got up.

Smoger refused to rule it a knockdown.

Syd was screaming to *"Take a point!"*

Someone upstairs hurled a bottle of beer. It sprayed the canvas logo with suds.

After the mat had been wiped with a towel and The Cobra warned for rabbit punching, the action resumed. Momentarily reeling, the fighters sized each other up. Jack yelled for Roddy to stay on his guard. Jones mocked him, smirking defiantly. Roddy lowered a booming hook. The Cobra stumbled into a corner. Roddy continued by smashing his jaw, then chasing him halfway around the ring.

By now, the roar of the crowd was made up of laughter as much as of wild cheering. Another chant for Roddy went up. Most of the house was on its feet . . .

In the ring, The Cobra was hotdogging: gyrating, crude undulations around the mat—like a Palm Street club rat working the disco—that scarcely concealed his evident caution.

From 1:15 to 1:03 not a single blow was thrown or landed. Roddy, having scored two knockdowns already—three if you counted the last as a double—appeared less rushed, more calm and deliberate.

Dropping his hands in a moment of quiet assessment, he shifted.

And that's when it happened: a barreling straight right cross to the chin. Roddy hit the canvas flat on his back. A cry of horror swept the club. Jack and Owen leapt out of their seats.

Roddy, propped up on an elbow at center ring, gazed into space for an instant, then, finding himself at the count of three, looked over to Jones, in a neutral corner, and smiled with a nod, as though to say, *"Good shot."*

A network commentator's voice carried over the din, announcing: *"Now we've got a fight, folks!"*

Roddy got up. He righted himself and nodded to Smoger, then glanced at Owen.

"Are you OK?" shouted Smoger at the count of eight.

Roddy turned back to him and nodded.

Resuming, he landed three jabs in succession. Clearly, his legs were still under him—even though his game had been thrown off abruptly. Jones seemed willing to settle for even.

In the last twenty seconds of the round, both fighters appeared content to wait for the bell.

Finally, the networks cut to commercials. Roddy came back to the corner frustrated. Jack got a look at him and knew not to worry. The kid was all right. He was simply angry. If not for the knockdown, he would've been given that round on the scorecards big, no question. As it stood, he had probably lost it, based on his solid trip to the canvas. But, no doubt, most of the crowd would much rather have been in his shoes by the break in the action.

"OK," said Jack as Roddy sat. "That's why we keep our hands up. Right?"

It might've been a good thing he'd been knocked down.

"Have some water."

Roddy swished and spat in the bucket. Jack saw blood.

Syd applied a compress to Roddy's cheek.

Owen spoke up. "He's trying to lure you in." He stopped and deferred to The Coach, as though to say, *Right?*

After a moment's hesitation, Jack nodded. "That's right." He looked from Owen to Roddy. "He's trying to wear you *out,* is more like it. He's leading you halfway around the arena . . . All I can do is repeat myself: you need to work him into the corners. *Then* start taking advantage of your openings. He's *way* too cagey to walk around with. He'll slip you all night if you give him the chance."

"*Manhandle* this guy!" Syd chimed in. "All you have to do is get ahold of him, Roddy."

He squeezed more water on Roddy's head. It rolled down his back and then into his pants, to the canvas, which Owen continued to wipe.

Jack drew back, relaxing for a moment. "Breathe," he said. "You're doing well, son."

Then Smoger was yelling: "Ten seconds, gentlemen!"

Jack leaned over. He whispered in Roddy's ear: "Don't take any shit from this guy."

The opening moments of round three passed in a flurry of ineffective jabs, both fighters blocking, dodging and clenching, and both looking overwhelmed momentarily. Jones managed to land a decent jab at one point (2:35), but he ate as much leather in return in doing so, and set himself up for a solid left. Again, The Cobra's chin had been carelessly upturned, exposed, an invitation. It was hard to believe he kept making the same fundamental mistakes, over and over. Green Dog was either incredibly off this evening, or Jones wasn't listening to him—or maybe he just didn't know how to box. He was making some awfully basic errors.

He took a solid hook to the ribcage, but landed a lunging counter-right. This led into a flurry of blocked jabs and punches at center ring.

"Don't let him get his bearings!" yelled Jack. And for once in the fight, Roddy listened: he landed a menacing hook to the body. Jones staggered back, falling into the ropes. He took another jab on his upturned chin. Then he got caught in a clench.

Smoger stepped in. "Break it up!"

Jones took a swing on the break. It missed. There was booing.

Smoger called time-out.

Shaking his head, Syd leaned toward Jack. "He *really* is a snake, this kid."

After dragging Jones down the road with a warning, Smoger signaled time-in. The action resumed.

Through a lift in the booing, Jack overheard a commentator speaking: "Jones seems less unorthodox now than simply confused."

But as though in reply, The Cobra lowered a right down the pike that snapped Roddy's head back, followed by a crisp hard left to the body.

They circled each other. Roddy pressed forward with both hands up, honing for his distance. Jones retreated, committing to a hard left cross. Roddy slipped it. Jones followed through with an elbow first, then a head butt—smack—to Roddy's forehead. A gash opened up on it, splattering blood.

Smoger called a halt to the action and this time, finally, deducted a point. The doctor was called to the apron to wipe off and take a good look at Roddy's forehead. He did so, swamped in a chorus of booing. After a brief examination, Smoger was told that the fight could continue. He checked with Roddy. "Are you all right?"

Furious, Roddy thumped his gloves, squinting through partially blurred vision.

"Time in!" Smoger called, backing up.

At once, ignoring The Coach's cry to "Keep your guard up!" Roddy pressed forward. He threw a jab, then let fly with a haymaker, missing. The Cobra backed into the ropes and sprung forward with two hard lefts.

Roddy went down.

He rolled to his back and got up right away, both legs still under him. He gestured to Jack and Owen and Syd not to worry, then turned to wait out the count. At eight, his gaze was clear enough for Smoger.

But Jack could see that all wasn't well.

Roddy had taken this fight too soon, and that's all there was to it. It was evident now. Six months down the road, with good training, he might have been able to pull this out . . . But right now, he was drowning in ring rust. It would take a miracle to turn this around . . .

The action resumed at a blistering pace. Right off, The Cobra landed a hook, followed by two stiff jabs to the forehead. Roddy absorbed the punches fully. He countered with a trademark hook of his own, dropped to the body for a shot to the liver, then jammed a short right hand to the temple that lifted and set up the chin for an uppercut. Jones wriggled and flailed like a noodle. He pitched back into the ropes, but rebounded with a lunging right that caught Roddy square on the jaw.

This time he went down hard.

Howling, the crowd was back on its feet. Owen, Syd and Jack stood up.

Roddy looked dazed.

The crowd watched, horrified.

Jones leapt onto a turnbuckle, spreading himself to the roaring disdain of all. Roddy managed to get to one knee by Dale Smoger's count of five. He flexed, fell back and hesitated, then barely made it up to his feet. He was hurt. As Smoger beckoned him forward, his eyes were glassy. He barely responded.

To Jack's relief, though to most of the crowd's disgust and rage, the match was called.

Almost at once, a fight broke out in the balcony. Shouting went up on all sides. More bottles rained down in the ring—but on Smoger this time, and on Green Dog and Jones's seconds.

As Jack darted into the ring ahead of the network cameramen, edging them out, he caught a glimpse through the uproar of Jerry Blye, seated at ringside, laughing.

Even though, afterward, the crowd at the Dogboy couldn't agree on the grisly specifics, they would have to concur on several points. First and foremost among them being: the individual who entered the tavern that evening had a hairline down to his brow. Not an inch of the skin on his forehead was visible. Most of his skull was covered with hair. One patron claimed that it looked like a dirty old toupee nailed through the bridge of his nose. More clearly: "His eyes let off where the pompadour started." He looked like a "hammerheaded Nixon."

Another feature in little dispute was the smell he exuded. Everyone agreed that he stunk to have lost control of his bowels, with overtones of cleaning solvents. Moreover, his hygiene was visibly poor. His neck was marked with infected cuts. His clothing, a ratty old sport coat and field pants, was streaked with mud and torn at the seams . . .

Other details—his cryptic verbage, his darkly, otherworldly aura, his outturned nostrils and gnarled hands that were covered with coarse, bristly hair—would be subject to heated disagreement, as Lamepeter Officer Keiffer noted. Reports of his "glowing eyes" and his frothing mouth would be listed as "drunken conjecture." After a point, collective memory folded on matters of visual detail. The stranger's behavior, however, was generally agreed upon, running, chronologically, as follows:

At approximately ten o'clock, the individual in question—variously referred to as "It," "The Shitbeast," "The Devil," "The Corn Dog" and "Dutchies' Revenge"—entered the tavern. At that time, fifteen persons were present, including the bartender, Freida Baylor. A group at the counter was watching a boxing event on the TV, above the bar. According to Ms. Baylor, the "intruder," as she called him, sat down and yelled for what sounded like food, though in some other language—"Dutch" (meaning: German, most likely) by the twang of it. He beat on the counter with a napkin dispenser. His manner was forceful, crude and belligerent. Baylor nervously gave him a menu . . . He pulled out a pile of dollar bills. He slid them across the counter toward her and, reaching over it, snatched up an unopened bottle of bourbon. The group to his left couldn't help but notice. He leered at them, snapping in "Dutch" again.

Everyone glanced away uncomfortably.

The intruder motioned to Baylor, jabbing the menu with one of his crooked fingers. He seemed to be placing an order for steak and potatoes. She took it, keeping her distance.

Next, he got to work on the bottle, pulling in horrible, slobbering gulps. He drank over half of the contents directly. His pallor was blanched when he came up, grimacing. Closing his eyes, he appeared to be choking back vomit. He belched, breaking into a smile.

Moments later, he snapped from his toxic rapture, shifting, annoyed. He was restless. He bellowed for service. *Where was his food?*

"Coming," Ms. Baylor assured him uneasily.

Looking around, he continued to shift on his stool, panting. He looked like a "madman."

Beyond the counter, Ms. Baylor considered her options. Had she thought it would do any good, she might have called the township police. But as it was: this "asshole" had already been in the Dogboy on several occasions, and even though, every time, he had threatened the general peace to a legal extreme, complaints to the sheriff's department had proven useless. No one had come by for hours.

And anyway, the cops were a "nuisance" themselves. And to add to matters, they didn't tip.

She wasn't about to go calling them now, directly in front of this jabbering lunatic. Nor would she try to eject him herself—not without someone to back her up. And certainly not without a gun . . . . Only one thing remained to be done: to sit there and wait for her boyfriend, a member of The Heathens, the "dreaded" biker gang, to arrive with a pack from their chapter, as per nightly custom, at 10:15.

"Wench!" The intruder slammed the bar with the empty bottle of Maker's Mark. He had drunk it in less than five minutes. *"Another!"* He stiffened upright on his stool. *"Another bottle!"* he yelled this time.

Suddenly baring his teeth, he squinted in irritation. He let out a sneeze. A cloud of mucus sprayed the counter. Again, he squinted and bristled and, this time, his body rocked forward upon release. His skull hit the bar. He squawked in pain, gripping his forehead. He nearly fell over.

Pulling together, he went for a basket of pretzels. He buried his face in them, chomping. Crumbs were scattered everywhere—all down the front of his jacket, across the counter. He tossed the basket over his shoulder and blew a glob of snot on the floor.

Then he caught sight of the television—the boxing match—and started to laugh.

While that was happening, Freida Baylor was standing at the end of the bar with her back turned—dosing a second bottle of bourbon with high-powered Valiums from her own prescription. Discreetly, she crushed the pills with a beer glass and dumped the powder into the bottle. A customer seated nearby saw her do so, but didn't object. He looked away.

By now, every soul in the bar was nervous, at best—too frightened to leave, in truth.

Baylor delivered the spiked bourbon.

Five minutes later, the intruder's order of beef and potatoes came up from the kitchen. Already into his second bottle, he didn't appear to be slowing down.

According to Baylor, he devoured his meal like a "God damned pig," then ordered another, this time with *"double the mutton and beer."*

No one had left the tavern, as yet.

At a quarter past, a couple came in: Dwayne Gibbons and Valerie Dollup, both in a state of intoxication. Gibbons, a regular Dogboy patron, was said to be particularly loud upon entry. Apparently, he and Ms. Dollup, a woman, by local renown, of "loose morals," were arguing back and forth over something. The source of their conflict wasn't apparent.

They sat at the bar and continued to bicker for several moments, not looking up, until, finally, the uncanny silence around them began to creep in, dissolving their argument. It was actually Dollup, annoyed that she hadn't been served a drink, who noticed it first. As Gibbons continued to air his grievances, Dollup quietly scanned the bar, picking up on the lack of conversation, first, then spotting the wild-eyed stranger across the bar, staring at her . . . Grinning drunkenly, she elbowed Gibbons and pointed. Annoyed by the interruption, Gibbons, in a wavering stupor, looked up. His eyes were glazed, half-lidded and bloodshot.

The moment he spotted the stranger, the color drained out of his face, by all accounts.

From there on, eyewitness testimony clashed.

Freida Baylor, who would own up to having been no fan of Dollup or Gibbons for years, would insist that Ms. Dollup had only made matters worse by "batting eyes with the stranger."

Other patrons agreed to a point, but insisted Ms. Dollup could never have known or suspected the trouble she was getting into. Even while flashing "alluring glances" across the bar, as one man claimed, she had seemed more intent on punishing Gibbons than soliciting shows of real affection.

Whatever the case, the regulars tried to wave her off, with no success. Baylor motioned an urgent warning. Which only egged Ms. Dollup on.

Swaying, she met the stranger's gaze. Her addled focus eventually sharpened. She stared intently into his eyes. Her coquettish grin began to dissolve, giving way to a look of vague discomfort.

Gibbons started to lose his cool. The regular patrons braced for disaster as the stranger, fueled by evident lust and intoxication, grew more excited.

He called on Baylor, demanding gruffly: *"Who's the trollop?"*

Baylor shrugged.

Again, the intruder spoke in "Dutch." It sounded like some kind of horror movie. He motioned to buy Ms. Dollup a drink.

Aggravated, Baylor was slow to respond.

The stranger pushed some money toward her, slamming the counter. *"Do as you're told!"*

Startled, she took a step back. Behind her, Ms. Dollup, as though coming out of a reverie, laughed out loud. "Give me a whiskey."

Gibbons intruded. "Don't give her a whiskey."

The stranger snapped at him, *"Quiet, vermin!"* He looked to Baylor. *"You heard the lady."*

Silence hung over the room momentarily, thick as a pending hostage crisis. Ms. Baylor frowned. "You're crazy, Valerie."

Dollup retorted, sneering nastily. "Fetch me a whiskey." She giggled. *"Freida."*

Livid, Baylor proceeded to mix a whiskey and water, shaking her head.

The stranger threw back his head and let out a "horrifying" laugh.

In a flash, he got up and carried his bottle around the counter toward Valerie Dollup. A wave of panic swept the room.

Dollup sat up on her seat, looking startled.

In an instant, the stranger took Gibbons by the back of his neck and ripped him off of the stool. Gibbons hit the wall and dropped to the floor with a yelp. A gasp went up, but no one stepped forward to intervene. The stranger slid onto the stool beside Dollup, grinning obscenely. *"Greetings, fräulein."*

As Gibbons struggled to get to his feet, the front door opened and the first of The Heathens appeared—at last, a half hour late. Taylor Blake, Ms. Baylor's boyfriend, was just in time to see Gibbons, whom he "couldn't stand," pull a cue stick down from the wall and smash it over the stranger's head.

The Heathens might have been spurred to action—i.e., beating Gibbons to a pulp—had the stranger not tended to matters himself. Uninjured, apparently, he whirled on Gibbons with a backhand, dropping him straight to the floor. He reached for the broken cue stick and bore down repeatedly. Squealing with every blow, Gibbons attempted to crawl for the door. Despite Ms. Baylor's appeals for help, The Heathens stood laughing. It caught them off guard. Parting ranks, they allowed the "worm," as Gibbons had always been known to them, to be "horsewhipped brutally" out the door. They even slammed it behind him, still laughing.

This was an unexpected, and welcome, surprise for them—a good start to the evening.

Even though Freida Baylor insisted the stranger had been causing trouble all night, and even though he looked "kinda freaky" and "stunk like shit," The Heathens liked what they saw.

"What are you drinking?" Taylor offered.

Again, the stranger responded in "Dutch." Nobody understood, but his overall bearing was less than deferential. He seemed unimpressed by their leather-clad brawn. He was fearless, this one: "a credit to bad-ass-dom."

Baring his teeth, he whirled back into the tavern and stalked toward a hedging Ms. Dollup. After another disgustingly long pull of bourbon, he let out a piercing laugh, then took her by the arm and pulled her down the length of the counter to the ladies' room . . .

For the next few minutes, a frenzy of banging and screaming let out from behind the door. While it was happening, Freida

Baylor cursed not only her boyfriend, Taylor, but the rest of his chapter for not stepping in. They dismissed her, insisting that Dollup was getting not only what she asked for, but what she deserved—and enjoying herself in the bargain, at that.

Which may or may not have been true, by report, given the cries of what sounded like "pleasure."

Either way, Ms. Baylor was fed up. She blasted her boyfriend's chapter for cowards. When one of them started to chop out a line of methamphetamine there on the counter (which all of The Heathens would later deny), she gave up and placed a call to the police.

Booing, The Heathens called her a "buzzkill."

In fact, the police had already been summoned—first by a pummeled Dwayne Gibbons, then by the first two patrons who were able to flee the bar while the coast was clear. The calls had been placed, one after another, from a pay phone, outside in the parking lot. Officers Kreider and a newly-returned-to-duty Beaumont were now en route.

Back inside, the thrashing and wailing from the ladies' room peaked to a sudden crescendo. A silence followed, interrupted by the roar of a boxer being knocked out on the TV.

Soon, the door swung open abruptly. The stranger reemerged —disheveled, deranged and "smelling worse than ever."

What's more, his complexion appeared to have "darkened." His posture was slumped. His eyes were "scarlet."

He didn't respond when The Heathens beckoned him over to blast "his share" from the counter. He didn't appear to understand—neither their speech, nor their intentions.

Finally, according to subsequent testimony, someone (Taylor Blake) produced a rolled dollar bill to demonstrate.

"It ain't the best," he was said to have claimed. "But it's good enough for a weekend in Blue Ball."

That caught the stranger's attention, at last. Accepting the outstretched dollar bill, he followed Blake's example, honking not only the line of crystalline powder intended for him, but three others beside it. He pressed his entire face to the counter. He snorted and slobbered in wild abandon.

Which didn't appear to bother The Heathens, even in light of the mess he made.

He came up with powder all over his face, blinking and twitching in breathless spasms.

The Heathens laughed as a few more disgusted regulars made for the exit with haste . . .

Then Ms. Dollup appeared from the ladies' room. Everyone looked at her—standing in the doorway, ravaged, despondent, her clothing in tatters. The stranger ignored her—along with the angry cries of Ms. Baylor to *"Get her a jacket!"*—pitting his face, instead, to the counter to slobber and snort at the powder some more. He stiffened in place, almost seeming to choke. He gripped the counter and craned his neck with a heaving, then *snapping* esophageal roar. A scream went up from the pit of his diaphragm.

Whether by cause of cardiac overload, the tavern's notoriously greasy cuisine, the two-fifths of whiskey downed in an hour, the three tabs of Valium ingested unknowingly—or, of course, the muscle relaxant the quadruple dose of crank had been cut with—a blast of flatulence ripped the air, followed by the pungent stench of feces.

Groaning, Ms. Baylor implored Jesus. The Heathens backed off in sudden alarm. Only Valerie Dollup's thousand-yard stare remained unchanged throughout.

Appearing "subhuman" by now—as one patron would claim, he had changed in an hour's time (*"He came in as a man and left as an animal"*)—the stranger / intruder snapped from his spot at the counter and shot down the aisle, scampering—past the jukebox, over the welcome mat, out the exit and into the night.

. . . startled cries from behind, diminishing. Open air. Wind from the north, through fields of aster and sumac and nitrogen—underfoot asphalt, slapping—trash on the road, moving over it, into a ditch—clogged with oil and sewage and rainwater . . . up the embankment, craggy with limestone and quartz toward power lines humming above—a blinding glare, more voices behind, more tires on asphalt, approaching directly—urgent calls to the driver—continuing up and then over the rim of the bank and then tumbling downward, downward, down—to a plateau of aster and jimsonweed, old rusty wire on appendages, puncturing flesh—then release—a pounding inside, as of moving again . . . through bull-thistle, knapweed and dogbane to aorta / ventricle, hammer and anvil. Surging. Thirst and palpitations. Overload, onward—till heavens above yawning wide in the darkness: trains in the distance, motorized traffic delayed at a crossing—of burning downwind, of exhaust and of cellophane—carbon monoxide, fiberglass, vinyl—wafting through fields of Queen Anne's lace, over islands of oak and hickory trees—bull thistle tearing the shredded finery, hanging in strips from the briars behind—until, fully divested, and running as brought into searing existence, alone, at birth: naked and bloodied and wailing and here without limit, though thirsty, terribly thirsty—down on all fours at the edge of a stream—the moon's reflection in ripples, a furnace of streamlined combustion, gulping, burning, fueling, steadily waxing to term . . . Up again. Blackness. A gap in movement—more briars, more sow-thistle, gouging and

tearing—a break in the tangle, a crumbling fence post—and over—a clearing of gentler grass—clover and goldenrods, sweet even now in the brittle of autumn, soothing of hazel welts—pressing at length to an island of white oaks and hickories—milkweed exploding on impact—over a gritty forest floor, covered with bitter green walnuts and pine cones and kudzu—a canopy overhead, white oak and maple crowns, gently obscured by the layers of dogwood and sassafras—opening up to the sky . . . Croppings of granite, spotted with red-green lichen and moss—slick on the incline—slipping, tumbling down until—BANG—to the cankered remains of a chestnut stump—coming to in the splash of a darkened corridor—getting up, pressing north . . .

Blackness . . .

Bounding through fields of squash in the moonlight, and pumpkins, and cattle manure underfoot—pavement again, of passing below: of honking and screeching and swerving and SLAM—to a pole—and, still racing, with thunder behind—to a pain in the flank and of stabbing, unbearable—onward, continuing, moving, flight . . .

The aroma of hay and confinement: of stables and holding pens, rank with the heat of manure—lumbering bodies, tense with fear and ripe for the tearing of flesh and crimson . . . of thunder and booming—and voices now, furious—squalling in starts—and then bounding again . . .

More blackness . . .

. . . weeds overlooking a lot full of half-completed modern dwellings. An engine cutting across the sky. Automobiles in the clearing below. Men inside. Patrolling the property. Grounds defiled. Moving again . . .

The clatter and rattle of falling beams. A door being torn from its hinges, on end.

Floodlights, shouting, more thunder, more booming . . . pellets of lead hissing by, off target . . .

. . . into a field of nettles and ivy. Moving through tangled thickets to clearings of nightshade, Saint John's wort and charlock . . . beyond to a blackened line of evergreens: cypress and hemlock and larches and spruce—a carpet of needles and cones underfoot, the sweet aroma of hardened pine sap . . .

An increased roar of motors ahead . . .

Evading them easily, back up an untraveled road to a field of pungent nitrogen . . . churning downwind from the ugly man's home, now approaching, his absence abundantly clear—in spirit, in purity—nobody home: down with the gutter trims, out with the windows, off with the pump handle, up with the waterwheel—spraying the porch from one end to the other, then off again, moving away . . .

Blackness.

. . . cockleburs, goldenrod, milkweed—continuing north over water, through ditches and granite—to darkness in terrible thirst and beyond: for the ugly man's fortification of sorrow—the place of captivity, home of the killing . . .

PART FOUR
Bring It In

Syd had been able to stitch up the cut over Roddy's eye in the dressing room, downstairs. But due to the number of blows he'd sustained to the head, he would still need an MRI. Syd had to work at the clinic early, and couldn't spend the rest of his night in Philth Town.

On leaving, he wrapped his arms around Roddy and told him, in no uncertain terms, how honored he'd been to serve in his corner, how well he had done by himself and the gym and how all of Stepford was sure to be proud of him too. He had nothing at all to feel bad about.

"Go to the hospital," Syd finished up. "And then go home. This town eats its young."

Jack drove Roddy and Owen to the Jefferson General's emergency room on 8th Street. There, they would sit in a packed lobby, surrounded by every battery victim and drug overdose for miles around—during which time they might have returned to Stepford, been treated and gone home to bed. Roddy was finally admitted at three, at which point the trouble with billing had begun.

While Roddy—who, black-and-blue and oozing, was able to keep his cool throughout—was rolled away in a wheelchair and left to sit in another hall for an hour, Jack and Owen attempted to deal with the desk receptionists, who were maintaining, despite what anyone else may have promised, that neither Travers's productions, The Network, the Blue Palomino nor anyone involved had insured their fighter with medical coverage. And seeing how the records reflected that Roddy, through a prior, boxing-related admission, already owed the hospital in excess of two thousand dollars, there was definitely a problem.

Exasperated, Jack started shoveling change into the lobby's pay phone to call around town. But at that hour, naturally, no one picked up. Three machines and a wrong number later, he broke down and pulled out his wallet, furious.

So much for one more chunk of their purse.

With orders to rest for a couple of days and a handful of over-the-counter aspirin, Roddy was finally released from the Jefferson General just before five a.m. Jack drove them back to the hotel to pick up their bags, only to find that their bags had already been moved to a storage room, down in the basement. Their rooms had been occupied. Sensing a lapse in communications, and taking note of Roddy's condition, the clerk offered all of them cots in a janitor's break room.

Jack had to *not* laugh . . .

An estimated one and a half million viewers had watched their fight on TV that evening, yet, first, the club had failed to provide them with proper equipment and decent quarters; second, the show's promoters had either bungled or lied about medical coverage; and third, now that the three of them were ready and, finally, cleared to get some rest, the hotel staff could provide no more than a pay phone to seek out alternative lodging.

"This"—Jack turned to Owen, remarking for what, undoubtedly, would not be the last time—"is why you stick with the amateurs, kid. This is a generation of vipers."

On which note, Owen was given pause to consider The Coach's manner of speech. Until this evening, Jack hadn't spoken, directly, more than a dozen words to him. From off to the side, his vocal inflections had sounded, for the most part, flatly neutral. However, in the past few hours, his accent had hinted directly at regional tendencies—that is: an upward lilt in statements, a puckering, nasally anal twang. Earlier, Owen had taken these intonations for specific to Pennsyltucky. Even though he hadn't been able to determine, through Roddy, The Coach's place of birth, he assumed that Jack had grown up in the area. If pressed as to *where,* Owen probably would have wagered on either New Holland or Lititz—one of the prominent farming boroughs. Jack was most likely a native of Stepford. Only at the mention of "vipers" did Owen begin to sense just *how* native. The tip-off lay in pronunciation. That is: the v in "viper" had a vaguely, if tangibly German w edge. And "generation" came through as "cheneration." In full: "a cheneration of wipers."

To outside ears, for those who had grown up elsewhere, it might not have been detectable. But for Owen, who had spent his whole youth on the outskirts of Stepford trying to make sense of the language, Jack's vernacular, however streetwise, had definite shades of the Pennsyltucky Dutch. (And Stumpf was a Dutchie name.) Maybe The Coach had grown up in the sticks, outnumbered by Plain Folk—or even as *one* of them . . .

He wouldn't have been the only hayseed to end up on King Street.

Still, it was odd.

And so was his pickup: a massive old F-150 with overly sensitive brakes, even touchier shocks and a souped-up engine that took off from under them, light after light. All the way out of town, Owen bounced on the passenger's seat, gripping an armrest. Roddy lay braced in a clench in the backseat, facing away—still awake, though silent. The window above him was draped with a blanket. At every turn, what sounded like piles of metal shifted around in the hatchback. Again, it was strange: The Coach, as a city rat, owning a pickup truck and all—but nowhere nearly as strange as the proposition he was about to make Owen.

To wit: at dawn, with the first rays of sunlight creasing the flatlands of Valley Forge—just after pulling onto the turnpike, from out of nowhere, as though in a dream: would Owen consider watching (which seemed to mean *running*) the gym for a couple of weeks? Apparently, Jack had emergency "family matters" out west that couldn't wait. He needed "some brains" to hold down the fort. Roddy already had keys to the building, and Rhya, who worked full-time as a florist, would still run her noon class three days a week. The regular crew would remain in the house. But someone was needed to answer the phones. Somebody had to take care of the club—someone accustomed to "fending off (w)ultures"—and more: the whole building (the sewer, the heat, the electric) would have to be monitored daily. As well, there were matters of scheduling (an amateur tournament was set to begin in five weeks) and sponsorship issues in need of attention.

And somebody had to bring in the mail.

Jack pulled out a roll of twenties, most of his coach's commission for the night. He apologized for not having more to work with. Thing$ had been tough at the gym, of late. He handed the money to Owen. It must have been two thousand dollars in cash . . . In time, if required, he might devise some way of upping the rate of compensation. For the moment, however, he needed somebody with love for the game, someone he could trust.

For Owen, the only thing left to consider was whether or not The Coach was serious.

Once he had settled on *yes,* he accepted without even blinking.

The Luck of the Celts.

The rest of the ride was spent outlining daily procedure: security, contacts, keys—guidelines for dealing with Jerry Blye.

Jack dictated while Owen took notes. They were finished before the Stepford exit.

The last few minutes passed in silence. A series of images flashed before Owen, dancing now in the oncoming road lines of 222 through his bleary-eyed drifting: his first week in "training," and how little Jack had acknowledged his presence, much less addressed him. The sudden offer to work Roddy's corner, which Jack had extended without warming up to him. And now, an appeal to run the club.

All of this had happened in twenty-one days.

And still, The Coach was decidedly distant—as pensive, distracted, preoccupied as ever. Of course, he'd been fully attentive to Roddy that evening, and all through the week in training. But every time he had turned away—if only to glance at the clock for a moment—a cloud of gloom had rolled back over him. Owen had watched it right from the start. This was the only Jack he knew.

It was seven o'clock when they dropped him off at the house. Every car on the east side of Mulberry Street had been moved—*except* for his Subaru. The city sweepers had already passed. Another ticket, the fourth of its kind, had been slipped under one of his windshield wipers.

He turned to Roddy, who was still in the backseat, propped on an elbow. His eyes were black. The cut on his forehead was oozing pus.

Owen shook his head, at a loss for words.

Roddy, grinning, mumbled: "I hope I didn't let you guys down."

"Shut the hell up."

Owen reached over the backseat and wrapped an arm around Roddy. "You did us all proud, brother."

"I love you, buddy."

"I love you too."

Owen got out of the pickup, nodding to Jack. "I'll call you this afternoon?"

The Coach pulled away without responding.

Mulberry Street was still littered with trash.

Owen turned and walked up the stairs to his front door. He unlocked it, went in, collapsed on the couch and lay there for twenty-five minutes.

As much as he might have preferred to bask in his optimum fortune (once again)—and maybe drift off to sleep with a shit-eating grin on his face for a couple of hours—there was much to be done, including a thorough review of The Basin's scanner material. Owen had set his machine on "record" at four p.m. the day before. He may have been gone from his post for a night, but his bases were covered. It was all in the timing. For as long as he stayed on his game, he could handle this: everything—the gym, the paper, the Sabbath . . . The only thing it would cost him was sleep. And that wasn't a problem. For over a week, he'd been up until five a.m. every morning—either roaming The Basin or wielding a spit-bucket—then walking grooves in the floor back home, unable to stop his mind from racing.

The scanner results only bolstered his mania.

By now, Owen's hypothetical musings regarding the moon had played out to a tee.

The first disturbance report in The Basin—a livestock attack in the hills of Ronks—had been filed on the night of September 25th. Six days later, on the first of October, a rash of follow-up killings, mostly of goats and chickens, had reached a climax—along with an outbreak of property damage and small-time robberies. The moon had been full.

For the next few evenings, the level of public unrest had shown a marked decline. By the weekend (October 9th–10th), The Basin appeared to have gone back to normal. The moon had entered its last quarter. The calm had extended for several days.

Then, in the early hours of Friday, the 15th, the livestock attacks had resumed—and along with them, over the weekend, a new wave of Blue Ball Devil hysteria. This came to pass in the new moon phase, which peaked on the evening of Saturday the 16th.

From there, the disorder had trailed off again, diminishing all through the following week. Even while media coverage had surged, the turbulence seemed to have ebbed momentarily. This coincided with the moon's first quarter, which had fallen on October 23rd. Again, disorderly conduct in not just The Basin, but all across the country, bottomed out when the moon's gravitational pull on the earth had been at its weakest. And again, it resurfaced a few days later, increasing in the nights leading up to the full moon—in this case, a blue moon on Halloween, which, on average, occurred every nineteen years.

The scanner reports from the previous evening concurred, including, among other incidents, sexual assault at the Dogboy Tavern, as corroborated loosely by fifteen witnesses, evasion of police at the same address, another attack on the Holtwood Development—this one resulting in six private guards open-firing upon (and missing) an "invisible maniac" trashing their grounds (again)—a farmer named Dougan's claim to have shot and wounded "The Devil" for groping his heifers—the arrest and disarming of nine local residents, most of them stopped in a single procession of minivans cruising Old Laycock Drive, for the unlicensed wielding of modified firearms—the subsequent arrest of an Amish youth, now being held on suspicion of vandalism—a high-speed automobile pursuit by Sergeant Billings of a navy-blue Hornet (Billings gave chase, but was left in the dust between Smoketown and Ronks on Lynwood Road), two complaints of harassment and one of a death threat, lodged by resident "protesters"—three reports of breaking and entering, one from a couple who swore up and down that an overgrown rabbit had robbed their icebox—the unexplained theft of one police radio from an Officer Nelson Kutay's patrol car (two of the officers called him a fat boy and "king hell dipshit" over the air)—and dozens of similar "sightings," with less specific details of property damage.

If these events were an indication of what lay in store for the coming evening—meaning: were they exceeded by 12:51 a.m., when the moon was full—then tonight would belong to The Sacred Chao. On that note, Owen felt nervously certain.

With a five-minute shower, a guzzle of java and a quick change of clothing, he got back to work.

To start with, the Dogboy was closed for repairs. Nobody answered the business number, and of fifteen listed witnesses, only one could be reached: Dwayne Gibbons. Owen hadn't forgotten the name: that sniveling rat who had tried to milk him for printing the motion detector photo. He didn't expect any better this time—which was good, as he wasn't about to receive it. A wildly distraught Gibbons raved about devils and horseshit and "killing that bastard."

Owen, lost in the muddle of spluttering histrionics, hung up the phone.

Attempts to reach Officers Keiffer, Beaumont, Billings and Kutay were unsuccessful. Again, the sheriff was out of his office. Even the dispatcher hung up on Owen.

Thence, he moved on to Dane Dougan, the farmer who'd taken a shot at "The Devil"—and who, like others, claimed that the creature, indeed, bore the overall appearance of Nixon—only with "clotted fur and mange."

It wasn't any better with the couple whose icebox had been broken into. Most of the people who'd phoned in "sightings" were either asleep or at work or not home. The same went for six of the nine individuals charged with the unlicensed wielding of firearms. The other three, one sounding sickly hung-over, the second cursing the sheriff's name and the third forbidden from taking the phone by his angry wife, who called Owen a "Jew boy"—had just arrived home from a maddening, all-night detainment in the Lamepeter Township precinct.

At this hour, no one seemed ready or willing to help Owen piece together an update. Thus far, his only good quote had been taken from a shaken-up Holtwood Development guard. According to Donald Matthews, who ran a backhoe by day and who'd witnessed the previous evening's attack as a stand-in watchman: that "thing" was no hoax. It had "woven" through an unbroken, six-man barrage of shotgun fire—almost as though it had "seen them patches of lead shot coming, and danced between 'em."

Still, the statement wasn't enough. It didn't make up for an hour on the phone.

By noon, Owen had run out of options, along with most of the wind in his sails—something he tried to contend with by drinking entirely too much coffee again.

A final call to the Dogboy failed.

Then he spilled coffee all over his crotch. Scalded, he leapt in a fit of yowling . . .

Yes, it was time to get out of the house.

Today, he would work at the office.

Or not.

The building was quiet. Save for Bess and a pair of typists, the newsroom was empty. No sign of Kegel or Jarvik. No sign of their secretaries. And really no wonder, as Owen's belongings—a couple of folders, some papers and pens and a sack full of trash mail—were stuffed in a cardboard box, on the floor, blocking the aisle behind his cubicle.

He stepped over it, looking inside.

Now here was an all too familiar scene . . .

His desk had been scrubbed with cleaning solvents. On top lay a letter from Timothy Kegel—a letter announcing Owen's dismissal. His "services" were no longer needed at the paper.

Owen called to one of the typists. "What the hell is this?"

Bess turned around. Her expression was flat. "What's the problem?" she asked.

"Where's Jarvik?" he snapped.

She spoke in a flat-line monotone. "Mr. Jarvik was hit by an automobile last night."

Owen stared.

She continued: "As I understand it, he's in stable condition. But he won't be back for a while."

At this, a barely discernible grin broke the otherwise stony veneer of her countenance.

Owen might have gone after her—might have demanded an explanation, then cursed her—had it not been for a nagging suspicion that what she had claimed was, at least in part, true. What else would explain this? Kegel would never have gotten this far with Jarvik around. Something had happened.

But what? he wondered.

And more importantly, *how*.

Once again, Owen thought of the moon.

In the meantime, in less uncertain terms were his future and gainful employ at the paper. Indeed, the only thing standing between him and instant ejection had been the old man.

It might have been nice to stick around for the rest of the afternoon, waiting on Kegel. It might have been nice to land a good hook to his body, or right on the point of the chin.

In all likelihood, that was the reason why no one was here, in the newsroom: the staff was squeamish. Kegel had probably given them leave until Owen had come and gone from the building.

The chickenshits.

This was the *fourth* time Owen had been dismissed in fifteen months, and on every occasion, without exception—even in Gorbach, where, normally, no one had held back from verbally telling him off—the firing party had left him a letter, too spineless to deal with him face to face. Which, in itself, was unsurprising—and, for the most part, acceptably bearable.

But this time, he had been fired by Kegel—the native, the Stepford Anus incarnate. And Kegel would not only bury The Kornwolf, the slate would be cleansed of Owen entirely.

This situation was all too Stepford.

At least he had landed another job.

The Crossbills seated throughout the drug and alcohol counseling session room—Isaac, Gideon, Samuel and Colin—hadn't laid eyes on Ephraim in days. In fact, none of their friends or neighbors had seen him. He hadn't been home for a week. He hadn't attended these sessions, either. The four of them hadn't known what to think.

On Monday, he'd shown up at Gideon's barn after midnight—appearing as though in a dream—to announce a "masquerade ball" at the Schlabach Farm to be held on Saturday night. For the rest of the week, they'd been spreading the word, as ordered, to gang members all through The Basin. But when doing so, discretion was in order—as, recently, many young Plain Folk were finding it next to impossible to travel the roads. A majority of them, in fact, had been confined to the homes of their parents after dark. Others, like Isaac and Samuel, who lived on their own, had been subject to close surveillance. On three occasions, all after midnight, their trailer had been surrounded by Orderlies. And twice, the young men hadn't been home—so, naturally, both were under suspicion. As were the rest of the Crossbills, Colin and Gideon, as usual, in particular—as Colin owned a car that resembled a vehicle recently involved in the hit-and-run of an English portable toilet, and Gideon, only the evening before, had been picked up by township policemen for walking the roads of Paradise after "curfew."

Indeed, the Crossbills were proving themselves the bane of The Order, if not The Basin, the prototypes of exactly how *not* to raise your children—and none more unnervingly so, or with lesser assurance of actual fact, than Ephraim.

Between his recent disappearance, the traffic incident two weeks earlier and, now, as discovered that morning, an attack on his father's house (windows shattered, the gutters ripped down, the walls streaked with paint), Ephraim had managed to dominate much of the local Order's imagination. Fueled by rumors of family madness and bygone events of a generation—shady, bizarre events that could never be verified—speculation had raged.

And to look at him now, seated to the rear of the drug and alcohol counseling session—staring absently into space, dressed in what looked like a stolen jump suit, his pallor drained and the weeping abrasions about his neck more grievous than ever—would only have fanned the burgeoning flames of conjecture. His ghastly appearance invited it.

The session director could barely look at him.

The English, on the other hand, couldn't look away. Torn between fascination and disgust, they rubbernecked, marveling all through the session. The city kids, too, could only stare—along with the pair of Beachies from Intercourse, both of whom kept a wary distance.

The Pink Gorilla, of course, honed in.

Still rankled by events in the previous session—the speaking in tongues bit, the open defiance—the Pink Gorilla had seemed intent on payback right from the start of the class.

Toward the end, he gestured to Ephraim. "Man." He pinched his nose. "Did something *die* in here?"

A wave of snickering fizzled as Ephraim failed to react. He didn't move. His gaze remained locked on the desk in front of him.

Discouraged, the Pink Gorilla resumed. "Your mother's a bitch in heat," he whispered.

More laughter, yet still no response. The Gorilla shifted, appearing somewhat embarrassed.

His third attempt was no more successful.

Ephraim appeared to be in a coma.

The Gorilla thumped the back of his head with a pencil.

At last, he began to stir.

Distracted, the session director, whose back had been turned to the class, looked around.

Nobody moved.

Facing the board again, he kept talking.

The Pink Gorilla resumed by jamming his pen cap into Ephraim's ear. This time, Ephraim reacted, flinching. He looked around sharply. Colin and Samuel cast him an uppity, vigilant look. He waved them off. Thumbing his ear, he settled a glare on the Pink Gorilla.

The Beaver Street kid who had sold him the watch interjected: "Are you gonna sit there and take that?"

While most of the Crossbills squirmed uncomfortably, Ephraim turned back around in his seat. His knuckles, flexing white, wrapped over the edge of the desk. His expression was rigid.

For the next few minutes, the Pink Gorilla would work at the nerve he had managed to tweak. Over and over, he poked and prodded Ephraim's ears with the end of his pen. Seething, Ephraim did nothing to stop it. He sat there, gripping the edge of his desk.

Samuel and Colin were crazed with frustration.

For two months, Ephraim had risen in rank—from an addled, outwardly sullen mute to a terror of men—within their gang. He had deified sowing the wild oats.

So watching him hedge from the Pink Gorilla, as such, was more than they knew how to bear. With four of his strongest companions on hand to assist him, if needed, it didn't make sense. The English, even and especially the big ones, were flabby and slow. Their valves were bloated. They wouldn't have lasted a day in the fields.

Yet Ephraim did nothing to halt the mistreatment. He sat there, taking it, taking it, taking it . . .

Even as the session director, with a glance at his watch, indicated the class's end, Ephraim stood for dismissal without ever looking over.

Why was he doing this?

Out in the hallway, Colin and Samuel attempted to step in and cover his back. But Ephraim himself veered away from them, seeming intent on remaining an open target.

He was limping, they noticed: plodding along in discomfort, favoring one of his legs.

The Pink Gorilla closed in from behind. "That's right." He breathed down Ephraim's neck, reeking of grease. "Just keep on walking."

Someone, a Redcoat beside him, said, "Get on him, Gary!"

And another one: "Kick his ass!"

Ephraim was shoved from behind. He stumbled.

"Oh, yeah," said the Pink Gorilla.

Laughter.

Once in the stairwell, Ephraim was blindsided—punched in the face. He fell to the landing.

The Gorilla stood over him, taunting and slapping and pushing. "Come on, then, Dutch! What's the matter?"

A roar went up from the mob overhead. Bodies jostled for better positioning. Ephraim, still waving the Crossbills off, got up and continued down the stairs. His expression was blank. He looked hurt, but uninjured . . .

Once on the ground floor, he walked (to avoid being shoved) out the door, with the mob at his heels, to the half-empty lot behind the building. Bordered by thickets, a creek and fields, blocked from the road with no cameras in sight and the guards on the opposite end of the building, the half-acre plot of cement was unmonitored. No one remained to stand in the way.

The Pink Gorilla was bigger than Ephraim. He must have outweighed him by ninety pounds. He was brawnier, taller, wider and seemed to be able to throw his weight around. On appearance, it looked like a massacre waiting to happen. As happen it would, directly.

He bore down by driving his elbow into the back of Ephraim's head from behind. Ephraim dropped to the ground and rolled. Gripping his skull, he flopped to a halt. The Pink Gorilla lost his balance. Ephraim struggled to get to his feet. Weaving, he made for Samuel's buggy, tied to a pole across the lot. He managed to clear more than half of the distance before the Gorilla was on him again. He was seized upon, spun around, picked up and head-butted.

Then he was dropped.

His head hit the pavement.

Again, the English howled with laughter.

Colin, Samuel, Isaac and Gideon watched in powerless mortification as Ephraim, grimacing, rolled to his side and spat out a tooth on the lawn.

They screamed.

He nodded his head, coughing hoarsely.

Isaac, reaching his limit, stepped forward.

Still coughing, Ephraim waved him off. *"Get back!"* He glared in terse refusal.

His order was heeded, however reluctantly.

Ephraim got up, shook off and turned, regaining his stance. The Pink Gorilla shoved him against a custom van. He rolled with the impact, leaving a streak of blood on the siding. Again, he was punched in the face. He went down.

The Redcoats cheered.

The Gorilla added a kick for good measure. Then he turned to a round of praise . . .

Gawking, the devastated Crossbills watched them gather around and congratulate him. Most of the Beaver Street League, disappointed at not having witnessed more back and forth—and not really up for expanding the cast while outnumbered four to one—walked off.

From out of the building, the session director appeared. On the way to his car, he caught sight of the crowd and stopped. He was spotted at once, and as quickly, the mob began to disperse—the Redcoats turning to walk to their cars in a huddle, the city kids panning out and the Orderlies standing behind, near their buggies, angrily calling after the English.

Ephraim was lying inert on the pavement behind the van, concealed from view. He didn't move until the session director was gone, and in doing so, quietly, slowly. Nobody saw him get up. Nobody spotted him hobbling over the pavement. The first one to notice him routing around in the trunk of Samuel's buggy was Colin. Gradually, the others turned to see. He lifted a portable stereo out of the buggy. He placed it on top of the seat and, with trembling fingers, inserted a tape.

The moment the leader began to roll, he turned to them flashing a crooked grin. Caught unawares, they could only gawk. As the chain saws commenced, he took off bounding.

The Pink Gorilla, along with the rest of his gang, heard the sound of a trash can lid being struck with a hammer, and froze in his tracks. Before he could turn, he was slammed from behind.

His cohorts leapt and scattered around him.

Peeling himself from the asphalt, he whirled around, stammering, wide-eyed, incredulous. *"What?"*

Ephraim was standing there, leering indulgently. One of his teeth had been chipped in half. It was bared as a jagged, oozing fang. His tongue curled over it, flickering wetly. His lips were a bluer shade of gray.

The sound of a fan belt slapping against an engine hood blared out of the stereo.

The Gorilla landed another punch. Ephraim's head snapped back with the impact. He swiveled, then came around laughing, his smile giving way to a fiendish, wavering cackle. His eyeballs protruded. A vein divided his forehead, meeting just over the brow.

"Verdammis!" he hissed, dribbling blood through the gap in his teeth.

The Gorilla stepped back. The circle of English widened around them.

"Get on him, Zeke!" hollered one of the Beaver Street kids.

The rest of them came back to see. There were no other people in sight, no cops.

The vocals approaching: 3, 2, 1 . . .

Even while cocking back to strike, there was fear in the eyes of the Pink Gorilla. His punch was sloppy, an off combination of pulling and reckless overcommitment. At first, it appeared to have packed enough wallop to cave in the front of Ephraim's head—it seemed to have planted, *embedded* itself in his face with a hollow, sickening crunch . . . But then came the screaming—both from the music, of ten thousand demons plummeting hell-bound, and the Gorilla, flailing about like an open nerve on the end of a string. A moment of disbelief washed over the mob, Crossbills and English alike. The Beaver Street kids, from the edge of the gathering, craned their heads for a better look. The English were already screaming for help, as the blood had already begun to flow when they saw what was happening, front and center: the Pink Gorilla's knuckles were jammed in Ephraim's teeth. His punch had been *caught*. His fist had been *eaten* in mid-extension . . . He screamed in agony—kicking and flapping, his face a deeper shade of crimson, with tears streaming down it, his jugular bulging—while Ephraim continued to maul his hand . . .

Under any other circumstance, Grizelda would never have gotten into an automobile. Although she had always been thought of as liberal-minded within her own district, and never more than in recent weeks, she was still, after all, a member of The Order. The *Regel and Ordnung* had to apply. Normally, the sight of Gideon's beat-up vehicle approaching the Hostler home would have triggered a show of her indignation.

Tonight, however, would prove an exception.

With Fannie, Hanz and Barbara watching from one of the kitchen windows behind her, Grizelda stood in the gravel driveway, tensely hearing out Gideon's report. On conclusion, she turned and hurried up the porch steps.

Fannie opened the door. "What's the matter?"

Hastily pushing past her, Grizelda waved, as though to say, *Not now, child.* Instead, she ordered: "Fetch me your keys to the schoolhouse."

Then she ran up the stairs.

Fannie was left behind with her siblings. She could tell something was terribly wrong. A feeling had haunted her all afternoon—a queasy, dread-filled sense of foreboding. Seeing her mother carry on thus confirmed it. Something was happening now.

She turned to her brother and sister, addressing Barbara, the older: *"Please, if you will—fetch me the keys from my coat upstairs."*

They complied, disappearing. She stepped out the door.

The horizon was streaked with bands of yellow and orange. Clouds rolled over the sky. A gentle, chilly breeze was blowing—field hay tumbling up the drive.

Across the yard, a spark lit out from the darkened car window Gideon was sitting behind. After a moment, the flaring glow of a cigarette cherry lit up his face. His expression, clearly directed toward Fannie, was one of snide, sardonic amusement.

"Good evening," he spoke in Py. Dutch, at first barely audible. Then, more deliberately: *"Wonderful night for a ride in the country."*

Fannie came forward, eyeing his beat-up car with an air of decided mistrust. *"Why do you drive this thing?"* she asked, running her gaze from bumper to bumper.

He grinned, pausing to drag on his cigarette. *"Well, you know . . ."* he shrugged nonchalantly. *"Necessity dictates."*

Drawing closer, Fannie could see he was sweating profusely.

"What does that mean?" she asked.

He said nothing. Changing the subject, instead: *"You should have seen your cousin today."* He shook his head. *"You would've been proud."*

She looked at him nervously. *"What do you mean?"*

Leaning forward, he turned on the radio.

Fannie jumped at the blast of music. *"Turn that off!"* she snapped, afraid that her mother might hear.

He turned it off.

It was quiet again. He leaned out the window. *"You know—you really should try to relax."*

She rolled her eyes.

"Not good for the nerves . . ."

"Shut up, Gideon. What are you doing here? What's going on?"

He leaned back in. His bearing was darkly intent, if sarcastic. *"Concerned, are we?"*

"You know I am."

Slowly, he tapped his ash out the window. *"Like I said, he did us all proud. Not to worry. He's fine . . . And the party's still on."*

Fannie leaned forward and grabbed his arm, overriding his gaze. *"What happened to Ephraim?"*

His smile faded, gradually sinking to poorly concealed discomfort. He answered: *"He got in a fight with a Redcoat. They're holding him downtown, in jail. We need your mother."*

She tightened her grip. *"Is he hurt?"*

"Not really."

She waited for more.

He shrugged. *"We just have to get him out, that's all."*

Relaxing her grip, she stepped away from the car.

His look of discomfort lifted.

"So, then—" He motioned toward the house. *"Quilting party this evening, eh?"*

Fannie, lost in thought, looked around again. *"What?"*

He nodded. *"Doesn't your mother hold quilting parties on weekends?"*

"No."

He dragged on his cigarette. *"Too bad."* He spoke with a tone of somber nostalgia. *"Patterns."*

Clearing his throat, he resumed with purpose. *"So, I guess you'll be at the party then."*

She ignored him, staring across the field.

"Come on," he coaxed her, cooing melodically: *"Come on—your verschproche will be there."*

That got her attention.

"At midnight."

She turned away, feigning disinterest. *"You boys be careful,"* she mumbled. *"You've already been arrested once this month."*

Smirking, he answered in English. "Don't worry about that, Miss Fannie. Just come to the gathering."

Behind them, Grizelda appeared in the doorway. Hanz and Barbara followed her out. They handed the schoolhouse keys to Fannie, who handed them off to her mother in turn.

Grizelda took them and, pausing, looked into her daughter's eyes. Her tone was solemn. *"I want you to stay inside this evening."*

Fannie nodded.

Grizelda shook her head. *"I'm serious. No exceptions."*

"Yes."

"Your father will be home soon."

"Yes, Mother."

Grizelda turned and walked down the stairs.

Her children watched her go from the porch.

She plodded around to the side of the car. She opened the passenger door. She stuffed a knapsack into the seat, then crawled in after it.

"We need the Bishop," she said to Gideon. Her tone was strictly business now.

Then, leaning forward, she called from the window: *"Good night, children!"*

Gideon looked to them, grinning.

His eyes had gone milky white.

As the car pulled away, moving steadily west through a browning expanse of tobacco fields, an aching nausea welled up in Fannie.

The moon would be up in a couple of hours.

Owen swung by the house on his way across town. There, he dropped off his things from the office and picked up the bag of grass he'd been saving for just the right occasion.

Finally, a blast of smoke—be it ever so wanting in nicotine. This would be hard-earned.

He twisted a comically bulbous joint and, while grooving to Miles en route to the West Side, sucked on it, choking and yukking it up as if the fate of a species hung in the balance. The smoke on the back of his throat was a miracle, ripping its way to the pit of his lungs.

He was stoned off his noodle on reaching the gym.

His neurons shouted a million thanks.

The building was tall as an aircraft hangar. The lights were out. The place looked empty.

Owen parked his car along King Street. He turned off the stereo and glanced in the rearview mirror. His eyes were grotesquely bloodshot. A bottle of Visine was stashed in the glove box. He used it.

With smoke wafting up all around him, he stepped out and, tripping, locked the doors.

He walked up the alley. A cool autumn breeze rolled through. It was quiet. No pushers. No people.

While turning his key in the back door's lock, he realized the gym was as empty as it looked. Rhya's class didn't run on Saturdays.

None of the juniors had shown up to spar. Jack was out for the afternoon. And Roddy was home in bed, recovering.

Speaking of whom: Owen had forgotten to check if the paper had covered the fight. No matter, really—as nothing in print would have shed any light on his evening's experience. Goodall would have assigned a reporter to follow the match on television, then dash off an article by midnight, at best. *If* they had run a piece at all . . . Owen, having worked the corner, probably wouldn't have suffered the coverage well. He could picture it now: *"In the end, the pressure was simply too much for our hometown boy"*—which was *true,* admittedly, though none of the hacks at *The Plea* would have understood why, or how. Roddy's performance *should* have been as far beyond their grasp as their word on the matter.

Thinking about it made Owen's experience back at the paper seem insignificant. His mind, his tangible worth was still back at the fight, in the corner, jumping and hollering. Nothing would ever contend with that—certainly none of the Stepford Kegels . . .

Owen stepped into the darkened expanse of the training room and looked around. A feeling of confirmation went up in him.

This was what it was all about.

The room was cool and enormous around him. It almost emitted a silent hum: the slapping of leather on leather, the music of discipline, momentarily suspended.

He stood in the half-light coming to terms with the fact that he now played a part in this world. He'd landed a role in the fight game, at last. He felt like a kid in a candy store. True, his exhilaration was cut with a nagging concern as to how The Coach's regular fighters might receive him, the "rich" white kid from the suburbs, initially. But Owen felt genuinely up to the challenge, and by that, his efforts were sure to pay off. In time, he would win them over, ho ho. All it would take would be perseverance.

Once in the office, easing his way into Jack's chair was the strangest part. He had to remind himself that he wasn't intruding. He wasn't sneaking around. The Coach had asked him, directly, to be here. He was *supposed* to be watching the place.

As discussed, emergency contact numbers were filed away in a flash card box. A security console was mounted behind him. Keys were stashed up under the desk. A .45 automatic was tucked in a subcompartment of the top right drawer. Dossiers, tax records, files and photos were stored in the cabinets to either side.

Everything was exactly in order.

Owen leaned back in the chair, at last allowing himself a moment's respite. Slowly, he ran his gaze across the opposite wall, photo by photo: Jack with Vito Antuofermo. A younger Jack with Earnie Shavers. Jack in the corner of numerous amateurs, in between rounds, barking instructions . . . Jack in a spat with a referee . . . His Golden Gloves Hall of Fame certificate . . . Trophies, ribbons, plaques, inscriptions and eulogies lining a row of shelves . . . And, front and center: a photo of Jack, beaming with pride alongside of Rodrigo Velazquez, the West Side's prodigal son—holding the lightweight belt between them . . .

Slowly, as the fear that somebody might barge in and find him there without written consent and work him over began to subside, his exhaustion, brought on by the match and the joint in his system and so forth, overtook him. Soon, the photos along the walls had begun to fade and blur in his vision. The chair beneath him softened and cradled his worn-out body. He closed his eyes. The opening shots of an inner-eyelid movie in lavender—which felt to be warming up to a great escape in blue—appeared to him just as he started to drift.

Then the telephone rang.

He jumped.

He hadn't expected a *call,* Jesus.

He glared at the phone: a battered old rotary deal hooked up to an answering machine. The portable unit appeared to be broken. Actually, just the receiver was gone. The ringer jangled and tore at the calm like an air horn, echoing up the stairs.

Quickly enough, the machine picked up.

"Hello, you've reached the West Side Gym. We're not available to take your call . . ."

Owen relaxed as the tape started rolling. For a moment, he thought about picking up the line—mostly because he could.

But he didn't.

He went back to settling in for a doze—back to the land of lavender safety . . .

Suddenly, from out of the speakers sounded a vaguely familiar woman's voice. "Hello?"—pausing to wait out the screening routine. "Jack. Hello, this is Scarlet." Another delay for good measure. Then: "Jack, are you there?"

Owen sat up in the chair.

Scarlet . . .

She exhaled. "No. I guess you've left already." Her tone was confidential. "All right, then. Everything's ready on this end. We'll see you tomorrow. Or Monday." Another pause. Then: "Please be careful."

The line went dead.

Owen stared at the answering machine for a long, inconclusive minute.

To start with, he offered himself belly-up to the sanguine, echoing lull of her voice. There was no mistaking it: that was The Coach's lady friend. She was mesmerizing.

But then her warning (*"Please be careful"*) succeeded in growing to wear on his nerves.

He grabbed the receiver. His first act in office, per se, instead of taking a call was to *trace* one.

Class, he thought . . .

This was shameless.

He should have been minding his own business.

The call had been placed from the area code 812. He dropped the receiver and reached for the phone book.

812 was Indiana.

What the hell was she doing out there?

Owen had taken Scarlet for more metropolitan—or possibly rural Southwestern. And Jack had claimed he was going out west.

Confusion.

They must have been related. Was that it? Jack had mentioned family matters, and she had said: *"We'll see you tomorrow. Or Monday."*

In response to which, Owen was filled with a strangely perturbing, ineffable sense of relief.

Feeling no less underhanded, however, he sat back down in the chair. He couldn't be trusted. You couldn't leave people like Owen alone with your wife or business. Ever.

More out of guilt than exhaustion now, he forced himself back into a slumber. But try as he might, he couldn't drive Scarlet's voice from his mind. *"Please be careful."*

Why would Jack ever need to be (*please* be) careful? The man was a fucking giant. Maybe his driving was scary, but still—her message had seemed more specific than that.

Whatever, the sound of her voice was enough to leave Owen drifting in hammy-eyed rapture. The Indiana fertility goddess. Already, she had invaded his dreams. And there she would stay, awaiting his drifting return . . .

But not if the phone could ruin it.

This time, he didn't fly out of his skin when it rang. Instead, he sat up expectantly. It might have been her again, calling back. If so, he would force himself to answer.

But no. The call was from someone named "Jarret." He sounded Caucasian. His tone was urgent.

"I need you to be there, Jack," he said. "Come on, now. Unexpected news. We're due in court in twenty-five minutes." He trailed off, waiting.

Owen hesitated. He didn't know where Jack was at the moment, and he didn't want to deal with a heated emergency . . .

Still, this guy sounded plenty distressed—he could have been told, at least, to look elsewhere.

Owen decided to pick up the line.

Yet, just as he reached for it, the voice started into a series of guttural blurts that sounded, at first, like static interference. Owen, confused, held off for a moment. He stared at the speaker, cocking his head. What *was* this? . . . He drew in closer . . . What was this person saying? What language was that? Was it . . . German? Was he speaking German? . . . Or worse: was that Dutch? . . . Was that Py. Dutch? . . . It was ugly enough: lilting and plummeting nasally . . . It sounded like Stepford Anus . . . It *was* . . . That was Pennsyltucky Dutch . . . Someone was leaving a message in Plain Folk . . . Wasn't he? Yes . . . That was definitely Plain Folk. Owen could hear it . . . .

The caller hung up.

Owen rewound the tape and listened again. Confirmed. He could *see* the pucker.

But that gave rise to the question, then: why was Jack receiving this message? One could only assume it implied that he spoke the language. But where had he learned it?

Owen peered around the room. An older photo of Jack in what seemed to be his early thirties, standing with the junior Olympic team of 1980, hung next to the door. Owen got up and went over to check it out. Jack looked as young in that photo as anything filed away in the paper's archives. While writing his piece on Roddy and Jones, Owen had come up short on available bio material for Jack at *The Plea*—specifically childhood information. Regardless of the stream of publicity he had received in Stepford over the years, nothing on record pertaining to Jack predated November of '78. Panning around the office now, that seemed to be the case here too. No photos of Jack in adolescence, no trophies, no amateur boxing awards, no evident memorabilia from childhood, nothing at all appeared on display. Roddy had offered little help, saying only that Jack was from somewhere in western Ohio. Owen hadn't pushed it. At the time, it just hadn't seemed important.

But now, with this call, he was starting to wonder.

He dialed the Stepford Personitary.

As long as his press badge was still active, and he hadn't been blacklisted locally (yet), this would be the quickest and easiest way to ascertain the facts.

A secretary answered. Owen provided his access number and waited for clearance. It came. Relieved, he placed a request for the deed of sale on the West Side Gym.

While holding, he scanned the wall again. The fog in his head was beginning to lift. He was wide-awake now. Any hopes for an inner-eyelid movie in blue had vanished.

The secretary came back, reading the building's deed of inheritance from Mortimer Zane, the previous owner and head coach, to Jack Stumpf—dated April 20, 1981. Owen bypassed the terms of inheritance, proceeding directly to the recipient's claim. There he was able to ascertain The Coach's social security number.

Next, he called the historical society. On credit, he was able to contract a research assistant to pull up a resident file. The assistant, taking note of The Coach's address and social security number, told Owen to give him twenty minutes. He would call back with the file in hand.

In the interim, Owen was able to examine The Coach's awards, piece by piece. Again, he found no inscription dated prior to 1978. There was something hanging, though, up on the wall to the right of the trophy rack, surrounded by photos—something so small that, until then, it had eluded his attention—as even now, it seemed out of place, otherworldly, bizarre. He had to look closer to verify, thinking at first that he'd spotted a mason's broach. But the metal pin in the small glass case before him spoke for itself, on appearance. Leaving little room for doubt, it was cast in the form of a purple heart. Even though Owen had never laid eyes on a Purple Heart, he was left to assume, by deduction, that a small metal pin in the shape of a purple heart was, in fact, just that, as the name inscribed on a small gold plaque beneath the piece reading Corporal Jack Stumpf, April, 1975, suggested that Jack was a Vietnam vet.

When the research assistant got back to him, sooner than expected, the emerging pattern persisted: there was no birth certificate, no medical history and no academic record on Jack. There was, however, a certificate of social security instatement. Dated February 3rd, 1975. Which seemed to suggest to the research assistant, based on cases he dealt with frequently, that Jack might have grown up within, then left, the Old Order Amish or Mennonite communities. Confirmation could be obtained at the Paradise Basin's Heritage House . . .

Before the assistant had even stopped speaking, a series of images overwhelmed Owen: the Paradise Basin's Heritage House—or the Stepford Mennonite Historical Society . . . The Basin as home to the Blue Ball Devil, more recently known (or mistaken) as The Kornwolf . . . Shady reports of armed Plain Folk conducting searches in Lamepeter Township . . . The Amish youth suspected of vandalism . . . The other one—the Bontrager kid—who had driven the Sprawl Mart trailer into a ditch . . . The beverage delivery man's insistence that the Blue Ball Devil, the original, was gone, as *"Uncle Sam had hauled it away . . ."* And the constant reference, wherever he went, to The Dutchies, The Dutchies—*"Beware of The Dutchies."*

And now, Jack . . .

How many Anabaptists could crowd the shot arbitrarily?

So then, continuing / picking up right where he'd left off:

What *about* Uncle Sam?

Circa, 1974: toward the end of the conflict in Viet Nam . . .

As the Dogboy's delivery man had recalled of the Blue Ball Devil, now coming to mind: *"His name was Jacob Speicher. He died in The Nam."*—which led into Jack's Purple Heart on the wall, having escaped his attention . . . Jack Stumpf, wounded in action. Jacob Speicher, killed in action. Jack Stumpf. Jacob Speicher. Jack. Jacob. Speicher. Stumpf . . . J. S . . . . The same initials . . . Jacob Stumpf? . . .

Coincidence?

Backing up:

Legally speaking, the Plain Folk weren't obliged to pay social security taxes. Only when shunned from The Order for life would an individual lose that exemption. Likewise, only when shunned was a person made eligible for military conscript and service. The Old Order Amish were recognized as a nonviolent, deeply pacifist sect. Their members qualified as conscientious objectors. If, hypothetically, Jack had grown up Plain, then his excommunication would have preceded by a matter of months, if not weeks, his instatement in the social security system—and from there, his registration for the draft. As the research assistant had asserted, that instatement was enacted in February of '75. According to the paper's archives, the last known sighting of the Blue Ball Devil had fallen on November 3rd of the year before. Meaning, by sheer coincidence or no, the Blue Ball Devil had ended roughly three months before Jack had "begun." One marked an end to "The Time of the Killing," as printed in *The Budget* ("*The Time of the Killing Is Back*"), the other, feasibly, *could* have marked the start of Jack's career in the military . . .

Deciding to risk it—or maybe too freaked out *not* to—Owen picked up the phone. He dialed *The Plea* with trembling fingers, was transferred to Bess in Layout, connecting. She answered. Forgoing the schmooze, he offered her fifty dollars, whatever she wanted, to access The Coach's military file. The fact checker, Riggs, could dig it up for her. She would just have to persuade him.

"You know," said Owen. "Use your feminine charm."

She hung up.

Stupid. Stupid. Stupid . . .

He had to calm down now. Take a deep breath. This was all hypothetical: *remember—go easy . . . Don't burn your bridges before you've reached them . . . And don't offer payment for services rendered. She may be swamped in student loans—but that doesn't mean you proposition her . . .*

Now he would have to call Riggs himself. And Riggs, like the others, couldn't stand him.

Bungling. Reckless. Foolish. White.

Too many leaps to conclusion. Slow down . . .

If Jack had grown up Amish or Mennonite, as assimilating details appeared to suggest, and *had* left the fold in connection somehow—and this was a leap—with the Blue Ball Devil—and *then* been drafted, not to return for the better part of the next four years—assuming all of that to be true, it would follow, as well, that he wasn't involved (directly) with the panic now sweeping The Basin—as Owen had been in Philth Town with Jack on the previous evening. The Coach had an alibi. Maybe in youth, that wouldn't have been the case. Indeed, plausibility allowed for Jack (as a Speicher—the change of names had yet to make sense) as an angry young man—whether spurred by worldly envy or material greed (desire for the English neighbor's pickup), defiance of elders, rejection of principles, alienation, creative ambitions, irreverence, wanderlust, secular interests or even an untreated chemical imbalance (Jack had been popping pills at the fight)—either losing his mind or, more probably, waging a campaign of terror locally. If so, then what a campaign it must have been. For a copycat syndrome to spring up now, without his involvement, almost twenty years later, he had to have pulled out all the stops. And then been caught, shunned and drafted . . .

On a larger scale, hypothetically still, the above assumed that on the afternoon of October 8th, out of 500,000 people in the county, Owen had blundered haphazardly into Jack, one of the (as-yet unknown) central figures in a story that, only the day before, had surfaced (by way of Gibbons's photo) on the other end of town, and then been published, under Owen's name, in the paper that morning.

How likely was that?

A half a million to one, for starters.

If Jack was involved in the Blue Ball Devil, in whatever manifestation, per se, then Owen's appearance at the West Side must have thrown him, The Coach, for one hell of a loop. To glance up from trying to make sense of the article only to spot its (unsuspecting) author sauntering into the building. Jesus . . . What *must* he have thought? What a mindfuck . . . Owen could only have looked the freak . . . And since then, Jack would have watched him closely . . . Which *would,* come to think of it, explain a few things . . . Jack would have kept a quiet eye on him—probably not speaking a word to him, initially. Then, once Owen hit too close to home, he would have been lured in, cornered . . .

He was now sitting in The Coach's office.

He suddenly felt like a thousand eyes had been watching from every side for weeks—and here he was poised for sentence and delivery: into the river with concrete boots . . .

Or *stoned,* perhaps. Again, he was getting ahead of himself. Delirious. Paranoid.

He needed to retrace his steps, go back. Annul the hypotheses, void the instinct—operate solely on logic and likelihood—back through the fearful conjecture to (cringing) his conversation with Bess before: to October of 1974, right where he'd left off: "The Time of the Killing."

The term had emerged in numerous contexts. First in *The Budget,* by outlined passages citing a "*Time of the Killing*"s return. And second, somewhere in his research, if memory served: from the pages of *Bad Moon*.

Owen still had that book in his bag. He reached for it just as the telephone rang.

Without screening, he answered. "Yes?"

It was Bess.

At first, he assumed she was calling to give him a piece of her mind. But apparently not. She sounded more bored than bent out of shape. "You've really got fifty bucks?" she asked.

Amazed, Owen nodded: "I do. For *that* information, I've got fifty dollars."

"Aren't you going to ask me what happened to Jarvik?" she popped the question. There was scorn in her voice.

He slapped his forehead. "Of course. Of course!" He had nearly forgotten. "What's going on?"

She reverted to a bored, disinterested tone. "He wandered out into traffic on King Street. The cops say he wasn't wearing shoes."

Owen thought about it. Yes, he could picture it: all too clearly.

But that explained nothing.

"They're running some tests," she continued. "His wife thinks it might be the early onset of Alzheimer's."

Owen pondered the thought for a moment.

She cleared her throat. "It runs in the family." Shuffling papers, she was. Owen heard them. "Whatever. Let's see . . ." She had already dropped the subject. "About this fifty dollars."

Owen nodded, awaiting her verdict.

"The problem is—" She sounded uncertain. "I've got something here, but it's not really much. And I still want *some*thing for my efforts, you know?"

"Name it."

She exhaled. "Well, I'll tell you, then you decide." She cleared her throat. "Jack Ezekiel Stumpf, right? Social number: 442-09-3002."

"That's the one," Owen nodded.

Ezekiel?

"I thought so." Her tone went as flat as Ohio. "All of his military files have been classified. Top Secret. They've got him in a minefield."

Owen waited, expecting more. "So?" he asked when it didn't come. "You can't hack into it?"

She scoffed, laughing: "Not without every federal agent in town at my door. And sorry, honey, but you're not worth it."

He hung up the phone.

Classified.

What the hell did that mean? "Top Secret"? That could be anything: limited only by the widening scope of the hypothetical. Hence, it meant nothing.

He pulled out *Bad Moon,* flipped to the index. His heart skipped a beat at the sight of "The Time of the Killing": pp. 70–71, 237–241.

Page 70 opened with an entry on *"The Burning of Heretics During The Reformation."*

Following Luther's split with the Catholic Church, a century of religious, political and cultural persecution ensued. Defined as heretical—and thereby *"silenced, confined and eliminated"*—were, among others, The Adamites, who ran naked in the forests; The Free-Livers, who practiced polygamy; The Weeping Brothers, who held tearful ceremonies; The Bloodthirsty Ones, who indulged in sacrifice; The Devil's Children, who worshipped Lucifer; and The Anabaptists, whose radical stance to "reform the reformers" had been branded seditious.

There they were again. One more Dutchie and Owen would have to start baling fodder . . .

He continued: "The burnings intensified during *'The Time of the Killing,'* once defined in older German as 'The Age of The Werewolves.'"

Owen marked his spot, then turned to page 237—twenty pages beyond the point up to which he had read. There, he found several woodblock prints, circa 1590, eight in total, depicting, in sequence, an upright, shaded creature apparently stalking the fields; the creature pursued by a hunting party; the creature, in human form, at trial; the creature, in human form, condemned—then tortured and, finally, beheaded and burned at the stake, underscoring the entry's title:

"The Execution of Peter Stubbe."

The article opened by noting that, according to George Borer's account, *The Damnable Life and Death of Stubbe Peter* (c.1590), a man by that surname (pronounced Shtoo-bay) was born in the Bedburg / Cephardt area of Germany in 1520. For most of his earlier life, he would verse himself in the arts of necromancy. At trial, he would *"freely confess"* to accepting a belt from The Devil, which, when worn, would transform him into a savage wolf—and no ordinary wolf, in stature, either: the creature was *"strong, enormous and cruel, with eyes that glowed and razor sharp teeth."* In this form, he stalked the countryside, killing and mutilating, even devouring travelers. Once the belt had been removed, the monster would quickly revert to the form of Peter Stubbe, who posed, by most accounts, an inconspicuous figure. Though odd in demeanor, he had never been suspected of, much less questioned in connection with murder: not even when several of his victims were known to have angered or insulted him prior to their deaths.

The court records maintained that Stubbe was driven by insatiable cravings for the flesh of young women. In human form, he would *"ravage them in the fields,"* then *"shape-shift into a wolf and kill them."* He was later judged guilty of incest, having taken his daughter as a concubine daily, and by her bringing forth a child. *"Furthermore,"* according to Borer's chapbook, this *"insatiable and filthy beast, given over to works of evil with greediness, lay even with his own sister. He frequented her company long times according to the wicked dictates of his heart."*

Stubbe had many women, as lovers and victims both. He was found to have killed and partially devoured eleven women in a single season. Two of them were pregnant and *"tearing the children out of their wombs in most bloody and savage sort, he afterwards ate their hearts, panting and raw."*

Next he was charged with, and found guilty of, killing three travelers, mutilating two and devouring entirely the third, a woman.

This was followed by Stubbe's murder of his own son, his *"heart's ease,"* whose brains he *"ate right out of the skull."*

The killings continued for many years.

Then came a day when a wolf was spotted abducting a shepherd boy near the town of Bedburg. A party of men with dogs assembled to track the beast. On approaching a clearing, they heard the cry of a terrified child. Then, as they swore under oath subsequently, a wolf appeared, yet soon, *"the beast shape-shifted into the form of a man."* The party quietly followed him back to his house, then seized and delivered him, Stubbe, to authorities in nearby Bedburg for questioning.

Peter Stubbe was found guilty by confession of sorcery, werewolfism, cannibalism, rape and incestuous adultery. His daughter and one of his mistresses were tried as accessories. All three were sentenced to death.

On October 31st (!), 1589, with a crowd of in excess of 4,000 persons from all over Europe in attendance, Stubbe was stretched on a rack. The flesh was torn from his body with red-hot clamps. His legs and arms were severed. He was decapitated. His body was burned to ashes. And, later, his head was impaled on a stake for public display in the town of Bedburg. In total, the "monster" had claimed fifteen (other sources contended twenty-seven) victims during a period known as *"The Time of the Killing."*

Today, as Stoner went on to note, historians theorized that Stubbe, in fact, had been a wealthy, prosperous and, not least important, *Catholic* landowner living between the predominantly protestant villages of Bedburg and Cephardt in a time of great famine. While, according to church records, many townspeople had starved to death during this period, Stubbe was said to have lived in comfort and relative ease, untouched by misfortune. For that, the villagers had grown to resent him. He was rumored to have been in league with The Devil . . . When, in the century's final decade, a string of murders—mostly of shepherdesses tending their flocks—broke out in the surrounding countryside, deafening cries for revenge had been raised all across the miserable, famine-wrecked province. Even though the fields, at that time, had been crawling with fugitives, bandits and deserters (or kornwolves) who might have ravaged and murdered the girls, then left their bodies to be torn apart and scattered about by the wolves of the forests—Stubbe was singled out for arrest, interrogation and execution. Many would now consider him a scapegoat, a victim of the prejudice inherent to his age.

The only catch was: the Bedburg / Cephardt murders had *ceased* upon his arrest . . .

Whatever the story, Peter Stubbe (also known by the surname of *Stumpf*!) was probably the best-known werewolf in history . . .

Owen looked up.

Visions of terror and execution danced before him.

Peter Stumpf.

Killed on October *31st,* 1589 . . .

Gradually, Owen's focus returned to the wall, spurred by a faraway clopping of hooves and the grating of steel-rimmed wheels over asphalt, approaching from down the street.

An image of Jack and Rodrigo sharpened. Owen stared at the photo, searching. The Coach had been shot in Vietnam . . . Jacob Speicher, an Amish youth, was said to have been the Blue Ball Devil . . . The Anabaptists had formed in Germany and Switzerland during the sixteenth century . . . The Werewolf of Bedburg was tortured to death, with his daughter and mistress, in 1589 . . . No mention was made re: the fate of the child begat by Stubbe (Stumpf) and his daughter—nor of the sister with whom he had practiced "carnal, unholy" relations daily . . .

And, come to think of it, wasn't the "Kornwolf of Possum Turn" from Indiana?

Again, Dr. Diller had been on the money: *"They'll call you a madman. Don't be a fool."*

Still deaf to the rumble of hoofbeats, Owen zeroed in on Jack's photo . . .

Nothing about his appearance was off. His expression was clear, rational, lucid. He looked pretty good for a Vietnam vet.

And, again, he had been in Philth Town on Friday.

This was giving Owen a migraine.

The unmistakable grating of horse-drawn carriage wheels ground to a pivot outside. The clatter of riding gear moved up the alleyway, gathering speed as it closed on the parking lot.

Owen remained transfixed on the photo, having just caught a peripheral blip.

Beneath a jubilant Jack and Rodrigo, holding the lightweight belt between them—Rodrigo's olive-complected hand to the right, supporting the central plaque, Jack's enormous hand to the left, clamping that end of the belt with his fingers . . . His fingers . . .

Something about . . . The knuckles: aligned in a perfect row, horizontally. (Backwards?) Something was wrong with the fingers . . . One of them looked to be out of place . . . His hand was off balance . . . The ring finger. That was it . . . Jack's fourth finger was longer than the others . . .

Owen's lungs refused to draw breath.

At last, a commotion erupted outside, jolting him back to the here and now. He got up and went out to see what was happening. People were shouting. A crowd, by the sound of it.

What was this?

Fido Jones *again*?

He wouldn't have shown up to rub it in . . .

Blye then?

Doubtful.

Pushers.

Carefully now . . .

He opened the door to a brick in mid-flight, coming at him. He dodged. It banked off the ring post behind him and fell, tearing into the canvas.

It could have killed him.

He looked back around, incredulous, braced for a follow-up shot.

From the murk of his reverie, several Amish men spilled from three different horse-drawn buggies. They let out a murderous yell at the sight of him.

Owen slammed and locked the door. A window shattered above the free weights. A brick came through. Glass on the floor.

They were pounding the door now, trying to ram it . . .

Terrified, he ran back into the office. Out the window, he spotted another buggy, positioned in front of the gym.

The phone started ringing. A security alarm went off. Lights on the console flashed.

He ran up the stairs. He crawled out a third-floor window and dropped to the neighbor's roof.

The first of the sirens went up in the distance, approaching. The cops were on their way.

After fifteen minutes, Judge Talmud Percy's alarm re: the freak show sweeping his courtroom had settled to a feeling of muted bewilderment. A district judge for twenty-five years, Percy thought he had seen it all, that every conceivable walk of life—from white-collar bond thieves and errant physicians to math teachers, wife beaters, mobsters and drunks—had appeared before him over time.

But nothing compared to this evening's cast.

First, at six p.m., the bailiffs had brought in a *thing*—a bruised and battered young man by the name of Ephraim Bontrager. Though he'd been stripped, hosed and clothed in prison garb before entering the room, he was still in a visibly frightful state. His skin was a paler shade of blue, with multiple cuts, abrasions and bruises. One of his teeth was chipped in half. And clumps of hair had been torn from his scalp.

Next had come the arrest report—and plenty bizarre, as grisly fiction . . .

The arresting officers, Cole and Collins, had arrived on the scene (Joseph's Hall) to find one "victim," Gary Reed, a quarterback for Hempland High, unconscious and bloodied, facedown on the pavement, with a career-ending trauma to his throwing hand, a second "victim," J. R. Beltzer, crawling across the pavement, "wounded," and a third, Ford Campbell, in the process of being "beaten" by the "perpetrator," Ephraim Bontrager. All three victims had been expressed to the hospital. Still unconscious, Gary Reed had been admitted for emergency work. Beltzer and Campbell were listed as "injured by multiple blows to the head and body." Their condition was "stable." The prognosis: "pending." The perpetrator, Bontrager, described as "possibly rabid" by both responding officers, had been detained at the Stepford City Precinct on charges of attempted murder.

To thicken the plot, the defendant was listed as belonging to the Old Order Amish community. Percy had never tried a member of The Order for assault of a non-Amish person. Of course, many cases involving the Plain Folk had passed through his courtroom over the years. But none like this one—none predicated on a physical confrontation with the "English."

Stranger still, this young man had been arrested at the juvenile detention center, where, it now came out, he hadn't belonged—as, first, he'd been charged with a traffic crime, not underaged drinking, three weeks earlier, and second, his age was listed as eighteen. He didn't belong in a juvenile program. If anywhere, he belonged in jail . . .

Exactly how this had bypassed administrative notice was not at all clear—though it may have had something to do with the fact that his record defined him as a registered mute. Maybe the cops hadn't known his age. Maybe he hadn't been able to tell them. More likely, his crime—having challenged a tractor trailer to a head-on game of "chicken"—was, even in light of the glaring absence of subsequent Breathalyzer results, deemed too bizarre to be chalked up to anything *other* than threshold intoxication.

No sooner had Percy reviewed the report, occasionally halting to glance with a cringe at the young man seated before him, below, than a slew of attorneys began to appear, only adding to the overall sense of confusion.

First, unsurprisingly, came juvenile defender Jarret Yoder, an old acquaintance and personal friend of Judge Percy's. Yoder himself had grown up Mennonite—even though he hadn't been long for the church. His peripatetic yearnings in youth had borne him away to the city for years, during which time he had earned his master's in psych, then gone into juvenile counseling. Having returned to Stepford in Gipper Time, he was now versed in, and dealt with, the trials and tribulations of urban street youth as much as the Plain Folk of Eastern Stepford.

His colleague, Public Attorney Davin W. Stutz, was the next to arrive. But with less than a minute's exchange between the two men, it was clear that they wouldn't be representing common interests today. On the contrary, as per norm, they would end up on opposite sides of the courtroom, tearing into one another. In fact, by the time Gerald Metzger, assistant D.A., showed up, they were already at it—back and forth in a flurry of hissing. Metzger, sure to appear on the victims' behalf, would only complicate matters.

While that was happening, the crowd that had started to form in the courtroom continued to grow. First there appeared a mob of angry suburban parents, now gathered to the rear of the room in a tense, murmuring huddle. Then came a group from the Beaver Street League who had witnessed the confrontation first-hand. Followed by one, then two, then six, then eight Amish persons—most of them young. And finally, a drove of random spectators. All for what, in theory, *should* have been a brief, routine arraignment. Percy was already overwhelmed by the time he broke down and called for order.

Jarret Yoder's opening statement had done very little to clarify matters. Amid a constant barrage of objections from Stutz, Yoder had opened proceedings by first paraphrasing that afternoon's altercation according to eyewitness testimony—all of which maintained that Mr. Bontrager *hadn't* started the fight, and had only fought back after being assaulted.

At which point, Percy hit the brakes.

"Mr. Yoder, first things first: how *old* is Mr. Bontrager?"

"Eighteen, Your Honor."

The judge's expression was stern, unamused. "Then what was he doing in juvenile counseling?"

Jarret's nod rolled into a shrug. "It appears there's been a mistake, Your Honor. This young man was referred to counseling by the Lamepeter Police Department. One can only imagine *how,* as this should be a routine matter. But it *is* interesting to note that, according to several by-standing witnesses, the arresting officer, Rudolf Beaumont, had beaten Mr. Bontrager so severely that any resulting prosecution would have been voided at or before first hearing. Meaning: the authorities would have jinxed their case by dint of excessive force. If true, then admitting him for juvenile rehab here in town would appear to have been the sheriff department's manner of trying to sweep this incident under the rug. Already, the sheriff has denied the charge. But his denial is shaken by the fact that Officer Beaumont has since been charged with *another* beating of a juvenile "offender," this time in a case of mistaken identity, for which the department is set to face a costly and public brutality suit."

Percy shook his head in confusion. "What are we dealing with here, Mr. Yoder?"

Jarret hesitated. "On the whole, sir?"

Percy nodded. "If it answers my question."

Yoder drew in a steady breath.

Then, in so many words, he proceeded:

The defendant's mother had died giving birth to him after extended (*"nineteen hours of horrifying homebound"*) labor complications—something for which his father had always blamed him in full, and with an active vengeance. Several witnesses, herein assembled, would testify to as much under oath, citing occasions on which the elder had struck, pummeled or beaten the boy. One needed only regard his battered condition at present to bear out their claims. The young man's entire body was marked with the signs of severe and continual abuse. He was also a mute. He'd been terrified into a state of speechless, glassy-eyed shock. This, Yoder intended to prove, had contributed to the events of that afternoon.

To which Stutz, of course, raised a howling objection. The judge agreed to hear him out.

First, he responded, the young man in question was widely known to be mentally defective. His status as a mute was accepted as having resulted from an accident in early childhood—a blow to the back of his skull sustained in a fall down the stairs, a common blunder. Likewise, his "present condition," the bruising and such, was the product of a childhood bout with a genetic disorder inherent to the Amish—a disorder from which he had suffered violent recurring flashbacks ever since. This added to his inability to speak—and, moreover, his general "feeble-mindedness." It also accounted for his lack of motor skills, which had resulted in numerous mishaps—many resulting in physical injuries . . . All of these matters had been addressed by the young man's district council already. Less widely acknowledged, though certainly known, was the fact that, since early adulthood, he'd been in trouble with the law on a regular basis. At eighteen, his record already included one arrest for under-aged drinking, four charges of violating curfew, one count of hedging a truck off the road, and now, the brutal, unwarranted assault of three "unsuspecting" individuals . . . His father, the Minister Bontrager, on the other hand, was a respected, upstanding member of the community—a minister appointed by his own congregation—whose curse in life it had been to attempt to control this boy—with little success.

Scoffs went up from the group of Orderlies seated directly behind the defendant. Somebody blurted, *"The old man's a drunk!"* It managed to catch the judge's attention.

Percy thumped his gavel and called the group to order. They settled down . . .

Turning back to Davin Stutz, the judge asked, "So where is this father now? This—" Squinting, he leafed through his papers. "What was his name?"

"Benedictus Bontrager, Your Honor," said Stutz. "We haven't been able to locate him."

Barely able to keep his seat, Yoder signaled. "Your Honor?"

"Yes, Counsel?"

Jarret stood up. "Your Honor, as of forty-five minutes ago, Minister Bontrager has been in police custody on charges of attempted arson."

A wave of gasping swept the room. Percy straightened up in his seat.

Yoder lifted a yellow paper and read from it. "Yes, sir: 'Attempted Arson.' 'Destruction of Property.' And 'Breaking and Entering.' He was arrested with five other men here in town for attempting to burn down an athletic center."

The silence to follow was thick with confusion. The judge leaned forward: "You'll have to do better than that, Mr. Yoder. What's this about?"

Shrugging, Yoder held up his hands. "We just received the call, Your Honor. We don't have any specifics, as yet. We can only present the arrest report. Permission to approach the bench for that purpose?"

The judge nodded, beckoning stiffly. Yoder moved forward to deliver the report. Percy took it and started to read, looking even more perplexed than before. He muttered under his breath discreetly, "Do you know what you're doing, Jarret?"

Yoder whispered back, "Just ask me about his job."

While a stern-faced Percy continued to try and make sense of the hastily filed report, Yoder counted his stars for the last-minute gifts that had just fallen out of the sky. Even though Jack hadn't been available (some day the bastard would carry a cell phone), even though now was the worst of all possible times for the kid to have gotten in trouble, and even though Yoder had not been fully prepared to appear in court, just yet, he *had* been graced in being arraigned before Percy, not only a personal friend, but a judge who had garnered a reputation as hell on domestic-abuse offenders. Along with that distinction he had a well-known aversion to Davin Stutz.

What's more, the Bontrager kid, through his actions, had laid the foundation for a plea of insanity—which, most likely, would be upheld, at present, by his ghoulish, unholy appearance. He looked as bad as his uncle ever had. He looked like fucking Linda Blair . . .

To continue, his father, with several accomplices, had been arrested an hour earlier—something so perfectly timed, it defied explanation, and couldn't have served them better.

Then, out of nowhere, Franklin Pendle had wandered up, wearing a Beaver Street jacket. Apparently, he and "his boys" had seen the whole thing and would testify gladly, if needed.

Which was reassuring, although it was still too-little-too-late for Franklin . . .

And last, from beyond, a pair of middle-aged Plain Folk had shown up to aid in the case—the first, Johann Schnaeder, a bishop in Minister Bontrager's own congregation, and the second, a woman claiming to be the boy's aunt and former guardian.

Yoder remembered her vaguely from childhood. She was Maria Speicher's friend. Jarret himself had never known her.

Whatever the case, he admired her courage. Testifying in an English court against a member of her family, not to mention the church, would be no laughing matter within The Order. Surely, there would be hell to pay—possibly excommunication.

Whatever the penalty may have been, Yoder wasn't about to talk her out of it. She was probably the only thing left between Ephraim and Cell Block Five for the evening. She was the stronsgest card in their deck, by far—with the bishop in shining second. Between them, Yoder had only been able to wrangle ten minutes of preparation. But in that time, with the notes he had taken, their case had been fortified many times over.

"You may return to the floor, Mr. Yoder," Percy announced at a normal level.

As Jarret walked back to his table, the judge continued, addressing Stutz. "Do you mean to tell me then, Mr. Stutz, that on entering this courtroom you knew nothing about this incident?"

"Your Honor?"

Percy held up the report. "This, Counsel. You know what I'm saying."

Stutz hesitated, then swiveled his head. "Your Honor, yes . . . in a manner, I did. But we really should hold off judgment until the men in question have been arraigned."

The judge frowned. "It says here they tried to burn down the building with gasoline."

Stutz, flinching, could only repeat, "We should hold off judgment till the facts are in."

As Percy exhaled and removed his glasses, assistant D.A. Gerald Metzger, who, until then, had held his tongue quietly, at last stepped forward to announce at full volume:

"Your honor, may I point out that while my colleagues are so earnestly discussing the defendant's home life, three young men lie injured in the hospital, one of them critically, due to his actions. With or without a pattern of abuse, *some*one must be held to account here."

A roar of agreement went up from the crowd of angered parents to the rear of the room. Judge Percy waved them to order, yet somewhere above the diminishing sizzle, the voice of a Beaver Street kid went out:

"Sounds like a load of BULLshit, yo!"

Percy pounded his gavel. "Quiet!" he yelled. His voice boomed over the courtroom. "This isn't a peanut gallery, people. One more disturbance and everyone goes." He glared at the crowd to drive home his point. Then he returned his attention to Stutz.

"Now, Counsel. The man you're defending. This . . ."

"Benedictus Bontrager, Your Honor."

Blinking, Percy shook his head. "Right. You say this man's an ordained minister?"

"Yes, Your Honor. Mr. Bontrager's been an Old Order minister for seventeen years. Dozens of fellow community members would readily stand to vouch for his character. The same cannot be said for the defendant."

Again, Yoder raised his hand. Percy waved him off. "One moment." The judge wasn't finished with Stutz, apparently. "What is this minister's line of work?"

Stutz hesitated, shifting uneasily. Then: "He works in livestock, Your Honor."

Another collective scoff went up from the group that was seated behind the defendant. Percy flinched. He looked ready to hold the whole crowd in contempt.

Jarret cut in. "Your Honor?"

"*What,* Mr. Yoder?"

"Permission to offer remarks at this time?"

Frowning, Percy looked away from the crowd. He nodded. "Let's get somewhere."

Jarret dropped his pen on the table. He picked up a folder . . . He hadn't had time to prepare, much less rehearse . . . At this point, he was just hoping to get all the names right . . . He couldn't afford to slip up. If anything—even one detail—was off, Davin Stutz would call him out, as Stutz had defended the mill for years.

"Your Honor, please excuse the defendant's friends and family for their verbal outbursts, but as each of them is well-aware, Minister Bontrager works in, and co-owns, the most intensely scrutinized puppy mill operation in the greater Stepford area."

"OBJECTION!" yelled Stutz,

"Overruled!" snapped Percy.

Stutz, wide-eyed, regarded Yoder in baffled amazement as much as rage. Jarret was turning the tables on him, beating Stutz at his own game.

"Thank you, Judge." Yoder proceeded, crossing his fortune to get this right. "Since 1970, Benedictus Bontrager and four associates have been operating the Blue Ball Canine Emporium. In 1980, a court-ordered search of the premises revealed deplorable sanitary conditions—massive overcrowding of cages, sometimes four or five dogs to a unit—malnutrition, disease, neglect and broad indications of physical abuse. Studies have shown that dogs being raised in the mill—and later sold to distributors—have significantly higher rates of, among other ailments, heart disease, bone marrow cancer and blindness than dogs being bred and bought elsewhere. For many years, this facility has been under watch by numerous organizations. Mr. Bontrager has personally driven off members of the media with a baseball bat. A petition signed by six hundred persons against the Emporium was filed last year. A national coalition of pet owners has cited the mill as the 'epitome of evil.'"

Yoder paused to lay the file on the table and dig back into his case. Producing another folder, he began his summary:

"Your Honor, in light of all of these factors—along with the testimony from today's incident, and more importantly, the defendant's condition—I'm obliged to remark at this time that his recent behavior can hardly be seen as surprising. Attributing blame to a medical disorder, as, predictably, Counsel Stutz has seen fit, is a standard recourse, tried and tested here in this courthouse on many occasions, and is no more confirmed, at present, than a more likely diagnosis of schizophrenia. On that note, at least, a history of mental illness *does* exist in the family . . .

"Whatever the case, we have every indication that the young man's father is a grievous threat to him—and, by way of same, a community hazard. We also have members of the Minister's own congregation"—Yoder refrained from naming or pointing out the Bishop directly—"who are pressing to have him shunned from their church for rejecting its code of nonresistance—which is to say, in common terms: for advocating the use of violence . . . Bear in mind that, within the fold, ordinations are determined by a drawing of lots—which is to say, by random chance. To be nominated, less than a fifth of the district body's recommendation is needed. We know that the Minister's standing in his own congregation is anything but unilateral.

"We also know that, at this moment, he's in custody on charges of attempted arson. We know that this man and his colleagues have faced repeated charges of animal abuse, and we intend to submit the photographs herein . . ." Yoder held up a second folder—and now, he was pushing his luck a bit (he still hadn't figured out how he was going to render these prints admissible, legally, as Jack had broken into the compound to take them)—

nevertheless, he proceeded: ". . . to prove that existing conditions at the mill are in gross violation of federal standards."

"Your Honor!" cried Davin Stutz, getting up. "Exactly *who* is being charged?"

Percy fixed him with a glare of contempt. "Sit down and shut your mouth, Counsel."

Furious, Stutz sunk back in his chair.

Percy returned his attention to Yoder. "Is there anything else you have to add?"

"Yes, Your Honor. One last thing." Jarret reached into his case and pulled out a copy of the footage that Jack had shot from an Intercourse Getaway's third-level window. "In conclusion: we intend to prove with this videotape—and with the cooperating verification and assistance of Bishop Johann Schnaeder—that Minister Bontrager has used the collection funds of his own congregation, as well as a tariff in homemade whiskey, to pay off members of the Lamepeter Township Police Department—again, Officer Rudolf Beaumont, specifically—in exchange for police cooperation."

Whereupon, Yoder held his peace.

In place of the expected objection from Stutz, along with outbursts from parts of the crowd, to say nothing of lengthy appeals from Assistant District Attorney Gerald Metzger, a heavy silence fell over the room. All eyes fixed on Judge Percy, as, leaning back in his chair, he clamped his brow with an overwrought sigh of bewilderment.

"Well, Mr. Yoder," he mumbled. "This is quite a can of worms you've opened."

After a moment, he lowered his hand, leaned forward and took one look at the defendant.

At last, he followed up: "And how exactly are you proposing this be resolved?"

Nodding graciously, Jarret placed the cassette on the table before him and, turning, signaled Grizelda to come forward.

All eyes watched as, clothed in traditional Amish garb, she

approached the table. Yoder leaned toward her, whispering: "Don't worry. I'll do the talking." He turned around.

Hoping to get this right, he commenced: "Your Honor, this is Grizelda Hostler. She and her family live in New Holland. Her maiden name is Bontrager. She is the defendant's biological aunt. For almost three years of the defendant's childhood, Mrs. Hostler served as his caretaker. The boy was sheltered and raised in her house. He was brought up as one of the family's own . . . It was only when Benedictus Bontrager had become a minister that the boy was returned, by council decree, to his father's home. Ever since, Mrs. Hostler has pushed—often to the scorn of her whole community—for her nephew's removal from the Minister's custody. She claims to have personal, firsthand knowledge of numerous attacks on the boy by his father—including being struck with a shovel, and even branded with a red-hot fire poker—along with dozens of senselessly drunken beatings which couldn't be deemed excusable. In light of all of this information, Your Honor, I propose the following: obviously, this case will have to be tried within your chambers in due course. With no disrespect to the victims intended . . ." Yoder turned to the crowd of parents and students, nodding. "All of whom will see their complaints addressed, to be sure . . ." He turned back to Percy, ". . . something will have to be done with the defendant in the meantime . . . As you know, I myself work with juvenile cases. We provide treatment and counseling programs. We also provide emergency housing—on which point, in this case, a far more effective alternative to prison is available already—and in my opinion, warranted, sir. That is to say, with your compliance: Mrs. Hostler might assume temporary guardianship of this young man. I myself could thereby work with him on an immediate, one-to-one basis. A community service assignment might be arranged. There are many options. But prison, Your Honor, should not be one of them. If, indeed, as the adage contends, "The bias of the father runs on to the son," then this young man is in need of treatment. Affording him less would be criminal negligence."

As Yoder rested his case, an unexpected calm settled over the courtroom. Amazingly, no objections went up. Stutz appeared resigned to the fact that this wasn't to be his day in court. Gerald Metzger, too, seemed oddly moved by Yoder's testimony. Even the white suburban parents along the wall were strangely quiet.

At length, having reached a decision, apparently, Percy exhaled and sat upright. Before speaking, he dabbed his brow with a handkerchief. Then he lowered his gaze to Yoder.

"Counsel, perhaps against my better judgment, I'm going to grant your request."

A whooping cheer went up from the group of Plain Folk seated behind the defendant.

"Quiet!" Percy hollered, waving his gavel—thrusting it, *jabbing* it toward them.

He almost looked ready to call out the bailiffs.

Scowling, he turned back to Yoder and resumed his ruling. "As I said, I'm going to grant your request. But on three conditions."

Jarret nodded.

"First, the defendant will remain confined to house arrest on the property of Mrs . . ."

"Hostler, your honor."

"Mrs. Hostler. Any attempt to leave the premises without due clearance will annul this ruling. Understood?"

Having expected as much, Yoder nodded. "Understood."

"Second, the defendant will wear an electronic ankle bracelet, by which his location might be determined. Any attempt to remove the device will result in immediate incarceration."

Again, Yoder nodded. "Agreed."

"And third: I want detailed notes on this young man's progress in therapy—as conducted by you, Mr. Yoder—delivered to my office on a weekly basis. Breach of this agreement will result in a ninety-day suspension of your license to practice law. Are we in accord on all of the above?"

"Absolutely, Your Honor," said Yoder.

Percy picked up his gavel. "This trial is scheduled for Tuesday, November 16th at one p.m. Arraignment dismissed."

As the crowd rose, Jarret Yoder stood and shook his head in disbelief. In fifteen years, he had never handed Stutz a more decisive whipping. In truth, he had only argued the bastard to a standstill on four or five occasions, and less, only once or twice, had he actually come out on top by a clear margin.

As the Orderlies huddled around him in gratitude, grinning, then quickly surrounded Ephraim, and Metzger faced the tempered wrath of the quietly nervous victims' parents, and Mrs. Hostler, openly sobbing with joy, thanked him over and over, Jarret Yoder regretted only that Jack wasn't there to share in the moment.

It wasn't as a journalist that Owen got caught up in traffic en route to the Heritage House. In theory and practice, he was no longer flogging his wares in the field of reporting. The tapestry falling together at last would find no place in public print. And the truth, he felt certain, would only get stranger. The scanner served to assure him of that . . .

The whole way down 30, he tried to make sense of the drama unfolding on Channel Twelve. Seven men had been apprehended dousing the walls of the gym with accelerants. The building was unmarked; that was the good part. Everything else just fueled the confusion: mentioned among the raiding party's principle members was someone named Bontrager. Owen had trouble placing the name until, out of the static, a dispatcher relayed the fact that this Bontrager's son, one Ephraim, had also gotten in trouble downtown. He'd just been picked up for "grievous assault" and was presently being arraigned at the courthouse.

Now he made the connection, did Owen: that rampaging Amish buggy driver . . .

Another familiar name on the page—and, for that matter, one more reminder that, yes, the truth belonged in a padded cell.

It was dark by the time he pulled into the lot. Leaving the glare of oncoming traffic, he parked, got out and ran to the building. It was open, thank God. One more hour.

A tiny old woman was seated behind the front desk, next to a postcard stand. The skin was hanging off of her bones. She looked like a prune. A Mennonite prune.

The walls were lined with books for sale. Handmade quilts were on display in a case. Down the hall to the right, a sign hung over a staircase: "Library in Basement."

Owen bought a ticket and went down. A door led into the reading room. A row of tall, aluminum off-gray bookshelves spanned more than half of the floor. The rest was an open seating area, set against glossy, whitewashed brick. Two individuals were sitting at tables—one, an older portly man with his nose pressed into a big black book, the other, a pale young waif in a bonnet and second-hand Pumas, reading a paper. Neither paid Owen any mind as he draped his jacket over a chair. Soon, he would look up to find them gone—both, it would seem, without making a sound.

The shelves were packed with books of every size, shape, age and condition: modern, updated historical texts, original maritime passage logs, hundreds of genealogical volumes, district records and family studies, countless editions of *The Ausbund,* the *Regel and Ordnung* and other prayer-related books, sailing charters, land deeds, birth and death certificates, tax records, court records, service records, diaries, memoirs, maps, accounts and letters . . . This was the most comprehensive base of data on the Pennsyltucky Dutch in existence: available information on every acknowledged Anabaptist in history, including all Amish, Mennonite and Hutterite residents of Stepford, from past to present—as well as a good many (thousands) of non-Anabaptist families who had emigrated either from the Rhine/Palatinate region of Gemany or Switzerland during the eighteenth, then mid-nineteenth centuries.

All of this, Owen was given to understand by way of a free brochure.

With his pulse in a flutter, he walked to the wooden card catalog along the wall.

He found a drawer with a faded label reading "STA—SUR." He opened it and started flipping through cards. Not surprisingly, the surname Stumpf filled a third of the drawer. There were dozens of entries, and even a couple of Stubbes to boot. But no Jack in the lot. And only one Jacob, d.1905. Long deceased.

Having expected as much, Owen moved up a couple of drawers to the label reading "SI—SPO." Similarly, half of the drawer was filled with Speichers. But this time, some Jacobs appeared—too many, in fact: the total number of listings came to forty-one. A brief examination revealed that, of that figure, thirty were listed as having been born in the twentieth century—ten of whom had died before '74. Of the twenty remaining, three were under the age of thirty, four were over sixty, one was in Utah, five were in Indiana and three were scattered through Ohio. The rest lived somewhere in Stepford County. Jacob Abraham Speicher (b. 1953–) was a resident of Stasburg, a shoe smith by trade. Owen took note of his reference number. Jacob Berman Speicher of Bareville (b. 1947–) was listed as belonging to District Sixteen. Owen wrote that down, as well, though the card appeared newer, updated, maintained. Neither seemed very likely as, first, Jack's middle name was (allegedly) Ezekiel, and second, both cards made reference to current religious or trade affiliations—*un*like the last two names, which included no middle initials and no occupations. The first was a Jacob Speicher, b. 1952, of New Holland. No occupation. No listed baptism . . . Only a reference number: volume 21 of *The Pennysyltucky Dutch Unabridged.* Duly noted . . . The second was Jacob Pfaff Speicher (b. 1941–) of 249 E. Lime St., Stepford, downtown. A definite possibility. But that would put Jack at fifty-two . . . And Jack was an early forties, at best. As well, he didn't live on Lime Street.

Uncertain, Owen noted the family research volume number anyway. Then he turned to the line of bookshelves, going, on a hunch, for the dead man from New Holland. 1952 sounded right . . .

Volume 21 of *The New Holland Pennsyltucky Dutch Unabridged* sat at eye level, deep in the fourth row of books. The series of fat, hardbound volumes took up nearly a third of one bookcase—four and a half shelves, in total. A place to begin, however daunting.

With trembling hands, Owen reached for the book. It peeled from its slot with the crackle of hardbound covers clung together with age. Curious, he checked the copyright date. The series was less than ten years old. It hadn't been used much. Or maybe the place just needed a dehumidifier.

Owen continued by finding the Lime Street Jacob Speicher's family tree: a slender paperback that didn't look promising. It spoke for itself on the opening page: "How My Father's Life in Mechanics Gave Birth to the Speicher Ford Dealership," by Jack F. Speicher, senior president. The man was a Lamepeter car salesman . . .

Having determined as much, Owen picked out an empty table and had a seat. He placed the unabridged volume in front of him. Squaring off, he fixed his gaze on the cover. He opened to page 610.

As expected, he came to a genealogical tree, as represented here in the literal: vertical lines and horizontal dashes connecting minuscule blocks of dense, almost microcalligraphic print, each of which indicated a given member's name, date of birth and address. It made for extremely rugged deciphering. Owen had already strained his eyes to their limit before something caught his attention—but not the name of Jacob Speicher. First, he discovered (amazingly not overlooking) one Ephraim Elias Bontrager, b. July, 1975.

There he was again. There was that crazy kid who had charged the Sprawl Mart wagon—the kid who was now in court downtown . . .

According to the chart, he was the son of a Benedictus Daniel Bontrager, (b. 1946–) of Bird-in-Hand (who must have been the one arrested for trying to burn down the gym that afternoon) and Maria Elanore Speicher Bontrager (1951–1975) of New Holland . . . Panning to the left horizontally, Maria Bontrager, b. Speicher, was seen to be one of three children born to Devon Speicher (b. 1927–) and Emma Louise Stutzman Speicher (1928–), both listed as current residents of Birdseye, Ohio. From right to left, it read: first, Maria, then Aaron Daniel Speicher (1953–) of Cedrick County, Iowa, and last, Jacob Ezekiel Speicher (b.1952–).

That was it.

Returning his attention to the diagram, Owen was overwhelmed by the family's size: Jacob Speicher had seven uncles and at least forty cousins, all of whom were represented as tiny, floating, sometimes overlapping blots of information—each wired into a larger, darker, overhanging penumbra of forebears. Even when limited solely to the patriarchy, tracing it back more than three generations without the aid of a magnifying glass presented a lengthy, exhausting task. As well, the volumes contained very little or no biographical information. Most important, Owen didn't have enough time. He returned to the card catalog.

After a good deal of flipping, comparing and ruling out names by date of birth, he settled on two of four possibilities, both in the form of family studies: the first compiled by a Katie Speicher of Turbon, Indiana, from 1968: "The Speicher / Mueller Connection," which, it turned out, traced a parallel (not directly related) branch of the namesake back to the purchase of a ninety-acre land deed in Chester in 1807 . . . The second was dated 1930, and compiled by an Elton Abraham Speicher (b. 1870–). Following his reference number, Owen opened the book to page 17, and there, discovered that Elton Speicher had twenty-five grandchildren, among whom, of seven siblings in the eighth and youngest generation, was a Devon Speicher, b. 1927, of New Holland.

That was Jack's grandfather. Devon of New Holland.

Every lead continued to score . . .

Elton Speicher, one of seven children born to John Speicher (1832–1910) and Catherine Shiffer Speicher (1845–1907), was raised on the family's 243-acre estate in Old Conestoga, outside of Stepford. Their house had been built in 1759 by Elton's great-great-grandfather, Johann Speicher (1731–1810), and had remained in family hands ever since. Back through the years, it had hosted a good many operations: from cider production / orchard farming under John and Catherine Speicher and family, to a dairy farm under John's father, Jonah Speicher (1800—?), and mother,

Ella (b. Lutz), to a sawmill under Jonah's father, Deacon Baltzer Speicher (1764–1850), who had started as a blacksmith in carriage repair, but later followed in the path of his father, Johann, an architect and carpenter by trade.

In 1759, Johann had purchased the land and erected a two-story house on the banks of the Conestoga River. There, he settled with his younger brother, Meldrick, and his infant half-sister, Josefina, who was under the care of his widowed grandmother, Susan Bechtel Speicher (b.1680), all of whom had survived and been misplaced by a random attack of "savages."

This was the last of a once-great family.

Heinrich Speicher (b. 1680) had succumbed to pneumonia during the transatlantic voyage from Rotterdam to Penn's Woods. His grandparents, Amos and Gwendolyn Speicher (b. 1635 and '37, respectively), had grown up in the town of Landau, in the Rhine/Palatinate region of modern-day Germany—one of the earliest havens for fugitive Swiss Anabaptist refugees. The colony's settlement had been fraught with peril. The second half of the Thirty Years' War (1618–1648), which, in the end, would claim over 40 percent of Germany's population, had devastated most of the area. Catholic and Protestant forces had plundered the land, razing and killing, continually. Then, with the signing of the Treaty of Westphalia (1648), which forced all citizens of Germany to declare a religion—even though the choices were restricted to Catholic, Lutheran or Reformed on penalty of exile, imprisonment, torture or death—the Anabaptists, lumped in with the Huguenots, Walloons, Witches, Muslims and Jews, were branded "sectarian," i.e., heretical: enemies of both the church and state. Such persecution, adding to the already untold misery of warfare and plunder, would then lead to seasons of plague and famine. All over Germany, once-fertile homesteads were pillaged by hordes of starving indigents.

This was the world in which Amos and Gwendolyn Speicher had grown up. For their children, the hardships would only continue—through the War of the Palatinate, during which the region was laid to waste again, through a pestilence that claimed several family members, through hunger, lawlessness, murder, religious persecution and untold miseries plaguing the *"God-awful shadow of Europe"*—a shadow which they would eventually escape at the beck and behest of William Penn, but only after twelve weeks of *"living hell"* on a charter ship across the Atlantic, during which not only Heinrich Speicher, but two of his children, one of them newborn, would die of pneumonia and be tossed overboard—followed by seven *"beastly"* years of servitude in a labor colony (a *"hive of malfeasance, evil and shame"*) before ending up on a farm in the borough of Northkill, where at least they could practice their worship legally, only to lose the property and half of their family during the Seven Years' War . . .

In her diary's final entries, Susan Bechtel Speicher (d. 1761) lamented a lifetime of woe. She looked to her coming death and to meeting her maker with weary and wavering hopes—hopes that, as Jacob Amman taught, she and her kin had been chosen to suffer, thereby securing their place in eternity. In eighty-one years, she had lived through greater turmoil, adversity, fear and sorrow than anything faced, in the narrator's words, by all but "her fugitive Swiss forebears."

Of course, those forebears weren't listed here. Susan's maiden name was Bechtel. The chances of finding them elsewhere, Owen had to assume, maybe wrongly, were slim. But her husband's ancestry, the peers of those fugitive Anabaptists, had been recorded—although in ever-diminishing detail the farther back in time they stretched. Notwithstanding the lack of firsthand accounts predating 1690, Elton Speicher's historical recap of Anabaptist survival in Europe upheld the narrator's claim as per even more wretched adversity faced by their forebears. During a time of famine, Amos's father, Emmanuel Speicher (1614–1653), had been shot along with sixteen "accomplices" for stealing and eating hay from the city. All but nine years of his turbulent life was spent tending the fields between warring armies.

His father, Joseph Horace Speicher (1584–1657), was among the earliest Anabaptists to flee Switzerland, and to settle north, in the

Rhine/Palatinate. Having escaped persecution in Bern, where most of his family had been disinherited, jailed, tortured, killed or driven out, he wound up in Landau. There, as the Treaty of Westphalia hadn't pronounced his people "sectarian"—*yet*—he joined the small, devout community of Anabaptists, the Troyer Colony—named for Deacon Hanz Troyer. Joseph Horace Speicher had worked as a farrier (a smith who shoes horses) by trade. He had lived on a sizeable plot of land that was shared between several extended families. In 1610, he married a woman described as "having escaped persecution in Bedburg prior to joining The Order." That woman (b. 1587) was listed as Clara Ava Stumpf.

Owen was already moving to push himself back from the table the moment the door behind him swung inward, sounding a buzz.

He fell off his chair with a terrified start. His head hit the backrest. He rolled with the impact.

Freezing, a middle-aged woman appeared in the doorway, looking down on him fearfully.

He *must* have been The Chosen One.

The woman stepped back. She looked ready to run.

Owen got up, spewing bitterly. "What do you *want*?"—more shaken than angry.

Braced to flee, she spluttered, "It's . . . our . . ."—steadily edging into the stairwell. Owen noticed her hairnet. Jesus.

She worked for The Prune. She was a Mennonite.

He rubbed his head in humbled annoyance. "Have you got something to say?" he asked.

She trembled. "We're closing in fifteen minutes."

He looked at his watch. It was 7:15 . . .

She was already gone when he looked again.

Still rubbing his head, he picked up the chair.

Everyone plays the fool.

Sometimes.

He returned to the Speicher log. Again, the name leapt out at him: Clara Ava Stumpf (1587–1622)—just as he'd dared to imagine it might, yet even more unexpectedly, somehow.

Owen wiped the sweat from his brow. He took a deep breath and continued reading.

The Troyer Colony Roster, printed in full in the study's closing pages, confirmed Clara's—and one other Stumpf, her mother, Helga's—church membership. Both women had been baptized in 1608. And both had come from the town of Bedburg.

The overall portrait of fact, conjecture and myth was now coming into focus.

As a documented fact: Peter Stumpf, or Stubbe, was executed in Bedburg.

As a myth, he was a bloodthirsty werewolf.

Conjecture provided for three possibilities:

One: the condemned had been innocent, and therefore a victim—effectively lynched by an ergot-blown, psychotic horde of Protestant villagers: someone whose case, for reasons unknown, presently lived in inordinate infamy.

Two: the condemned had committed mass murder: a sixteenth-century Jack the Ripper, of sorts: a frenzied libertine / sexual predator / cannibalistic degenerate sentenced to burn at the stake for his crimes.

Or Three: Peter Stumpf had, in fact, been a "bloodthirsty werewolf," a devil, a Blighted One . . . Which would have meant that, as much as Owen cherished regarding the age of Luther as one of wholesale paranoia, at least one case in an estimated thirty thousand executions was *not* fully innocent.

Fact: by parish record, his daughter and mistress were put to death along with him.

Fact: no mention was made of the child allegedly begat by Stumpf and his daughter, nor of the sister with whom he'd engaged in "carnal, unholy relations daily."

Fact: Clara Stumpf was born in the town of Bedburg in 1587.

Fact: Peter Stumpf was beheaded in the town of Bedburg in 1589.

Fact: the town of Bedburg was located in the province of Westphalia, forty miles north of the Rhine/Palatinate's border.

Conjecture: Helga of Bedburg was actually Peter Stumpf's sister and concubine.

Conjecture: in the wake of Peter's arrest, Clara Stumpf, as an infant, was smuggled out of Bedburg by Helga, her aunt.

Conjecture: lucky to escape with their lives, they took to the forests as wandering fugitives.

Fact: Helga and Clara Stumpf were baptized in Landau in 1608.

Fact: they were listed as having evaded persecution in the town of Bedburg.

Fact: Landau was set in a wooded stretch of the Rhine/Palatinate region.

Deduction: as fugitives, Helga and Clara, the latter under the care of the first, had wandered the woods of the Rhine/Palatinate hiding from church and state authorities.

Fact: in light of their situation, as well as existing political, religious and economic conditions in Germany, the Anabaptists, specifically, would have provided both Clara and Helga Stumpf with their clearest, if only, sanctuary. Both would have been baptized as adults. Both would have married and changed their names. And both would have then assumed the guise of pious Anabaptist wives.

Fact: Clara Stumpf married Joseph Horace Speicher in 1612.

Synthesis: three hundred fifty years later, a member of their fourteenth generation of descendants, Jacob Ezekiel Speicher, ran amok in Pennsyltucky—whether in jest or outlandish earnest—reviving belief in an ancient "curse," a phenomenon known as "The Time of the Killing," while spawning, at once, a new urban myth—and passing it on for reenactment . . .

Question: but passing it on to whom?

Answer: someone within the family.

That was Jack's excuse, wasn't it? "Family matters"?

Owen stopped.

Family matters?

He looked at his watch.

Damn it.

He should have gone to the courthouse . . .

He looked at the pile of books on the table. He would just have to come back for them later: he'd never be able to sneak them past The Prune without busting a seam in his trousers. As much as he hated to leave this material out in the open where someone might find it, he just couldn't bring himself to steal it . . . Besides which, the footsteps now coming down the stairs sounded unmistakably male: probably a janitor fetched by the stammering middle-aged woman who worked for The Prune.

Owen pulled on his coat, gathered the text and walked back into the aisles. He was drenched in sweat. With trembling fingers, he placed each book in its slot on the shelves. And none too soon, it appeared, either: as, moments after the door had buzzed, most of the lights on the ceiling went out. Only a single, low-watt bulb in the middle of the reading room glowed dimly.

Typical Stepford bullshit, that: instead of announcing *"Closing time!"* the janitors (even the service staff was frosty) would sooner play dumb and, afterwards, once it was obvious, *inconvenienced.*

"Hold your water!" Owen grumbled, annoyed.

Anal, queeny bastards.

He emerged from the aisle and followed the length of the catalog back across the room. While cutting through the darkened maze of tables, he spotted a figure in the doorway—a man with his features obscured. A very large man.

Owen slowed down. A prickle of fear shot through him. The oxygen caught in his throat.

Exhaling in clear exasperation, the man stepped into the light.

It was Jack.

When Fannie arrived at the Intercourse Market at seven o'clock, it was nearly empty. The auction building was cold and drafty, providing for no more than twenty-five persons. Jan Pratt was up on the block, bidding away a crate full of chickens. The crowd before him consisted primarily of English farmers and livestock merchants. Jonathan wasn't among them; Fannie determined as much with a cursory sweep. She found herself standing alone, for the most part, if flanked by a few familiar faces. On one side, Jonas Kachel, who'd hosted the district's last, ill-fated service, stood grinning toward her, seeming at peace with his lot in life as a miserable wretch. While, down the row, Horace Grabers and David Ziegler were muttering grimly—neither, by any account, more miserable, though lacking all pretense of neighborly love. Between them, a dwindling mob of English bidders accounted for worldly prospects. Fannie felt out of place among all of them. She couldn't relate to a soul in view. To her eye, life with the Zieglers or Kachels was no more feasible than leaving The Order. Yet, for as far back as she could remember, these had seemed like her only options. Sure, there'd been *Rumspringa,* during which time she had gotten a chance to loosen her bonnet. But *Rumspringa,* finally, had served to compound her overall sense of isolation. Very few of her daily associates seemed to share in that isolation. If one thing linked her, indissolubly, to Jonathan, it was their genuine piety—their steely, unwavering Christian faith—from out of which, all blessings had flowed. In ways, it had set them apart from their peers. To be sure, it had set Jon apart from the Crossbills. *And* it distinguished them, both, from Ephraim.

By nature, they truly belonged in The Order.

As much as she cared for her cousin, Fannie was certain his faith in God had been compromised. (For that, she blamed her uncle in full.) The same applied, for different reasons, to a good many members of District Seven. Yes, Bishop Schnaeder, and others, were there. But they had been steeped in opposition for longer than Fannie had been alive. Only in recent days had the Bishop made clear his intention to break with the church.

This turn of events had been loaded with paradox.

Whereas fear of The Devil had cast a shroud of gloom over much of The Basin, Fannie and Jon had been given a glimpse of a brighter life in the days to come. Out of this ordeal, she had assumed, at least the district would be reconfigured. Whole new assemblies would come into being, and one of them, Bishop Schnaeder's, was sure to be suited ideally to Fannie and Jonathan. They would remain in the fold, as intended. All they had to do was survive this season . . .

But first, they had to get through tonight. Which hadn't gotten off to a very good start.

Having defied her mother's orders, along with taking the bait from Gideon, Fannie had come to the market to find, by way of a shrug between sales from Pratt, on the block, that Jonathan wasn't working. He had already left the market. He had withheld his plans from Fannie—having said he would be there till after eleven. Were she not entirely clear on his rationale, she might have felt betrayed. But she knew that his highest aim, in this case, would have been to spare her excessive worry. She trusted Jon as only his *verschproche* might, and with understanding.

Still, she would give him hell when she found him. *Provided* she found him without any trouble.

Standing with David Ziegler, Horace Grabers had spotted her, and the two were now glaring. Fannie's appearance had halted their conversation. They were fed up with the Hostlers.

She nodded to Pratt before turning away. Then she walked down an aisle, overshadowed by empty crates on either side. Behind her, a halfhearted bidding contest had begun. Pratt's auctioneering resounded, filling the vacant expanse of the building. It faded away as she passed through the exit.

There weren't enough people outside, in the parking lot, to justify the overhead lighting expenses. A couple of funnel cake stands were still open, and two or three vendors were milling about. Otherwise, it could have been midnight in Ronks—save for the hum of distant traffic. Indeed, as Fannie had already noticed, the roads were congested throughout The Basin. Beyond the sprawling expanse of asphalt, 342 was a blur of activity.

Fannie's buggy was one of three Amish wagons tied to the hitching station. She stopped to untether her father's pacer. The sound of music caught her attention. She glanced out over a field of corn that bordered the lot to a bluff in the distance. The lights from a Lutheran church's steeple were visible, etched on the darkened horizon. The congregation inside was singing. Fannie could hear them clearly now.

For a moment, it brought to mind Jonathan's voice. And, as such, she was instantly captivated. Jon could do things with his voice that most people could only dream of.

Unlike Ephraim.

As quickly, (on that note) her stomach dropped. She was soon overcome by the insistently nagging dread that had plagued her all evening: a feeling that something was terribly wrong—that a travesty into which she was bound up inextricably hovered with imminent closure. She didn't know how to interpret the feeling, exactly—or, more so, how to believe it. Her only tangible sense was that someone would die tonight.

She had to find Jonathan.

Jack arrived back at the gym by 8:30, several hours behind schedule. Originally, he had planned to be out in the fields, concluding matters, by then. For a couple of reasons—including his personal safety—he'd waited until this evening. But, soon enough, he would overshoot moonrise, defeating the point.

He was terribly frustrated.

From the time he hit the plank at a clip out of Philth Town that morning, what would have begun as a hectic day had been complicated further by numerous unforeseen delays.

First, he'd been summoned by phone to the city precinct to talk about Franklin Pendle. Jack had already considered this matter settled a couple of days earlier. But, apparently, an Officer Bolton, who was new to the force, wanted firsthand confirmation. He'd needed The Coach to look over "the merchandise"—the gloves and equipment brought in from the pawnshop. For this purpose, Jack had been made to wait in the lobby for over an hour and a half. Franklin himself had been questioned already—and had insisted, as Bolton relayed, that Jack had given him everything—all of the goods in question—freely, as a "gift." If *not* corroborated, Franklin would be in Joseph's Hall in time for dinner.

Once The Coach had been called to the evidence room, he'd taken one look at the headgear and bag gloves—and even his busted portable—and thrown in the towel, more disgusted than heartbroken.

No more. Franklin was on his own.

Second, Jack had then driven to West Chester County to visit the farrier there, only to find that a bridle had been misplaced, transported to Downerstown. While waiting for a young man to fetch it (by buggy), Jack had remained in his truck, down the road. Originally, he had placed this order outside of Stepford County deliberately. Forty miles to the east, fewer questions were bound to be asked—and he wouldn't be recognized. Such had been his initial logic—but that had been back at the start of the month. By now, word of the blight had spread—to the point where Plain Folk all over the country, if not the world, were sure to be talking—all it would take would be one of the farrier's young assistants to shoot his mouth off, or one of the incoming Amish locals, or anyone, getting a look at the product, then asking who had placed the order—and what for—and God only knew what would happen.

Jack had felt fortunate once it was over.

Third, more alarmingly, he had returned to the gym to find it blown for a whirl. Three of the training room windows were shattered. The back door was nearly torn from its hinges. A sizeable patch of the outer wall had been torched, then hosed with extinguisher foam . . . Right away, Jack had thought of Blye. But then he had noticed the horse apples scattered and caked in the alley behind the gym—along with a wide-brimmed hat lying torn and dirty beneath the fire escape . . . And with that, he had realized that, just as he'd dreaded might come to pass one fateful day, The Crow had finally come to the city. An old suspicion of Jack's was confirmed: although he had never been listed in Stepford's directory, and never, excepting in recent days, gone back to The Basin for anything, he, as a coach, had garnered enough publicity over the years to alert even old man Bontrager, and many others, by the look of it, as to his whereabouts.

And if not, then Brynmor had filled them in.

And fourth (to speak of whom), the kid had been present and, in short, made a mess of everything. His jacket lay on the floor of the office—stinking of grass from across the room. A chilly draft had led Jack upstairs to the roof hatch, hanging wide open to the sky. Thus, the kid had made his escape, uninjured, presumably. No problem there.

But in covering his tracks around the office, he had failed to abysmal excess. Which might have been prompted in part by Yoder's message in Pennsyltucky Dutch. Given its content, Jack understood the intended rationale, as it were: normally, he and Jarret spoke German or Plain Folk only, if ever, in private—and as more of an arcane novelty than anything. In this case, however, Yoder had been more at ease with divulging specifics in code—which, ironically, had only spurred the Brynmor kid to investigate.

And that was exactly what had happened—as evidenced clearly by the other two messages, the first from a mumbling research assistant at the Stepford County Historical Society, who was phoning to "reconfirm" directions to the Amish Basin's Heritage House, the second from an angry-sounding lady at the paper: (*"Don't ever call here again, you asshole!"*)

After he listened through them, the messages started to fall into place for Jack. His dilemma shifted from catching up to *recovering,* and how to proceed—in what order . . .

Finally, he had placed a call to Yoder. But Yoder's phone was down temporarily. Ridiculous portables never worked . . .

He looked at his watch. It was seven o'clock.

He had to get down to the courthouse, fast.

He managed to ring through to Marty who, stupefied, promised to come watch the gym right away. It was strange that the whole place hadn't been sacked already. Marty was there when you needed him.

The courthouse was seven blocks away. It took longer to drive than it would have to run there.

Jack had arrived to find Percy at dinner. The entrance guards were unable to help him. But a passing stenographer had overheard their discussion, and done her best to summarize: the defendant had been released on house arrest. The details would come out on Monday.

Jack had then placed another call to Yoder, and left a message this time. What was the use of having a portable phone if you didn't leave it on?

Then he'd moved on to his second dilemma: the Brynmor kid. The Heritage House.

He'd managed to get there in twenty minutes. And none too soon: the place had been closing. Owen had been in the basement, prowling around in the aisles, the resourceful bastard. Jack had been ready to stand corrected for underestimating the kid. But not without giving him such a scare, he would dream in black and white for a month.

Forty minutes, an offer he couldn't refuse and a shocking enticement later and humbly, graciously, Owen had conceded to keep his fucking mouth shut.

Which, as it turned out, was easily assured: he had just lost his job at the paper.

Still, that wouldn't prevent him from snooping. And Jack could suffer no further intrusions. Owen would stop asking questions, for the moment. He would make no attempts to report his findings. Also, he would attend to the gym, as already discussed. No change in the deal . . . In return, providing he upheld his end of it, he would be let in on matters that surely exceeded his wildest flights of fancy—matters which, by himself, he would never be able to get to the bottom of. Whatever faith he may have placed in his own investigative prowess, Owen had scarcely begun to scratch the surface on this one, and *wouldn't* alone. The only way through to the marrow was Jack. But Jack, in turn, would have to demand unconditional, *total* cooperation.

By the end of it, Owen looked queasy, either with fear or relief—it was hard to tell which. He'd seemed to be overwhelmed completely. But he'd also appeared to understand, and be up for, the task and position assigned him. Not that he'd ever had much of a choice. Or so The Coach would've had him believe.

Jack had left him sitting there, white as a sheet, in his Subaru, staring at the diner where the two of them had just spent an hour talking. Jack talking. Owen nodding.

The Coach had pulled away from the parking lot, opening up on westbound 30.

By then, he'd been feeling nauseous himself. The medicine vial in his pocket weighed heavily. In twelve more hours, by early morning, he would've been cleared to resume his dosage. In the meantime, he needed all the help he could get. For the moment, he had to endure the fever.

To either side of the road, glaring electrical lights had flared in trails: billboards, traffic lights, lanterns on fences, a sign reading: "HARVEST SABBATH TONIGHT."

To think, he would live to see the day . . .

Nothing was sacred, not even the profane.

At least the training room door was fixed, or, in any case, momentarily barred. Marty had fashioned a row of sliding bolts to the door jamb. Solid enough. He was now at work on the windows, nailing boards over the top of the shattered panels.

Jack, having thanked him, was free at last to turn his attention to preparations.

The hatchback was ready, the locks and bars and chains—and the farrier's product—secured. He needed to take a last walk through the building—a final cursory sweep to confirm that he wasn't forgetting anything, or, more specifically, leaving it out in the open. Brynmor was scared enough, at the moment, to hold back from digging around too insistently. Of course, he would never sit perfectly still. That wasn't to be expected or asked. However, in light of certain prospects, already mentioned, the kid would cooperate. As long as nothing too blatant was left behind—down in the cellar or up on the wall—Jack could rest assured that Owen's briefing would unravel systematically.

Meanwhile, The Coach had to check his machine, fix the alarm, if needed, and get out.

Yoder's message began optimistically. His voice boomed out of the speaker in triumph.

"Jack, Jack, Jack . . ." He was laughing. "Jack. Hey. We did it! Jack. Come on, now, pick up the phone. You called."

A humming static silence followed.

Judging by Yoder's tone, The Coach almost braced for a burst of applause in the background. "Jack?" Again, the hum. Then, sighing: "God damn it. You need to buy a cell phone."

Why? thought Jack. *What good does it do* you?

Yoder continued, as though in reply. "I'm down at the courthouse. You just placed a call to this number . . . fifteen . . . minutes ago. I was caught up in signing release papers, sorry. Phones aren't allowed in the judge's chamber."

Jack refrained from breathing a sigh of relief just yet.

Yoder hadn't finished speaking.

"Here's the story—" He began to explain. "We brutalized Stutz. You should have seen it. Percy ripped him a whole new valve."

That, alone, was cause to rejoice. But what about the kid? What *about* those release papers?

Laughing: "He told him to shut up and sit down."

Come on . . .

"It was beautiful." Yoder coughed. "Excuse me." Clearing his throat, he finally got on with it. "So, then: the bad news is . . ." He faltered, catching himself. "Well, first, the *good* news—why rush matters, right?—(I'm killin' ya, right?)—The *good* news is: a restraining order went through against Senior. He's out of the picture. The kid almost murdered somebody today. Yet Percy took one look at him—Jesus, the state of him, Jack—you'd better be careful—Percy took one look and, I don't know—everything seemed to go our way." Yoder paused for a moment, then added: "And I daresay, I wasn't so bad myself."

With that, The Coach started loosening up. He still had a hard time believing it possible, but it looked as though someone had finally managed to snare The Crow by legal means. It would now be a matter of nailing him proper.

Still, Yoder wasn't finished. "The bad news is . . ."

And here it came.

"We didn't get custody. The reason being: he would have wound up in jail, guaranteed. I didn't even push for it: especially after his aunt showed up. The Minister's sister. What's she to you?"

Jack stopped breathing.

"Your sister-in-law, I guess. She, more than anyone, disabled Stutz. She might have been *the* deciding factor."

A cold panic gripped The Coach. He tipped back, wobbling—jolted with sweat. His heart boomed into the wall of his ribcage.

No, Jarret—please say you didn't . . .

"And not only that," he continued buoyantly. "She's willing to work with us, starting tonight. Man, she answered all our prayers. It's too bad you hadn't kept in touch with her. She could have saved us a lot of time."

No, Jarret knew nothing at all about—

"Grizelda Hostler, that's her name. The kid's under house arrest with her family."

Jack had never told anyone . . .

"We're due in court on the fifteenth."

He ran out the door.

PART FIVE

Put It Down

The whole way home, Ephraim squirmed in a feverish state of semiconsciousness—traffic lights panning across his field of vision in the backseat, his posture slumped, his ear cocked into Auntie's bosom, his forehead slick with perspiration. Gideon Brechbuhl was driving their Hornet. The passenger seat beside him was empty. The rest of the Crossbills were back in the city, having deferred to the Bishop's order: they would be finding another way home—if needed, by rail, or the public bus. Ephraim's condition was "top priority." He was running a fever, apparently.

Auntie mopped his brow and gently ran her fingers through his hair. He drifted in spells—here again, gone again—dipping in and out of awareness. Through every lapse, he was conscious of movement outside, rolling by in the early evening. 342 was alive with activity. Most of the bar lots were filled with cars. Children in costumes wandered the streets. And the ceaseless, glaring hum of traffic . . .

Turning south onto Laycock Drive, he spotted an outdoor fire in the distance. On either side, the backyard parties and cookouts and field bashes started appearing: the first of which showcased a pack of already stumbling Redcoats with microphones huddled behind a towering wall of speakers, one of them horning a four-hundred-decibel message across a field of stubble, beyond which glowed another fire, beside which stood more giant speakers and through which another pack of Redcoats bellowed back their replies. Above, what looked like a deep-sea emergency spot beam probed the underside of a choppily rolling shelf of clouds. More fires appeared along the horizon.

Around the next bend, a rock band was filling a crumbling barn with torrents of feedback. Dozens of pickups surrounded the building. Bodies were moving around in the darkness. Blankets of smoke wafted over the road.

The English had gotten started already.

Finally, the schoolhouse appeared up ahead. Gideon slowed to a stop by the fence. He got out, holding a leather bag, and opened the back door. Grizelda accepted his hand. She stood to position and turned. Together, they managed to drag a listless, sweat-soaked Ephraim out of the backseat.

Off to the north, a jagged, tree-lined escarpment was etched along the horizon. A low-riding shelf of cumulus clouds drifted over the sky, moving steadily east.

The hinge of a seesaw creaked in the wind. The light from a pole down the road cast a network of shadows across the facade of the schoolhouse.

Halfway up the stairs, supported by Auntie and Gideon under both arms, Ephraim began to find his legs. Once on the porch, he caught his balance, though still in a feverish, wobbling daze. Auntie turned to Gideon, bidding him leave. He bowed in quiet deference. He placed the leather bag at her feet, and without hesitation, backed down the stairs to the car, got in and started the engine.

Ephraim watched him drive away.

Kicking up spirals of dust, the Hornet vanished around a bend to the south.

Auntie unlocked the door. It swung in, dimly breaching a wall of darkness. The smell of hickory tables, candlewax, ashes and moldy books drifted out.

"Come, then, Fastnacht." Auntie motioned.

The term resounded in Ephraim's head: a relic from deepest, fading memory. That's what she'd called him. Before the fall—when Fannie had lain on the bedding beside him: *Fastnacht,* after the dough ball fried in lard and coated with powdered sugar. *"Hello, Fastnacht,"* Grizelda would coo, standing over their crib. *"Fastnacht Sweet."*

She closed the schoolhouse door behind him. She led him to a chair at the front of the room.

"Sit here," she spoke in Py. Dutch.

He did as she ordered, still wrapped in the blanket.

Grizelda placed her bag on a chair. Ephraim watched her root through a drawer of the wooden cabinet along the wall. The shelf above her was lined with Bibles.

On either side of the kitchen's door frame, iron candelabras were mounted. She lit the wicks and backed away. The wall before her glowed into focus: cabinets, fixtures, an alphabet chart . . . Next to the Bibles, a marble cross hung perfectly centered, lit from below.

As Auntie made for a kindling bin in the corner, Ephraim studied her movements. It was amazing to look on her now without any fear of retribution . . . Although she had never left his side, in spirit, she hadn't been there in person, in body, for almost fifteen years. In essence, they had been barred from—or otherwise terrified out of maintaining—contact. Being together, now, in this place, in this circumstance, unleashed a flood of images: learning to walk in the Hostler kitchen, stumbling, tripping and falling toward Auntie, his first attempts at speech with Fannie, a tractor ride with Abraham at harvest . . .

Auntie came back with a bundle of sticks. She walked to the woodstove and opened the door, then proceeded to break the wood into pieces and carefully place it inside, over straw . . . The flare of a match went up in her fingers . . . The flame brought her countenance into relief.

She was older now. Strands of gray jumbled out of her bonnet. Jowls were beginning to form.

Ephraim felt like he'd missed, or been robbed of, an age. The feeling was all too familiar.

The past few days had passed in a series of free-floating, grisly, disjointed episodes: moments of clarity buried in voids from which only occasional flashes emerged: like a stone skipping over the lake of fire: hours, whole evenings, were gone from his memory—with only abrasions and puncture wounds, adding to already torturous thirst, to show for it. And every awakening growing ruder, more violent, deeper into the fray than the last . . . As had been the case that very morning . . . He couldn't remember the night before—aside from a terrible scene in a toilet. But he *did* remember waking up. He recalled having come to his senses entangled in willow roots, lying beside a creek—bleeding from granules of lead in his backside. And running home naked he wouldn't forget. And digging his overalls out of the stable. And the state of his father's house, Jesus, Mary and Joseph . . . But after that, there was blackness again. Emerging from which, more horrible injuries. Onward, thence: to a moldy, floodlit shower room under the blast of a hose. Somebody taking his fingerprints, shoving him. Then the arraignment.

Or part of it, anyway.

Auntie closed the door of the woodstove. She stood up, turned and walked to the kitchen. The white of her apron ties faded to black, disappearing. A pump handle broke the silence. A gurgle of well water rose through the pipes, increasing in pitch. It splashed onto metal. The handle was pumped, again and again. A steel container was filling steadily. Drifting, the water thinned to a trickle, then cut.

Auntie emerged from the dark. She placed a pan on top of the stove. She drew the flap on the range beneath it.

"Now." She glanced to the bag on the floor beside Ephraim. Her eyes came to rest on him squarely. Candlelight flickered across her face, throwing overblown shadows against the wall. Her silhouette moved in distorted passes.

"You've been injured," she said. *"And you're running a dangerous fever. Take off your clothes."*

Ephraim stared.

He could no longer place any faith in his senses: treading the waters of reason while caught in a tailspin of harrowing sensual derangement. He couldn't distinguish between the illusions of sound, or of optical subterfuge. In his mind, Auntie had just announced (or guessed) that he had been wounded, shot. But that was something she couldn't have known.

Still, she appeared to be waiting for something.

Dispelling all doubt on the matter, she added, *"We mustn't allow for blood poisoning."*

After which, turning, she walked to a window and drew the blinds. *"There's too much at stake."*

He didn't know how to interpret that either.

"Quickly," she said.

He took off his shirt.

Looking away so as not to embarrass him, Auntie walked to the leather bag.

"And remove your trousers," she said while unzipping the bag and producing a towel and soap.

Ephraim removed his trousers, snaring one cuff on the plastic ankle bracelet.

Grizelda returned to the basin on the stove. She lifted and brought it around behind him.

Standing naked, his skin was an off-shade of gray now—with yellowish splotches of brown—and a patchwork of blood-crusted lacerations. Light glowed in from the roadside windows, touching on every abrasion and welt, every puncture, the gouge on his inner thigh, the hundreds of scratches all over his back—and the weeping, pitted, angrily swollen shot wounds marring his lower backside.

Auntie set the tub on the floor and got down on her knees. She reached into the bag. She pulled out a household medical kit. Ephraim sensed her fingers running on metal—on the polish of surgical instruments—followed by glass—a bottle: liquid (traces of iodine) splashed into fabric.

Water was wrung from a larger cloth. Then came a dab of liquid, the texture of fabric and, finally, a spear of fire.

Ephraim screamed.

Auntie gripped his leg and held it. *"Be still."*

He shuddered, clenching his jaws. The burning persisted. *"Verdammte Scheisse!"*

Auntie said nothing. The sound of his voice triggered no response. She didn't even flinch.

At last, the pain began to subside, settling now to a burning rash.

Ephraim wondered how Auntie had known about this—his condition, his festering wound.

Could talk of a shooting have reached her attention?

Had somebody sighted and drawn a bead on him?

Or had it been one of the city cops in the decontamination room? Had one of them spotted his injuries during the hosing and mentioned them, later, to Auntie?

None of these scenarios seemed very likely, yet none was discountably far-fetched either.

As for the sound of his voice not perturbing her, rumors could have been circulating.

Moreover, Auntie may never have placed any faith in his diagnosis to begin with. That is to say: she might not have believed he was mute in the first place—and so, not reacted.

Again, these explanations were feasible. But Ephraim had trouble believing them, somehow. Auntie had always known more, he felt, than anyone living might have suspected. There was an air of omniscience about her. Maybe, then, she could help him now.

But first, the lead shot would have to be dug from his backside. The tissue was badly infected. The pain to come would be nearly unbearable.

He leaned forward to grip the desktop. His fingers dug into the wood. He braced himself.

Slowly, she started working the tips of a pair of tweezers into the wound.

Locking his gaze to the floorboards, he held on in rigid suspension as, one at a time, a half dozen pellets were dug from his backside.

He almost vomited.

Forcing his mind back to Auntie Grizelda, he searched for an out . . .

While either he couldn't remember clearly, or hadn't been conscious for most of the arraignment, one specific remark by the juvenile attorney who'd represented him lingered: the reference he'd made to some unpronounceable madness running within the family.

What did that mean? The *Bontrager* family? Or did it have something to do with his mother?—his mother, about whom he knew so little, and most of whose family had moved away—with the rest thinning out to distant cousins from outlying districts. Virtual strangers . . . On several occasions in youth, he had seen them in wagons, exchanging words with his father.

He'd once met his uncle Aaron too. But Aaron hadn't seemed crazy at all.

Surely, there had to be some explanation. Auntie Grizelda might know what to make of it . . .

The final grain of shot was extracted. It plinked in a tray from the medical kit. Water splashed into the metal pan. The towel was wrung out again. Dabbing gently, Auntie washed his wounds with soap. She rinsed and carefully dried the skin. Then she applied more iodine. Once again, Ephraim winced.

The procedure was over.

Behind him, Auntie stood and continued dabbing his shoulders and back with the towel. "There," she mumbled under her breath, as though to say, soothingly, *Better, much better . . .*

She put down the towel, uncapped a bottle and began to rub his neck with oil.

He hadn't felt anything less disturbing, more soothing, since Fannie had held him last.

"Auntie?" he broke the settling calm. He spoke in German. *"Who was my uncle?"*

Her fingers lifted away from his skin. Ephraim sensed a flash of surprise in her. Slowly, he turned to regard her expression.

She looked surprised, if somewhat amused.

But before she could answer (or not) his question, a rumble of hoofbeats and carriage wheels pounding on asphalt sounded from down the road. A patrol was approaching. Grizelda shot to attention. She leapt to the candles and snuffed them. She doused the fire in the stove with water. Then she pulled Ephraim away from the window. She ushered him quickly into the kitchen.

There, they couldn't be seen from the windows.

She motioned to keep down.

They waited.

After a minute, three sets of wagon wheels rolled to a stop in the driveway outside. Shouting from carriage to carriage in Plain Folk. Footsteps advancing along the walk. The glow of approaching fire. Torches . . . Up on the porch now: silhouettes peering in every window. More voices behind them. Surrounding the house. Had they spotted the smoke?

Ephraim's heart was booming. A gouging sensation was tearing his brain to pieces. Auntie wrapped her arms around him. Gripping his temples, he choked back a scream.

Finally, the footsteps receded, retracing the path down the staircase, back to their wagons. Carriage wheels pivoting, steel on gravel, and off they rumbled: the glow of their torches shimmering past the schoolhouse windows—panning the ceiling in arcs of yellow, into which Auntie emerged from the kitchen. She stood by the window to watch them go. Ephraim, cross-eyed, stumbled behind her. He tripped on a table leg, fell to it, rolled over, belly-up, and clamped down, not letting go.

The blood in his veins had begun to boil. It felt like his spine was hyperextending.

A series of turbulent flashes commenced, each of them striking a cardio thunderbolt—booming cacophonic, fragmented crashes of falling timber and echoing foghorns—beaming erratically in between fire and blackness, the stench of decay and malevolence, deafening, blinding, burning his nostrils—whirling adrift in it, slipping away . . .

On coming to, he thought that a good deal of time had elapsed. Auntie was still at the window, but now she had opened the blinds. She no longer seemed concerned with the road patrols.

Slowly, she stepped away from the window and mumbled: *"We don't want to block your light."*

Again, it was such a bizarre remark, he had trouble believing she'd actually made it.

Along the horizon, a gentle glow appeared behind the retreating clouds.

Doubtfully looking him over, Auntie returned to the subject. *"You really don't know?"*

He shook his head.

Again, she appeared surprised, though not altogether amazed, by his incomprehension. Maybe she'd always assumed that community rumor had filled him in on this matter. Maybe she thought he'd been able to distinguish between fact and fiction.

If so, she was wrong.

At last, with an air of sardonic mirth, she went on: "I guess there's no harm in telling."

She took a deep breath and turned. Exhaling slowly, as though to say *"Where to begin,"* she proceeded from what he could only assume was the start, in a time when his parents were young . . .

The year before Ephraim's birth, it had been—when his mother Maria's beloved brother, Jacob, was called up for military service. As a member of The Order, his term had been delegated to public utility work. For many families, "road patrol," as this option was known, was no better than combat—as, even though young men were spared active duty (which wasn't at all to be taken for granted), their terms of service were such as, too often, proved wholly disastrous to life back home.

That was what had happened to Jacob.

Growing up, he had never been known as a menace. Not unlike most other boys, he'd been given to occasional acts of mischief.

But never had he gotten in serious trouble. The youngest of three, he was seen to have come from an upstanding, disciplinarian family; through proper rearing, he and his siblings had always been thought of as even-tempered.

The war would bring all of that to an end.

Less than a month before the "draft" (as the English referred to being conscripted) had been discontinued as a government policy, Jacob's number had been called up.

The whole situation had been absurd, said Auntie. The conflict had been almost over.

Nevertheless, he'd been ordered to service, pending a lengthy appeal in the capital.

Ten months later, he'd found himself pounding railroad ties with a traveling work gang.

For almost a year, he would live in a boxcar with ten other men serving terms of their own. By day, their labor would be demanding. By night, their hours had been twice as long. The only relief would come on the weekends, when most of the crew had been granted leave. Their meager pay would carry them into the nearest urban port of carousal. Familiar, already, with bottled spirits, the Orderly roadmen were soon falling prey to the worldly temptations of song and the flesh. For most of them, life in The Basin would not resume without definite complications. Some would find the transition impossible; dozens would leave the community thus.

Now, said Auntie (the rate of her breathing slowed with her carefully measured speech). *Now then,* she went on in Py. Dutch: *"Most of the stage had already been set . . ."*

On arriving home, unannounced, for a seven-day leave that autumn, Jacob—scraggly, unshaven, wearing a leather jacket and clipped with an earring—found himself up against not just the hazards of "decompression," as it was known—including an edict of social avoidance for breach of dress and lack of humility—he was to find out, at once, of his sister's engagement to Benedictus Bontrager.

Auntie paused to allow her narrative proper time to register for Ephraim. In silence, she walked from one end of the floor to the other.

Benedictus, she said, had been one the oldest bachelor males in the district. At least three women were known to have spurned his proposals of marriage—and more his advances. He'd been renowned as a drunken letch, the bane of an otherwise God-fearing family. In youth, he'd spent many years in transit, steadily moving around the region. Once his family had settled in Blue Ball, he'd already come of working age. He had landed a job in a livestock yard. Soon, he had left the home of his parents. He'd lived in a one-room cabin, alone, on an overgrown hillside west of Paradise. Grizelda, his newborn sister—his junior by fourteen years—would grow up in Blue Ball. He would have little in common with her. He wouldn't relate to her sense of grounding, her evident faith in object permanence. Matters of kinship would breed his resentment.

In time, he would drift away from his family. Auntie would never consider him kin. Neither would both of their younger siblings, who grew to regard him with muted contempt.

Ephraim's uncle, Jacob, for his part, had always distrusted Benedictus.

And *in that,* Auntie said, moving again, *he certainly hadn't stood alone . . .*

Even before the mill had opened, Benedictus, Grabers, Tulk and the Stoltzfi were rumored to have been involved in shady dealings with English farmers—matters so crooked, allegedly, so illegal, the church had refrained from addressing them. Likewise, Benedictus was known to have plied his trade at the Soddersburg market, a cattle yard widely renowned by area farmers for high rates of stock mortality. Many district councils forbade their members even to visit the grounds.

That being the case, a substantial number of Plain Folk resented the mills and their owners. Even though Jacob's parents may not have shared in that sentiment, they were outnumbered.

In time, he would learn to accommodate for their notable excess of gullibility. But he would *never* forgive them for allowing "The Crow" to so much as *look* at Maria, let alone for conceding her hand in marriage . . .

Auntie halted in mid-pivot, stopping to loom over Ephraim, her profile starkly etched in the yellow glow of the streetlights. Her posture was rigid.

Exhaling, she went on:

She and Maria, Ephraim's mother, had grown up together, one year apart. Their families had lived down the road from one another. Their parents had been members of Old District Seven.

Over the course of their childhood, Auntie had watched the uncanny bond that existed between Maria and Jacob develop.

In *Rumspringa,* even though she had been older (by two years, a critical leap in seniority), Jacob had cast a suspicious, disapproving eye toward her every suitor—even the older and bigger heads of the supper gangs—without fear of reprisal. It was a given that anyone sweet on Maria would have to contend with him . . .

One of his closest companions, at the time, had been Ephraim's counsel, Jarret Yoder—and no, the recurrence had not been at random. Now, as then, Yoder was clearly watching out for Jacob's interests. Just as he'd shown up in Percy's court that evening, armed to the teeth for battle, he had met Jacob at the bus station twenty years earlier, hoping to ward off disaster.

It would have been difficult for Jacob to process what Yoder had then been obliged to tell him. At first, he would've been hard-pressed to think that his friend might *dare* to be so rude. Even in casual jest, the notion of Bontrager's going anywhere near his sister would've come through as aggressively rude.

But, after a while, it would've been clear: Yoder, in fact, was telling the truth.

Whereupon, he would have been forced to explain how The Crow had moved in on Maria less than a month after Jacob had left The Basin. His parents, it would've come out, had been lured by the thought of a well-established suitor. They had approved of The Crow's designs on Maria.

That much, he might have processed.

But never could Jacob have thought to envision that Benedictus's every advance might have prompted other than Maria's scorn.

Neither would Auntie, for that matter. Likewise, most of their friends would disapprove. But try as they would, one and all, to dissuade her, something had gotten ahold of Maria.

By nature, Maria had never distinguished herself as naive. Nor overly gullible. In many ways, she had been keenly intuitive. The problem was: she'd also been a fool for love. Benedictus had seen this, and capitalized on it: his approach had been straightforward, simple, direct: flattery, diligence, patience, consistency and most important, coaxing her parents. If nothing else, a decade of spurned advances had taught him how *not* to proceed. By dint of elimination, at last, he would manage to hit on a working formula: gifts to the family, clean, untattered garments, perfect church attendance. And never forgetting to smile—not until marital vows had been exchanged. As hard as this might have been for Jacob, on hearing about it, to comprehend, it was something The Crow had been planning for years. The groundwork had all been laid in advance.

Livid, Jacob would have ordered his friend to drive him home at once. And after a year of pounding ties, he would've been no one to argue with. Yoder would have taken him through New Holland, past the gorge, to the Speicher lane—doing his best, all the while, to quell Jacob's anger with reason. To little avail.

This would account for Jacob's temper on showing up, out of the blue, at his parents' home. Said to have been in a spluttering frenzy, he'd frightened his mother "half to death" and even threatened his father with violence before running out of the house in tears.

Maria, *"thank God,"* had not been home.

By the end of the afternoon, Auntie continued, a long-haired, muscle-bound, bearded Jacob in denim, a T-shirt and dark sunglasses had been seen in the back of an English vehicle, looking the worse for wear and tear.

By dusk, he and Yoder—a young man said to have lost his faith in God already—had been spotted at a bar on Old Route 30, drinking themselves into blind confusion.

By midnight, they'd been arrested for public misconduct, then locked in a precinct cell. And, by morning, Jacob's district council was set to convene and rule on his case.

With nowhere to go, estranged from his family and penniless after their wild night, he would have been left with no choice but (as rumored) to sleep in a ten-acre plot of forest belonging to Jarret Yoder's uncle. For the first few nights, Yoder might have brought him blankets and food, and even kept him company. But nobody else would've known (or been sure of) his whereabouts. *Or* of his worsening condition.

However, once he had missed his date of return to the highways, that would change.

Within ten days of his last known appearance in Blue Ball, a pair of military officers had come around, asking questions at market. Rumors would circulate, rumors that Jacob had left the country, or maybe gone west. Members of District Seven would humor the officers, up to a point, with conjecture. But nothing would come of it. Eventually, they would be left with no choice but to go on their way. By early October, Jacob's fate would have been consigned to the great unknown—yet one more innocent lost to the war.

One week later, the killing had begun.

To start off, one of the Stoltzfi's layer houses had fallen under attack. A flock of hens had been ripped to pieces. No explanation would come of the incident.

Three days later, it would happen again. But this time *fifty-one* birds would be killed. A warning would quickly go up through The Basin: a mountain lion was stalking the poultry.

In days to follow, many acres of corn would be ravaged, uprooted and ruined.

Then, less widely acknowledged, Mary Ann Schnaeder, the Bishop's sister, had been assaulted by a "foul-smelling, devilish beast."

Over the course of the next weekend—all inside of forty-eight hours—three herds of cattle would be attacked, a goat would be mangled and left on the highway, a storage bin would be drained of corn and a "rabid bear" would be seen chasing traffic . . .

"Does any of this sound familiar?" Auntie spoke, interrupting the flow of images.

Slowly, she stepped away from the window. Something about her was different now. Her eyes were lustrous, wide, unhinging.

Behind her, the moon had appeared through a break in the clouds, washing over the tree-lined escarpment. The Basin glowed in a milky haze. It was radiant, luminous. It spilled through the window.

Facing it, Ephraim sat breathlessly comatose. Both of his arms were unresponsive. His body felt shackled, entombed and increasingly distant with every passing moment. He hadn't been conscious of Auntie's voice or diction through most of the preceding narrative. Even now, he couldn't rely on the testimony of his perceptions—i.e., her question, and his having heard it. All he could summon was one of his own. In German, with difficulty:

"Und meine mutter?"

Slowly nodding her head with a flexuous look of *now we're getting somewhere,* Auntie came forward. *"Yes. Your mother,"* she said. Her voice was palpable finally.

The floorboards groaned beneath her advance. *"Your mother was already living at home—in your home—when Jacob returned that autumn. Benedictus had bought the estate from the Nolts, who'd gone to Kentucky in April. His plan had been to move in as soon as he and Maria were wed in November. Meantime, she would attend to the house. Her mother would help her equip the kitchen. Her father would till and nourish the land, and her friends and relations would sleep in the back room.*

"For all of our apprehensions, Jacob would only appear on one occasion."

Auntie stopped to catch her breath. This seemed to be taking a toll on her nerves—her voice was cracking now, torn with sickening dread and what sounded like anticipation.

"Your mother and I were upstairs that evening. By rueful coincidence, Benedictus and Bishop Holtz were down in the cellar. The two men had been taking structural measurements. Normally, they wouldn't have been in the house. The timing couldn't have been any worse—as, at that moment, seemingly out of nowhere, a desperate cry had gone up in the woods. We ran to the window . . . We spotted him there—on the lane, at a hobble—approaching the house. He looked like nothing we'd ever seen—like a tortured ghost. He looked like an animal . . . Your mother let out a scream at the sight of him. At once, she ran for the door to go after him. But Benedictus barred her way. And when I intervened, the bastard hit me. Then he locked us both in a closet. Wailing, your mother collapsed in tears."

Auntie leaned forward: *"And that was the last we ever saw of the Jacob we knew. In his place"*—she settled her gaze on Ephraim firmly—*"days later, came forth your progenitor."*

Ephraim blinked in sudden confusion.

She drew in closer. Her breath smelled of blackening apples and vinegar. *"Yes,"* she said. The veins on her neck were like ruts in the candlelight. *"Yes . . ."* she repeated, and this time the word was drawn out as a hissing gaseous emission.

"I don't understand," Ephraim muttered.

Scarcely able to summon his breath, he rocked on the desktop. He felt like a giant, throbbing artichoke beached in silt.

"I don't understand."

Repeating himself . . .

Auntie closed in, beaming, exultant.

She seized his testicles, clamped down and *twisted.*

The jolt that tore from his thorax to every appendage so far exceeded all previous forays into the world of pain—a cross of electrocution, impalement and ratcheting steadily flush in a vice grip—the regents of hell would have squirmed in discomfort.

Auntie brutally wrenched his scrotum. Crying out, he fell to his knees. She wrung both hands. Her fingernails gouged him. Something popped. He went into convulsions. He felt himself losing control of his bowels.

Speaking out there, she was—hissing and warbling off in the storm.

What was she saying?

He couldn't distinguish her words in the hammering downpour of images flooding his mind. Panels of black and white now alternating to complementary colors: red, green—red, green—orange, blue—purple, yellow—purple, yellow—orange, blue—red, green—red, green . . . Increasing in frequency, slowly dissolving in tone and uniformity, darkening, withering, smoldering in from the edges: blossoming ringlets of cancerous black—out of which shades of light and movement began to materialize, gelling to form . . .

. . . through a hazy, vaporous, moonlit field sat the Bontrager home. His father's house. But the Minister didn't appear to be present. The place looked newer, less gone to the dogs . . .

The motionless figures of two young women stood, side by side, in the sitting room window. Staring across the yard, toward the forest. Something was out there. Beckoning, calling them . . .

Fade to black.

Return: both women in nightgowns, walking across the clearing, familiar somehow: both seeming absent within the moment—unconsciously driven . . .

Fading again.

Then there was jostling bulk in the grass—snorts and labored panting in time, a soft, impassioned gasp on the wind. Succeeded by steady, labored breathing . . .

More darkness.

The women, divested of garments—Auntie (and Mother?), impossibly younger—lying still on a bed of lilac . . .

Darkness.

Then a primal scream *. . . A torrent of deviant, carnal excess: requited in full, among three with abandon: two vestal maidens, one blighted pariah. The odor of sweat and ammonia, rancorous. Slapping of tenderized flesh on bone—and of writhing. And thrashing. And snarling. Fluids.*

Rapture: flaring to white-hot emptiness—out of which seed would take root in each vessel . . .

Ephraim, screaming, exploded from both ends.

And *now*—she warbled, out there in the maelstrom, her voice at a squalling, murderous hiss—*now, after so many years of silence, bearing the burden of knowledge exclusively, after an age's charade in The Order—at last, the cycle would be completed. With the sacrificial lambs of marriage and motherhood fully consigned to the task, the tragedy set into motion by Jacob years earlier would enter its final act. Tonight, the blight would be consummated. Tonight, the curse would come to term—though not by way of Ephraim's sister. No one would ever know about Fannie. Fannie herself would remain unsuspecting. The blight would never awaken in her. Auntie had seen to ensuring as much. Her daughter had been given every amenity, every security, growing up—a faith and a future within The Order . . . As Ephraim might have been given the same . . . But, through circumstance, Ephraim had been destroyed. There was only one purpose left for him: he alone would complete the cycle. All he required was a jolt to ensure it . . .*

"You pitiful bastard," Auntie spat.

She twisted his mangled scrotum a hundred and eighty degrees, then tightened her grip. She pitted one foot to his torso and *heaved* with all of her strength. He brayed like a hinny. A snapping of bone sounded, growing louder. All at once, the candles blew out.

A howl went up from Ephraim's throat.

At last, his testicles hardened and swelled in her grip. A blow to her jaw disengaged it. She fell to one side, hitting the floor.

Above her, the moonlight was blotted out suddenly.

Stumbling around in the dark, he was. Moving now. Painfully. Coughing and hacking, he shuddered, then turned on her.

"Fastnacht Sweet." She laughed.

With the riding gear straining and rumbling under his buggy the whole way out of town, Minister Bontrager lashed his reins across the back of the lurching pacer. The underfed animal, having been held in police impoundment, neighed defiantly. Cursing, the Minister lashed again. The leather held taut in his clammy grasp. His feet were moving, flopping around the trunk.

He had been in this state all day.

Just after dawn, on returning from the most tumultuous nightly patrol so far—a patrol during which the entire party had spotted The Devil in flight from the ridge of one bank along Hollander Pike, on the left, toward another, a full twenty yards to the right—suspended above their wagons, cutting across the moon in a lopsided profile, then dropping, vanishing, leaving the party below in a startled, hollering panic—he'd found his whole property littered with garbage, the waterwheel broken, the porch in shambles, the hinny, untended, wandering hungry, and the house siding blotted with streaks of paint.

Whereupon, he had taken leave of his senses, storming around the yard in fits. By eight o'clock, Jonas Tulk had appeared in a manner of no-less-livid duress. His pantry house had been burned to the ground. Both men cursed and spat in the dirt.

Within minutes, Emmanuel Stoltzfus appeared in his wagon, also raving and jabbering: someone had tossed a dozen empty field traps over the compound wire. The alarms had gone off, but Ezekiel Stoltzfus, guarding the building, had seen no intruders. Emmanuel insisted The Devil was taunting them, promising wrath in the hours to come.

Thereupon, joined by Grabers and Cleon, they'd set out for town to find the beast.

For years, rumors had been in circulation that, in fact, it was still alive—and, moreover, hiding in residence locally: several community members vouched to have spotted it prowling the streets on occasion.

Initially, talk of this kind had been somewhat predictable, given the subject in question. Most of The Order, at least in The Basin, dismissed it as baseless superstition.

However, on that matter, most of The Order knew very little about The Devil—including the name that it went by now. Only a handful of elders, among them Tulk and the Bishop and Benedictus, would have been able to recognize it. And normally, none of them would have been reading the English papers. The Ordnung forbade it. The month of October had been an exception only by cause of circumstance. At market, Orderly vendors had followed the daily coverage with vested interest. Too much stock had been in peril for all concerned, including the mill owners.

Earlier on in the week, Benedictus had spotted the article indirectly. Jonas Tulk had left the sports page out on a table to be discarded. The Minister, never intending to look at it, only caught sight of the photo by chance. The text verified it. And Tulk would concur: The Devil, dressed in street clothes, walking away from the camera as though in disgust.

It was older and bigger. Yet unmistakable. Benedictus would never forget: he had seen that face from his window, had barred it from entry, had turned it away at the door. The mark of the damned would remain with it always—the look of a blighted, contemptible wretch. Even when tempered by age, it was evident.

Now it was simply a matter of finding it.

By mid-afternoon, their efforts had paid off. An Orderly vendor downtown, at the market, on reading the article Tulk had presented them, pointed them west toward an athletic center.

Ten minutes later, Cleon Stoltzfus, the idiot, had set the building on fire. No one had seen him produce the gas can. Everyone else had been ramming the door. By dousing a patch of the outside wall, then lighting it, he had set them back hours. And, seeing how The Devil hadn't been in the building, their time in confinement had served no purpose.

Reviewing it now, while driving east on 342, getting closer to home, Benedictus was seeing the gravel-strewn shoulder ahead through a blood-red tint.

He was furious above all with Davin Stutz, who had shown up to represent them (late) unprepared, disheveled and oddly spooked. He looked as though he'd been beaten up. The Minister didn't know what to make of it. In fifteen years' worth of dealings, he'd never seen his attorney in such a state. Normally, Stutz would've been on a roll. He would've been storming the floor at a clip . . .

But not this evening, it seemed. Effectively worthless throughout the proceedings to follow, he never *once* consulted his clients. He never made eye contact with the judge. It seemed to be all he could summon to qualify three of the five men in question for bail.

In the end, he argued (without conviction)—and, once more, forgoing their consultation—that Cleon Stoltzfus and Ivan Grabers had succumbed to a "momentary loss of reason." His logic, by force of deduction, being: through placing the blame for the less circumstantially clear—and thus, more easily contested—charge of attempted arson on *two* of them, the others might be released for the evening. And somebody had to get back to the mill. It was now under the insufficient guard of the younger Stoltzfi, James and Ezekiel.

The three of them might have thanked their attorney for posting bail with his own money—as, otherwise, all of them could have remained in jail overnight, if not through the week. Benedictus understood that part. What he *didn't* get was why Stutz had been so ineffective, so utterly worthless in court: watching him mumble his way through their plea, frequently trailing off in midsentence, engendering awkward vacuums of silence while fumbling over his notes, had been torture.

He was sitting in a town car, parked across the street from the precinct, upon their release. Slowly, he got out and motioned them over. They waited for traffic, then crossed in a pack.

As they gathered around him, huddled in the shadows of the parking garage, Benedictus demanded: "What in the hell is *wrong* with you, Davin?"

Stutz, looking less than impressed, explained.

Then, after fifteen years, he dropped them.

Veering into the driveway now, the Minister stewed on his parting remarks. "If it weren't for the video footage, we might have a chance. My condolences, gentlemen. Good luck."

Their bail had been part of a "severance" package—a parting gift, an attorney's farewell.

Trying to piece it together was maddening.

Apparently, the boy had gotten himself into serious trouble that afternoon. And that atheist lawyer, that renegade Mennonite hippy, Yoder, had jumped right in. And so had Sister Grizelda, the trollop. And Bishop Schnaeder, to complicate matters. They had all gone before Talmud Percy, Lord deliver, early that evening. Foreseeably, Ephraim had been pronounced a "victim" of too much corrective zeal.

The irony there may have lay in the fact that, of late, the boy had been *under*disciplined. True, a proper thrashing had followed the superstore incident, naturally enough, but no further measures, aside from a public shaming in church, had been implemented. Aside from that, the Minister hadn't laid eyes on Ephraim for over a week. The boy had vanished. His obligations around the house had gone unperformed. The hinny had wandered into the forest. The tobacco that hung in the shed was ruined. The mail had been piling up for days, during which there had been no sign of Ephraim. And the Minister hadn't bothered to look for him, either. His time had been spent otherwise. By day, he'd been occupied guarding the mill, and by night, he'd been out on the road patrols. Surely, whatever condition the boy may have been in, at present, was self-inflicted.

But Percy, the bleeding heart, wouldn't have known that. And, as the arraignment that evening had played out, his vision might have been clouded the more.

Nothing was clear, as of yet—no clearer than Davin Stutz's report on the case, which included a felony bribery charge purportedly backed up by video footage.

Although, as the Minister understood it, Davin hadn't *viewed* that footage—hadn't verified its admissibility—he had, nonetheless, withdrawn in the face of the mere allegations presented by Yoder: namely, that Rudolf had taken a payoff in "cornhome" and District Seven's offerings.

Benedictus would never have thought to imagine that someone might catch them on film. The idea was so far removed from his scope of conjecture, he didn't know how to consider it . . . Someone (or something) had caught them on camera from one of the hotel windows. Was that it? The possibility dawned with increasing alarm on the Minister: it would've been easy. Those windows were twenty-five yards from the porch. That building had shadowed his house for so long that he often forgot it was even there. But it was. Assuredly. Anyone could have checked in and recorded their whole exchange.

But who in the world would have done so? And why?

The list of possibilities rolled.

Bishop Schnaeder was the first one who came to mind. There was simply no telling the measures to which he might opt to resort in "cleansing" the church. And again, according to Stutz, he *had* attended Ephraim's arraignment that evening.

Yet, supposing that he might have disregarded the Ordnung's stance on graven images, he still wouldn't know how to operate a camera. He wouldn't have known how to turn on the power. Years in Schnaeder's company told Benedictus it had to be someone else.

Grizelda, more likely. Yes: his sister. Deception had always been her greatest asset. In that, Benedictus himself had conditioned her: back in the years when he'd shown up to work in his parents' barn every Saturday morning—before he had fallen out of grace with them, back when Grizelda was only a child and could never remember—(*could* she?)—or attempt to resist though he might picture it now—she had followed him into the stables, and down through a hatch in the floor to the lower pens, through the shadows—he'd never forgotten—and into the corner, and down on her knees in the straw to where not crying out was rewarded with candy, and keeping her mouth shut was bartered in shame.

Thus, he had taught her the fundamentals of telling and thinking and living the lie.

And now she was using them all against him.

Was that it?

She certainly loathed him enough. As well, there was nothing she wouldn't have done for the boy. And she wasn't hung up, technologically.

No, he wouldn't have put it past her. But he wouldn't have put her *up* to it, either. Grizelda, beyond all the bluster, was not that resourceful. In truth, she was palpably dense. She wouldn't have thought to stake out the house with an English camera. Not as described. She might have *done* it, upon suggestion—but she wouldn't have thought of it. That much was certain. It had to be somebody else.

Beaumont?

No.

Unless he had been undercover for years, Rudolf was out of the question.

It might have been somebody out for his badge, though. Another policeman. Or maybe an activist.

Either prospect was bad enough—as Beaumont had never maintained any loyalties: one sign of trouble, and he would've cracked. He would have turned them all in on a dime—even though turning them in, in this case, wouldn't have cleared him of his own involvement. No, he wouldn't be able to worm his way out of this mess: not before Percy . . . It had to be somebody other than Rudolf. And probably not a cop, for that matter. The cops would never have handled it thus. He wouldn't be coming up, now, as an accessory—and not in a pending domestic case. At this point, Rudolf was one more culprit snared in a widely expanding net. He would pay, dearly, along with the rest of them, once his role in this matter was public. But Counselor Yoder would never allow him to cloud the prosecution's objective. Yoder was after the Minister, first and foremost.

Yoder was after him.

Why?

No matter how he stacked it, the picture still didn't fall together logically.

For one thing, Yoder had never gone after the mill. He may have done battle with Stutz, on occasion, but never with Benedictus. No grudge, to speak of, existed between them. Even though Yoder had grown up Plain, the two men were unacquainted personally. After all, Yoder had been raised as a Mennonite—and not only that, but a *Beachy* Mennonite . . . The Beachies drove cars. They used electricity. Their sons became English hippy lawyers . . . He would've been out of touch with most of the larger, more fundamental Old Order.

So somebody had to be working with him: someone who had it in for the mill. Yoder had claimed to have in his possession, with every intention of submitting them to Percy, highly incriminating photos of the premises.

Again, the "evidence" hadn't been cleared. Furthermore, as with the videotape, the source had gone undisclosed, as of yet.

At once, Benedictus remembered the odd disturbance at the compound two weeks earlier. Could someone (or something) have infiltrated the building and taken photos then?

Again, it couldn't have been Grizelda: she wouldn't have made it over the fence. And as much as the Minister would have preferred to believe that Ephraim was somehow to blame, he couldn't accept the idea that the boy had been able to breach their alarms undetected. No. The boy wasn't smart enough. No.

It had to be someone incredibly fast—someone skilled: someone clearly intent on riding the Minister's back as a personal curse . . .

The Devil.

Yes. That would account for it.

Just as the damage incurred on his homestead—the waterwheel torn from its axis, the fence in tatters, the property scattered with refuse—loomed on either side of the lane in the moonlight, as though in confirmation, Benedictus began to understand. After all this time, it was clear.

Thus, his only remaining option presented itself in direct appeal: he would have to find and kill it himself. Alone. Tonight. At once. With a gun . . . There wasn't much time left to settle the matter. Minister Bontrager's dealings with Beaumont, as captured on film and presented to Percy, would open a can of worms that would implicate all but the slickest of fish in The Basin. Benedictus would never survive, in community standing, the days to come. First, he would be excommunicated. Then run out of business. Then, possibly, jailed.

Likewise, The Devil's hours were numbered. With most of the township out for its hide—twenty patrols, by the latest count—and acknowledging claims by an English farmer to have shot and wounded it the night before, there was no way the killing would outlive this season. It probably wouldn't survive the evening.

The Devil and Benedictus stood to gain by naught but the other's demise.

With that in mind, the Minister trained his focus on hastening matters along. Beginning now: he would go inside, load his Mossberg and start walking north. In the fields between Welshtown Road and the mill, where most of the recent attacks had occurred, it would surely appear to him—*some*where, unable to balk at his challenge. And so, it would die.

He got out of the buggy and tethered the pacer to one of the only standing fence posts. He managed to kick in the front gate, which hung by a thread, then walk up the cobblestone path, surrounded by garbage and rotting vegetables.

Even before he climbed the stairs, he noticed a light in the sitting room window. A lantern was burning behind the shade. Someone had been in the house in his absence.

It couldn't have been the boy—not if what Davin Stutz had maintained was true. Ephraim had been confined to house arrest, with the Hostlers, pending inquiry. No one but Tulk had the keys to this house, and Tulk was en route to the mill, as agreed upon.

Benedictus paused on the porch. Standing between two holes in the floorboards, he gazed at a swipe of paint on the wall that had dried in the form of a question mark.

Straightening up, he opened the door to be met with an outpouring draft of rot. There must have been something dead in the house—a possum or groundhog that might have dropped in through the shattered windows and choked on a mothball. Benedictus hadn't smelled anything worse since their final congregation. Instead of triggering caution or fear, the smell just succeeded in fueling his rage.

He pulled out a handkerchief, buried his face in it. He jammed the door with an open palm. It swung in, banging the wall. A wave of rancid heat blew over and past him. A deep, soundless hum made the inside walls of his ear canals quiver and itch. Around him, as though in the path of a coming tornado: a static-charged calm hung heavy. Once he was inside, the sensation intensified. Here, the entire scale was off. The ceiling and floor looked out of perspective. The hallway's dimensions had shifted, it seemed. The walls appeared vaguely ephemeral, shrouded, as though bleeding through from a parallel vortex. The light spilling out of the sitting room, down the hall to the left, was an off-shade of burgundy—*un*like the glow of an oil lamp. There seemed to be something missing, as well . . . A coat rack? . . . A mantel? . . . Then, *added,* perhaps? He couldn't tell what, but something was different.

His head felt dizzy. He started to spin.

Again, he buried his face in the handkerchief. Squinting, he moved down the hall toward the light. His footsteps echoed ahead of him. A creak in the floorboards echoed all through the house. He was sweating. The back of his throat was parched and dry. His lungs felt tight and congested . . . There was something intensely familiar to all of this—every instant, a bygone whisper, every movement, a revisitation.

He reached for the heavy wooden cane that hung from a coat peg along the wall. He brought it down, taking hold of the handle, then slid his grip to the opposite end.

Approaching the doorway, he slowed his advance. For a moment, he thought he had heard something—grinding, a shifting movement—though whether from above or behind him, he couldn't determine exactly. In truth, it had sounded to be right *beside* him, moving along with him, aping his gestures. But that was absurd. He was standing alone. And the house was silent.

Nerves, he thought.

Breathing slowly, he rounded the jamb and, with watering eyes, peered into the light.

Candles were placed around the room in a distantly recognizable pattern. Their wicks had burned into the wax. They emitted a deep, reddish luminescence that flickered across the opposite wall—down the length of a faded patchwork quilt which, at first, he couldn't place, but which then took a turn for the identifiable—first as a blanket brought down from a box in the attic, then as a family heirloom, and finally, for just what it was, and exactly as had been displayed half a lifetime earlier: the bridal quilt of Maria Speicher, as woven with care by elderly spinsters . . .

Continuing down: a sheet was drawn back from a goose down mattress on a white oak bed frame. All four posts were staked with candles. Columns of wax ran down to the floor. At the foot of the bed sat a stool and a bucket, tools of the midwife's occupation.

A slam of imagery staggered the Minister: hot, fleeting streaks of intensity, straight from the furnace. Gone as quickly.

He teetered. His equilibrium stabilized.

Then it recurred—this time with greater impact and vivid, protracted clarity: a scream in the half-light, wailing hysteria, blood on the floor, on the mat, on the walls . . . He found himself gazing in tenuous dread from the doorway, over Grizelda's shoulder. Below, Maria lay screaming to Jesus. Her pallor was drained to a bluish gray. Her long red hair was matted and tangled and fanned out across the sweat-soaked pillow. Beneath her, the mattress was soaked in blood. The floor was awash in it, matted with towels. Grizelda's apron was splattered in thirty-six hours of amniotic discharge.

She cried out for help—more water and towels—from her brother, damn him. What was he doing?

She turned. Benedictus, now as then, could only gawk in speechless horror. Maria's body lay drained in a puddle of gore. She was dying, and nothing could save her.

"She's dying!" Grizelda screamed. *"You bastard! Help me!"*

He couldn't. He took a step back.

And, with that, as he watched in the role of his own captive witness, as though in a dream, he had fled—out the door and across the open yard to the fields in a shattered delirium.

Two days later, Jonas Tulk would find him passed out in a Soddersburg tavern.

For now, however, the image of Sister Grizelda persisted: cursing his name. He was still in the room with her, somehow—still looking down on them, frozen, unable to move.

He was trapped in the presence of all that had come to pass in his absence at Ephraim's birth.

Before him, Maria lay shuddering, too weak to scream, in the throes of imminent death. She managed to whisper discernibly: *"Please . . . Don't let it die . . . "* to Grizelda, begging. *"And never . . . ever . . . tell your . . . brother."*

Her eyes clouded over. In a moment, she was gone.

The breath had scarcely left her body before Grizelda seized a knife. Without hesitating, she wiped both sides of the blade with a rag, then turned on the body. She drew a forceful downward incision from over the navel to the lower abdomen. The skin opened up like a morning glory. There wasn't much blood. But the nerves were still active. The arms and legs continued to twitch as Grizelda traced the incision again, successfully cutting into the uterus. In she reached. Gray and puckering, Ephraim was pulled from his dead mother's womb.

Grizelda, having herself given birth to an infant daughter two weeks earlier, clutched the child to her lactating bosom, then stood and, with lifeless resolve, looked down on Maria's corpse.

"I won't," she promised.

Reeling, the Minister fell over backwards. His head hit the wall. He collapsed in the hallway. At once, he was back up, scrambling, gasping, losing his balance. He couldn't see anything. Groping in darkness, he swung the cane. It shattered a porcelain vase on the cabinet. (Where was his handkerchief?) Something was burning inside of his chest. The stench was unGodly.

Coughing, he stumbled back into the sitting room. No one was there. Yet, the quilt was still hanging. Someone, or something, had entered the house. He could smell it. He needed to get to his gun.

He picked up a candle and, gagging, returned to the hallway in search of his handkerchief. There it was: under the cabinet. The cane slipped out of his sweaty palm as he stooped to retrieve it. The candle flame singed his beard. He sneezed on smoking hair.

Again, he buried his face in the cloth. Quickly, his tremors of fear and astonishment led into semiconvulsions of rage. Maria's dying plea reverberated: "*Never . . . ever . . . tell your . . . brother—*" again and again. He couldn't silence it. Nor could he bury Grizelda's response:

"I won't."

The treacherous, filthy harlot . . .

Once and for all, she would die.

Tonight.

Leaving his cane on the floor of the hallway, Benedictus limped to the kitchen. Still holding the candle, he lit the wall-mounted oil lantern. His back felt exposed to the darkness. He'd left himself open.

He turned.

The kitchen, too, had been thrown for a whirl. Paint on the walls, more trash on the floor. Scattered crockery shone in the glare of the steadily brightening oil lantern. The Minister swallowed. His heart palpitated.

He made for the gun cabinet, off in the corner. He opened it. Both of his shotguns were there. He pulled down the Mossberg ten-gauge pump—"The Non-Differentiator," Tulk always called it. While loading the chamber with lead shot, the Minister's fingers trembled and twitched uncontrollably. His chest was still pounding. Something was wrong with his heart. His breathing felt sharp and constricted. He dropped the handkerchief, damning it. Using both hands, he finished loading the gun. Breathing the air was like siphoning shit through a mouth guard: waffled rectum in hog fat.

The Mossberg was loaded. He filled his pockets with extra shells. He made for the back room. There, every Bible he owned had been shredded to pieces. An overturned bureau lay smashed on the floor. And this time, the walls had been splattered with feces.

He yelled at the wreckage, then kicked the remains of an *Ausbund* across the floor.

A muffled, scarcely audible rustle of movement disrupted the silence to follow. The Minister stopped to listen. The house was quiet. Then the movement resumed: a definite shifting of weight upstairs, the groaning of floorboards, a steady creaking. Followed, shortly thereafter, by voices. Or maybe a single voice. More likely, yes—a single voice, by the sound of it . . .

Yes, and (incredibly, moreover:) laughing. A chilling cackle rolled through the house. There was something unreal in the tone of it, something so utterly insolent, so inappropriate, so out of place with the Minister's state that his rage was suspended momentarily, giving way to disbelief.

It was coming from just overhead, directly above him; jeering—it seemed to be taunting him. More: it was coming from Ephraim's room. And it sounded like Ephraim, however unlikely.

In equal breach of the judge's ruling as Minister Bontrager's household authority, the boy, that impudent, soon-to-be-choking-on-lead-shot whoreson was laughing upstairs . . .

Benedictus snapped from his trance. Quietly back through the kitchen he crept. As quietly, up the stairs he continued—gripping the Mossberg, his finger on the trigger—while, warbling madly, the laughter continued, discernibly muted inside of the room. Benedictus stopped at the top of the stairs to ignite an oil lamp. Again, the walls lit up to reveal a splattered assault of fecal matter: Ephraim's bedroom door, down the hall to the left, was marked with cryptic scribbles. Farther on, something had fallen through from the ceiling: a large black hole to the attic. A mound of plaster below, on the floor, trailed into the washroom, which seemed to be flooded.

The boy was still laughing. It made no sense.

Although insubordinate, Ephraim had never distinguished himself as suicidal. The current show of defiance gave Benedictus occasion to pause momentarily. What in the world could the kid have been thinking? Out of his mind, he was—must've been—crazy . . . And ready to die, by the look of the house.

The Minister found himself at a loss.

More alarmingly: *if* the boy had defiled the interior, thus, then it followed that he must have done the same to the outside—as the damage was nearly identical in nature. But, ceding as much, it also matched damages rendered to houses all over The Basin—houses, whole properties, widely assumed to have been desecrated by The Devil itself . . .

In the midst of which came another epiphany: the odor now filling the house was the very same stench that had filled the last worship service. (And Beaumont's cruiser the week before.) The whole congregation had choked on it. (*"Stunk up my whole back-seat!"*) And The Devil hadn't been there.

But Ephraim had—right down in front, on the Sinner's Bench.

Ephraim had been there.

No, thought the Minister.

Despite any rumors of family curses, Ephraim could never have hosted The Devil. Of that much, Benedictus had always felt certain. The Devil was cunning, elusive. The boy was a worthless, incompetent wretch. He couldn't have leapt over Welshtown Road. He couldn't have run up alongside of traffic. Or straight through a plate glass window at the superstore . . .

Benedictus refused to believe it.

Ephraim was nothing at all like his uncle.

(*"Never . . . ever . . . tell your . . . brother."*)

His uncle . . .

(but not)

The Devil.

His father.

As though in reply, a voice went up behind the door, in High German: *"What's wrong?"*—with a tone of impudent mockery. *"The family tree got away from you?"* Laughter. Then, hissing: *"Why not leave the perpetuation of kin to the able-bodied?"*

Trembling, Benedictus stepped away from the door. He had heard enough.

Hound of hell, delinquent brigade or crazed adolescent, it made no difference: whoever belonged to that voice was about to get blown in half.

"Come on, old man!" the taunting persisted. *"The only thing more hilarious than infertility—"*

The Minister tried the door. It was locked.

"—is an armed and murderous cuckold!"

He jammed the door with the butt of his gun. More howling went up on the other side: shrill peals of spite and hilarity laced with tones of inscrutable malice. Already dreaming of ways he would pummel, strangle and, finally, dispatch of this bastard, the Minister pitted one shoulder squarely into ramming the door from its hinges.

The voice lilted into a singsong delivery: *"Barren as winter, and nary a whelp . . ."*

And thereby, a realization—or more of a rudimentary *ob*servation, however delayed in forthcoming, as yet—began to dawn on Benedictus: something fundamental was wrong with this scene: something so basic, so simple—a break in the norm—that, until now, it hadn't occurred to him.

While ramming the door, it began to register, steadily creeping into the forefront: the voice behind the door was pronouncing articulate vitriol.

Ephraim was mute.

He hadn't completed a sentence—certainly nothing in German—in all of his life.

Yet now: *"Wir scheissen in die milch deiner Mutter."*

The Minister blew a hole in the door.

A scream let out. Then a cough. Then a chuckle.

The son of a bitch was *still* laughing . . .

Benedictus pumped the Mossberg and leveled it. Three more shots exploded. Gaping, jagged holes opened up in the wood.

The door was still on its hinges.

The silence to follow was thick with a sweetly caustic haze of gunpowder smoke. At once, Benedictus reloaded his gun. The lantern behind him flickered and dimmed for a moment. It caught. The air was still. Only the sound of the shells snapping into the chamber and, faintly, the Minister wheezing, disrupted the otherwise deafening calm. Quickly, he finished reloading the Mossberg. As quickly, he sighted the doorknob and fired. It exploded. A hole opened up. There was still something barring the door—what felt like a bolt. In a fury of reckless abandon, he emptied the chamber, then, flipping his grip to the barrel, followed up with a woodcutter's swing.

Once, he chopped at the splintered patchwork of holes, remembering Sister Grizelda, *twice* he jammed the butt of his Mossberg through the wood, recalling Maria, *three times,* a sizeable hole opened up, conjuring fleetingly Ephraim's image, and *finally,* the whole of the slab fell in, giving way, in flesh and blood, to The Devil.

It pulled him through on his own momentum. The barrel was seized and torn from his grasp. His arm was taken ahold of and twisted.

Their eyes met only for an instant: remorseless, glowing red . . .

Then it sprayed him.

His vision was blackened with bile. His scream gurgled into a choke. Something was lifting him—something was gripping his windpipe. He couldn't look down. He thrashed and kicked his feet.

A series of turbulent visions commenced: just as he felt himself hoisted and borne up and over and *slammed,* headfirst, into the wall—a fragmented image of Ephraim, thus treated, in youth, when he'd knocked a lamp from the table, appeared before him with vivid intensity, just as the beating led into release, into weightlessness, free-floating, end over backwards and *slam* on the door frame, twisting his back on the drop and cracking his ribs upon impact—this time for having been ten minutes late home from fetching the Minister's wandering pacer—just as he felt himself spluttering, blindly lifted again—the pain in his back like a nerve ending under the blast of a torch—to be held overhead in a straight-armed brace, carried into the washroom—where Ephraim had once dribbled piss on the floor—and dunked to his ears in a basin of burning, corrosive liquid, just as he felt himself tossed, then tumbling, down the hall toward the top of the stairs, soon to be lifted again, a thunderous backhand triggered an image of Ephraim, hoisted aloft and slapped repeatedly. Another blow, this one harder, shattered the bridge of his nose in a white-hot flash. A third tore into his gut, invoking a scene of the boy doubled over in agony; the last, a full-force kick to the jaw, sent him end over end down the stairs, precisely as Ephraim had plummeted, spiraling blindly—slamming his head on the ridge of a step—and the rest in a tumble, landing flat on his back with a slap at the foot of the staircase.

On lifting his head, he still couldn't see—blinded by burning gall and ammonia. He coughed in silence. Something was wrong with his voice. He was puckering, wheezing desperately. Straining to cry out, he only succeeded in gulping air. He choked.

He was mute.

Only now, this late in the game, were his fears confirmed beyond a doubt: The Devil had always been after *him*. Exclusively. Benedictus Bontrager . . . All other incidents, every attack in The Basin had happened on *his* account. Dozens of unwitting neighbors were victims of guilt by association with *him*. Beaumont, Grabers, Tulk and the Stoltzfi, with hundreds of farmers all over the county, had been ensnared in a noose originally fashioned for *his* neck alone. And now, as it tightened, the rancor and weight of an age-old conflict came to bear.

Yes, The Devil had been *his* curse—in the strictest, most literal, worldly sense: it had hounded his trail for nineteen years, using every available fissure, all openings, every weakness in gaining a foothold, acting through constantly shifting mediums, vessel by vehicle, host after host, guise upon dupe after innocent victim; beginning first with Jacob, already weakened by drink and worldly exposure, who'd borne him a grudge from their first encounter, relapsing into the blight of his ancestry—second, Maria, the "virgin bride," seduced into carnal hosannas therewith, then murdered while giving birth, as attended by Sister Grizelda, third, the chameleon, whose life in The Basin would take on the role of a masquerade in preparing for this, The Return: The Devil's Final Coming, through fourth and last, the boy, Ephraim.

The Minister's vision cleared to confirm it: slowly descending the staircase, cloaked in a shadow of stark, impending malevolence, closing to blot out the lantern above him. It looked like the boy, from a certain angle. The dip in its forward stride was evident. Shades of Jacob came through too.

But mostly it looked like Richard Nixon.

Whatever was happening off in the forest, in fields or on back roads for miles around, the bars along Route 21, Old 30 and 342 were oddly calm. The neighboring English developments, too, for the most part, had been devoid of unrest. By now, it was almost appearing as though the entire evening might just blow over—most of the first half had passed without serious, or even the standard, expected incident. Curfew had brought trick-or-treat to an end with a sigh of relief across The Basin. Amazingly, now that the tally was in, a much lower level of vandalism had been reported than many had feared—substantially lower than in previous years. In part, this was thought to have been the product of so many nightly patrols on the road; between the development crews, the superstore guards, the police and the black bumper squadrons, an estimated seventy mobilized parties—an unlikely body of interests known, unofficially, as the Lamepeter Coalition—was combing the township in search of trouble. As well, the field bashes, parties and barbecues had served to contain the local youth. So far, the greatest discernible threat to the public was run-of-the-mill drunk driving.

Inside of most taverns, no matter how crowded, the vibe was decidedly anticlimactic. At first, it reminded Owen of New Year's Eve in an all too familiar sense: everyone hell-bent on pulling out all the stops, thereby ensuring a flop . . .

But after a while, it started to look as though much of the crowd—in costume, sifting through baskets of now complimentary korn puppies—hadn't shown up for a party so much as in spite of The Coalition's insistence that everyone stay indoors for the evening. The Coalition did *not* run The Basin. That was a point which most of the locals appeared intent on making clear. For a week now, they had been subject to constant harassment while driving home at night. Concerned as they may have been with the situation, they seemed even more resolved on living, for an evening, in defiance of it. The Lamepeter Coalition be damned.

But once that notion had been established, the rest of the evening began to lose steam. As though in corroboration of all of his worst assurances, Owen watched as, in bar after bar, the atmosphere steadily leveled off to a vacuous hum. In several establishments, sales were beginning to drop by as early as ten o'clock. Indeed, the "keepers of song and flame" had been spared the (*lo, but for korn meal*) wrath. They'd also been spared much entertainment . . . Bars like the Villa Noeva were filled with drunks nodding off to third-rate honky-tonk. The Visigoth's "karaoke explosion" was dead in the water by 10:15. The Dogboy, though somewhat more lively, at first, wound up full of half-lidded regulars, most of them looking embarrassed by the state of their appearances.

A man in a pink flamingo suit may have said it best when, on losing a game of pool to the likeness of Long John Silver, he settled his tab with a word to the bartender: "Sorry, Freida. But I look like an asshole."

Owen had shown up in Lamepeter Township expecting a riot on every corner. Instead, he had found that, despite his efforts, no one was up for the Harvest Sabbath. Stepford simply wasn't game. Surprise, surprise. There had been no disturbances . . . Not one tavern brawl. No burning scarecrows or overpass drops had come up on the scanners. There was no way of knowing what calls had poured into *The Plea* that evening, for practical reasons, but as for the public airwaves, no Kornwolf sightings had been relayed whatsoever. A total of seven reports of vandalism—four window soapings, two drive-by eggings and one toilet paper attack—accounted for Halloween in The Basin this year. A single arrest had been made hours earlier: the charge was "failing to signal a turn." The offender was seventy-eight, and sober. It hardly amounted to bedlam in Blue Ball.

Normally, this would have been embarrassing.

Aided by storybook-ideal conditions, bathed in the radiant glow of a Blue Moon and buoyed along by a week-long, $25,000 advertisement campaign, and he *still* hadn't managed to kindle the flames of pandemonium in Stepford Town.

Normally, this would have sent him packing.

But right now he couldn't help feeling lucky—lucky not only to be alive, but for every passing moment of calm.

It wasn't until 11:30—seated in his Legacy, parked in a tavern lot, staring at the moon in vague disquiet—that a garbled exchange broke the scanner's silence, hinting at the first, however initially vague indication that maybe, just maybe, the evening wasn't entirely over.

One of the voices had mentioned a fire.

Owen, starting his engine, thought *here we go . . .*

Ten minutes later he arrived on the scene—the Holtwood Development headquarters trailer—to find its exterior paneling scorched and the front porch smoldering, stinking of gas.

The company spokesman, whom Owen had met once before, was shouting at a pair of officers.

A guard behind them dispensed with the last of a portable fire extinguisher's foam. Two other property guards stood watching. The charred stoop was coated in lather. From what Owen gathered, the trailer had just been nailed in a "drive-by Molotov cocktailing." One of the guards had spotted the vehicle: a "light blue Hessian-mobile," as he put it.

The smaller of the cops stepped back from the spokesman to ask for Owen's press credentials. Before they were checked, however, the spokesman flew off the handle, blasting both officers, along with the sheriff, as incompetent *scumbags*. With that, the officer went back to arguing, forgetting all about Owen's clearance. Watching them go at it, Owen began to sense what felt like a coming storm—a drop in the air pressure sweeping The Basin: something approaching with terrible certainty.

Two miles north, on Eby Hess Road, just south of Bareville, driving west, Officer Rudolf Beaumont was so deranged with agitation, he was having trouble keeping his grip on the wheel.

Over the course of the past ninety minutes, he'd taken a blindsiding: first, by way of a call from the sheriff demanding to know about "bribery charges," the details of which were scant and confusing, at best, however directly alarming. Beaumont had lied through his teeth, of course. The sheriff knew nothing about the mill. Beaumont alone had been working with Tulk and the Stoltzfi and Grabers and Benedictus. His involvement amounted not only to turning the other cheek to their operations—but to strong-arming, ushering off and / or bearing false witness against their opposition—i.e., overly persistent intruders. Over the years, he'd made seven related arrests, and administered even more beatings. Most of the suspects, what Tulk called the "animal activist prowlers"—had wound up in jail. In exchange for testifying against them, Rudolf had been given monthly payoffs. Essentially, this arrangement had always been simple, if undemanding enough. On select occasions, when circumstance dictated, Beaumont had even guarded the mill. Today had been one such occasion, as most of its keepers had been locked up, evidently. The idiots. Something had happened in town that morning to land them in Stepford's prison. Ezekiel Stoltzfus had contacted Rudolf at 5:15 in search of his father. By that point, Beaumont had already heard all about the attack on his cruiser radio. Ten minutes later, he'd been at the mill. A distraught Ezekiel had filled him in while, behind them, the hounds had been wailing chaotically. The timing couldn't have been any worse.

Sheriff Highman, braced for a loaded evening, was calling out all of his units. In moments, Rudolf would be assigned to "crowd control" at the Blue Ball Devil maze. From there, he wouldn't be able to steal away for more than a couple of minutes. Hence, the mill would be left under insufficient guard for most of the evening.

He managed to slip away from his post at ten, right when the call had come in: Sheriff Highman's voice crackled over the radio, demanding explanations.

By this point, Highman was fed up with Rudolf—what with the beatings and all, and the bad publicity they had brought the department.

But *these* charges, *felony bribery* charges, if true, were a whole different game altogether.

Rudolf, parked in the compound lot with his headlights cut, listened in horror—all the while, pretending to be at the fairgrounds (minus the carnival roar), which didn't sit well with the sheriff—*"Where are you?"*—as Rudolf replied: *"In a portable toilet."*

He blew his cool in the conversation. He might have done better to simulate bad reception for all of his grace under pressure. And Highman wasn't about to let up. His interrogation was only suspended, momentarily, due to distraction: a call had come in on a situation apparently pending in Bird-in-Hand. This left Rudolf standing at a loss with a frazzled Ezekiel, who couldn't enlighten him. It wasn't until—by stroke of fortune—Jonas Tulk pulled in behind him, rocking along in his family wagon, that hope for an explanation surfaced. But Tulk, for that matter, would be in the foulest of moods himself, and for solid reason: Beaumont and Benedictus had landed them all in a world of shit, he said. And with that, the picture began to unravel, however imbued with acrimony.

Back on patrol at the maze by 11, Rudolf began to register the full implications. Beaumont would surely be called to the stand to account for his role in accepting the offerings. Someone had caught him on film, red-handed. And knowing Benedictus, he'd botched their arraignment—Rudolf could hear the old windbag raving of Devils and hippies in Percy's courtroom. The harder he thought about Minister Bontrager taking the stand, the more nervous he grew. And the crowd around him was no help at all—hundreds of drunks in masquerade walking by, some lipping off to him (*"Look, it's a pig!"*) from behind their veils of anonymity—as, all the while, the park's director, now seated inside of the ticket booth, glared at him. Rudolf felt himself flushing over. A simmering inner panic welled up in him. Presently, Sheriff Highman's voice came over the radio, calling for Kutay.

Allegedly, the city police had issued a warrant for violation of house arrest on an Ephraim Elias Bontrager. The young man and his aunt, his legal escort, had been due back at her house by ten. Officer Kutay was ordered to check on it . . .

Finally.

Rudolf broke for his cruiser, blasting himself for not realizing earlier: yes—of course. The kid, that bastard . . .

He and those Dough Balls—or Crubbills, or whatnot—had carried this whole thing out with a camera.

Resourceful, they were. Every one of them: crafty. Punks.

Beaumont knew where to find them.

He slowed on approaching the old gravel lane that cut into the woods from a bend in the road. A trail of dust hung over its weed-choked corridor. Someone had just driven through.

Rudolf turned off his headlights and slowly drifted up the rising incline, shadowed on either side by deciduous trees, their silhouettes etched in the moonlight—around a bend to a break in the forest, then out to a narrow path between cornfields. From there, he slowed his advance even further. An acre of stalks moved by at a crawl, beyond which a floating expanse of darkness harbored the glow of a distant bonfire.

Yes. Exactly as he had suspected: the Schlabach Farm. They were gathering here.

The last three barn party raids had been launched against out-in-the open, high-profile targets. In light of foreseeable heightened police opposition to underaged drinking this evening, surely the Dough Balls would have relocated operations to somewhere secluded. The long-abandoned Schlabach Farm was the obvious choice, to Beaumont's reckoning. Situated 500 yards from the northernmost bend in Eby Hess Road, behind him—and a mile to the nearest lane in all other directions—the place was nearly invisible. No one could see it from any road. The nearest house was miles away. And the aging couple who owned the property lived in Ronks and didn't patrol it.

Across the field, a couple of figures were moving around in a haze of firelight. Stacks of what looked like boxes dotted the yard. A car was parked to one side. The southern wall of the barn was faintly discernible, patterned with networks of ivy. Beaumont cut his engine and stared for a minute.

Yes. This was it.

He reached for a sack on the floor of the passenger's seat. Inside, there were ten pairs of handcuffs—as issued by Sheriff Highman that evening—one box of .45-caliber bullets, one canister of tear gas, a stun gun and Mace. Perching the load on his lap, he unpacked it. Everything snapped or slid into place.

Then he went for his cruiser's radio.

"This is Unit 4." He gripped the receiver and waited. No answer came back. Again, he spoke. "Unit 4."

Still nothing.

Annoyed, he checked the volume. All systems were go.

He didn't have time for this.

"This is Beaumont, Unit 4," he growled. "I'm switching my handheld off . . ."

A glitch in the static came back in response. Rudolf stared at the radio's digital equalizer in puzzled annoyance. One of its ranges peaked abruptly. The speakers crackled. What sounded like laughter filled the cruiser. The officer flinched.

"Hey, Rudy—" An unfamiliar, oddly accented voice of a young man spoke. *"What are you doing out there in the bushes?"*

A twitter of laughter went up in the background.

The tone was insolent, thoroughly spiteful. Beaumont could scarcely believe his ears.

"What do you call ten thousand cops at the bottom of a lake?" the voice continued.

Dead air spanned the gap to the punch line. Then: *"A good start!"*

It howled uncontrollably.

"Give me that thing!" came another voice. *"What's up, Rude-oaf?"* More defiant: *"How long's it been since you slept with a woman?"*

Which *really* made them laugh out loud—as though the idea were beyond preposterous.

"How about a man, then?"

They roared all the more.

Beaumont sat there, paralyzed, watching the figures double over around the fire.

Passing the mouthpiece again, someone else started in: *"You ought to be grateful for asthma. You wouldn't have lasted a week in boot camp."*

"Yeah."

"He'd be crying for his teddy bear."

"BAH!"

Rudolf could feel something twist in his bowels.

"Rudy. Hey, is it true that your father wore women's clothing?"

That did it.

He grabbed the receiver and fired back. "You sons of bitches!" He squawked, overloading. Then: "I swear to Jesus, I'll kill every one of—"

He seized up, choking.

They crowed in triumph.

Again, Beaumont flew off the handle, but this time, he ended up puckering mutely.

Snapping at last, he reached for his keys. He was starting the engine just as the radio cut to silence. A moment later, a voice returned, unencumbered by static.

Calmly: *"Hey, Officer—look to your right."*

He froze.

"It's coming . . ."

Cringing, he turned.

His cruiser was slammed on the passenger's side by what felt like a hurtling fire hydrant. The vehicle went up on two wheels, lurching. Beaumont's head hit the ceiling. His scalp opened up, spraying blood all over the dash.

The cruiser teetered—wheels in the air and, suspended, leveling off, then—

Returning momentum and falling—*crashed* back down.

A chorus of wild cheering went up.

"SCORE!" came a call from across the field.

Coughing, blood-soaked and losing his vision, Beaumont reached for his door handle. Jammed. The entire frame of the car had been twisted.

He couldn't see ten feet ahead through the darkness.

"Hog roast tonight!" came a drunken holler.

Another round of cheers went up.

A shadow passed in the rearview mirror. He craned his neck for a look, but was stopped by a sharp, unbearable pain in his back. He gasped. The blood dribbled into his eyes.

He unholstered his .45. Something appeared to his right. It was coming. He pointed the barrel . . .

A mile and a half to the south and closing, over the hill, approaching on foot via Old 18, between Ronkers Lane and an overly active Stumptown Drive, Jonathan Becker had already been on the frayed end of calm when the shot rang out. Having opted to walk, as opposed to driving his buggy, for dread of police entanglement, he'd found out the hard way, and quickly enough, that the township police were completely outnumbered. In the past twenty minutes, he'd managed to elude one black bumper squadron—a five-man party from District Nineteen, well out of its loop—two security vans from the Sprawl Mart, and a couple of Redcoats spotting the ditches with a high-powered halogen lamp—eluding them all by dodging into the corn as their wagons or vehicles passed; an act which, in all probability, would have gotten him strung up and whipped, were he spotted. To add to the tension, an amplified hollering match between warring English camps down the road was filling The Basin with hair-raising, overextended belches of feedback. The whole thing had put him on edge to begin with: fear of reprisal had kept him going. Ephraim's final admonishment (*"Midnight. Alone. No excuses."*) still rang in his head. He knew to take that warning to heart. He knew they would seek him out, were he absent. Visions of Colin Graybill waking his family at midnight spurred him on.

Just as the fear of search and seizure had kept him on foot, so the traffic had frazzled him. Then came the gunshot, followed by a booming metallic SLAM that rang through The Basin, then something worse: a shrill, though equally deep-ended, wholly phantasmal howl. It carried across the fields in an echo. A haunting silence fell over the night. The English hollering match desisted. Everything seemed to rear up for a moment, as though to say, nervously, *What* was *that?* . . . The calm to follow was thick with portent. Yes, this evening would come to pass, and all within it to resolution: but not without facing the music first. A purge was in order.

The moon was full.

Jonathan picked up his pace, moving nervously east at a shuffle, down the fleetingly empty stretch of Old 18, past where the end of the field on his left gave way to a jagged incline that grew to a high, craggy, barren escarpment, the bank of which shimmered with quartz in the moonlight. Ahead, maybe two hundred yards, an overgrown pathway led up and over the ridge. Jonathan focused on getting there quickly.

By morning, this nightmare would all be over.

The roar of a motor preceded the burst of movement from over the ridge by an instant: launching as quickly into the open air, on a downward angle and plunging, its engine a whining combustible blast in flight, the vehicle shattered the silence.

Terrified, Jonathan leapt in his tracks.

The Hornet's bumper tore into the downgrade, ripping through silt and gravel. It glanced off a boulder, upended, went over and flipped. It cleared the ditch and came down in the road on its side, grinding across the asphalt. A shower of sparks went up underneath it. The tearing of metal on pavement resounded—and, lost in the rumble, a voice crying out.

Finally, the vehicle ground to a halt. Still on one side, it swayed momentarily, the driver's seat cocked toward the belt of Orion. Then it fell back to its base with a crash.

At once, hysterical laughter rolled out of it. Smoke wafted over the road from the engine. The road was now quiet. In place of the rattle and crash, there was Gideon's voice, in stitches: *"That's what I'm talking about!"* in Plain Folk. Colin joined in with a whoop of accord: *"I can't believe you fucking did that!"* A door came open. In English: "Ach! Let me out . . ." Still laughing. Gideon tried the ignition. "Hold on—" He coughed.

It started.

"Damn, this thing is incredible."

"That's the *second* time."

They got out of the car. From a distance, Jonathan watched them circle it. He didn't know whether or not they had spotted him. As such, he hung back in the shadows.

Gideon came up for air with a belch.

He dabbed his brow with a shirtsleeve and looked at it. *"Hey. I'm bleeding . . ."*

Colin laughed. *"We ought to get back."*

They returned to the car.

Breathlessly, Jonathan watched them move. They had already climbed in, shut their doors and shifted into gear when they called to him.

"Well, come on!" Colin shouted impatiently. *"You're the fucking guest of honor."*

The back door opened. The engine rumbled and spat. They were waiting.

"Ach! Get in!"

Officer Kutay, who, so far, had spent his evening responding to noise complaints, received orders to check on the Bontrager kid at the Hostler residence just before midnight. A few minutes later, he rolled down the gravel drive, feeling vaguely insulted by the order. While everyone else (some thirteen officers, along with a five-man squad from the city) was out and about—whether chasing a Holtwood van that was clocked running ninety in a thirty-mile-an-hour zone or responding to a rise in complaints re: rampant drunk driving along Route 21—Fatty had been assigned to check on a missing eighteen-year-old Dutchie.

He rounded a bend in the drive to spot someone, a hatless, bearded figure in black, wandering circles around the yard. As Fatty's cruiser slowed to a halt, the figure looked up, bathed in the headlights. The look on his face shone of tormented worry.

As expected, his name was Abraham Hostler. His wife, it followed, was named Grizelda. And no, they hadn't come home—neither she nor Ephraim, their nephew: Ephraim Bontrager. Both were a couple of hours late. A social worker had already come by to check the house and living conditions. Then a city policeman had come to install an electrical boundary network (the "bracelet line") around their property. Ephraim was now in violation of house arrest, an annulment of same. And if Mrs. Hostler didn't appear in the next hour (by one a.m.) a warrant would go out on her, as well.

For the life of him, Abraham couldn't understand it. This was unlike his wife, he claimed. Normally, he would've had to assume, by now, that they'd gotten into an accident. But no reports of a crash had been filed, and the hospitals hadn't admitted them either. It didn't make sense. Half of their district was combing The Basin in search of an answer. The Hostlers' oldest daughter had set out to look for them only moments before, while Abraham himself, with two of their children, had been left behind to watch over the house. So far, no update—not one piece of news—had come back. It was driving him mad with worry.

Fatty was just beginning to feel for the man when a roar broke out from the west: what sounded at first like a chain saw at three hundred decibels, tearing and grinding in starts, soon to lead into a gigantic trash can lid being smashed by a hundred-pound hammer, and on—to a ruptured fan belt slapping the underside of an engine hood . . .

Fannie was emerging from a narrow path through the corn to the edge of the Schlabach property the moment a scream pierced the deafening roar, like a thousand demons plummeting hellbound . . .

The first things she saw were the torches: what looked to be three different martin houses wrapped in gas-soaked bedsheets, burning on twenty-foot poles. An array of movement proceeded within their field of illumination below. Even from two hundred yards, she could make out the overturned cruiser, off to the left. Figures were gathered around it, thrashing in time with the music while beating the vehicle's underside with sticks and pipes. Their movements flared in a wash of red. They were baying like coyotes. One of them reared up and, hollering, shattered a passenger window.

Behind them, between a stack of boxes and what had to (appeared to) be a tractor, standing directly beneath a torch, someone (a young man) dressed in a flowing gown was spinning around in circles. Somebody else (a young woman) ran by with a sack on her head, trailing a parasol. Surrounding a second pile of lumber between the house and the barn stood a crowd. A couple of barechested young men were splashing the wood with pints of lighter fluid. Behind them, piles of assorted merchandise filled the clearing. On drawing nearer, Fannie discerned the outline of common garage appliances: rubber hoses and motorbike helmets, and plastic rakes—and everyone freely picking through them, throwing together unlikely costumes: a couple of girls in inflatable life jackets, bathed in the firelight, guzzling spirits—behind them, young men with pails on their heads, thrashing in time with the hellbound descent.

Fannie had never heard anything like it. The tempo was unbelievably furious. The instrumentation was truly unreal. It sounded like some kind of killing machine: a corn thresher vaulted by nitrous oxide, storming the hills at a thunderous charge—visions of indiscriminate slaughter, a marching of thousands, unbridled savagery.

Fannie couldn't begin to conceive of it—even though, yes, it moved. It *rocked.* There was something so wholly malevolent driving every measure, it made her sick.

The young men, with cans of kerosene, gas or whatever it was they were splashing the wood with, backed away from the pile as a pair of headlights spilled from the opposite cornfield. A match was struck. The side of the barn flared up in a blaze of yellow and orange. The vehicle, badly beaten, a junker, slid into a fishtail, spinning mud. Over the amplified clamor of music, a buzz of cheering arose from the crowd. Several more people came out of the barn for a look of their own, stepping into the light. Most of the field was now glowing yellow. Fannie could make out the vehicle now—the one Colin had picked up her mother in while driving.

Something was wrong with her equilibrium. Suddenly, the world was stuck on an angle. Her legs felt weak underneath her, like she was slogging through quicksand. She struggled to keep her footing. The closer she drew to the gathering, the more she could feel herself drawn by the madness sustaining it. Just as, in turn, she felt strangely aware, as never before, of the glow of the moon—that atrocious music, damn it to hell, continued to pain and captivate her.

She halted, trying to gather her wits—to breathe, to recover / regain her senses. She was still thirty yards away from the barn. No one appeared to have spotted her yet.

Hundreds of objects all over the yard were now visible. The most conspicuous being: a towering stack of beer cases, flanked by a pair of metal kegs, and surrounded by people in varying states of undress, all rearranging their makeshift costumes. Around them, a line of English bicycles lay like dominoes splayed in the grass. Someone ran by in a sequin dress. Somebody picked up a pogo stick, laughing. A group of young women—Mary Brechbuhl, Fannie's replacement instructor among them—sat routing through baskets of jewelry and hatpins. A giant rug was spread out in the grass. There were Styrofoam coolers and kerosene lanterns and TVs and dozens of bottles of liquor. Someone was casting a rod and reel. The door of a soda machine hung open. The stuffed head of a moose was lifted above the crowd and twirled about. A grandfather clock was thrown onto the fire. A body—what looked to be Samuel Hoff—leapt over it, cutting through roaring flames. Uninjured, he came down, whooping. He turned on the others and shouted.

And here they came . . .

A second and third body shot through the flames. Soon to be followed in rapid succession—from every direction, hooting and hollering—over the blackening grandfather clock. Somebody's costume—a fabric streamer—caught fire. Then came a midair collision, a crunch that left Amos Yoder (by the sound of his squalling) in the coals below, at a scramble. Around him, shrieks of laughter went up. The car was still spinning mud by the creek. A mob was still beating the cruiser with sticks: its windshield hung together in shards. The impact of iron on buckling steel carried over the fields in a rhythmic clatter. Someone appeared from the barn in an officer's hat. He pointed a gun at the overturned vehicle, shouted and, waving, fired. Everyone jumped on him, kicking and yelling. Disarmed, he was forced to the ground and beaten. The car horn wailed from the edge of the field. The music's tempo quadrupled explosively.

Fannie knew that this couldn't last. The Crossbills were making a big enough racket to draw every cop in The Basin in minutes. One could only assume they'd intended as much.

Or were they completely oblivious?

Yes, she decided at length, they were. They were out of their minds: whirling amok in a poisoned delirium, gone to the world—they appeared to be under a spell of sorts: hedonic enchantment.

She skirted around them.

Blocking the open door to the barn, a back-turned Samuel Hoff stood, chin to the sky and a bottle of whiskey upturned, with his legs spread, urinating all down the door frame. Somebody nudged his back in passing. Fannie managed to squeeze through the opening.

Into a corridor, flanked on either side by stables and pens, she tripped. The music was painfully loud. Bodies were moving around in the dark all around her. Some were lined up on the stable railings, peering down in motionless silence.

She crept to a gate and looked over the wall. There were three of them. And one old goat.

She backed off.

Stumbling on in disbelief, she emerged from the stable hall into the open, torchlit expanse of the barn's interior. The roar of the chain saws cut as she entered. A beating of drums rumbled out of a column of speakers and ricocheted all through the building. The smoke from the torches went up through a hole in the roof, obscuring the rafter beams. A staircase ran from the highest loft down three crooked flights to the scene on the ground floor . . .

The roar of the chain saws—again, a rampaging thresher at large—resumed from the speakers: sure to brand the attending image indelibly / brutally / clearly / eternally: strung from the rafters, bound by his ankles and wrists in an upended fetal knot—maybe five or six feet off the floor—hanging gagged with electrical tape in a quivering, naked mass of lashed and bleeding fat: the English policeman—the one they called Beaumont.

A large red candle was jammed in his rectum. The gap in his buttocks was clotted with wax. The wick of the candle was burning, searing the flesh on the backs of his legs and ankles. He squirmed on the rope. But in trying to redirect the flame, he worked up momentum. He started to spin. He was squealing in pain. Below, three figures stood lashing him with switches. Behind them, a girl in a ski mask was shoving a sweet potato into a sock. Over by the stereo, gathered directly in front of the speakers, in the blast of it all, a couple of boys lobbed rotten onions, targeting parts of the cop's anatomy.

All the while, the music continued, screaming and tearing its way to conclusion:

Angel of death
Monarch to the kingdom of the dead
Infamous
Butcher
Angel of Death . . .

The final line was repeated as Fannie backed away in mortified silence.

The rope from which the cop hung bound by his ankles and wrists twisted into a knot. Slowly, he drifted out of his spin. His face was blue.

The music ended.

Groaning went up from the stables—a muffled, heavy breathing . . .

Soon, the girl in the mask came forward to pummel the cop with her sweet potato. Hovering still, he whimpered. He looked like a bulging maggot in possum wire. For an instant, he lifted his face to the light. One of his eyes had swollen shut. The other rolled back in his head as he gulped in voiceless futility.

Silence lingered.

And in that silence, Fannie heard Jonathan.

Back from the blackening void came the chain saws. The group by the stereo speakers jumped. Slowly, the cop drifted into a counterspin, flinging mucus and tears in an arc. The hurling of onions resumed. Along with a rain of blows from the sweet potato. Followed as soon by the lashing of switches. The music was even more frightening now.

Yet still, in plummeting hellbound again, Fannie was certain she'd heard his voice: somewhere in here, adrift on a break in the chaos, Jonathan's cry had gone up. Bound and gagged, he must've been—tied up in one of these pens.

She reentered the stable hall.

Ephraim was nowhere in sight. And her mother would never have been here. But Jonathan was. She could feel his despair. Somewhere, in one of these pens. He was calling.

She walked to the end of the main corridor, past the spectatorship lining the rails, into darkness, clear to the opposite end. And there, bound by his neck to a watering trough on the floor of a stable, he lay.

His hands were tied. His mouth had been gagged with a handkerchief. His face was beginning to bruise. Someone had beaten him up, to be sure. But his bearing was clear. He looked rational, sober—if greatly relieved by the sight of Fannie.

Gasping, she fell to her knees at his side. At once, the look on his face was clear: she wasn't to worry about his condition. His injuries, none of them permanent, might be tended to later. Right now, they had to get out of this place while they still had a chance.

In compliance, she fumbled to untie his bonds. But the rope was too tight. His eyes went wide. He was signaling to take off his gag at once. She worked at the handkerchief, pulling it out.

He gasped.

"What is it?" she asked.

He nodded across the hall. *"There's a knife over there."*

Never flinching, Fannie crept through the dark and lifted a knife from a rack. She came back quickly, dropped to his side and started working the blade to position. The rope around his neck was thick. It took her a minute to make the cut. Freeing his ankles and hands was easier.

Standing, she helped him get to his feet.

They embraced for an instant. His body was trembling.

"We've got to get out of here," Fannie told him, turning slowly around toward the gate.

With one arm clutching his ribs and the other in Fannie's grasp, he followed her lead. They emerged from the pen. They cautiously followed the opposite wall toward the exit door. The stalls to their right sat empty, the doors wide open. The hallway around them was clear. Torchlight spilled through the herding gate, up ahead, lighting the path in a wash of yellow, beyond which a line of backs surrounded a four-way exhibition in progress—everyone huddled in rapt attention. Fannie and Jonathan moved to elude them by staying in the shadows to the edge of the doorway.

They might have made it, too—albeit to God only knew what next, outside—had Isaac Hoeker not stumbled by at that instant, the worst of all possible moments.

As it happened, his passing was so abrupt, and so shadowed, he almost missed them. In fact, he *did* walk by altogether, and was heading for the door—when it started to dawn on him. Flinching, he slowed to a halt. He was already turning before they could break to run for it.

"Fannie?" He squinted in visibly drunken confusion, gripping a bottle of spirits. *"What are you doing?"* He swayed, then caught himself, snapping to attention on noticing Jonathan. Looking him over: *"What is he—"* Uncomprehendingly, Isaac turned to Fannie. *"What are you doing with him?"* His expression had shifted from puzzled to fully alarmed.

He dropped the bottle and started forward.

Bracing, Jonathan edged away from him.

Fannie stepped in between them. *"Stop it, Isaac."*

He pushed her out of the way and continued for Jonathan.

She jumped in between them again: *"Stop it!"* She pitted her weight against him. *"NO!"*

He still didn't listen.

A holler went up from the crowd on the railings, lost in the blast of the hellbound descent.

Isaac pivoted, whirled by Fannie and dove for Jonathan. Down they went. Jonathan's head hit the floor with a crack. Isaac scrambled to straddle him, pinning his arms down. Then he was punching his skull—repeatedly, blow after blow, with abandon.

Fannie jumped on his back and, screaming, clawed at his face and eyes from behind. Jonathan managed to squirm out from under his weight, then level a kick to his stomach. Isaac heaved.

He went over—and along with him, Fannie—sprawling headlong to the floorboards.

Jonathan heard her cry out on impact. She rolled, gripping the back of her head. Recklessly, Isaac struggled to get to his feet, falling over her. Once more, she cried out . . . Everyone crowding the stables looked over.

It was the first time Jonathan Becker had ever thrown a punch in anger. It would have surprised him no less than the crowd to see Isaac, the bully, go down before him had Fannie's honor not been at stake. Never would Jon have struck anyone, much less Hoeker, without such provocation.

Isaac went stumbling backwards, falling. Into the column of speakers he crashed. They tumbled. He fell to the floor, unconscious. The music died with an echoing clang.

For the very first moment all night, there was silence, if only for one resounding instant. Everyone crowded around the pens had turned to gawk in breathless shock. The pounding outside was in deafening absence. Then came a rumbling rush through the doorway, everyone flocking to see what had happened . . .

The crowd would be left to deduce as much by the overturned speakers across the floor as by Isaac, beside them, flat on his back, as by Jonathan, now, carefully helping Fannie, his *verschproche,* get up.

Holding on to one another, they turned to the crowd on wavering legs.

Before them, eleven Crossbills and two dozen others—many of whom they had known since childhood—gazed back in quiet alarm. Their expressions were suddenly clear—as though Jon's uncharacteristic use of force had triggered in each of them an awakening.

Sensing as much, Jonathan broke the calm with an open-ended suggestion: *"You know, it's not too late to get out of here."*

No elaboration was needed: only the as-yet sirenless calm—itself underscored by the incontrovertibly damning spectacle Beaumont presented.

Lord, Beaumont. Someone would have to pay for that. There was no way around it . . .

But better to deal with it elsewhere and later than up against the police tonight. One look at Rudolf and Buster Highman would probably have had them all shot on the spot.

Such, in essence, was Jonathan's point.

And, just for an instant, they paused to consider it: everyone standing in wall-eyed shock, as though lifting from ages of senseless derangement—some of them draped in feed sacks, others with buckets and snowmobile masks on their heads, most everyone painted (or charred) in some manner, and all looking frightened, bewildered and lost.

In the midst of which, a patter of trickling liquid rose into audibility.

Everyone looked around. The floor beneath Beaumont was spotted with blossoming droplets. Still in a spin, he was urinating—hosing the air in a figure eight. It sprayed down his chest and face to the ground. The trickle ebbed as he slowed from his whirl.

That's when they heard it: up from the dwindling pitter-patter of liquid in dirt: an arrhythmic slapping of footfalls, approaching from the south in lengthy, bounding strides.

A unified gasp went up. The crowd backed away from the wall. A slam rocked into it.

Everyone screamed.

Something was scuttling up the sideboards—clear to the roof. Obscured by smoke and shadow, it dropped through the hole in the ceiling. It landed on a rafter beam, then darted left.

Jonathan made for the overturned speakers. He dug into one of his pockets while moving. Around him, people were scattering blindly—off to the corners, they huddled in terror.

Fannie was left at center floor. Standing alone, with a drained complexion, her hair in a sweat-soaked jumble—as frightened as anyone, clearly—she lifted her gaze.

At the top of the staircase, her cousin appeared.

On emerging, at last, from the loft, he was nearly unrecognizable, even to her. He was scarcely a thing of this world anymore. His eyes were alight with a hatred so intense, no human being could harbor it.

And nothing with such an atrocious hairline belonged in an upright posture at all . . .

Nonetheless, there could be no doubt: it was Ephraim. Sure as the evening was strange. A bigger, more menacing Ephraim, perhaps—turned inside out and then loose on the world—but Ephraim, as everyone present had came to know him, in recent days, all the same. Gazing down on them now, as a wrathful captain assailing a mutinous crew (soon to be walking the plank, every one of them), sheerly imposing. Omniscient. Indomitable.

Any collective awakenings withered. Pangs of conscience were forced into recession. Moments of clarity soured to fear.

In spite of which, Fannie was prompted to sympathy.

Even before she began to sense Jonathan moving around in the shadows behind her, she'd already lifted her hands to Ephraim, intent on coaxing him down alone—as only she could: beckoning gently.

But Ephraim responded as never before: with a snarling lunge down a third of the staircase. He reared up, fixing a closer gaze on her.

A startled commotion went up from the crowd.

Gasping, Fannie took one step back, feeling suddenly vulnerable. All of the earthly compassion had left her cousin's eyes. He was absent, ruthless, full of lascivious intent, and focused on *her,* apparently.

She couldn't contend with such force on her own: not without Ephraim's recognition.

On that, her mind returned to Jonathan: back in the mound of toppled speakers, behind her, under the overhang, out of view—what the hell was he doing back there?

She turned for him.

Plugging a power strip into a generator box, he signaled: *keep going!*

The receiver was working, apparently. Only the speaker cord had been ripped from its socket. The system had been reconnected by Jonathan: down on his knees at the tape deck, waiting for the leader to roll . . .

She understood.

Outside, Officer Kutay was quietly passing the western wall of the barn from a distance of twenty yards to approach, more directly, the crumbling southern side, when he heard, or, with disbelief, could have sworn he was hearing the opening notes of a tune that ran all the way back to his father's tool shed (long afternoons with an AM radio, stripping and sanding and polishing woodwork), from out of the cracks in the building's sideboards, drifting, with flickering creases of torchlight: what sounded like / had to be George Jones, no matter how seemingly, *madly* impossible . . .

Back to back with the chain saw massacre Fatty had heard while approaching the barn, and given the state of Beaumont's cruiser, and everything Kutay had seen being done to it, Possum's voice sounded almost *too* rational. Fatty had trouble believing his ears.

Back up the overgrown lane, a half mile through the corn, his cruiser was stuck in a ditch—the product of trying to drive without headlights. From there, he had crept down the rest of the path with his .45 drawn, moving straight for the chain saws. Once at the edge of the clearing, he'd come into view of the gathering, just as expected, and, much less predictably, Rudolf's cruiser. The sight of it upside down, being beaten, had prompted Fatty to call for backup. His call had then been confirmed by the dispatcher.

"Wait for us, Nelson. Sheriff's orders."

Whereby, Kutay had turned down his radio.

Intent on complying with Highman's order, he'd held his position.

He certainly wasn't about to go in there alone. *No way.*

It was only when, after a couple of minutes, a booming explosion had filled the barn, stopping everyone dead in their tracks outside, soon to be followed by weighted silence, then by a massive stampede through the door—that Officer Kutay suddenly found himself overlooking an empty yard and, whether in fear of losing his quarry or simply out of curiosity, crossed the field to investigate: over the creek on a wooden bridge, around the cluttered, fire-lit clearing, through scattered garments along the periphery, into the shadows, behind the barn . . .

And that's where he'd heard "A Good Year for the Roses."

Which brought him right up to the moment, confirmed.

In a wavering crouch, with the gun in one hand and the pork rind gut sagging over his belt, he made his way up the barn's embankment. He probed for a crack in the building's sideboards. At first, there was something obstructing his view: a stack of paneling maybe—old insulation or boarding stacked up on the inside. He edged his way down the wall to where shimmering light spilled out of the vertical cracks. He peered through one of them. Slowly, his eyes adjusted. He started to take in the scene. To begin with, all he could see was a line of heads, turned away: a motionless throng, and the flickering glare of what must have been torchlight . . . Then he began to notice their costumes: somebody dressed as Christ on a signpost. Someone in drag. Someone else in a gas mask . . . And all of them poised apprehensively, seeming to cower, almost.

They looked out of their minds.

Kutay shifted a few yards down to his right. He peered through a higher crack. This time he saw something moving above them, descending a staircase slowly, its overblown shadow at large on the opposite wall. It was big and dark. Yet he still couldn't make out the details. It looked like a burned animal. Again, he shifted his stance for a better angle. He peered through a crack in the wood that was only a couple of feet off the ground. And *now* he saw it, though what in the name of Jesus, he couldn't begin to wonder. It looked like a charred and decomposing shit monster out of a toxic spill . . .

While descending the stairs, it appeared to be weakened. Or maybe just swaying in time with the music. Then, more than weakened, it seemed to be sick. Or wounded. Or poisoned, perhaps. Or drunk . . . It brought to mind something that Fatty had seen on the TV: a program on Indian snake charmers—out of a basket each serpent had risen, entranced by the plaintive wail of a flute—or in this case, the "Possum," George: crooning in sanguine perfection, into the chorus:

It's been a good year for the roses
Many blooms still linger there
The lawn could stand another mowing
Funny, I don't even care . . .
And when you turn to walk away
As the door behind you closes
The only thing I know to say:
It's been a good year for the roses . . .

The figure dropped below Fatty's line of visibility, obscured by the crowd. Fatty, unconsciously mouthing the words to the song, continued to probe the wall. He discovered what looked like the hole from a .22 slug. He looked in. There it was again: dragging its hindquarters over the floor in starts: an abomination of chance. It was gurgling, gasping. The life force appeared to be draining right out of it. It seemed to be dying—and *sorrowful,* wilting, out of its element, stricken to an excess of vulnerability. The girl at center floor—the only one dressed in standard Dutchie garb—with her arms outstretched in protective assurance, appeared to be holding it under her sway—as toward her it staggered, its energy dwindling with every passing step in advance: the Blue Ball Devil. It had to be. That was no costume.

Kutay could smell it now.

It sank to its haunches before the girl—again, out of sight.

Fatty cursed. He moved to the right. His heart was racing . . .

Where was backup?

He looked though a penny-sized, hollowed-out knot in the sideboards. Now he could see the floor: in the middle of which, the girl stood sobbing, leaning gently over The Devil—itself in prostrate, inert submission—as all around them, the crowd began to blink and stir, as though from a nightmare—proof that music could soothe the soul, it appeared. But then Fatty began to look closer: something was twirling just over the crowd—something he couldn't distinguish at first. Squinting, he strained for a clearer look . . .

. . . bloodied and quivering, oozing, inverted and swollen to threshold retention of fluids . . .

Kutay staggered back from the wall, reeling down the incline. He managed to catch himself. Gagging, he gripped his pistol. *"Rudolf!"* he cried out. An avalanche rolled through his focus. He lifted his barrel and shot through the sideboards. He fired again. And again. And again . . .

The first slug ripped into Isaac Hoeker's prostrate body, lodging into his spine.

The second blew harmlessly over the crowd.

The third shot actually grazed The Devil . . .

And the fourth tore straight through Fannie Gwendolyn Hostler's shoulder, dropping her instantly.

Jonathan was already halfway across the room by the time she had hit the floor. He dove to her side in a scrambling panic. Gasping, he scooped up her motionless body. Her shoulder was bleeding, opening up in a patch of crimson beneath her blouse. Her eyes were closed, but her lips were trembling. She was alive, it appeared. And suffering.

Around them, the crowd was stampeding in terror. A throng of bodies jammed the doorway.

Jonathan cried for an end to it all. His voice was lost in the pandemonium. Something was blocking the torchlight above. He looked up.

Ephraim was standing over him: staring intently down on Fannie. A definite look of recognition, of worry, flared in his gaze for a moment. As quickly, on sniffing her body, that look gave way to an air of devastation. Jonathan watched as the last he would ever see of his oldest friend disappeared. In the place of whom, something more horribly pitiless rose to its full, unbridled stature . . .

It tore through the wall of the barn, with a splintering racket of boards, in a single leap.

Halfway across the field now, running in blind terror, Fatty could hear it: directly behind him, closing fast. He scarcely managed to turn his head before it was severed, leaving his body. End over end, the earth and heavens jumbled. The spinning slammed to a halt.

He was staring up from a clump of thickets. Behind him, the creek was trickling gently. The side of his face was perched on a stone. There was some kind of horrible noise from above.

In his fading moments, he watched his headless corpse being mauled to shreds and trampled.

Back in the barn, "A Good Year for the Roses" faded.

Finally, the sirens were coming.

Owen was just north of Intercourse, trailing a Holtwood patrol car on Harvester Drive, when an APB went out on a place called the Schlabach Farm on Eby Hess Road. The sheriff had summoned all units to respond. There was trouble, apparently—serious trouble, as Owen deduced by the dispatcher's tone. But on following up, he found that the township police had sealed off the gravel drive leading into the fields of the property in question. No one was being allowed to pass, and the cops weren't remarking on the situation. In spite of the livid demands of the Holtwood crew, which was soon to be followed by Sprawl Mart patrols, then a black bumper squadron and no less than thirty "concerned"—meaning armed—citizens, Sheriff Highman's officers staunchly, aggressively refused to impart any details.

Finally, one onlooker, fed up with arguing, stomped to his vehicle, claiming that he knew a "back way" in, if the cops wouldn't help him.

As most of the crowd, including Owen, was prompted thereby to follow his lead—down Eby Hess Road to Old 18, then right for a quarter of a mile, then right again—onto a darkened gravel path on the opposite end of the property in question—it wasn't until they spilled through a gap in the corn and down a bumpy slope and across a field toward a crumbling barn, encircled by flashing cruisers and cops, that a damage report was made available.

Which, evidently, ran as follows:

Thus far, according to Officer Christopher Keiffer's unofficial assessment—offered up only to keep the incoming motorcade at bay for the moment—one Lamepeter officer, name undisclosed, was dead by cause of decapitation. An unidentified Amish girl had been killed by gunfire. Another young man, also Amish and shot, was in an ambulance, paralyzed. A second officer—one whose identity wasn't to be disclosed, at present—had been discovered in a "highly compromising" position inside of the barn. That officer's cruiser, presumably, lay overturned in a heap of devastation. A second cruiser was said to be lodged in a ditch somewhere, back up through the field. A third vehicle, a '72 Hornet, was also marooned in a pile of itself. Thousands of dollars' worth of "suspected robbery" goods lay scattered about—from bottles and clothing to furniture, tools and recliners and boxes of fishing lures—everything, probably down to the final item, reported stolen from barns and garages throughout The Basin that month—collected, at last, in a sprawling array . . .

Keiffer went on to explain how, upon their arrival, the township police had found only two conscious individuals present: an unidentified young Amish man, and a young Amish woman, wounded by gunfire. Neither had spoken a word as of yet. The police were still trying to pry them apart.

Several juvenile suspects, four in total, had been caught fleeing the scene—yet every one of them seemed to have been in the clutches of some kind of drug-induced madness. Filthy, jabbering, wide-eyed and unrestrained, they were bound for a season in the psych ward. The cornfields were said to be crawling with similar, equally crazed young men and women. Two more, both in masquerade, had just been stopped on Ronkers Lane, and from them, only one person's name had been spoken with any clarity:

Ephraim.

With that, the crowd surrounding Keiffer, who would later take a pranging for making a statement—had heard enough. The Sprawl Mart patrol was already familiar with *that* name. Half of the black bumper squadron on hand had been searching for someone named Ephraim all night. The last order Officer Kutay, now deceased, had received was to check on the home of one Abraham Hostler for a young man in breach of house arrest named Ephraim Bontrager. Three of the city cops in attendance had orders to find and catch him, as well . . .

Suddenly, a name had been thrown to the mob, and, at once, that name became an objective—so much so, that the moment a Stepford detective pulled up in a silver Land Rover, everyone crowded around his vehicle, shouting demands, thumping the hood.

Alarmed, the detective rolled down his window. There, on his passenger's seat, in open view, was a portable tracking box.

A couple of officers slowly emerged from the barn, looking notably pale and unsettled. Instead of dispersing the crowd that had grown to encircle the nameless Stepford detective, they joined it with heated demands for involvement. Everyone wanted in on the kill.

Dragging the box from the passenger's seat, the detective placed it on top of his hood. He activated the power. It glowed to life. A digital grid appeared. The program was loading. A moment passed . . . Then came a tiny electronic blip.

Adjusting a dial, the detective looked up. He pointed west: "He's over there."

* * *

Unlike what a good many district members, and Plain Folk in general, had grown to believe, Jonas Tulk knew The Devil was vulnerable. A fleeting eternity might have elapsed since he'd shot it, but that wouldn't alter the fact: at a time when the compound had been much smaller—a twenty-cage facility—and far less secure, when the dogs had provided their only alarm, and the doors had been poorly (uselessly) fortified, Jonas alone, armed only with a .22 rifle, caught totally unawares (sleeping) and firing into the dark, no less—had crippled the beast in a single shot. He remembered it yowling off into the night—alive, but wounded: as quick to be driven away as it had appeared.

It was flesh and bone.

Tonight, after so many years, he was better prepared. Tonight, there would be no surprises. The compound was fully equipped at present. Now there were floodlights, reinforced doors, security cameras, alarms and a phone. Jonas himself, wide awake, stood armed with a sawed-off shotgun in hand and a .357 revolver tucked into his belt. Every electrical light in the building, both inside and out, was glaring intensely. All four cameras were working. As well as the alarms. And all of the doors were locked . . . Cleon and Bontrager may not have been there, and James and Ezekiel were roaming The Basin, but Jonas felt ready to hold down the compound alone. In fact, he preferred it this way.

From the ground floor's office, a cubicle packed with camera screens, he could survey the property. Nothing would enter—or pass—undetected. All systems were go.

And none too soon.

All through the evening, he'd waited with tortured impatience. At one point, he'd almost jumped the gun, when, from out of nowhere, a figure had crossed the highest screen of his monitor: a vaguely familiar woman's image in tattered white—partly obscured by darkness, stumbling east on the road . . .

The experience had left him on edge. But maybe, he decided, that was where he belonged. Ghostly apparitions wouldn't contend with the flesh and blood of The Devil. Tulk knew enough to expect a direct attack. It would probably storm the doors. As well, it would probably appear after midnight, when most of the roads were beginning to clear. The Devil had always relied on instinct more than intelligence—even though, recently, *some*thing had entered the compound through one of its ceiling hatches.

Those hatches were blocked now.

The only way into the building was via the main entrance, directly ahead.

In one of the cages, a Labrador puppy lifted its head from the slumbering cluster. It stared at the wall for a moment. Ever so gently, it thumped its tail on the mesh. Then again. It sat up.

Two cages over, a collie stirred from sleep with a growl.

Tulk stood in silence, gazing around at the angular, sheet metal walls of the building as though in the gut of an English whale.

The Labrador barked. The others around it began to sit up. They stared at the wall.

It was quiet again.

Jonas walked to the office and looked at the camera monitors. No sign of movement.

He returned to the floor.

He drew a corncob pipe from his pocket.

Maybe this would steady his nerves. He lit the bowl.

The alarm went off.

Every dog in the building sat up.

Jonas ran back to the office.

A light was flashing and buzzing under the monitors. He looked at the screens. There was nothing. No movement, no glitch in transmission. Unless the fence had been climbed already, it looked untouched. *Except* . . . (as it nearly eluded him)—maybe for: what was that jag in the pattern out there?—in the northeastern corner?

He flipped to manual. Zooming, he saw it: a gash in the wire.

That alloy was meant to be indestructible.

He flipped off the twelve-gauge's safety—and no sooner done than the pounding commenced from outside: a giant *slam* on the wall, to his left—and then, coming around, on the right . . . Or behind him? . . . Again, on the left . . . (?)

He ran back to the office. The monitor screens were jolting with static. The impact was coming from all sides at once. With the fence alarms blaring and every dog in the compound baying off its rocker—he wasn't even able to hear himself think.

He tried to deactivate the alarm. But something was wrong with the console, apparently. Something had locked up. It wouldn't respond. A honking blast tore out of the wall-mounted speakers above him. He fled the office.

Out on the floor, the chorus of howling had welled to a level, atonal crescendo. From every cage in the building it rose.

There were three aisles, each running twenty yards back to the loading gate. All of the units were stuffed with puppies. And all of the puppies were howling.

Furious, Tulk called out for silence. He walked down the aisle, ramming the gate handles. The wailing rose, as though to spite him. Then there was pounding again, on the walls. The mounted alarms continued to blast. The Labradors wouldn't pipe down, God damn them. He rattled their cage. They snapped at him, then resumed howling, undaunted. He flushed with rage.

He leveled the twelve-gauge and fired.

Silence.

As quickly as Tulk had reacted, the sirens let up. Along with the pounding outside.

A whimper rose from the quivering mound of Labrador puppies, most of them dead.

Twice more, he fired.

The rest of the cages were still.

Jonas moved to reload. He thumbed a lead slug into the chamber and pumped it. While digging more slugs from his pocket, he suddenly thought of the cameras. He turned around, took a step back toward the office and looked in. The static was gone from the screens. They were still on. And something was moving on one of them. Jonas drew closer. It took him a moment.

Then he saw it.

It was looking right into the camera—grinning . . .

Jonas screamed.

His lifted his twelve-gauge to blow the whole board in response. But as quickly, the lights went out.

Which wasn't supposed to be able to happen.

Benedictus had gone to ridiculous lengths to safeguard their power supply. The only way to disrupt its flow would have been to sever the main to the generator. And no one could do that without a key. The access box was made of titanium.

Tulk, in a panic, fumbled blindly in search of the office. He ran into something—a chair. Sliding past it, he got to the door. He lifted an oil lamp down from a hook to the right of the frame. He lit it. The objects around him glowed back into view. He continued reloading the shotgun. Before he could finish, the puppies resumed their lament—from one corner, first, though scarcely perceptible, then from another, in tandem and rising: soon to engulf the whole building.

Here was a genuine call to the damned.

Jonas returned to the floor with the lamp. On approaching the cages, he slowed his advance. In confusion, he lifted his flame and, shivering, peered around. Something was different here. None of the lights was working. But more than that, something had changed. The scene appeared as though through a tinted, burgundy filter.

His balance wavered.

Slowly, he bent for a look to his right. A cage full of snapping huskies lunged at him. Something was wrong with them: milky-white gazes by lantern light. Cataracts. Blind, they were blind . . .

As he backed away, his gaze fell over the unit behind them. A rottweiler stood where a litter of puppies had sat moments earlier.

As with the huskies, it snapped at him viciously, foaming at the mouth. It appeared to be diseased.

Down the aisle, they proceeded, thus: on either side of him, baying obscenely.

Golden retrievers with scoliosis, hunched in defiance, gnawing the gate. A tick hound with some kind of skin condition. An Irish setter vomiting bile. Dobermans crippled with bone marrow cancer in squalling heaps. Arthritic dalmatians. And, underfoot, rivers of filth and feces.

The stench was impossible, even for Tulk.

Again, he leveled the shotgun and fired.

The tick hound's image was sawed in half. In its place lay a mound of bloodied puppies.

He pumped the gun and turned around.

An enormous *slam* hit the loading gate door: Once. Twice. Then three times—it buckled, steadily tearing away from the frame.

Each impact was staggering. Never had Jonas imagined such force. He shot at the door.

The last of his slugs tore into its lining. He dropped his twelve-gauge and went for the pistol. Tearing from its hinges, the door rushed inward—advancing upright, being pushed from behind. He fired. Sparks went up. It kept moving, unstoppable: straight up the aisle . . .

Here it came.

He unloaded his chambers at once.

It flattened him.

He wound up pinned to the floor underneath it. The handle had gouged and torn his scrotum. A broken rib tore into one lung.

He strained to cry out. But his voice was gone.

Through his agony, all he could sense was The Devil. Standing over him. Moving around.

It wandered down one of the aisles: repugnance incarnate / brimming with foul intent.

On every side, the howling welled into a final sustain, above which, almost inaudibly, Tulk heard the unmistakable sound of a cage door sliding open.

It took him a couple of minutes to catch up, but Rudolf managed to overtake—and edge his way to—the head of the line. He was driving Nelson Kutay's cruiser. The needle was pushing 105. Part of a candle was lodged in his ass. He had burn marks all over his body. Bruises. Cuts. Abrasions. Fractured appendages . . . Veering all over the road, he was murderous. Everyone tried to steer from his path. A man in a Chevy had almost gone into the ditch while attempting to let him pass. None of them mattered now. Only one thing was imperative: kill the Minister's son. Wherever he'd come from, whatever abominations of chance had conspired to produce him, and disregarding all ramifications: Ephraim, The Kornwolf, the Blue Ball Devil, could not be allowed to survive this evening. There could be no risk at all of his capture. And critically: no one could get to him first . . . The killing stroke was reserved for Rudolf, for whom all remedial notions of personal human integrity hung in the balance. Already, he wouldn't be able to face his fellow Lamepeter Township officers, nine in total, who'd cut him down from his shame in suspension, ever again. Even now, he could hear them laughing. For the rest of his life, he would never escape it. Some things simply cannot be lived down. Rudolf's career as a cop was over. Aside from the charges pending, as yet—the Bontrager / Yoder / Percy debacle—he would never set foot in the precinct again. That much he'd come to terms with already. What bothered him now was the mere possibility that someone might get to the creature first: without sending it back to hell himself, Beaumont, undoubtedly, would never even be able to *kill* himself in peace. He wouldn't know how to face his maker. Or The Devil.

Bitch of eternity.

His uniform stunk of sweat and urine. His wrists and ankles were chafed with rope burn.

He *slammed* into one of the Sprawl Mart vans. It swerved to the shoulder. He pulled ahead of it. He gained on a truck full of locals with high-powered spotting lamps, probing a field to the south. It jarred to one side as he passed. He accelerated—soon to be rolling by Officer Kreider—then Sergeant Billings, and onward, hurtling—up the procession in reckless abandon. His wheel base straddled the dotted line. The ditches passed at a rumbling blur. Finally, he pulled up beside the Land Rover, leading the pack. He looked over. He pointed.

The city detective scowled—as though to say: *What the hell do you think you're doing?*

Beaumont ignored the gesture, demanding, in turn, with a show of hands: *Where is he?* He pointed to the tracking box. *Which direction?*

Annoyed, the detective pointed north: *Over there*—then added insistently: *Slow down!*

Rudolf disregarded him.

Roaring ahead, he crossed the junction at Peterville Drive and Shelty Run Avenue. His radio garbled with angry shouts. The pavement steadily rose before him. Just ahead, it was: *right over there* . . . He could feel it now: over the hill. Almost there . . .

Sheriff Highman's voice exploded: *"Beaumont, you son of a bitch!"* from the radio: *"Cool your jets, God damn it! Slow down!"*

Rudolf floored his accelerator. Cresting the hill at 110, he continued. The road leveled out. Then, abruptly, it started to dip.

That's when the woman appeared.

Her crazed expression, her tattered dress, the slash marks running from shoulder to torso flashed in the headlights from nowhere, rising. A vision of madness, blocking the road.

Soon she was up on the hood. The windshield exploded. Beaumont's vehicle rolled.

Her body was tossed.

Through the slam and jumble, Rudolf could feel himself splattered in blood.

* * *

The next driver over the hill, the detective, plowed right into his overturned cruiser. It spun with the impact, tearing the pavement.

The Land Rover ended up jammed in a ditch.

Then came a Sprawl Mart wagon, dead-on. It went end over end.

The pileup commenced:

Officer Kreider collided with three different vehicles—Sergeant Billings's cruiser, the truck full of locals with deer spotting lamps, and Kutay's vehicle, with Beaumont inside of it—consecutively, all in attempting to steer clear of one: the upended Sprawl Mart wagon. Seven more vehicles—three patrol cars, two pickups, one Holtwoodmobile and a Rabbit—were added. Thirteen vehicles lay in states of ruin before it was over.

Bodies began to appear in the wreckage, crawling from windows, cursing Jesus.

The headless corpse of the woman lay sprawled on the road, hosing blood all over the pavement.

Inside of the overturned cruiser, Rudolf found her head.

The Minister's sister.

Yelling, he scurried out of the heap.

On his feet now, he couldn't determine where all of the blood was coming from. Given the pain, he assumed that his right arm was broken. And something was wrong with his neck. But he didn't feel cut. He was covered with blood, but it didn't appear to be his . . .

He had killed her.

To hell with it.

Dozens of people were mobbing the road. He hobbled across the pavement, managing, somehow, not to be singled out. Over the shoulder and down the embankment. He opened the Land Rover's passenger door. Inside of it, clutching his ribs, the detective scowled. "What kind of an asshole *are* you?"

A .45 auto was pressed to his skull. Beaumont demanded: "Where is he?"

Coughing, the detective shook his head. "I already told you." He pointed across the field. "He's right over there. We were almost on top of him."

Rudolf followed his gesture.

Back to and over the road he proceeded, down the bank to a field of weeds. Before he could blend into darkness entirely, somebody called his name. He'd been spotted.

No matter.

The field was awash in moonlight. He ran through the weeds. There was mud underfoot. It was marshy and black.

He fell on his face.

Plastered in oozing grit and sediment, he got back up. He shook off his pistol, groaning. He clutched his arm. It was broken.

No matter.

He pressed on.

After a break in the weeds, an incline lifted steadily out of the marsh—up, up—to a dry plateau. From the edge of which, Rudolf finally spotted it.

Moving away in the dark, maybe forty yards up: in a streak of white. It was stumbling.

Wounded.

It must have been shot.

It was breathing erratically, wheezing. Beaumont could hear it.

Ignoring a cry from behind, he went after it.

"Rudy!" somebody yelled for him. "Stop!"

They were chasing him . . .

No matter: this was the end.

He dropped to one knee and took careful aim. He squeezed the trigger.

The figure collapsed.

Slowly exhaling, Beaumont looked over the trembling sights of his smoking barrel. He squinted, then stood up. Ahead, the motionless figure lay sprawled in a clump of thickets.

Kreider ran by. Then Officer Hertz . . .

He followed them over to look at the body.

Facedown in the weeds, it was perfectly dead. The bullet had gone through the back of its chest.

The problem was: even in death, it was bigger than Beaumont expected. Bigger than Ephraim. And whiter. And older: with sagging buttocks.

Most notably, it was a human being.

And worse: its hands were bound with wire. As well, it was gagged with electrical tape. And something was literally pinned to its shoulder—pinned into place with a finishing staple.

He stooped to look closer. The object was plastic. It looked like an ankle bacelet. It *was*—a police-issued ankle bracelet: tagged to the bone with a staple.

Kreider whistled. "Whoa. Jesus Christ, Rudy . . ."

Officer Hertz shook his head, bending forward.

A couple of people ran up as the body was rolled over, onto its back.

Benedictus.

In spite of his noble intentions, along with his moral authority in court that evening, there wasn't much left to this whole affair that could have gone worse for Jarret Yoder. Assessing the damage, now, at the mill—and all it implied, indirectly or not so—he realized he hadn't made one right move the whole way through. His failure was total. Had he listened to Jack at the outset, weeks ago, the worst charge they might have been facing now would be (arguably justifiable) kidnapping. Had he left the floor to Stutz that evening—or better yet, turned the case over to Metzger, as intended, or even pled guilty as charged—he wouldn't be facing potential disbarment, he wouldn't have doomed his reputation, and he wouldn't have placed his trusted colleague, the judge, in the line of the coming shit storm.

More, had he kept his mouth shut, the kid would be holed up in Joseph's Hall right now—maybe strapped to a chair in the psych ward, or locked in a padded cell, full of tranquilizers. Sixteen injuries, four of them critical, wouldn't have been sustained in the pile-up. An unidentified Amish youth wouldn't lie in paralysis, shot in the back. Dozens of Orderly juveniles probably wouldn't be roaming the fields either. The only decent cop in Blue Ball, Nelson Kutay, wouldn't be dead. Jane Doe from the Schlabach Farm wouldn't be on the floor with a gunshot wound. One of Yoder's targets, Beaumont, wouldn't have mowed down another, Bontrager—*after* he'd already killed the defense's witness, Grizelda Hostler—in public. And, last: the body of Jonas Tulk might not lie mauled to a gurgling pulp . . .

A heartbreaker, that one.

Yoder was watching them scoop his remains from the compound floor.

At least this answered a few of Jarret's oldest questions, however egregiously.

Since long before he had left The Basin, moved to the city and enrolled in law school, he had been suffering, *agonizing* over his role in what had become of Jacob.

In the end, he had always been forced to accept the fact that there'd been no choice.

When, finally (after not having been seen for a week), Jacob had stumbled out of the forest that early November morning, appearing to Yoder on his grandfather's property, he had been less than half alive. A rifle slug had been lodged in his chest. His tattered shirt had been soaked in blood. He'd been writhing in fitful, delirious starts.

Without medical attention, he wouldn't have made it. Jarret harbored no guilt on that matter. How to *get* that attention had been the dilemma—as it haunted him still, after all this time.

He couldn't have reported his friend to The Order, as District Seven had shunned him already. More alarmingly, rumors that Jonas Tulk had shot The Devil the night before had been drifting around the Intercourse Market. For Jacob to show up then, the next morning, with a bullet wound would've been suicidal.

In light of ongoing events in Blue Ball, he couldn't have turned to the cops either. The Basin had been much smaller back then—less populated by a factor of three. One look at Jacob and the local police might have dragged him out back, if given the chance.

Jarret could not have accepted that risk.

But what had that left him, then?

The army.

Initially, the mere idea had sickened him. That Yoder, of all people—first as a Mennonite (albeit a doomed, if still pacifistic one), and second, as a young man of worldly ambitions growing up in the dawn of the Age of Aquarius—would even *consider* contacting government "hippy catchers" felt tantamount to blasphemy.

Yet, for that matter, he hadn't been a doctor. And Jacob had been dying.

There had been *no choice.*

Jarret had driven his car to a filling station. From there, he had placed a call to the Stepford County recruiting office. An MD had been dispatched to accompany him back to the shack on his grandfather's property. There, an unconscious Jacob was placed on a stretcher, then loaded into an ambulance.

Jarret had watched them roll away.

And so had gone Jacob's life in The Basin.

On the good side, Jack would not only forgive him (though Yoder wouldn't know it for years), he would later commend him for acting sensibly. More, he would thank him for saving his life—and, far more still: the lives of others. On that point, Jack would remain insistent.

And now, at last, Yoder understood why.

On the bad end, Jacob would lose almost everything, beginning with his status as an Orderly CO. Having violated the terms of his service ("1–W" work), he was no longer eligible for road patrol. Normally, this would've relegated him overnight to basic training. But Jarret, through months of dogged persistence, would never be able to confirm as much. The closest he would get, via dozens of phone calls to army spokesmen all over the world, was an indirect suggestion that Jacob, his friend, was "possibly"' overseas. Jarret would never have any specific knowledge of Jack's career in the service. Aside from a claim to have "spent some time in Asia," Jack himself wouldn't speak of it. Only one thing was dependably certain: he had been gone for the next four years.

In its wake, his disappearance would fuel conjecture throughout the whole community. In spite of his exile, his name would come up (with solemn reserve) during talk of The Devil. His involvement in numerous livestock attacks would be rumored. Tulk would be said to have shot him.

Such hearsay would only inflate when a government agent appeared at market that winter. By asking around about Jacob, he (the agent) would manage to kindle a good deal of panic among the Intercourse vendors. Thus, he would be directed to District Seven's council, as expected. Bishop Holtz, who had lost three acres of corn at harvest, would turn him away, insisting the council could only pronounce the surname that Satan had given *that* creature—a title to ring in damnation forever, as forebears in infamy—the surname of Stumpf.

The agent would take note.

And that was how Jacob had lost his name.

From there on out, he would fade from Orderly recognition altogether.

His parents, who had always been staunch fundamentalists, would start by refusing to acknowledge his name. This would be followed with icy resolve by most of his friends and former associates. Probably his staunchest remaining defender, his sister, would die giving birth that spring. One by one, his fellow supper gang members, "The Rutles," would join their churches. Thereafter, rising property taxes would lead to the relocation of many of his family members to the rural Midwest. Ephraim, the boy, would know less about Jacob, his uncle, than Jack of his nephew's existence. The boy would grow up at a time when The Basin would lose a third of its Amish residents. The whole community would be redefined. Diminishing congregations would merge. The First and Eleventh Districts would join to form what became the Twenty-first. The Tenth would dissolve, pouring into the Fourth, as the lay of the land itself would be altered. Once reconfigured, the Seventh District would bear only shades of its former likeness. Less than half of its membership would have any tangible memory of Jacob. His image would have dimmed to a sketchy anomaly, just as The Devil would have faded.

Yoder alone, in the whole of the county, would recognize (and greet) him—albeit with speechless disbelief—upon his unexpected return to Stepford.

He often took solace in knowing that Jack had resurfaced "unblighted," as he referred to it. That is: sound of mind and body.

By appearances, he had been in form. His bearing had been direct and clear. What's more, he had gained about seventy pounds of muscle. He'd come back as big as a house.

Beyond all of which, in a baffling twist, he had learned how to fight—and to fight like a pro: almost as though he'd gone down to the crossroads.

Even though Jarret could only imagine what Jack had lived through "overseas," he felt certain of one thing: the truth would be sure to exceed his wildest flights of fancy.

He knew that whatever had happened out there, he himself was, to some extent, responsible.

That had been quite a load to bear, for many years.

It still made him cringe.

Tonight, however, the consequences of not keeping one of those . . . *things* . . . locked up were apparent—all too horribly apparent.

Never again would he doubt Jack's word.

Four state troopers, three downtown cops and a mob of disgusted township patrolmen were roaming the filthy aisles of the compound with handkerchiefs clutched to their blanching faces. Outside, a half dozen volunteer firemen jockeyed to peer through the guarded doorway. Behind them, a black bumper squadron of no fewer than twenty members—including the band of four that had chanced on the scene when, in passing, a scramble of dogs had poured out of the building—was gathered with torches and clubs in the parking lot. As was a growing crowd of locals.

Everyone present could smell the facility. Those on the inside were viewing the cages. And once the sheriff had arrived with a crime scene photographer, Jarret considered it settled. The mill would never recover from this.

After a couple of minutes, he noticed an officer kneeling by one of the cages. Inside was a Jack Russell terrier: one of the puppies that hadn't been freed to devour its keeper: whimpering frantically, scratching. The officer spoke through a handkerchief. "What's this?" He leaned forward, poking the cage. The puppy licked his fingers. It started to bark.

Around it, the other dogs joined in.

Shaking his head, the officer lifted the bolt on the door. He opened it slowly.

Over his shoulder the animal sprang.

It touched down running: across the aisle and into the clearing. Past Yoder. It weaved through a tangle of legs and coattails.

The sheriff yelled, *"Somebody stop that dog!"*

Too late: it was already out the door . . .

In the parking lot, startled, a couple of volunteer firemen tried to step in its path. But the terrier slipped them with ease, cutting left—under buggies, then up to the road in a flash. The crowd, seeming unsettled more than curious, watched it stop to sniff at the pavement. Slowly, it lifted its snout to the wind. A couple of men from the squadron pointed. The others stopped talking. Everyone stared.

With his head thrown back, the terrier howled in a shrill, resounding cry to the moon. The rest of the dogs in the building joined in.

Sheriff Highman came out of the mill.

For a moment, the chorus welled up in the night, as a pipe organ filling a roofless cathedral.

The crowd stood motionless.

Then, abruptly, the terrier bolted up the road bank.

A voice went up: *"He's on to something!"*

The black bumper squadron dispersed in a scramble: on foot, they went after it, most of them—hollering: straight up the bank at a charge with their torches. A half dozen Englishmen followed along. The volunteer firemen ran for their cars. Behind them, the city and highway patrolmen spilled from the compound and into their cruisers. Followed by most of the township officers. Sheriff Highman ran back inside. Yoder got into his ATV, determined to stay behind a wheel.

On pulling away, he saw two of the sheriff's men leading a pack of dogs from the building.

Sergeant Billings's radio blared from the otherwise battered heap of his cruiser. It sounded across the pileup scene. A crowd of hundreds was standing by: what looked to be every person the Holtwood corporation had ever employed. Several more Plain Folk in family wagons. Five infuriated Sprawl Mart crews. A growing fleet of locals on four-wheelers. Members of the press (*that reporter from town*). A motorcade of "registered marksmen" deployed by the Reemsville Pistol and Fishing Brigade. And a phalanx of drunken drivers and urban degenerate trash in masquerade, joy-riding . . .

Everyone heard or got wind of the message in moments: the hellhounds were onto The Kornwolf. Foraging south, they were: just over there . . .

The Coalition began to roll.

Owen wound up toward the front of the line. Which he knew better than to want any part of. He edged over, letting the pickup trucks riding his ass move around him. They drifted ahead. Then, before giving up too much placement, he got back in line. He was keeping the pace.

Above, on the right, moving steadily down an embankment toward him, he spotted fire. There were people with torches, on foot. They were running. And shouting in anger. They looked to be Amish.

Brake indicators appeared in the road. Owen slowed down. Headlights glared from an intersection, directly ahead.

Leading the Orderly mob, Emmanuel Stoltzfus shielded his eyes in the glare. He reared up, waving his torch in the road. Behind him, his sons, with various members of the Brechbuhl, Kachel and Hostler families (an unlikely grouping, if ever there'd been), came out of the downhill charge at a stumble. Coughing, they tripped to the opposite shoulder and, lifting their torches, looked into the forest. The puppy was gone. Too fast, it had been for them: last spotted booming ahead, toward the ridge up above and behind them, and over and gone.

Stoltzfus was livid. He stormed in circles, waiting for someone to make a suggestion. Around him, jamming all four of the roadways, the English motorcade rumbled and honked.

A furious Damien Hostler—brother of Abraham, whose daughter had just been shot, demanded in German: *"Where did it go!?"*

The parents of Gideon Brechbuhl shouted: *"What have you done to our children, Emmanuel?!"*

Bishop Schnaeder appeared from the crowd, stepping forward to ward off impending violence.

From out of the motorcade, even more Plain Folk rushed toward the argument, ditching their buggies.

The honking rose to a deafening blast.

Finally, a siren let out from the west. Flashing lights appeared in both lines. Traffic parted, crowding the shoulder. The sheriff's cruiser broke through the line.

Buster Highman got out of the vehicle. Two of his men, Billings and Kreider, were there to meet him. Their cruisers were hammered. He led them around to the passenger's side.

He opened the door.

Each of them brought out a pair of dogs.

A cry went up.

Everyone mobbing the road looked over.

The dogs were howling into the forest, straining on leashes, the same way the puppy had . . .

Dwayne Gibbons, from behind the wheel of his Chevy Blazer, watched everyone scatter: over the pavement and down the slope in a trailing rush of flame they went. They were following Highman, two of his men and the hounds. Gibbons floored the gas . . . His Blazer lurched to the right—off the shoulder. He drove on an angle past three other pickups. Then he swung back up the incline and onto New Holland Avenue, leading the pack.

Through a break in the trees on his left, he could still see them moving. Torches flared in the overgrowth. Four-wheelers shot down the bank in pursuit of them. Everyone else in the motorcade fishtailed the corner, following Gibbons's lead.

The torches were starting to drift, dimming into the forest.

A lane forked off to his left. He swung onto it. A van shot past him before he could level out of the turn. He sped up.

The torches appeared from the north, approaching.

Again, the mob poured out of the forest, spilling across the road in his headlights. Again, it continued moving south, with Highman running the hounds among them. And again, the motorcade followed along in tenuously pending loss of contact.

This time, however, a break in the foliage opened up to the side of the road. Gibbons trailed after those in the lead—turning left, down a gravel path through some evergreens: straight for the edge of a broad clearing.

Having caught sight of an island of trees, Gibbons pulled ahead of the pack. His Blazer bounced over rows of stubble. Behind him, the Holtwood crew followed up. They circled around to the rear of the multiple-acre plot of chestnut trees. A couple of pickups cut to the left. The rest of the Sprawl Mart wagons followed them. A phalanx of gas hogs surrounded the island. Their high beams illuminated the overgrowth.

A driver in camouflage hunting fatigues got out of a jeep and waved in the headlights. Gibbons lifted his M-14 from the backseat and went to see what was happening . . .

A terrier was yapping into the bushes.

The black bumper squadron had only crossed half of the field when a torrent of gunfire erupted. The sheriff, ahead of them, felt a patch of lead shot cut the air above him. He jumped in his boots with Billings and Kreider beside him, then ducked and continued forward. While closing the gap, there were four more shots in rapid succession, then panicked shouting. A moment of silence. A call from the opposite end of the plot. Somebody screaming. The roar of an engine. Two more shots.

Then: a curdling howl.

On the sheriff's orders, Kreider and Billings released the dogs and unholstered their weapons. They ran with their pistols extended in straight-armed braces, stumbling recklessly forward. They passed a van full of volunteer firemen lodged in a cornrow, spinning manure: ahead, the rest of the motorcade rumbled and ground to a halt, surrounding the trees.

Jarret Yoder got out of his muddied 4x4 and looked around. He saw Holtwood patrolmen arrayed in the headlights, training their guns on a clump of thickets. Then he saw cops running up to them, yelling to cool it—as dozens of torch-wielding Orderlies followed from every direction at once.

Yoder moved forward to see what was happening. Several policemen and one of the Holtwood officials were arguing back and forth—soon to be joined by the mob all around them.

Another barrage of shots went up. A horrible cry let out from the darkness.

Dwayne Gibbons ran into the bushes. A moment later, his rifle boomed. Then it came flying back out of the ecotone—followed as quickly, end over end, by the lifeless body of Gibbons himself:

it slammed into one of the Sprawl Mart wagons and dropped in a splayed array of limbs. Officer Billings ran over and, crouching, checked for a pulse.

Gibbons was dead.

Across the way, on the northern edge of the plot, Owen saw someone collapse. It was one of the Holtwood droogs. He was screaming, clutching his chest in the weeds. He'd been shot.

Everyone scattered, leaving him there. Owen ran back to his car. Some Plain Folk were hiding behind it in terror already. He crouched in their midst. A couple of volunteer firemen hit the dirt behind them.

The shooting and screaming continued: along with that sickly, curdling howl from the darkness. Then, over the top of it, multiple bullhorns issued an order to *"Hold your fire!"*

The shooting desisted. From out of the calm rose a scream. The Holtwood droog was in agony. "*—shot* me! Bastards."

A voice followed up in the bullhorn: *"Everyone out of there! Now!"*

A moment of silence gave way to more shouting: "What are *you* gonna do about it, Sheriff?"

"Yeah, Buster!"

More voices: "To hell with him!"

"*—SHOT* me!"

Confusion.

Again, from the bullhorn: "We'll *torch* it out, that's what!"

And Highman wasn't the first to have thought of it. Off to his left, a pickup truck driver had lifted a gas can out of a hatchback. Behind him, a growing mob of Orderlies muttered in understanding compliance: such had been their intention, it seemed.

They parted, spreading in both directions. As the Holtwood droog was pulled to safety, they probed the brush for brittle thickets.

The sheriff repeated: "We'll *torch* it out then!"

A Sprawl Mart official emerged from the plot, looking terrified. Then came a tall man in dungarees.

When no one else stepped from the darkness, Highman resumed. "Is everyone out of there now? Where's Manny?"

"Dead!" someone called. "Forget him."

"Now hold on . . . "

Down the row, they were dousing the brush with accelerants.

Highman repeated: "Hold *ON*!"

They ignored him, backing away.

A wall of flame leapt up in the brush.

The sheriff started forward: "No! You idiots!!"

Tripping, he fell on his face.

On the southern end, several Orderlies, aided by superstore guards toting gallons of gasoline, managed to link the blazes. The flames rose quickly. The heat forced everyone back.

For the first time, a cry of grim jubilation went up from the crowd.

"BURN!" someone yelled.

A roar of agreement.

The sheriff's orders were lost in the cheering.

Again: *"Burn, you son of a bitch!"*

And chanting: *"DIE! DIE! DIE!"*—in unison.

They fired their guns in the air . . .

Owen looked around in amazement.

There were hundreds of people now—most having left their vehicles back in the traffic or jammed in the mud at the edge of the field, and come running: a motley procession of firemen, farmers, cops, Plain Folk and honky suburbanites.

Just when Owen had thrown in the towel on The Sacred Chao in Stepford Town, enter: The Devil, as advocate *par extraordinaire*.

He still hadn't seen it.

After all that had happened, he would never lay eyes on it . . .

He could *hear* it, though: screaming like something washed up on the wrong end of Pluto's moon.

Owen couldn't help but relate.

Part of him felt to be in there with it.

Slowly, he emerged from the shadows behind his car. He turned away from the blaze.

A feeling of homesickness—or maybe of home*less*ness: pangs of the uprooted—overtook him. Ready to sit out the final act, he spotted the glare of headlights approaching . . .

From out of the woods to the north—through which, so far, no other automobiles had materialized—barreling over the rows in a lurching of high-powered beams and the roar of hydraulics: the F-150 was already turning heads. It was closing too fast for the distance—approaching dead-on. The cheering subsided. A wave of alarm swept over its path.

The crowd divided, dodging to either side in a chorus of panicked hollering.

Never veering, the vehicle shot through the ecotone, crashing through thickets and limbs. One of its wheels caught a rut in the soil. It launched through the flames on an angle, then came down, kicked to the left, inside of the plot, out of view of the mob, encircled by fire.

Fortunate not to have rammed a chestnut (or to have blown the tanks) coming through, Jack leapt out of his driver's seat. At once, the heat was nearly unbearable. Hiking his collar up past his ears, he darted ahead toward a break in the trees. On every side, he could hear them shouting: *"Get the hell out of there!"*—*"Crazy!"*—and, one and all: *"Who was that?"*—in a garbled roar. But they wouldn't come after him. Not in these flames. They were out of the picture.

He looked around.

A fallen chestnut lay in the clearing before him, etched in a haze of smoke.

As could only emerge from the starkest reality, there it was. Crouched on the trunk, its outline black in the flaring heat . . . It was panting. Wild-eyed. It looked to be wounded. And burned . . .

It was glaring right at him. *Jesus . . .*

It really *did* look like Richard Nixon.

Jack had spent all evening chasing this thing, always lagging behind by a critical step. He had been all over Lamepeter Township—from Bontrager's home to the Schlabach estate to the Hostler address to Cry in the Dark—and now that he'd found it, the blighted one didn't appear to sense anything different about him.

Good.

This would be tricky enough. In its present condition—wounded, cornered and frightened—it would be at its most dangerous. This would take perfect timing. And accuracy . . .

And here it came, down the length of the trunk at a scurry, lunging directly for Jack: as quickly as he could sit down on a right-handed bomb up the middle.

The impact was flush.

The blighted one dropped like a sack of apples.

Jack hovered over the motionless figure to make sure it wasn't playing possum.

While doing so, he waited for the pain to creep into his hand. But it never materialized.

He straightened up gradually, breathing.

Scarlet would be impressed.

He That Still Wallops.

He should have just done this to start with—skipped the formalities and simply abducted the kid. They would have been in much less trouble now, all of them—especially Jarret, the sorry bastard.

As it stood, they were placing themselves at risk of exposure on too many fronts. And if either man were *ever* connected with this, they would both go to prison for years.

In which case, essentially, there was no telling what might become of the boy . . .

Still, he couldn't be left to die. The Crow was dead. And Jack wasn't God.

The Coach had spent most of the second half of his life atoning for much of the first. And, as part of it, this matter wasn't for him to decide. The rest would be up to Ephraim.

He crept back over to his truck, still shielding his face with his collar. He opened the cab door and reached inside. He dragged out the wolf girdle . . . Here was the fruit of the farrier's labor: two hundred pounds of iron plating welded into a body harness. Once strapped in, there was nothing alive that could ever bust out of it. Even a kornwolf.

Jack was locking the bridle in place when, above the roar, he heard a sharp, insistent yapping. He looked around.

A spotted terrier was stamping its paws in the dirt before him. It snapped at the blighted one. Then it challenged Jack. It was fearless.

No other creature had braved these flames.

It followed him back to his truck, still yapping.

The bridle was latched and bolted down. The arms and legs were chained to the floor. Jack was moving to lock and bolt the door the moment he noticed the watch . . .

He didn't know how to believe his eyes. He wouldn't have thought there was anything left to this month, on the whole, that might have surprised him. But here was the damnedest thing he had seen: the blighted one wearing his watch—the watch that had disappeared from his office, the watch he had blamed on Franklin Pendle . . .

Now *this* would take some figuring out.

Almost choking to death in the meantime, he slammed, locked and bolted the cab. The terrier followed him into the driver's seat.

Of course it did.

Saint Jack.

He turned, craning his neck for a glimpse through the hatchback window. Already, it stunk.

This young man was in for a wild ride: the next twenty hours would crawl by as a veritable hell on earth of unparalleled intensity: probably the most excruciating ordeal he would ever undergo.

And no walk in the park for Jack either. He had packed earplugs, incense and Lysol.

And plenty of Benny Goodman, of course.

And Randy Newman.

And Call of the Whale.

But first, he would have to get out of here: back through the wall of flames without slamming headlong into one of these oaks, or igniting his fuel tanks—or killing some fool on the other side, maybe.

From there, he could make it across the field without snapping an axle, or blowing his tubes—keeping one step ahead of the mob, all the while.

The nearest lane was a hundred yards through the forest, and led directly to the highway.

Once on the road, with a jump on the gun and his mojo in form, he could outrun these honkies . . .

this story never ends . . .